A Gathering at Oak Creek

Walt Davis

The original cover art for *The Gathering at Oak Creek* was done by Mike Pinson of Hugo, Oklahoma. Mike is a rancher/saddle maker/ artist. As a working cowboy in New Mexico and Oklahoma for most of his life, he knows his subject matter well. Limited edition prints of the cover and other prints are available. Contact Mike Pinson, 2430 Tanglewood Lane, Hugo, Oklahoma 74743 Cell 580-317-5016

For information on other works by Walt Davis see www.waltdavis ranch.com

A Salute to West Texans
Past and Present
When and where ever they live

By

Walt Davis

"West Texas is less an area
Than it is a state of mind"

WD

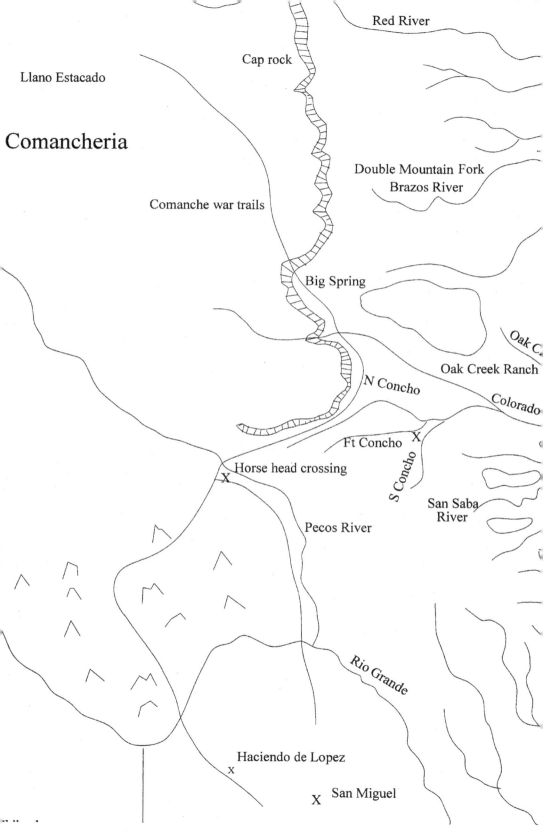

CHAPTER 1

Northern Coahuila Mexico 1875

All men know Alejandro Rios as a brave man but at the moment he was close to panic with fear. Fear not of something he saw or heard but rather fear because of what he could neither see nor hear. He turned in his saddle and searched the narrow canyon floor stretching away behind them; he scanned also the tops of the vertical canyon walls seventy feet above them. He saw no movement, no sign of life of any kind and this worried him greatly. In this dry country, the narrow stream of running water threading through the canyon was a magnet for life of all kinds and there was no life present. In the mile that they had ridden down this canyon, he had seen no animals either large or small and the only birds to be seen or heard were in the air high above. The canyon floor here was deep sand with very little vegetation, the result of the runoff from the mountains above being funneled into boiling destructive torrents by the narrowing of the canyon walls. Rios was becoming almost claustrophobic from his inability to see beyond the walls that seemed to be closing in on him like the jaws of a trap and they narrowed even more in the stretch ahead. He was mentally berating himself for taking the short cut through the canyon but it was too late to do anything but hurry through. This route cut miles off their journey but clearly put his party at risk if the Apache caught them in this narrow confine. The sand was deep and loose so that it was impossible for him to accurately read tracks. He knew that a number of horses had recently passed this way but he could not be sure how many, whether they were shod or unshod, how long since they passed or even, for certain, the direction of their travel. Looking forward, he could see his entire party moving single file down the canyon and he could see that his men were alert. Every man had his rifle in his hand and all were searching for hostiles just as intently as he.

There were twelve well mounted and heavily armed men in the group with five big pack mules and five extra horses. They were four days into a ten day journey from La Hacienda de la Campana de Santa Maria on the headwaters of the Rio Conchos to the city of Monterrey in the State of Nuevo Leon. They were to deliver the cargo carried by two of the mules to the Banca de Guzman y Guzman in Monterrey. Don Philippe Ramirez-Santos, Patron of La Campana, had entrusted this task to Rios, telling him that its' success was a necessity if La Hacienda de la Campana de Santa Maria was to survive beyond the six generations that his family had owned it. Rios was greatly honored by the trust shown in him by Don Philippe; Rios, like every man in the party, was born on La Hacienda and was totally loyal to his Patron. So far, there had been no trouble but two days ago, they had seen the sign of a large group of Apache and yesterday they passed a small rancho where the jacales had been burned with the people inside. Los Brutos were surely in the area and Rios would feel much better when they were in the open where their horses and their rifles could be used to advantage. They were entering the narrowest portion of the canyon now but in four hundred yards would reach the open plains.

As Rios watched from his rear guard position – his group quickened their pace in anticipation of being free of the constraints of the canyon. Before the entire string could come up to the new pace a single gunshot rang out and his second in command, who was leading the party, fell from his horse in a lifeless heap. The shot was obviously a signal as a hail storm of arrows, gunfire and even rocks descended on them from the top of the canyon walls. His men returned fire but with little apparent effect; the Apache would pop up, fire and disappear in an instant. Men were falling and men and horses were screaming; Rios saw that their only chance lay in getting clear of the canyon and shouted for his men to run for the plains. Those of his party still able spurred for the open ground and Rios followed driving the pack mules ahead of him. The men still alive reached the mouth of the canyon and Rios began to hope that at least this small part of his command might survive. Just outside the canyon mouth, were ricks of driftwood on either side of the trail – left there when flood waters dropped their loads of flotsam as they spread out and lost velocity. As the riders approached, these drifts exploded with gunfire from the Apache hiding within them. Rios saw the remainder of his men and most of the horses fall before a shot to the head ended his consciousness.

Luis Robles-Ramos reined in his horse at the first gunshot and, as the sound of what was obviously a major battle intensified, waved for his men to follow and rode rapidly off at a ninety degree angle to the route he had been following. He had no idea who was fighting who but, for certain, he and his group wanted no part of the fight. Federales would shoot them just as quickly as would Apaches and townsmen from the little dump where they robbed the store might still be following them. For the sake of their health, they needed to get to a calmer area so he turned his horse to the north and away from all the activity. The question of the identity of at least one participant in the fight became clear when a panicked mule came running into their midst with an Apache arrow stuck in its rump and two more stuck in the pack it was carrying. One of his men caught the mule and pulled the arrow, which had barely penetrated the hide, from its rump; even if the pack held nothing but parched corn, the mule was more valuable than everything they had stolen in the last two weeks. They spurred their horses and concentrated on putting distance between themselves and the Apache.

CHAPTER 2

New York City 1992

It was unusually warm for an early spring day and Bart Ryan was looking forward to coming out of his jacket and having a cold beer. Bart grew up in New York City but the older he got, the more the crowds bothered him; on the walk from the subway stop, he was always in a mob at this time of day and in the five blocks, he didn't see a single person smile. He shouldn't let it bother him but sometimes he wanted to stand in the street and scream, "Smile damn it." If he wasn't careful, he would become as crotchety as his neighbor, old man Higgins. Bart was startled out of his wool gathering when – just as he reached his apartment door – a voice close behind him asked, "Mr. Herbert Barton Ryan?" surprised, Bart jerked around; fumbling and almost dropping the keys he had ready to unlock the door. He was Bart to his friends and the people he worked with and "Little Pat" to the older people in the neighborhood, at least those who had known his parents and watched him grow up. The last time he had been called by his full name was by the process server for his ex-wife's lawyer. Before that it was by the man from the city attorney's office with three hundred and eighty-five dollars and sixty-five cents – including penalty and interest – worth of his unpaid parking tickets from the time when he still had a car. This fellow had a lawyer look about him and an envelope in his hand as well when he repeated "Mr. Herbert Barton Ryan?" You expected to get mugged occasionally in New York City, even in old family neighborhoods like this, but he was beginning to get a little paranoid about the legal muggings. He considered denying that he was him and even thought about jumping the porch railing and taking off. Neither idea seemed too bright since he was standing at the door of his apartment with his name on the mail box and wearing the name-tag from SaveWay Electronics SuperStore that said "Hi, I'm Bart." "Who wants to know?" sounded lame even as he said it. "I am Roger James of the legal firm of Stilwell, Cohen, Caudle and Kaufman and I am attempting to locate Mr. Herbert Barton Ryan whose mother was born in Texas." He was sure something unpleasant was about to befall him but couldn't for the life of him imagine what it might be or how to avoid it. His Mother came from Texas but it was forty years ago that a fifteen year old orphan girl had caught a train in San Angelo Texas and started north and east on the journey that would eventually bring her to New York City and a home as the wife of William Patrick Ryan and mother of Herbert Barton Ryan. Curiosity overcame apprehension and produced "I'm Bart Ryan." "If you please, Mr. Ryan, what was your Mothers' maiden name?" "Moms' name was Mary Alice Barton before she and Dad married." "Capital Mr. Ryan! It seems my search is successful. I am to give you this letter of explanation and ask you to call at the offices of Stilwell, Cohen, Caudle and Kaufman at your earliest convenience. The address and telephone numbers are on the letterhead." Roger James handed Bart a letter and walked away with an over the shoulder "Good day, Mr. Ryan." Bart looked at the envelope in his hand and back up to where James had been. Questions swirled through his head like dry leaves in a whirlwind but Roger James was gone in the traffic of people coming home from work.

Bart let himself into the apartment, relocked the door and shucked off his bright orange SaveWay Electronics SuperStore salesman's jacket. He tossed the letter on to the kitchen table and went to his bedroom to change out of his work clothes. Feeling much better in old soft jeans and worn moccasins, he got a beer from the refrigerator. A pungent odor followed the beer out, "I really have got to scrape that thing out this weekend." Taking his beer and the letter, he went back into the front room to the one really comfortable chair in the apartment. As usual, the scruffy gray tomcat, who really belonged to Mr. Higgins down the hall but that had adopted Bart when his wife moved out, was there first. Damn Cat (D. C. for short) was ill tempered, smelled bad and had fleas but all and all Cynthia for him wasn't a bad swap. Bart managed to evict D.C. without losing any hide and sat down to read the letter.

Stilwell, Cohen, Caudle and Kaufman
Attorneys at Law
1716 North 51st St.
New York City, New York 10007
212-555-6578, fax 212-555-6579

July 16, 1992

Dear Mr. Ryan:

Our firm has been retained to locate the heirs of the late James Thomas Barton of Maryneal, Texas. It is our belief that you are such an heir. If so, it is possible that you may be eligible to share in the estate of the late Mr. Barton. Please contact me at your earliest convenience.

Sincerely,

George A Hendricks

George A. Hendricks III Attorney

Bart didn't see how he could be kin to anyone from Maryneal Texas even if they did have his Mothers' maiden name. Mom was an only child and he knew that she had supported herself without help from the time she was orphaned at fifteen. Bart picked up the big road map atlas (his favorite prop for daydreams) from the bookshelf and opened it to the index of cities and towns. "Under Texas let's see, Marshall, Mart, Martindale, here we go- Maryneal- Wj-13." Opening the atlas to Texas, he found four full pages of maps; two for the western half and two for the eastern half of the state. Wj-13 led him to Nolan County in the western half and there in its' southwest quarter was Maryneal. A small dot in the middle of what looked like a whole lot of empty space; it was at least twenty miles to the nearest other little dot and he didn't see anything that looked like a city for sixty or seventy miles in any direction. To the south about that far was San Angelo, from where he knew his Mother had left west Texas, but there could be a lot of people named Barton in an area of that size and none of them kin to him. Still he was intrigued with the mystery and the possibility that this might be a chance for him to see a different part of the country.

Bart had always had the wanderlust; he joined the Army right out of high school in order to see the World but after boot camp spent his entire hitch in a motor pool just across the river in New Jersey. When he and Cynthia fell in lust and got married, he did his best to get her to move with him to California or Montana or anyplace different but there was no way she would leave her Mother and the neighborhood where she grew up. After they split up, he thought about taking off on his own but with debts and alimony to pay, it was too easy to fall into the rut where he found himself now. Even when he got the debts paid down and Cynthia did him the tremendous favor of marrying

Marty Katz, he couldn't seem to work up the energy to start his Grand Trek. Bart looked at his watch, 5:35, too late to catch the lawyer tonight but SaveWay Electronics SuperStore was going to be short one sales clerk in the morning.

Both of Bart's parents were dead, his Father in a construction accident when Bart was sixteen and his Mother from cancer four years later. He tried to remember everything that his Mom had told him about her family, about west Texas and her early life there. It wasn't a lot, it had not been a happy period in his Mothers' life and she seldom spoke of it. All he knew for sure was that her Dad had worked in the oil fields and that both he and her Mother had died in a car wreck when Mom was fifteen. There were no brothers or sisters. She had once told him that what she remembered best was the constant moving through a series of old rent houses always reeking of the crude oil on her Daddy's work clothes. Her dad was a roughneck, she told Bart when he was about ten and then had to explain that it didn't mean that they had rough necks though she said with a little smile "Daddy was a little rough around the edges." Roughneck was just what they called the men who manned the drilling rigs in the oil patch, and they were the kings of the workingmen. They commanded a wage at least twice what common labor could expect plus the prestige of being of the elite. Many a west Texas boys' greatest ambition was to get out of high school and to catch on as a worm — or rookie — on a drilling crew. Instead of $1.00 an hour for a forty hour week you could be knocking down $2.25 an hour eight hours a day seven days a week. If you had the nerve to be a derrick man and work ninety feet in the air you could make even more.

Life in the west Texas oil patch was a hard life in a hard dry empty land and with her folks gone Mary Alice wanted to go someplace where you could drink the water without having to first boil coffee in it and where you didn't have to constantly be on the lookout for rattlesnakes – they turned up even inside the rickety old houses that they rented. With her parents dead and no other kin around, the county judge decided that the county would bury her parents and that Mary Alice should go to a state orphan's home at least until her sixteenth birthday. Mary Alice didn't argue she just went home and sold what she could of her folks' possessions (mostly to the members of her Dads' drilling crew) who didn't really need any more clothes or pots and pans but did feel a need to do something for the orphaned child of one of their own.

Mary Alice packed her clothes and the tin box that her Mother used to store all their birth certificates and her and Toms' marriage certificate and set off into the world. With the proceeds of the rummage sale and what was left of the money that her Mother had squirreled away $.50 at a time and made her and her daughters' secret, Mary Alice caught a ride with her Dads' driller into San Angelo and then a train north. She had no idea where she wanted to be except out of the dust and grime of the oil patch so she decided to just look around until she found someplace that felt like home.

A fourteen dollar train ticket took her out of the oil patch and into another world. She might not know exactly what she wanted but she did know that she wanted to be somewhere greener and cooler than west Texas so she went east for greener and north for cooler. She didn't do badly for a fifteen year old on her own; she waited tables (or washed dishes if she couldn't find a waitress job) and always made sure that she more than earned her pay. Whenever she moved to a new town the routine was the same, find work, find a room preferably with a widow lady and then get a library card from the local library. Her Mother had loved to read and had passed this love on to Mary Alice. At first reading was just a way to escape into other worlds but then she learned that anything she felt a need to know was available and that librarians everywhere loved to help people who wanted to learn. In the little town of Vinita in northeast Oklahoma, a librarian discovered that Mary Alice had not finished high school and told her about the general equivalency degree program. A little more than a year later, Mary Alice had a certificate from the state of Oklahoma attesting to the level of her education and a new sense of confidence and purpose. Finding that she liked studying and learning opened a new world and soon translated into a degree from a business correspondence school which proclaimed that Mary Alice Barton was a fully qualified commercial bookkeeper. Tulsa Oklahoma was booming so armed with her new degree and the classified section of the newspaper Mary Alice sallied forth determined to find employment in her new field. She steeled herself against the expected rejections and was more than a little surprised when she was hired, twenty minutes into her first interview, as a bookkeeper for Osage Tool and Supply Company. Eight months later Mary Alice still had the title of bookkeeper but her real job had become office & personnel manager- troubleshooter-saleswoman and indispensable girl Friday to old Mr. Ike Cowen who owned the business. By this time, she could talk to company reps about the comparative strengths and weaknesses of forged end sucker rods vs. threaded and welded end rods, to high riggers about the proper size and length of choker cables for different loads and to the construction men about how much rebar was needed in various thicknesses of concrete slabs; if she didn't know the answer to a question, she would the next time it was asked.

After the first time, she could turn the tables on and make a laughing stock out of the smart aleck that wanted a "sky hook" or a "left handed Stillson wrench." She was "little sister" to all of the regular customers and any clod that used foul language in her presence was straightened out right quick by Mr. Ike or any of her "big brothers" that were close. The one drunken roustabout boss that failed to heed the language warning found himself turned into an "airplane" by two burly roughnecks and flown halfway across the gravel parking lot before coming in for a landing on his nose. To add insult to injury, Mr. Ike went out with a 24 inch pony rod in his hand and made him come back and pick up the teeth he had scattered on the lot. Cheerful, well groomed and smart Mary Alice changed the atmosphere in Osage Tool and Supply from coarse to that of the home life that the men who came in wished they had. This was the situation when Mary Alice met William Patrick, "Big Pat", Ryan as the first customer of the day for Osage Tool and Supply Co. on a Monday morning in October. Big Pat was a crew chief for the Empire State Bridge and Iron Co. of New York City and had come to Tulsa when his company won the contract to refurbish the bridge across the Arkansas River. He came into Osage Supply to order materials needed on the bridge job and then came in nearly every day for the next three weeks to see Mary Alice. He joked later that he didn't have a choice; it was either marry the girl or get fired a long way from home because he couldn't keep his mind on the job. First Mr. Cowen blustered calling Big Pat a cradle robbing Irish hooligan, then he begged for them to wait until Mary Alice was older until finally Mary Alice stomped a foot and said "enough, I love him and I am going to marry him." So Ike paid for the wedding, gave the bride away and sent the new couple on their way with a five hundred dollar dowry in the brides' purse.

CHAPTER 3

Oak Creek Ranch 1992

Mac Connley woke – as always – an hour before daylight and reached a hand out to the apple box beside his bed for his makings. After fifty years of practice, even flat of his back in pitch darkness, he could roll his first smoke of the day and not lose enough tobacco to make a cigar for a cootie. As he smoked, he thought about what needed to get done today. First thing should be to ride up to the windmill in Reese canyon and check on the water level in the reservoir. It had been three days since he was up there and while the wind had blown real strong all week, things could go wrong with windmills. It was probably all right but like all good stockmen, Mac had a horror that he might let stock run out of water. Even though it happened forty years before, Mac still got a sick feeling whenever he thought of the time Slick Black got drunk in a line camp and let six penned horses die of thirst. Slick had to quit the country, he couldn't get a job; nobody wanted to be around him much less work with him. After he got his chores done and checked the water in Reece canyon, Mac thought he had best ride into town. He was getting low on groceries but also he needed to see the lawyer and find out if he had a partner yet. With his day planned out, Mac was ready to start the painful process of getting out of bed and moving. A lifetime of being bucked off, knocked down, run over, kicked, and stepped on had given him a goodly assortment of joints that didn't bend when they were supposed to and some that bent when they weren't supposed to; it took longer every year to get things moving. At least, unlike some old cowboys he had known, he didn't yet have to find a stump or a bucket to stand on when he mounted.

As he enjoyed – soon as the coughing stopped – his first smoke Mac thought that all in all he was lucky that he wasn't broke up worse than he was or even dead. He had been in some serious wrecks over the years, most of them coming before he and his running buddy Windy Barton got old enough to have a little sense. Cowboying is not the world's most genteel profession so they had both acquired the normal amount of broken bones, rope burns and mesquite thorn punctures in their everyday activities but looking back it was their recreation time that did a lot of the damage. Like the time that they got enough beer in them at a rodeo in Pecos to make entering the wild mare race seem like a good idea. The way it worked, they turned eight wild mares out of the bucking chutes at the same time and two man teams were to catch a mare, get a surcingle on her and have one team member ride her across the finish line at the other end of the arena. They planned it out that Mac would rope the mare and Windy would help him get her stopped so Mac could go up the rope and ear her down. As soon as Mac got a hold of her, Windy would drop the rope, put the surcingle on and ride her across the finish line with Mac hazing her in the right direction. It started out alright, the mares came busting out and Mac caught a little dun mare right behind her ears and had her almost stopped by the time Windy could get hold of the rope. They both set back on the rope and had her dead stopped when another mare came charging from the other side of the arena and hit their rope running full speed. The collision jerked both of them and their mare down into a pile with the mare mostly on top. Mac recovered first and jumped on the mares' head just as she got to her feet and shouted for Windy to "Get your rigging on her" but since he had most of the mares left ear cinched between his jaw teeth it came out more like "Et yu iggin n hu." It didn't really matter; Windy had lost the surcingle in the wreck and just swung up on the mare and hollered, "Let her go, I'll ride her with a mane hold." Mac turned the mare loose and jumped at her with a shout to run her toward the finish line. It was looking good, their mare was making tracks toward the finish line while only one other rider was mounted and his mare was sulked up and not going anywhere; Windy was reared back on his mane hold looking like a real bare back bronc rider when a coil of the lariat rope the mare was still wearing pulled up tight on Macs' right leg. The mare hit the end of the rope just as she downed her head to do some serious bucking and things happened fast for a while; Mac flew fifteen feet through the air to land flat of his back with one leg, he was sure, a whole lot longer than the other, the mare turned a half flip to land on her back with her tail stretched out straight in front of her and Windy flew through the air plumb graceful like before landing on his nose to roll head over heels three times and come to rest sitting up with his hand still full of mane hair. That little deal kind of put them off rodeo for a while but as Windy said, "It could have been worse, we could have had jobs and had to miss work while we healed up."

It almost was worse one time when they got drunk in a Bohemian dance hall down near La Grange. They had been having a fine time drinking beer and dancing with the girls but about midnight all the families and the nice girls went home so there wasn't anybody to dance with and Windy came up with the idea of starting a little fight just for the fun of it. He and Mac got back to back in the middle of the dance floor and Windy announced that they could "Whip everybody in this joint." They were doing pretty good, they were big and young and stout and most of the young guys had left when the girls went home. They had knocked down two or three men apiece and were feeling pretty salty when the old gal that ran the joint came out from behind the bar with a 30-30 saddle gun. That gun was probably old when she took it away from Poncho Villa but it worked just fine when she put a bullet through the roof to add to the collection of bullet holes already there. Evidently the locals knew what to expect because suddenly Mac and Windy were all by themselves on the dance floor and the bar-maid was racking home another round and the gun was pointing at them instead of the ceiling. They both broke for the door and jammed up there just long enough for her to get off another round before they got through and were running free. It was dark outside and they didn't think that she could see them but she still sent two more bullets towards the way they were headed. They made it to their horses and got back to their camp ok; they took a vote and decided that they were partied out for a while. When the sun came up, Windy found out that he wasn't crippled like he had thought; it was just that the heel of his left boot was shot off. The shirt Mac wore at the dance smelled like country girl perfume for two weeks; it surely smelled nice but they didn't feel any real need to go back anytime soon.

Mac finished his smoke and started the process of getting his old bones in a stand up position. As he creaked and groaned erect, he thought, not for the first time, "If I had known I was going to live this long, I would have done things different." Mac had been on Oak Creek Ranch for almost fifteen years. He came here in 1978 with Windy Barton after a letter from Susan George caught up with them in Montana. Mac and Windy grew up with Susan, she was Susan Sedberry then, and she and Windy had a thing going for a while. When it started to look like marrying kind of serious though, Windy spooked and he and Mac took off for New Mexico. For the next twenty-four years he and Windy cowboyed in just about every state west of the Mississippi plus a couple in Mexico and one in Canada. They did a little of everything from grazing big steers in the spring and summer on the bluestem pastures of Kansas to taking cows up to the high country of Montana in the spring and back down in the fall to loose herding cows wintering on the high desert of Nevada. They might be sweating in the brush country of south Texas today helping gather Mexican steers out of big pastures for the fall shipping and next week be in a Colorado high valley feeding alfalfa hay out of horse drawn sleds to a set of cows that would be snowed in until May. They spent several winters riding circle broncs for the big cow outfits in west Texas; they would start six or eight young horses on each of four or five ranches and then make a big circle from ranch to ranch riding each set of horses in turn. If things got hungry, they would light somewhere and build fence or work on windmills but as soon as a riding job opened up, they would be gone. They were soon known throughout the west and it was seldom that they had to go without work for long. They would never leave an employer in a bind once they signed on to do a job but they might whip somebody's ass when they left if they felt they hadn't been treated right. If they decided to go to Oregon or Mexico or anywhere else, they caught their horses, threw a tarp and a diamond hitch over their hot rolls on their packhorse and went.

Susan married Bill George and they moved to the old George home ranch on Oak Creek. Several times when she and Windy were courting, Susan said that she wanted a whole houseful of kids; Mac always thought that the idea of a herd of kids was what spooked Windy but Susan and Bill never did have any kids. When Bill died, Susan realized that she had to have some help if she was going to keep the ranch. Bill was sick for quite a while before he died and things were in pretty bad shape by the time Susan got him buried and had time to think of anything besides taking care of her husband. Bill never believed in over paying his help but the two hands on the place when he died weren't worth even what Bill paid. Susan sent letters to several outfits where she knew Mac and Windy worked on occasion; one letter caught up with them in Montana as they were helping Dumpy Lee, another transplanted Texan, finish his fall work. They caught a ride for themselves and their horses on a cattle truck that was running empty back to San Angelo and rode into the Oak Creek headquarters eight days after Susan mailed the letters. That was the start of some good years. Mac and Windy worked like the devil to get fences back in shape, windmills serviced, pens rebuilt, cow herd culled and to tend to all of the other things that had been let slide while Bill was sick. Susan worked with them when they were horseback but the rest of the time she spent cooking and gardening and pampering two old coots until their clothes didn't fit. It was still ok when Susan and Windy decided to get married and Windy moved out of the bunkhouse and in with Susan. Mac still took all his meals with them and they spent every evening together on the front porch, or in the winter, by the fireplace in the big house. Mac told Susan that the only problem with the arrangement was that he had to leave the radio tuned real loud to WBAP or it got so quiet in the bunkhouse that he couldn't sleep. Susan laughed and said if Mac had been a real friend he would have warned her about Windy's snoring before it was too late. Oak Creek didn't have but eight sections and with a stocking rate of a cow to twenty acres would carry about two hundred fifty cows. After they got things in shape, it was no strain for them to handle the work with just a couple of neighbor kids to help at calf working time. They were all three getting a little stiff and a little gray but Mac didn't believe he had ever been happier in his life. He and Windy had spent their lives working for the other man with no real claim to anything but their horses and their names. There are worse legacies than being known as top hands who always did the best they knew how but it was sort of nice to feel that what you did was more than just a job. Windy and Susan even talked of getting a little band of mares; mainly Mac was sure, so Windy could indulge in his all time favorite job of working with colts. Once when he and Mac were riding, Windy said, "Partner, you and I had a lot of good times and a lot of fun but the biggest mistake I ever made was not marrying that little girl when I first had the chance."

Suddenly Susan was sick and before they realized how sick, she was dead. Windy moved back into the bunkhouse and they cooked on the old wood stove in the lean-to; neither of them could bear the big house without Susan. A lawyer came out from Sweetwater to tell them that Susan had left Oak Creek and everything else she owned to the two of them fifty-fifty; everything except some jewelry and some china that had belonged to her grandmother; that she left to a grandniece in Alabama. The lawyer gave them a note in Susan's handwriting saying "You boys have been partners for forty years, this will make it legal. Love, Susan." There were papers for the two of them to sign and later the lawyer came back with more papers. The winter went past in kind of a fog, they did what had to be done to tend the stock but nothing else seemed worth the effort. Windy got real quiet, went off his feed and began to show his age bad. Mac was about ready to try to get him in to a doctor when the spring rains started. As the pastures greened up and baby calves started dropping, Windy perked up, started eating and taking interest in what was happening. It was the time of the year that all cowmen live for with new life everywhere; the hard old country was suddenly almost embarrassingly soft with new grass and brilliant wild flowers forming a backdrop for new baby animals and birds back from the south. No one who hasn't seen it can imagine the difference between west Texas before it rains and the same country after the rains come. The colors change from washed out straw colors and browns and grays to a dozen shades of green with sprays of pink and orange and white and the smells change from sweat and dust to moisture and the fragrances of cactus flowers. Windy was almost back to his old self when Mac rode in from the pasture to find him lying, face down, dead in the hall of the horse barn with a bridle in one hand and a curry comb in the other.

CHAPTER 4

Oak Creek Ranch 1992

Emiliano Cortez eased slowly around the cedar bush until he could clear the short bow in his left hand. The doe was walking from right to left across the mouth of the draw in which he stood and he would have a broadside shot in another ten feet. The bow and two flint tipped arrows he had made were not up to his Grandfathers' standards but since it was close to sixty years since his "Comanche" grandfather had shown him how to make and hunt with the bow and since he had nothing to work with but his pocket knife, Emiliano was rather proud of his efforts. The equipment was crude, especially the flint arrowheads, Emiliano had thought of making flint points after coming across a spot under a limestone bluff where from the number of flint chips on the ground someone had once worked flint. The Tonkawa lived in this area for many years and made flint points and blades for their own use and to trade with other tribes. He had already taken several rabbits with the bow and blunt arrows but needed a point with cutting edges if he hoped to kill larger game; his Grandfather had used points filed from hoop iron but Emiliano had neither iron nor a file. The two flint points took him most of a day and a lot of frustration but if they were not pretty they were at least sharp. The last rabbit was two days ago; he was hungry and really needed to kill this deer.

Emiliano was some twenty days into a journey brought on by loneliness and boredom; his two sons had long since left home and his wife of forty years was two years in her grave. He woke on his farm one morning to realize that his life was empty with no one to care about or need him and nothing to hold him to this place but habit. He made a deal with a neighbor to farm his field on shares and told the village that he was going north to see his sons. Emiliano had no idea where his sons were, there had been no word from either in all the years they were gone but this would do as an excuse to travel to Texas. He had not traveled that far, perhaps 300 miles, but this was a fair distance to his old legs and twice he had been forced to walk over twenty hours to the next water. After he crossed the Rio Bravo del Norte or the Rio Grande as the gringos called it, he traveled mostly at night to avoid Los Migros of the U.S. Border Patrol – twice he did not travel for several days when the patrols were out in force. He had misjudged the time it would take to get far enough from the border to be able to stop and seek work. He had some money but had not thought to change his pesos into dollars before crossing the border and he was afraid to do so now. His supply of corn meal and jerky lasted only two weeks and this was a bad time to be trying to live off the land. Last falls' pecans and sweet chinquapin acorns were long gone and few of the other wild foods were ripe yet; not the mesquite beans, the agarita berries nor the prickly pear tunas so he was reduced to eating whatever he could catch and as the old song about poverty said, "nopalitas sin sal" or prickly pear pads without salt. So far he had eaten two armadillos, several crawdads, a possum, three rattlesnakes and three rabbits. He had come up on two isolated ranch houses in the last week but both times he could not see any men as he watched from the edge of the brush and had continued his journey as he did not want to walk up on a woman alone. Twice before he had come north of the Rio Grande, once when his crops failed due to drought and he had to seek work to feed his young family and once ten years later when a man he thought was a friend returned with stories of riches to be gained by signing on with a labor contractor supplying labor to the big vegetable farms. The first time he returned home as soon as he had saved enough to see him through till his next harvest and the second time he was gone over a year before he could save enough to buy himself out of the contract he signed with the contractor and return home with nothing but a little English. Texas was not his favorite place and he was beginning to wonder just how wise was his decision to seek the treasure of his Grandfather. If truth be known, he was not even sure that the treasure his Grandfather described had ever existed; the story of bandit gold was a big part of his childhood but it was entirely possible that it existed only in the mind of an old man seeking to impress and entertain his grandson. Whatever the truth, Emiliano had used the tale to justify his journey and was rather enjoying his departure from a lifelong role as a stolid and rather boring small scale Mexican farmer and pillar of the community of San Miguel. The journey had not always been enjoyable but it had been challenging and he felt more alive than he had in many years. It did not compare to the adventure that his Grandfather had lived but it was a dramatic change from his previous life.

Chapter 5

Northern Coahuila Mexico 1862

At age ten Grandfather Juan was abducted from his parents' village in northern Coahuila by a Comanche raiding party. At this time the Comanche looked upon Mexico as their own private reserve for producing slaves to sell, women to rape, captives to turn into Comanche and most importantly horses. As soon as the fall hunt was over and while the ponies were still fat from a diet of rich summer grass, death with a painted face and a buffalo horn headdress would appear in northern Mexico; the first full moon in October was known from the Platte River to central Mexico as the Comanche moon and when it appeared, fear and dread ruled the land. The Comanche were not conquerors, they had no desire to own land or rule a country; they were pillagers pure and simple, swooping down on an unsuspecting populace to kill, steal and destroy and then vanishing back into an untracked wilderness known only to them.

At first Juan was sure that he would be killed as soon as the raiding party stopped but when the group did not stop and did not stop, only pausing for the briefest of moments to throw him up and tie him on a fresh horse and to change mounts themselves, he became certain that death would be preferable to one more hour on the back of a loping horse. The warriors chewed dried meat and drank from water skins as they rode but gave Juan nothing. The war party was driving a large herd of stolen horses and the warriors traveled at a rapid pace. They would lope a mile or so and then trot a while, changing horses frequently but never stopping. It was a full thirty-six hours from the time he was captured in his Fathers' corn field before he was finally taken from the horse and dumped, still bound, on the ground to fall into an exhausted state more like a coma than sleep. He was awakened by a kick from one of the warriors who jerked him to his feet, slapped him across the face and lifted him to the back of yet another horse. They paused at a flowing creek to water the horses; the warriors all drank deeply but did not offer to take Juan down or give him water. Juan didn't know it but he was seeing normal behavior for a Comanche war party. Few pursuers could match the pace set by Comanche leaving the scene of a raid; if they had enough horses, they would make fifty miles in the time that any but the most determined followers could cover thirty miles and this only at the cost of riding their mounts into the ground. The war parties routinely left a trail of dead and dying captives and exhausted horses in their wake. The brutal mistreatment of Juan was also part of a plan. The Comanche were always looking for boys who could become warriors and replace those lost in their warlike lifestyle. Not all boys had the physical and mental toughness to become a Comanche warrior and it was better to weed out the weaklings early. Juan was to live as a Comanche or "Nurmurnuh" as they called themselves until he was twenty-three years old but at the moment, he was just a miserable and frightened little boy.

Grandfather Juan was an old man when Emiliano was born, it was many years after Juan came back to the valley where he was born before he was even marginally accepted by the people, he even had to travel far to the south to woo and win a wife. It was not easy for the people to over look that a person had lived and fought with the godless devils that made life in northern Mexico even more harsh than the climate and poverty decreed. Having lived all but his early years in a warrior society, Juan had a hard time hiding his disdain for the mild mannered and self effacing Mexican peasant men. He was seen as arrogant and over bearing and was feared by many as dangerous; this perception was strengthened when Juan found farming too tame and signed on as a scout with the Federales in their campaigns against the Apache and the Yaqui. His standing in the polite society of the village was further damaged when he brought back fresh scalps from his wars and proceeded to smoke cure them as decorations for his horse. He was the best grandfather any boy could hope to have; full of tales of warfare, horse stealing and buffalo hunts and always ready to teach the skills needed to survive the wild life in Comancheria. From the time Emiliano was six years old, Juan took him on hunting trips into the mountains where they ate, sometimes for weeks, only what they could catch and what wild foods were available. Although Emiliano did not realize it, Juan was a man torn between two ways of life; the society in which he now lived could not even conceive of the joys and satisfactions of the wild and unfettered life that he had previously lived. The history of the west is replete with stories of children rescued after being captured by the Comanche and other tribes who returned to live with their abductors at the first opportunity; what boy wanted a life of following a plow mule when he could live as a hunter and warrior? Emiliano was the only person to whom Juan would tell stories from his days as a "hombre bronco" or "wild man" with "Nurmurnuh - The People" and Emiliano soon learned that it would not do to repeat these stories to his parents and especially not to the village Padre. Emiliano particularly liked to hear the tale of

Juan's last few months with the Comanche and his desperate flight from the "Buffalo Soldiers."

By 1875 most of the buffalo had been killed by hide hunters and nearly all of the Comanche and their Kiowa allies had come into the reservations starving and beaten. Juan — known then by his Comanche name "Sees Far" — was with a small group of Comanche not willing to give up and come in to the reservation. They were attempting to get to Mexico and beyond the reach of the black faced "Buffalo Soldiers" who were wreaking havoc on Comanche bands from their fort on the Concho River. These soldiers with their Tonkawa scouts were rounding up the last scattered remnants of a once mighty people, killing their horses and forcing them into captivity north of the Red River. The days when the Comanche were "Lords of the South Plains" and feared from the Platte River to Guatemala were at an end. The Buffalo Soldiers found Sees Far and his group just south of the Double Mountain Fork of the Brazos River and in a running fight killed or captured all but Sees Far and three other warriors. These four broke contacts with the soldiers just at dusk and rode south as fast as their weary ponies could travel for they knew that their ancient enemies, the Tonkawa, and the soldiers on their big grain fed horses would not be far behind. They might have been able to elude the soldiers but the Tonkawa knew this land as well as they did. The Tonkawa harbored an intense hatred of the Comanche for it was the Comanche who had killed most of the Tonkawa people and driven the rest from the home of their ancestors. The four fugitives stopped at a seep spring on a slope above the "creek where the sweet acorns grow" just before daylight to tend their wounds and rest the two ponies that were still able to travel. As the sun touched the horizon the breeze freshened, as it usually does at this time of day, and brought them the scent of wood smoke. Sees Far and another adopted Mexican named Slope went on foot to investigate and found — four hundred yards up the creek —three men still asleep in their blankets with three horses and a big mule grazing hobbled near the camp. Slope kept watch on the sleeping men while Sees Far went back to get the others. If they could get them, the fresh horses would give them a chance to escape from their pursuers. The two Comanche, Black Horn and Shadow were little more than boys who looked up to Sees Far as a seasoned warrior and readily followed his lead though both were wounded and Black Horn was weak from loss of blood. Stressing the need to maintain silence to prevent giving direction to the Tonkawa trackers, Sees Far led his group against the strangers. They had two bows with them and after creeping in close, killed all three men with arrows and knives with almost no noise. The men, two "tab-ba-bohs" or "white men" and a Mexican, were armed with two pistols and a rifle each and had the look of hard men even in this place where all men had to be hard to survive. Searching quickly through the dead men's possessions as the others were catching the horses and mule, Sees Far was pleased to find ammunition, dried meat, corn meal and even some coffee in their saddlebags. Reaching down sideways to pick up one of the two small packs that the mule had been carrying, he was surprised to find it was as if the bundle were tied to the ground. Sees Far moved astraddle the pack and lifting with both hands was amazed to find that it was as heavy as a grown man. After undoing the straps and brass buckles closing the leather pack, he found the inside filled with leather sacks full of gold coins. The small sacks were old, the leather they were made of stiff and cracked and each sack carried a brand shaped like the church bell Juan remembered from his childhood. Sees Far knew the value of the gold but it was too heavy to even consider trying to take with them, they would be lucky to outrun the solders with nothing but themselves, their weapons and a little food burdening the horses. The strangers had camped on a bench above the creek where a limestone ledge protruded from the base of a long ridge. Wind, water and animals had formed shallow caves in several spots under the ledge. Sees Far carried the gold packs to one of these, and after looking carefully for rattlesnakes, pushed them as far under the ledge as he was able and raked part of a pack rats' nest over them. To be sure he could return to the spot later, he made a mental note of the small creek running into the larger from the west just upstream, a smaller yet creek coming in from the east downstream and of the long flat-topped mesa off to the east. He had been close to this place twice before when the women of the tribe had insisted on coming here to gather the acorns that grew in patches along the creek bottom. Unlike the acorns of the live oaks to the south, the acorns of the jagged leaf oak were sweet and highly prized by The People. The four mounted the three horses and the mule and leading their two spent ponies headed south leaving the three dead men, their saddles and their camp plunder. As they left the main creek just south of the larger creek, Sees Far noticed a slab of rock shaped like a bear that had caved off from the rim rock above the bed of the creek; his heart jumped at the sight since the bear was his own special guide and such a sign could only be good medicine.

The running fight with the soldiers had taken the group farther east than Sees Far had intended going and now they were just northwest of the bluecoat soldiers camp on this same "creek where the sweet acorns grow" and a long days ride north of the Buffalo soldiers' fort on the Concho. Sees Far kept the group going south in single file until they came to a rocky ridge where he had the group string out still in single file and then turn due west riding abreast. It wasn't much of a ruse but maybe the Tonkawa would miss the turn and continue south for a ways looking for sign in the heavily grassed flats. They tied Black Horn to his horse when he became too weak to ride and he died just as they reached the Colorado River. In normal times, they would have tied the body high up in one of the river bottom trees but they knew that it would be spotted by the Tonkawa. If this happened they would cut off and eat the boys' hands thus making him their slave forever in the afterlife. Sees Far tied a large rock to the body and after opening the belly to keep trapped gas from floating it; carried the body as far out as they could into a deep pool and sunk it in the river. Not a proper burial for a Nurmurnuh warrior but better than letting him be found by the Tonkawa. Sees Far led his reduced group across the Colorado River and south until they reached a creek flowing into the river from the west. They rode west in the flowing water until nearly dark when Sees Far found a rock ledge where they could exit the creek without leaving an obvious trail and turned the party south once again. About mid night they crossed the North Fork of the Concho River; pausing just long enough to water their horses and themselves before continuing south. As it began to get light, Sees Far told the other two to go on while he waited below the crest of a ridge to watch their back trail. The country was rolling grassland with a few scattered big oaks. Brush grew only along draws and in the thin soil below the ridge crests so that from the elevation he could see a long way. He waited until full daylight without seeing any signs of pursuit and had just started to follow his companions when he heard shots and saw dust coming from the direction they had taken. From the ridge Sees Far could see Slope and Shadow being pursued by ten or more blue-coated soldiers who were firing as they

gave chase. As he watched first one and then the other of his friends'
horses went down and the soldiers were on the fallen warriors with
swinging sabers before either could more than began to run. Sees
Far concealed his horse and himself in a shin oak thicket below the
ridge crest and waited to see if the soldiers would back track their
two victims. The soldiers shot the two wounded horses and the two
Comanche ponies, caught the loose mule and rode east toward the
fort on Oak Creek. There were no Tonkawa with this group and the
troopers appeared to be white rather than black; evidently Sees Far
and his group had the bad luck to run into one of the roving patrols
from the camp on Oak Creek. If this was so, then the black faced
soldiers and Tonkawa would soon catch up and he was still in danger.
The Tonkawa would know that there had been four men in his party
from the sign left at the seep spring and at the camp where they killed
the strangers; they would also know that at least two of these were
wounded and that the party had three big horses, the two ponies and
a mule. Sees Far's best chance to escape was to follow closely the trail
left by his two companions to the point where they were attacked
by the blue backs and then to mix the tracks of his horse with those
of the soldiers by following them until he found a good spot to turn
south without leaving a plain trail. Not even a Tonkawa could tell
if a shod horse was being ridden by a soldier or a Comanche if he
rode in the soldiers' trail and was only a few minutes behind them.
With luck, the Tonkawa would waste time trying to find the trail of
the unaccounted for horse and would look in every direction except
that taken by the blue backs. Sees Far hated to leave the bodies of
his friends but knew that any attempt to hide them or carry them
away would only result in failure and his own death as well. There
was enough roll to the land so that he was able to stay fairly close

to the soldiers without being seen. Before he found a good place to turn south, however, he spent several nerve-racking hours expecting every minute to see the Tonkawa come charging up behind him. This was a new emotion for him; he was familiar with the rush that comes from combat with foes that are doing their best to kill you and with the tenseness of creeping up on an enemy horse herd at night but with all of his people gone, for the first time he felt fear. He wanted to get to Mexico as quickly as possible but after seeing a patrol of blue clad troopers headed south, Sees Far turned to the west. The country became increasingly dry as he traveled west; he was entering the northern edge of the Chihuahuan Desert. Water for his horse and himself was scarce but he had come this way before and knew where to find water. He came to and followed the Comanche war trail that began high on the Llano Estacado, came down on the rolling plains at the Big Spring and led southwest to cross the Pecos River at Horsehead Crossing. From there one fork of the trail went south to cross the Rio Grande into Coahuila Mexico and on south to Zacatecas while another went southwest to Comanche Springs and then south into Chihuahua. These trails had been used by the Comanche for more than one hundred and fifty years because of the reliable watering points along their routes. Sees Far crossed the Pecos and turned south toward Coahuila and the valley where he was born. By traveling mostly at night and avoiding all contact with people he managed to make it to Mexico without further problems; his last act as a Comanche was to use his bow to kill a traveling vaquero so he could have clothes and a saddle and become once again a Mexican named Juan. After nearly two hundred years of unrelenting raiding, rape and pillage by the Comanche on the people of northern Mexico, a Mexican captive may have killed the last Mexican to lose his life in this struggle. Juan never again ventured north of the Rio Grande and the only person he ever told his entire story was Emiliano; not even to Emiliano did he tell of the killing of the vaquero.

CHAPTER 6

Central Texas 1869

Seth Collins topped the last hill on the seven mile walk home from Navasota and could see smoke rising from the chimney of his mothers shack; he hoped Mama had something cooked – he hadn't had a bite since daylight when he ate some cold cornpone as he walked. Seth was tired – aside from the fourteen mile walk – he had worked three hours for the store keeper, Mr. Walker, unloading freight. He was tired but also, he was excited – about as excited as he ever remembered. Jethro – Mr. Walkers' regular hand – told Seth that this coming Saturday morning a man from the United States of America Army was going to be in Navasota to sign up black men to be soldiers and go fight the red Indians out west. Seth had trouble believing that the United States Government was going to give a bunch of black men guns and teach them to shoot. It was just a few years ago – in The War – that any black man caught with a gun was likely to get hisself shot. Jethro swore it was so; said two or three years ago his cousin Benny had been in one of the first bunches of blacks to join up. Benny was traveling around with a white officer looking for stout young blacks who wanted to be soldiers; Benny was a sergeant now with gold stripes on his uniform that was just like what the white soldiers wore. He told his daddy that he got paid fourteen dollars cash money every month besides getting his clothes free and them feeding him – feeding him good too.

Seth was close enough to the house now to smell fat meat frying and, for the last hundred yards, he was almost running. Mama was at the stove and looked over her shoulder when he came in the door; he grabbed her up in a bear hug and twirled her around – she was a little bit of a thing that didn't weigh nothing. "What is the matter with you? You big lout, put me down or I'll jab you with this fork." Seth put her down but not because he was afraid of getting jabbed; Mama had been smiling the whole time she was fussing. "Mama, I am going to be a soldier and learn to shoot and get paid." Bringing up pay reminded Seth and he dug the three pennies Mr. Walker paid him for unloading freight out of his pocket and gave them to Mama. The money disappeared into Mamas apron as she fixed Seth with that "Who do you think you fooling?" look that always got the truth out of him. "It's so, Mama the United States of America Army is looking for black men to be soldiers and I am going to Navasota Saturday and join up." "What they going to have you do? Wait on them white boys?" "No Mama, I am going to be a real soldier with a bunch of other black men and go fight the red Indians." Tom – Mamas' man now – spoke up from his chair in the corner, "You better stay away from them Indians, boy; they'll shoot a arrow in your black ass." "You watch your mouth, Tom Nelson; you don't talk like that in my house!" "Mama, Jethro has a cousin name Benny who has been in the army for three years; they pay him fourteen dollars cash money every month!" Tom snorted, "Ain't no black man ever got paid fourteen dollars a month." "Well, you looking at one who is going to."

Saturday, Seth left early and was waiting on the square with two other young black men when a little before dinner time, two mule drawn wagons being driven by black men in blue army uniforms pulled into the square. There were also two white men in uniforms riding good looking horses but it was the black soldiers that caught Seth's' attention. One soldier got down from the wagon seat to hold the officers horses; the man was wearing a clean uniform that looked brand new and Seth could see that his boots were clean and freshly greased. There were eight or so young blacks sitting on benches in one wagon; they were dressed, like Seth in ragged overalls and slouch hats. The soldiers sat, or stood head up and back straight as a flag pole; the men in the wagon sat slumped over like they were tired. Seth saw the difference, stood straighter and raised his chin. One of the white men turned to a black soldier with stripes on his jacket, "Sergeant Miller, Lt. Crane and I are going into Mr. Walkers store, get my folding desk out and set it up in the shade and then feed the men and our prospects here and see how many of them want to be horse soldiers." Sergeant Miller snapped a crisp salute, "Sir, yes Sir." The wagon drivers by this time had their teams tied to hitching posts and at Sergeant Millers instruction unloaded a folding desk with a stool and a chest from the lead wagon and set up in the shade of the tremendous old live oak on the courthouse lawn; they then took a larger chest out and set it by the second wagon. Sergeant Miller walked over to where Seth and now, three other others were standing. He stopped in front of them and said, "My name is Sergeant Miller and if you sign on with this man's outfit, it will be me that either makes soldiers out of you or kills you trying; do any of you think you are man enough to make a United States Cavalry man?" No one said anything until Seth snatched his hat off and said, "Yes Sir, I do." "Put your hat back on man and don't call me sir. I am a non-commissioned officer; you call me Sergeant Miller and save the sir for the officers. What's your name?"

"They calls me Seth Collins, Sergeant Miller." "They calls you Seth Collins? Is that your name?" "Yes sir, I mean yes Sergeant Miller that's my name." "Well if that is your name then tell the world; "My name is Seth Collins." "You join up with us and you not some head bobbing field hand, you are a United States soldier!"

The dinner bell at the headquarters of Moore Plantation down the road started ringing to bring the field hands in to eat and Sergeant Miller told the four of them to get in line where the other recruits were lining up to be fed. Each man was given a small baked sweet potato and a big white flour biscuit with a thick piece of fried bacon. The soldiers all took clean tin plates, cups and knives and spoons out of their mess kits while Seth and the rest ate out of their hands. This was the first white flour biscuit that Seth had ever tasted; the way that the black soldiers carried themselves had just about cinched the deal for Seth but the white flour biscuit didn't hurt.

Seth was late getting home, after making his mark on enlistment papers and receiving two silver dollars as a signup bonus, Seth had followed the wagons to the soldiers' overnight camp and spent some time talking to Sergeant Miller. He found that he could have part of his pay sent every month to his mother by way of Mr. Walker. He was to be back in Navasota ready to go on Monday morning and he was more than ready; half of his ten dollars a month pay was far more for his Mama than he could earn if he stayed.

Seth walked into the camp just as the teamsters were hitching up the teams; the recruits had already finished breakfast but Henry – the soldier who was acting as cook – gave Seth a cup of coffee and another of those biscuit and bacon sandwiches. He gave Seth his own mess kit and told him that it was his to keep clean and to take care of; the cost of anything that he lost would be taken out of his pay. Mama had gotten up and made him corn meal mush with bacon grease and molasses and a glass of buttermilk but that was a couple of hours ago; the biscuit was just as good as he remembered and the coffee was real coffee and fresh and strong. He finished his second breakfast just as Sergeant Miller boomed out "Detail, mount up." Seth helped Henry lift the grub box back into its place in the lead wagon and then climbed into the back of the second wagon with the other recruits. As he sat down on the plank bench, Henry reached under the wagon seat and tossed Seth a blanket roll wrapped in a piece of tarp. "Here is your bed, you might want it to sit on; we got more than three hundred miles to go before we get to Fort Concho and our horses.

The trip quickly fell into a routine; they rolled out of bed before daylight, had breakfast and were on the road before it got hot; they stopped at noon for an hour to eat and to rest the mules and stopped again around four or whenever they reached a good campsite. Each night, after the mules were tended and camp set up, Sergeant Miller and Private First Class Johnson would work with the recruits on marching and close order drills. The other recruits bitched about the drills but Seth found that he liked the sensation of moving in unison with the squad of men; he liked the feeling of being part of something bigger than himself. When they got to Austin, they lay over for two days waiting for another group of recruits to arrive from the north and they were issued uniforms. Each man received two new blue suits — two pants and two jackets —along with a set of old washed out blues for work detail, two sets of underwear and socks, fatigue caps, rain slicker and — best of all — new boots. Pfc. Johnson showed them how to stow the new clothes in duffel bags stenciled with their names. Seth watched as a garrison soldier stenciled his name on a bag; he memorized how his name looked and promised himself that he was going to learn to read and write. That night the recruits were allowed to go into the colored section of Austin if they were back by midnight; they found a dive down by the river that had home brew and whores and by ten o'clock most of the recruits were drunk and dead broke. Seth came back early. A new world was opening to Seth; a world where he could make things happen instead of just having things happen to him — he could learn to be a good soldier — he could earn stripes like Sgt. Miller — and he could save his money.

CHAPTER 7

Emiliano brought the bow to full draw and released his arrow as the doe, angling slightly away from him, stepped into the open forty feet in front and six feet below. The arrow struck just behind the last rib and angled forward through the deer's rib cage causing the doe to first hump up and then bound forward out of sight around the shoulder of the draw with her tail clamped tight against her rump. Emiliano knew that he should wait and give the doe time to bleed out and die but instead, he plunged recklessly down the draw dodging the rocks that littered its' bed; he was pleased with himself and anxious to follow and find his prey. He was agile for a man his age and was doing fine until, in a steep place, he came around a large rock to find a big rattlesnake coiled and alert right in his path. He was going too fast to stop so Emiliano took the only option he saw and leaped to jump the snake. He cleared the snake without a problem but landed on a rounded boulder and fell hard across the jumbled rock. Emiliano ended up on his back desperately trying to regain the breath that had been knocked out of him and with the smell and taste of blood in the head that comes from violent contact. As his breath and his senses returned, Emiliano saw, with a sick feeling, that his left foot was turned at an impossible angle to his knee. He was sprawled, head down hill, with his legs draped over some fallen rocks but with his back and shoulders in the relatively clear bed of the draw. He couldn't sit up or turn over from this position so he used his arms to push backwards off the rocks. He scooted far enough that he could get his good leg in play and with a push from it, slid off the rocks. Till now he had not been in great pain but when his broken leg fell from the rock, pain rolled over him like a wave of fire, he screamed and lost consciousness.

Emiliano drifted in and out of consciousness because of the pain but also due to the effects of concussion from the blow to his head. After some time, he had no idea how long; Emiliano came fully awake and found that by lying very still he could keep the pain to a bearable level. "Now you have done it you old fool. You will very likely die right here in this draw. No one knows or cares where you are, you have no food or water and you cannot travel with a broken leg. Even with your wife dead and all of your children gone; your empty little home in San Miguel would look awfully good right now."

Mac rode slowly up the trail to Reese Canyon, rapidly losing the good mood with which he had started the day. After light spring rains, last year had been as dry as he ever remembered and though it was late May, not a drop of rain had fallen this year. Even this early in the morning, it was already hot; there had been at least a dozen days so far when the temperature topped one hundred degrees. Mac knew that he faced another day of scorching sun in a sky totally devoid of cloud and a steady hot dry wind out of the southwest that felt as if it were blowing straight off the fires of hell. The perennial warm season grasses and forbs that had deep root systems had greened up briefly early on and even made a little growth but the annual plants, even the winter weeds, had not even germinated this year. Only once before in this country had Mac seen a spring green up as light and as short lived as this and that had been in 1957 in the seventh year of the worst drought of his lifetime. Mac had dug some post holes two days ago and the soil was bone dry as deep as he had dug; the air was so dry that there was no dew or scent of moisture even in that coolest part of the day just before daybreak. Since he and Windy had been on Oak Creek, the ranch had been stocked conservatively but this was the fourth year of drought and the grass reserve was gone. The cattle and the game were eating the forage faster than it could grow. He needed to sell some stock to reduce the load but hesitated to do so until the lawyers could find Windy's heirs. Mac had never had a partner other than Windy and was more than a little drawn up to be in business with someone he had never met. He didn't want to start off on the wrong foot by making decisions that affected both of them without his new partner having his say. Something would have to be done soon though; bare ground was beginning to show through the turf in more spots and he knew that if they lost their turf, it could take years (if ever) for the land to recover. Most rain in this part of the world fell as violent thunder storms; such rain ran off of bare ground and didn't soak in like it did on turf. Also bare ground became so hot under the summer sun that water already soaked in evaporated out before grass plants could drink it in. They could reduce the herd to match the slower growth rate of the forage but if it didn't rain soon they would have to sell all the stock and just hunker down till the drought ended. All ranchers hate to sell their breeding stock but holding animals too long in a drought can destroy a range. Even when being fed all they need, stock will continue to pick every green leaf as soon as it appears and in doing so will eventually kill the grass plants; they will even pick up the dead plant litter, leaving the soil bare and subject to killing heat and to erosion by wind and water. When nature was running things, in drought times the grazing animals either left or died; it was only after man took over with windmills and fences and hay and sack feed that stock could be held on land that could no longer feed and water them. You can always buy more cows but when grass and soil is gone, it's gone.

Besides drought, Mac also had to worry about money, when Susan died, Windy inherited from his wife with no death tax but the half that went to Mac was taxed and they had to mortgage the ranch to pay the government. Now with Windy dying, the taxman would be back, wanting his blood money again. The I.R.S. came up with a value of $300 per acre for Oak Creek even though this would mean a value of $6000 for a home for a cow, which was completely ridiculous. Any chance that they might have been able to negotiate a more reasonable figure was lost when Windy blew up and called the government man "a pot bellied, four eyed, blood sucking little piece of buzzard shit" and Mac and the lawyer had to drag Windy out of the room to keep him from making good on his threat to "Kick a mud hole in your ass and stomp it dry!" There had been times over the years when he and Windy had grouched about how this ranch owner or that one had it pretty damn soft; funny how the view changes depending on where you're standing. Between the drought, cattle prices and the government, Mac was beginning to think that being the boss was considerable overrated. With Susan and Windy buried out south of the house, he hated to even think about selling the ranch but couldn't for the life of him think how else the death tax could be paid again. Maybe his new partner would have money or at least be a good businessman.

As Mac came around a bend in the trail, Bald Hornet suddenly shied sideways blowing rollers in his nose and whirled to face to their left, in the process popping a crick in Mac's neck and jerking him out of his blue funk. "What's got into you, you old fool?" The "spook" turned out to be a dead deer lying just off the trail and Mac was wondering, "What killed a sleek young doe like that?" when he saw the arrow sticking out of her side. Mac could see that the arrow was homemade, not that different from the ones he had made as a boy. Mac got down for a closer look; the deer was fresh, still warm and the blood just now turning dark. Turkey feathers were fastened to the arrow shaft with bear grass fibers and mesquite gum just as he had done as a boy but this was a much neater job. Mac pulled the arrow out and was surprised to see the point was flint; Windy and he had beat a lot of flint into sharp pointed gravel trying to make arrowheads before they gave up and made some out of flattened nails. From the ground Mac could see a faint blood trail on the cow path coming down out of the canyon so, leading Bald Hornet, he began to back track the deer. They went maybe a hundred yards before the blood trail played out but Mac continued on up the path as the most likely way that the deer had come. They were passing were a draw came down into the canyon bottom when Bald Hornet snorted, stopped and pointed his ears up the draw. Mac couldn't see or smell anything but trusted his horses' keener senses; he looped Hornets' reins over a dead snag and started up the draw afoot. Just inside the mouth of the draw was a jumble of rocks that had fallen when the draw undercut a ledge and beside the rocks was a man.

He was lying on his back facing up the draw with blood covering his head and from where Mac stood, looking very dead. Mac stepped up beside the man and was startled when he opened his eyes and very softly said "Buenos dias, Senor." "Buenos dias, yourself but it looks like it hasn't been a real good day for you Senor." Mac squatted down beside the man and saw that the blood had come from a gash in his head that was now just seeping, that didn't look too bad but the leg was something else; the man's left leg was obviously broken below the knee with his foot turned out to the side. Mac was no stranger to broken bones, including his own, and knew that the leg would have to be immobilized before the little man could be moved. He also knew that there was no way in hell that he could keep those broken bones from moving while he got the man to somewhere he could get help unless the leg was set. He was five miles from the nearest telephone and at least a mile from the closest point that an ambulance could reach. If he went for help, it would be three hours or more before anything would be done for the man and the old fellow didn't look like he could last that long. "Senor, do you have water please?" "Sure thing friend, hang on a minute" Mac said and went back to his horse for his canteen. Mac knelt down and held the little mans' head up so that he could drink from the canteen. "Gracias Senor, my name is Emiliano Cortez; might I know the name of my benefactor?" "My name is Mac Connley, Emiliano Cortez but let's wait until we see if I can get you to some help before we title me benefactor." "The leg will have to be straightened and bound to something to hold it straight. Can you do that for me Mac Connley?" "I've done it before but it's going to hurt like hell when I pull it straight; are you sure you wouldn't rather me go for some professional help?" "The leg is already swollen and will soon be too swollen to set, I would be grateful if you would try to straighten it now." In his heart Mac knew the little man was right but he dreaded having to tackle the job. He went over the options once again in his mind before saying, "OK, let me gather up something to bind it with and I will be right back." Mac knew he had several pigging strings in his saddle pockets that would do for lashings but he would need something to hold the leg rigid after he got it straight. Neither the red berry cedar that grew on the slopes nor the mesquite down on the flats had straight limbs and Mac was wondering if he would have to go clear back down to the creek to find something when he remembered a stand of drought killed sumac a couple of hundred yards back down the trail. He stepped up on Bald Hornet and rode back to the sumac; the stems were about an inch in diameter, straight, dry and as he found when he broke several to length, fairly strong. Mac went back up to the draw and carried a bundle of twenty-four inch lengths of the sumac and the pigging strings up to Emiliano. To this point Mac had not really looked at the injured leg. "Let me look and see what we are up against." There was no blood showing on the leg and Mac was pleased to find when he pulled up Emilianos' pant leg that the bone had not come out through the skin. "It could have been a lot worse, if we can get it straight; it ought to heal without a problem." Mac sat down flat with his left leg between Emilianos' legs and the sumac and pigging strings close at hand. "Just lie easy, it will take me a minute to get everything ready." He bent over as if he were arranging the splint material and then with one smooth motion, thrust his left foot into the little man's crotch and grasping the twisted foot in both hands, pulled the foot toward him while rotating it back to its proper place. Emiliano screamed, jerked back and fainted but Mac had the satisfaction of feeling the bone jump into place with an audible click. Working quickly to get done before his patient came to, Mac smoothed the pant leg down and using all but one of the sumac sticks, surrounded the broken leg with a case of wood bound with rope. Mac lay the splinted leg down and using his handkerchief and water from the canteen began to clean blood from Emiliano's face. In a moment the little man opened his eyes and asked, "Is it done?" "It's done and the bone popped into place; I'm sorry that I tricked you but I didn't want you to tense up and make it harder to straighten the leg." "Senor Connley, I am in you debt. I was sure that I faced a long and painful ordeal before death would give me release." "The name's Mac and you don't owe me a thing. Let's get you turned around so your head is not downhill." Mac raised Emiliano up to a sitting position then picked up both his legs and pivoted him around 180 degrees. "Now you lie still while I see if I can figure out how to get you out of this canyon. I will have to go hunt something to make a stretcher with but I won't be gone long."

Mac remembered seeing a motte of honey locust with several dead trees near the creek and rode back to see if he could find material to make a sled or a litter or something that he could use to move Emiliano. The dead trees were twelve to fifteen feet tall and as big around as his wrist where they came out of the ground; not as large as he would like but Emiliano wasn't very heavy and Mac had no way to cut down bigger trees anyway. He broke off six of the dead saplings and rode back up the canyon dragging them with his lariat and stopping along the way to cut bear grass for lashing material. He first considered making a stretcher with Bald Hornet carrying the rear end while he carried the front and led the way but it would be a long two miles back to the house carrying that load. Also Bald Hornet was a steady old fellow but this would be something new for him and if he blew up there would be no way Mac could control him without dropping his end of the litter. Mac decided that he could use the two largest saplings as the frame of a travois and lash crosspieces from the smaller saplings to them with bear grass; one end would drag on the ground while the horse carried the other end and Mac led the horse. It would be too tight to get Bald Hornet up into the draw so he would have to build the travois next to where Emiliano was lying, get him on it and then drag it out to where he could hook it up to the horse. When he explained what he had in mind to Emiliano, the little man said that with help he could walk down out of the draw but Mac was afraid to take the risk; he didn't have that much faith in his jerry rigged splint. By scooting Emiliano over, Mac was able to build a horse wide travois on the floor of the draw but then realized that he needed something to cover the crosspieces. Bald Hornet stood quietly as Mac unsaddled him but looked back with a question in his eye as Mac re-saddled him without the saddle blanket. Unfolded Mac's old Navajo saddle blanket was almost as long as Emiliano was tall and stiff enough to make lying on the crosspieces bearable. Between the two of them they got Emiliano on the travois without too much pain and Mac pulled the rig out on to the cow trail heading down hill. Hornet wasn't sure what they were doing but backed up between the arms of the travois without a hitch and stood quietly as Mac lifted the front of the travois and tied it off to the saddle horn. Bald Hornet shied just a little when the travois first drug along the ground behind him but responded to Macs' reassurance and with Emiliano using his little bundle of possessions as a pillow they started down the trail. Emiliano saw the doe as they passed and called "Senor Mac it would be sinful to waste such fine meat, please dress the deer and put it on the travois with me." "Are you sure you want me to take the time to do that Emiliano? We are still a long ways from the house and any help for you." "Senor Mac, I have been dreaming of a meal of fresh deer liver for the last week; there is no medicine that could make me feel better, besides I can rest my leg on the carcass like a pillow." Mac field dressed the doe and using the last of his pigging strings, tied her to the travois below Emiliano with the liver, kidneys and heart safely stowed in the body cavity. It was a long two miles back to the ranch house with Bald Hornet walking very slowly and seeming to know that he must be careful not to jerk his load and while Mac heard several stifled groans, Emiliano did not complain nor ask him to stop until they came to the creek where he asked for a drink of the cool water.

When they reached the headquarters, Mac led Hornet and the travois right up to the bunkhouse door and after helping Emiliano to stand on one leg, carried him into the bunkhouse and laid him down on Wendy's' old bunk. The little man seemed to shrink into the bunk and said softly "Gracias Senor Mac, I did not expect to live, much less feel comfort again; I owe you more than I can ever pay." "You don't owe me anything, all I did was what anybody would do. I don't have anything for pain but some aspirin or some whiskey and as gaunt as you look one drink of whiskey might send you on a three-day drunk. When did you last eat?" "It has been a while since I had a full meal." "Let me get you some aspirin and something to eat and then I will see about getting you some help for that leg and cut head." Mac brought three aspirin and a glass of water and after getting Emiliano propped up with a folded blanket and a pillow, helped him get the aspirin and all of the water down. He then came back with a bowl of cold red beans cooked with bacon and two left over biscuits smeared with butter. Cooking had never been Mac's long suite, the beans were scorched and the biscuits had squatted to rise and got baked that way but Emiliano devoured the meal like it was food fit for a king. "I don't have a telephone," said Mac "so I will take the truck over to the neighbors and call for an ambulance to come and take you to the hospital." Emiliano paused with the last spoonful of beans almost to his mouth and said "Senor Mac, I am in your country sin papel, how do you say, without the proper papers? Also, I have no money for doctors. If you will permit, I will rest here until my leg is better and then I will do whatever work you may need done to earn my keep and to repay you for your kindness." "Emiliano, you are welcome to stay as long as you need to but we have to get someone to check you out and put a cast on your leg." "Senor Mac, my wife was curandera for our village, she often had to splint and cast broken limbs and I have helped her to do this many times. If you can bring me plaster of Paris and some gauze or soft cotton cloth, I can show you how to put a cast on my leg as well as any doctor. See the swelling has gone down a lot already; by tomorrow there will be no problem in putting on a cast and no need for a doctor. Then if you can find me something to use for crutches, in a few days I will be able to get around enough to at least help around the house." "I think you would be better off to let me get you to a doctor but ok, we will see how you feel in the morning. If you are not going to the doctor tonight, I need to find something to replace that broke stick and rope cobble job on your leg and to clean up your head." Mac brought soap and water and got the worst of the dried blood off Emiliano's face and neck then poured hydrogen peroxide into the cut and pulled the edges together with adhesive tape and covered it with a gauze pad. Then he gathered up some smooth lathes from a wooden apple crate, a soft towel and more adhesive tape and managed to replace the sumac and pigging string splint with one that fit much better and held the leg rigid without being uncomfortable. Mac worked as gently as possible but he had to slit the seam of Emiliano's pant leg and lift the leg to wrap it in the towel and by the time he had the splint taped on, Emiliano was gray with pain. Mac looked out the window and was startled to see the sun already low in the west; it was over six hours since he had found Emiliano. "You rest a bit while I unsaddle my horse and do my chores and then I will skin that deer and cook us some supper."

Mac had been alone more in the months since Windy died than at any time in his life. He grew up in a small house with a large and boisterous family where even the nights had a constant background of noise from the nocturnal snores, mutterings and movements of his parents and six siblings and while his working hours were often solitary there was nearly always someone around in the evenings even when he and Windy were batching in some remote cow camp. He found that he looked forward to having the gutsy little man around. The fact that he was "wet" didn't bother Mac, he figured anybody that was willing to walk two or three hundred miles looking for work had character if he didn't have nothing else. Besides, he and Windy had several times spent time working in Mexico "sin papel" just like Emiliano was in this country. Mac unsaddled Bald Hornet and gave him a bite of oats that he didn't really need but had earned a hundred times over and went to lock up what was left of Susan's chickens. Every time he failed to put them up at night, something caught another one of them and the flock was down to 14 or 15 hens and the rooster. He needed to get a dog or at least sit up with a light and a shotgun and make a good heathen out of the chicken thief. Susan's pet Jersey milk cow, Belle, had come fresh a month ago and the calf could not began to take all the milk she was giving so he had been milking her out at night to make her more comfortable. When Susan was alive, she and Belle had kept fresh butter and buttermilk and sweet milk and thick cream to put on hot peach cobbler in the walk-in cooler all the time but it didn't seem worth the effort with just him to eat it. Tonight though, he milked in a clean bucket and took the milk in, strained it and put in the refrigerator; maybe Emiliano would enjoy a glass of fresh milk with supper. Mac got a bucket of clean water and carried it, a clean tub and the doe over to the pipe rack where they skinned game and beeves when they butchered. It had not been used since Susan got sick, without her to organize and order he and Windy around like a drill sergeant and to can and grind and freeze and smoke the meat, with a pasture full of cheap cattle they had turned to living on bacon, bologna and for a treat, store bought hamburger. The deer was a small one and in a few minutes Mac had the hide off, the carcass washed ready to hang in the cooler and the heart, kidneys and liver trimmed and washed. He hung the deer in the cooler, wondering again if he should just turn it off, it held only some eggs, a half of sack each of potatoes and onions and a side of bacon. It was a far cry from the days when there was always a side of beef and usually a deer hanging in addition to the hams, smoked sausages and bacon. In those days, the shelves were loaded with food of all kinds from soft cheese and pickled venison to all kinds of fruits and vegetables from Susan's big deer fenced garden and orchard that she irrigated from the stone reservoir by the windmill. The first year Mac and Windy came to Oak Creek, just as soon as they finished the "got to do" things like fencing, Susan set Mac and Windy to hauling and spreading on her garden the mountain of manure that she paid James Coleman to bring her from the Sweetwater sale barn. Just when they had the mountain down to hill size and were looking forward to a restful job like shoeing horses, here came James with a huge truck load for the orchard. This turned into an annual event and while they grumbled to themselves about being turned into "clod hopping farmers", Windy and Mac were secretly kind of proud of "their" delicious tomatoes, and onions and sweet corn. They may not have had much money but the people of Oak Creek ranch ate like royalty when Susan was alive. Like most ranch people they ate a big breakfast before daylight of eggs with sausage or bacon and hot biscuits with cream gravy or pan cakes with butter and syrup then at noon, dinner would be the main meal of the day with usually a choice of at least two hot meats like steak fried in beef tallow or chicken and dumplings or pot roast plus all the side dishes of vegetables plus hot bread and a dessert. Susan's Mother was "Hill Country Dutch" from the German settlements to the south and Susan had carried on her traditions of setting out good food and plenty of it. Supper was normally lighter, sometimes just cold cornbread crumbled in sweet milk and maybe a bowl of ice cream to cap it off. Since he had been by himself, Mac ate whatever was easy and was looking forward to seeing if he could cook liver and onions without making a mess of it.

Every bunkhouse Mac had ever been in had at least one set of crutches and theirs was no different. Mac found a set in the storage room off the lean-to and cut them off to what he hoped was a suitable length for Emiliano. When Mac looked in on him, Emiliano was dead to the world asleep so Mac worked as quietly as possible to keep from waking him as he built a mesquite wood fire in the stove, mixed a batch of biscuits and sliced the liver, after first having to sharpen the butcher knife. How could a knife go dull just sitting in the drawer? He sprinkled on salt and black pepper then rolled the slices in flour and started them frying in hot bacon grease. When the liver was well browned on both sides, he added two onions cut into thick slices and a little water with salt, pepper and flour stirred in; when the gravy started bubbling, he put the lid on the heavy cast iron skillet and moved it to a cooler spot on the stove to simmer. He started water heating in the coffee pot and just as the coffee started to boil, heard Emiliano call his name. "Senor Mac, I would greatly appreciate some help. It is necessary that I get up and go outside." "Give me just a minute to get our biscuits out of the oven." Mac put the pan of biscuits in the warmer oven then picked up the shortened crutches and went in to the main room. "Let's see if you can manage these crutches; the bathroom is right through this door, there's no need for you to go outside." With Mac helping, Emiliano got stood up and holding the bad leg crooked at the knee managed to hobble down the hall to the bathroom. By the time he got back to the lean-to kitchen, Emiliano was shaky weak but he sat down in one of the three chairs and when the aroma of liver and onions hit him, started twitching his nose like a dry country rabbit with his first sniff of alfalfa. "Senor Mac if that tastes half as good as it smells, you will have created a masterpiece!" "No guarantee on taste, but it's hot and there's lots of it." Said Mac as he ladled up two plates of liver and onions with biscuits and gravy and warmed up red beans and placed them on the table with two cups of coffee. "There's fresh sweet milk if you want it and sugar and cream for the coffee."

CHAPTER 8

Bart woke much earlier than usual and lay wondering why until it hit him that today he went to the lawyer. He was up, shaved, showered, dressed and fed by the time he normally opened his eyes and then sat fidgeting and drinking coffee waiting until it was time to call work that he would not be in and to call the lawyers' office for an appointment. Looking for some way to kill time, Bart went back to his bedroom and browsed through his bookshelf. His Mother passed her love of reading on to him and over the years, he had collected a more than fair library even if most of his books were in paperback. As a boy he had devoured westerns, he was after all half Texan, so there were a lot of six-gun melodramas but as he matured, he found historical fiction and true history so that his collection ranged from trash to treasure but heavy on the western theme. Since his "maybe" relative, James Thomas Barton, had lived in Maryneal, Texas, he picked up his copy of Elmer Keltons' *The Time it Never Rained*, which he remembered was set in the San Angelo area. The book deals with the great drought of the 1950s and how people coped when not just their livelihood but their entire way of life was destroyed. Bart was fascinated by the strength of some of the characters Kelton described and decided that these were people he wouldn't mind claiming as kin. He started reading with the idea of passing the hour and a half until 9:00 when he could make his calls but quickly became absorbed in the story and in what seemed like only a moment his watch said

9:08. His supervisor wasn't thrilled with the late notice but said he would call in someone to cover for him. The secretary at the law office checked and then told him that Mr. Hendricks could see him at 2:00 and to please bring along a copy of his birth certificate. That wouldn't pose a problem, along with her love of reading his Mother had instilled in him her bookkeepers' passion for organization; his original birth certificate and some copies along with his army discharge, his high school diploma, his divorce decree and insurance policies were in the small fireproof lockbox that had belonged to his Mother. With the request for a birth certificate, Bart for the first time allowed himself to hope that this "inheritance" might amount to something. It might even be enough that he could take a trip and see the country where his Mother was born.

"Mr. Hendricks will see you now Mr. Ryan, please come this way." Said the pretty little receptionist that Bart had been furtively watching over the top of an old magazine for the last hour; if he had to wait; at least the scenery was nice. George A. Hendricks III was standing beside a desk as big as Bart's bed and looked as if he had been sent over from central casting to play a New York lawyer until he reached out his hand and with a big lop sided grin said, "Come in Mr. Ryan, sit down and let's see if we can make your day a little brighter." "Can I get you some coffee or something else to drink?" "No thanks", said Bart, "I'm fine." Hendricks looked in the folder on his desk and asked, "Did you have time to get a copy of your birth certificate." Bart handed over the copy which Hendricks read carefully and said with another grin, "This is the last part of the puzzle unless your Mother had other children that we don't know about", Hendricks looked at Bart with a questioning look on his face and when Bart shook his head No, said "We have found the only surviving relative of your Great Uncle James Thomas Barton. Did you know your Mother had an uncle?" "Mother told me that her Dad had one brother but that they were not close and that she never met him." "From what the law firm in Sweetwater Texas told me, your Great Uncle left west Texas long before your Grandparents were killed and evidently he did not know that your Mother existed. At any rate he died without leaving a will and the Court gave the firm of Walker and Walker in Sweetwater the task of tracking down any heirs. They traced your Mother to New York and hired us to find her or any of her heirs." "That sounds like a bunch of trouble for a lot of people," said Bart. "Did he leave enough to make all that trouble worthwhile?" "I don't have an inventory of the estate, you will have to contact the Texas lawyers for that, but I do know that there is a ranch of several thousand acres among other things." Bart sat very still for a moment before asking in a small voice "Several thousand acres?" Hendricks flashed another of his now familiar grins and said, "I told you we were going to brighten up your day."

CHAPTER 9

Mac drove the old pickup south toward home at his normal highway speed of forty-five miles an hour and like always marveled at the fools that went blasting past him even on the blind curves going up Nine Mile Mountain. If they were in such an all fired hurry to get where they were going, why hadn't they left earlier instead of driving like crazy people, blowing their horns and cussing him just because he drove like a sane man? His trip to town had been timed right as the lawyer did have news about his new partner; Herbert Barton Ryan was flying into Abilene from Dallas tomorrow on his way here from New York City and the lawyer would bring him out to the ranch the next day. Mac had been trying to remember if he'd ever met anybody from New York City and couldn't get any closer than a real strange duck from Kansas City. Still this fellow was the grandson of Windy's older brother Tom so he probably wouldn't to be too different from normal folks. Tom left home under some sort of cloud when Windy and Mac were about twelve and he didn't remember Windy ever having much to say about him.

He had bought a whole mess of groceries since there would be three mouths to feed instead of just one and had what he hoped was the right stuff to put a cast on Emiliano's leg. He would open up the big house tomorrow, light the hot water heater and check to make sure that there was propane in the tank; the bunkhouse had plenty of room but might not be up to New York standards even with the bathroom complete with bathtub and a shower that Susan had insisted on adding when he and Windy first got back. Mac fought it off but the same thought kept creeping back into his mind; this fellow might be coming just to sell the ranch as fast as possible and get back to New York. Well, as Windy used to say, "If you can't do nothing about it, there aint no use in worrying about it." Mac turned off the highway and rolled the truck up to the bump gate going into the ranch; he pushed against the right side of the center pivoted gate with the truck bumper and as the gate swung open, drove smoothly through the opening. A thought hit him as he drove through and the gate closed behind him and he broke into a big grin as he remembered the government tax inspectors trying to get through this gate. The one driving pushed too hard and the gate swung around and hit the rear fender of the car, he goosed it just in time to catch the heavy plank gate coming back on the front fender. He slammed on the brakes and the gate swung back to catch him in the ass again. This was repeated several times until he finally made his partner get out and hold the gate open so he could drive through. Their plain little government car would still run but Mac bet that they had hell explaining how they had gotten both the front and the rear fenders on the left side bashed in without touching the rest of the car. It was getting late; he would have to hurry to get the groceries unloaded and his chores done before dark. As he topped the ridge above headquarters, he saw smoke rising from the cook stove chimney and Emiliano coming back on his crutches from the lots where Bald Hornet and Grayman, the two horses he had up in the horse trap, were eating oats from their trough. "Hola, Senor Mac, the bunkhouse is cleaned up, the eggs are gathered, the chickens are put up, the water is running on the fruit trees, the horses are fed and there is a stew on the stove but I could not think where I could put this wooden leg so that I could milk the cow." "There wasn't no need of you doing all that, hobbling around with a broke leg." "Senor Mac, I must carry my own weight or I will not feel right about taking your hospitality." "Well, Hell, let's get this cast on your leg and you can start building fence tomorrow, but right now I better go milk Belle." Mac had not had much company lately but he thought; "If he was going to have company, Emiliano was sure the sort to have." With Emiliano giving instructions, getting the cast on turned out to be as simple as he had predicated, the swelling was down and the leg looked pretty good except for being black and purple from the bruising. When they were through, the cast started just below the knee and covered all of the foot except the toes. Mac had asked for something to protect the cast and the pharmacist sold him a strap on boot like thing that fit over the cast. Emiliano pronounced the cast to be as good as his late wife could have done and Mac had to argue him into sitting still while Mac served up the stew. "I could not find any chile, Senor Mac, so this guisado does not have much taste. I can do much better if you can bring me a few spices." "I don't know how fresh they will be but there are all kinds of spices and stuff in the kitchen of the big house. We will look tomorrow; my new partner is coming and I need to open up the house. It's been shut up a long time and will need airing out and the floor swept."

CHAPTER 10

Bart was so fascinated by the countryside that he was having a hard time carrying on a conversation with Donnie Walker, the younger half of the firm of Walker and Walker. He had never seen anything like what Donnie told him was called "the Big Country." Landing at Dallas-Fort Worth International Airport he might have been in any big American city but from the time he stepped off the plane in Abilene, he was in a different world. They were traveling west on a rolling plain that when you topped a rise, seemed to reach forever in all directions. They passed areas of farm ground with cotton just starting to break ground in gracefully curving rows and oil fields with pump-jacks nodding slowly up and down like feeding dinosaurs but mostly there were miles and miles of the feathery looking brush Donnie told him was mesquite. Rather than green, the grass along the roadside and what little he could see in the pastures was gold colored and even the weeds looked wilted. The only trees, aside from mesquite, were along the banks of the infrequent creeks and they looked dusty and seemed to have too few leaves for their size. Bart felt a thrill run up his back when after reading about them since he was a boy; he saw his first windmill off in a pasture pumping water for a small group of cattle. The highway crossed another creek and Donnie said with a sly grin "That's Bitter Creek where the town of Sweetwater gets its water. We will be there in a few minutes, find you some supper and a motel room and in the morning I will run you out to meet Mac Connley and see the ranch." Bart had been on the go for more than twelve hours but was still so wired and had so much running through his mind that he doubted he would sleep much tonight. Donnie had told him before he left New York that he now owned an undivided one half interest in the 5120 acres that was Oak Creek Ranch and in the cattle and equipment on the ranch but hadn't told him until today that the ranch carried a one hundred and twenty thousand dollar mortgage and that he would owe something like that more in death taxes. When he knew for sure that he really had inherited a ranch, Bart started a frantic search for information about the ranching business and what he found was not promising. The cattle market was way down and cattlemen all over the country were singing the blues. In addition, Donnie told him that west Texas was in the fourth year of drought and that if it didn't break soon not only the farmers and ranchers but also the entire economy of the whole area would be in serious trouble. Bart hoped that his new partner had some good ideas because he could see right now that he was in over his head and badly needed to talk to the accountant Donnie recommended.

Emiliano insisted on going with Mac to clean up the big house and after feeling of the cast to make sure the plaster was hard Mac gave in. While Mac went around opening windows, Emiliano started brushing off the dust that had sifted into the old house from dust storms and covered every horizontal surface like a thick coat of paint. When he got to Susan's' kitchen with its big double oven stove, commercial size refrigerator, racks of cooking and baking utensils and over sized cabinet top work spaces, Emiliano was like a kid in a candy store, hobbling from one wonder to the next and talking to himself ninety miles an hour in Spanish the whole time. "Senor Mac, in this kitchen you could prepare feasts for the King and all of his court. It is twice, no four times, the size of the one where I once fed fifty men three times a day." "The wife of my dead partner loved to cook and this kitchen was her one extravagance; she was never happier than when she had a crowd coming for dinner." Between the two of them, they got the place cleaned up, the hot water heater going and made up the bed in the master bedroom. The old two story house, once home to about half of the whole George clan had five bedrooms and unusual for its time, two bathrooms. Susan had joked once that if it wasn't so far from the highway, they could open a hotel. Emiliano found Susan's' spice inventory and some home canned green chilies in the pantry and set out to make another venison stew. The one from the night before made with only salt and pepper was an affront to his pride as uno cocinero and he felt the need to demonstrate his culinary skills to his new friend. For lunch, he fried up a batch of deer meat, made mashed potatoes, biscuits and cream gravy. As they ate, Mac asked Emiliano where he had learned to make and hunt with a bow. Emiliano told him the story of his "Comanche Grandfather" and the wonderful times they had together when he was a young boy. They spent most of the day cleaning on the big house and got things in pretty good shape with time to do chores before dark. As Emiliano promised, the new stew was much better and not long after supper two well fed but tired old men turned out the lights and went to bed.

Mac wanted to ride out to check on things but didn't know when the lawyer and his new partner would be out so after chores, he spent some time working on the corral fences and about 11:30 went back to the house to find Emiliano had warmed up the stew and started a fresh pot of coffee. The coffee had just finished perking when a car pulled up out front and Mac went out to meet his new partner. Bart was opening the car door when a tall gaunt old man stepped out on the front porch of the ranch house and in a voice surprisingly strong and deep boomed out "Get out and come in." Donnie Walker came around the car and with one hand on Bart's shoulder, said, "Mac Connley, meet Bart Ryan." Ryan stepped forward with his hand out "Mr. Connley, I am very pleased to meet you, Donnie has told me how lucky I am to have you for a partner." Taking the out stretched hand, Mac said, "The name's Mac, Bart and I'm surely glad you're here. You all come on in the house and we will have some dinner while we talk." The group went in through the living room and back to the kitchen where Emiliano was putting plates and silverware on the table; "Donnie Walker, Bart Ryan, meet Emiliano Cortez, he has been helping me around the place." Bart went around the table and stuck out his hand, "I am pleased to meet you Mr. Cortez." Emiliano first ducked his head looking a little abashed but then took Bart's hand and said, "Con mucho gusto Senor Ryan." Donnie just nodded and Emiliano nodded back. "You all are in luck", said Mac, "If Emiliano wasn't here, you'd be lucky to get boloney and rat cheese sandwiches. Get you a plate and help yourselves." Emiliano started to duck out the back door but Mac quietly caught him by the arm, handed him a plate and said "Get your plate and I will pour coffee so you don't stub that wooden leg and scald somebody." Mac noted Bart's smile at his little joke but he also saw the frown that crossed Donnie Walkers' face. Mac knew there were people who considered themselves too good to eat with the help and was pleased that his new partner wasn't one of them; if the lawyer didn't like it, he could eat on the porch. Mac had spent most of his life being "the help" and he'd be damned if he would see his friend put down in his own house.

The atmosphere at lunch was at first a little strained but lightened up quick as Bart peppered Mac with a barrage of questions about the ranching business, about Oak Creek Ranch and about his great uncle Windy. Mac felt like the weight of the world was lifted off his shoulders as it became clear that selling the ranch was the last thing Bart wanted to do. Donnie needed to get back to Sweetwater and asked Bart if he wanted to ride back into town and get a rental car. Mac spoke up, "There is no reason for him to rent a car, Susan's Buick is in the garage or he can use the pickup if he wants to go someplace." Donnie told them to check with him later in the week, as he would set up a meeting with the accountant, then said his goodbyes and left. Bart followed him out to get his bags out of the car and to thank him. As he got back to the porch, Mac opened the door and said "Take the main bedroom to the right there, we made up the bed yesterday." Bart carried his bags into the room and asked, "Where is your room? I'm not running you out am I?" "No not at all, Emiliano and I are out in the bunkhouse." "I wouldn't want to impose but is there room for me out there? Wouldn't it be simpler if we were all together?" "There's room a plenty and you're more than welcome if you can stand to hear two old men snore."

They left Emiliano cleaning up the remains of lunch and after putting Bart's bags under an empty bunk walked down to the pens where Bald Hornet and Grayman were dozing in the sparse shade of a huge old mesquite that grew just outside the corral. "Would you like to saddle a couple of horses and see part of the ranch before supper?" "I have never been on a horse in my life but I can't wait to see the ranch and I'll do my best not to fall off." "You're about Windy's size and built like him, we'll put his saddle on Grayman and start your education as a rancher. The cattle are up in Reese Canyon which is about two miles from here; we can see the cattle and a fair part of the ranch in two or three hours." Mac held his horse to a walk and after a few minutes Bart began to get comfortable with the novelty of having his head eight feet in the air and with the motion of the horse under him. As they rode, Mac told him about the drought and the need to sell cattle to lighten the load on the grass." I had hoped to lease some grass, the old 9R Ranch that joins us on the south is a really good forty-five section ranch and it still has grass. A couple of lawyers out of Dallas bought it several years ago for a play pretty and the first thing they did was take all the cattle off. I tried to talk to one of them about leasing some grass and you would have thought that I had asked him to sell me his daughter; all I got was a ten minute lecture on how cows have ruined the West but that he and his buddy were going to save at least a little bit of it. There is no way I could convince those two of anything but without grazing, in ten years or so, that whole ranch will turn to a brush thicket growing on bare ground. Anyway, that is the only grass anywhere around and I don't see anything for us but to sell some stock. I hate to sell cows with baby calves on them but if we don't sell some, we will run out of grass and wind up having to sell everything and probably at the bottom of the market. The market for cows with young calves has already broken here locally, nobody has any grass so most of the pairs coming in to auction are being split with the cow going to slaughter and the calf being sold for a little bit of nothing to farmers who will try to keep them alive until they get big enough to handle hay and sack feed.

We have about fifteen cows that won't calve this time and about fifty cows that are getting some age on them. What I had thought to do was to sell the empty cows and a handful of cattle with faults of one sort or another here locally then put the older cows together with the same number of younger cows and see if I can sell the package to some people I know up in Kansas where it's still raining." "Mac, you know that I don't know anything about ranching but even I can see that we don't need cattle that we don't have the grass to feed. I don't have any reason to go back to New York and I can't think of anywhere I'd rather be then on this ranch so let's back your judgment and get started with what we need to do. I'll have a little money when I get my apartment sold; I'm strong and not afraid of work. If you will have me, I would like to be your partner." Mac rode on maybe twenty yards before looking up and saying, "Son you don't know how big a load that takes off of my mind. I was scared that you would want to sell out quick as you could and get back to the bright lights. You won't get rich but there are worse ways to make a living besides ranching so let's see if we can't keep this one running." They rode on a little ways before Bart said, "If I am going to be a west Texas rancher, you better tell me what a section is, I've heard that term ever since I got here and have been too afraid of looking dumb to ask what the hell it means." "A section is a square chunk of land a mile on each side Son, 640 acres and in this kind of country about enough room to be a home for 30 cows."

When they got to the gate into the Reese Canyon pasture, Bart climbed down to open the gate and was startled to find how sore he was already. He didn't say anything but thought to his self, "If that little ride made me this sore, I may not be able to get out of bed tomorrow." He managed to open the gate, which Mac told him was a "wire gap", get his horse through and the gate shut again while losing only a little hide to the barbed wire on the gate. When he tried to re-mount, he pulled on the saddle horn so hard that Grayman had to shift his feet to keep from being pulled sideways and looked back at him with what Bart felt sure was disgust but he stood until Bart managed to clamor back on with brute strength and awkwardness. As they stepped off, Mac said, "You'll get the hang of it, just keep your back straight and lift with your leg while you pull up with your hand." They rode deeper into the canyon and began to see cattle grazing the broad canyon floor and along the banks of the small dry creek that wound back and forth across the creek bottom. Mac seemed to be concentrating and was silently looking at each group of cattle they passed, sometimes riding around a group in order to get a better view. Finally as they neared the backside of the pasture, he said, "I can't be sure of a quick ride through count like that but I think they are all here." "Mac, why are all the cattle locked up in one pasture? Why not just open the gates and let them roam the whole ranch?" "Two reasons, one it makes it easier and quicker to see all of the cattle and second it gives the grass on the rest of the ranch a chance to recover from being grazed. The first was real important when we still had screwworms to deal with, then somebody had to see every animal at least every couple of days to keep them from being eaten alive." "Eaten alive by worms? I thought that maggots only ate dead flesh. Is this part of my greenhorn initiation?" "Not funning you Son, the screwworm fly lays eggs in open wounds that hatch into worms that eat only living flesh and if they are not treated, they will kill the animal. It's hard on the cows to have to make milk without green feed, but we used to calve in the winter here, just so screwworms would not infect the navels of the new calves. Over half of all the baby deer would die every year even with their mamas trying to lick the worms out. One of the few things that the U.S Government ever got right was when they eradicated the screwworm in the early 1960's."

"How did they manage to do that? They couldn't have sprayed insecticide over the whole country." "Some bright fellow figured out that the female only mates once so they raised millions of screwworm flies in a lab and zapped them with X-rays or something to make them sterile. Then they dumped the sterile flies out of airplanes, the sterile males mated with the native females and over a period of ten years or so the screwworm died out not only here but clear down to Panama. We don't need to rotate the cattle through small pastures because of the screwworm anymore but we probably should have more pastures for the good it does for the grass. Some ranchers are using thirty or more pastures for each herd and are having real good results with both the grass and the cattle. They are trying to copy the way the buffalo grazed this country for thousands of years; a lot of animals on a small area for a short period of time followed by a long rest period." "Why would buffalo graze like that? They could go anywhere they wanted." "Wolves", replied Mac," If the buffalo didn't stay pretty close together, the wolves would pull down any stragglers. With a lot of mouths to feed on a small area, the herd had to keep moving on to fresh grass so all the animals could get enough to eat and for the same reason they didn't come back to areas they had grazed till the grass had a chance to get some growth. Things worked pretty slick when Ma Nature was running things; buffalo and other critters ate the grass and then moved on so it could re-grow and both the grass and the animals did fine. The wolves got fat catching the old and the sick but most buffalo got to live a normal life span until the Indians got the horse and things began to change. The plains Indians had the buffalo in decline even before the hide hunters got here just because it was so much easier to hunt and to follow the herds once they had horses. When we took over, the first thing we did was kill out the wolves. With the wolves gone our cattle lost the herding instinct and spread out instead of staying in compact herds. Since they were spread out, they didn't have to keep moving to find enough to eat and would graze the same grass plants over and over as fast as they grew without ever giving them enough time to recover. Also before man got involved, in drought times the grazing animals either left or they died so the grass was not hammered while it was in a weakened state. Charley Goodnight, who was an early day Indian scout and rancher in this country, told of riding across the high plains up in the panhandle for three days back in the late 1860's without ever being out of sight of a drought killed buffalo. The drought finally broke and the land came back like it had a thousand times before. It was only after man took over with windmills and fences and hay and sack feed that stock could be held on land that could no longer feed and water them. It is easier on the cattle but it is hell on the land. This country used to support way more animals than it does now. We have hurt it bad, not on purpose; we just didn't know any better. This can be a hard old country but it is a good country if you treat it right and mostly it has good people."

CHAPTER 11

Tejas Mexico 1824

Thomas Connley reined in his horse while he was still in the cover of the oak mott and sat quietly absorbing the sights, the sounds and even the smells of the prairie that opened in front of him and of the oak motts scattered beyond. He looked for men or horses and for any sign that men might have recently been here; he looked for carrion birds that might indicate a recent kill by hunters but also he looked for trails left through the tall grass that might have been made by men riding in single file. He both watched and listened of any sign of wildlife whose routine had been disturbed by humans and he watched his horse for any signs that it had seen or smelled something that he missed. When he was satisfied that he was alone, he rode slowly across the neck of open prairie that separated him from the next oak mott. Thomas was the point scout for a group of wild horse hunters and he took his duties very seriously. They were in dangerous territory and his friends relied on him for early warning of any threat. He had seen nothing to indicate there were people around since three days ago when he had stood hidden in a thicket, holding his horses' nose to keep him from whickering to the horses being ridden by two Indian men. The two were obviously returning from a hunt as they had a pack horse loaded with game but their route was at ninety degrees to that of Thomas and his friends and he waited and watched as they rode out of sight. The horse hunters came from western Arkansas and were headed for the open prairies to the west in this part of Mexico. It was early spring and the creeks and rivers of eastern Tejas were running high. The floods forced them to go west from the Arkansas settlements and cross the Red River on the ford at Fort Towson in the Indian Territories before dropping south. They could have saved a lot of miles had they been able to take the Trammell Trace southwest from Arkansas but with the high water, the area from the Sabine River down to the Sulfur River and on to past the Neches River was one big swamp. They had to swim the Trinity River but once across the Trinity, the country changed rapidly becoming drier with timber giving way to grassland. Since leaving the heavy timber of the eastern river bottoms, they had been riding southwest across a rolling grassland savanna, a sea of grass dotted with scattered big oak trees and occasional oak thickets where topography or luck had spared young oak trees from destruction by the wildfires that sometimes raged through this area. The creek bottoms had more timber than the uplands with pecan and walnut being common but even in these areas the timber was widely spaced with grass as the understory instead of brush. Wildlife was abundant; they saw deer and bear daily as well as large flocks of prairie chickens and wild turkeys. Buffalo and elk were less common but becoming more so as they went west and they had seen one small band of wild horses. Thomas was anxious to get to the true prairie where wild horses should be more plentiful and he wanted to get there before the wild horses had time to fatten up on the new spring growth after losing weight on dead grass all winter. It was a lot easier to catch and handle thin horses than it would be once they regained condition. He was enjoying seeing the new country but he wanted to get started acquiring the wealth that would restore to him and his three siblings the security and substance that they had lost with the death of their parents four years before. Both of their parents along with a baby brother and a little sister had died in one of the cholera outbreaks that regularly devastated the western Arkansas settlements; in some communities more than half the people, sometimes entire families, died. Thomas was the oldest at sixteen and had been doing a man's work and taking a man's responsibility since he was twelve years old. Their uncle David had taken in the four orphans but Thomas was determined that he and his two brothers and sister would not be dependent upon charity even from family. This trip was his chance to begin earning the resources he would need to gain their independence. He was the youngest of the group that had come to Mexico to hunt wild horses but he had earned his place in the endeavor by his skill, intelligence and hard work. There were ten men in the group and their plan was to find a good location on the edge of the open prairie and begin catching wild horses. The captured horses would be hobbled and loose herded until they had a good sized herd. They would then halter and neck yolk the horses in eight to ten horse units and lead them out. They would have to hobble the horses every night and re-yolk them every morning until they became gentle enough to be driven as a herd. Catching the horses and getting them back to market would be difficult enough but they must also dodge both the local Indians and the Spanish lancers that patrolled the area from the mission forts at Nacogdoches and other points to the south. The Indians were not that big a problem, the local tribes were not as warlike as the tribes farther west, but the Spanish lancers were a real concern. They looked upon wild horse hunters as thieves and tended to deal out summary justice by execution. The group was involved in a dangerous venture but delivered to the rapidly growing settlements in Missouri each horse would bring ten to twelve dollars cash money. Arkansas was the western frontier of the sudden expansion of the United States brought about by the U. S. purchase, twenty years before, of the Louisiana territory from France. Money was in short supply on the frontier; the most common cash being Spanish silver escudos, called Spanish dollars, which were often hacked into eight, more or less, equal pieces known as bits. Cash of any description was scarce and most commerce was conducted by barter or with paper script from one of the large trading companies that had been doing business on the Red and the Arkansas Rivers for many years. On the frontier, you could live and raise a family without money; many families on the outer edge of the settlements would not see ten dollars in cash all year and as with all rare things, cash had value. Bear grease was as good as or better than lard and buckskin breeches and homespun linsey- woolsey shirts served the same purpose as broad cloth and linen but while you could sell well tanned buckskins for a dollar each in the settlements, you could not buy a new twelve dollar Hawken rifle on the frontier for twelve buckskins. It was worth taking a few risks to obtain some hard cash.

The men on this expedition, most of whom were kin to Thomas, wanted and needed the money but also they enjoyed the opportunity to poke a finger in the eye of his most Catholic Majesty, the King of Spain. They were, to a man, Scots-Irish Protestants, though most of them had seldom seen the inside of any church and if truth be known more than a few of them carried almost as much Indian blood as they did the Scot or Irish variety. Many of their forebears came over from the old country as single men of very slight means; quite a few got to America by signing papers of indenture to gain their passage.

Most of them were not exactly prize catches for the few eligible young women of their own race; Indian maidens were more plentiful and less fearful of living the rather rough life of a frontier wife. The founding matriarchs of many of the Scots-Irish families had grown up speaking Cherokee or Shawnee or Tuscarora. The same drive to improve their situation that sent their grandfathers to Ireland from Scotland now pushed these men west in search of land and economic freedom. To a son of the old order where ownership of his own land had been a dream beyond his wildest imagination, this new world with its' land free for the taking was heaven on earth. They began a migration that was to last more than one hundred years; they moved west beyond the settlements as families and groups of related families and established their farms and their homes. Some settled permanently in favored areas but many, when the settlements caught up to them, loaded up and moved farther west. They made friends with, traded with and intermarried with the local Indians when this was possible and when it was not possible, they waged total war. They made the best of friends and the worst of enemies. These were the people Thomas Connley sprang from and they had become some of the most independent and most self sufficient people the world had ever seen. Every man was a stockman and a farmer, a hunter and an Indian fighter and like as not, able to do rough blacksmith and carpentry work, make a fair run of whiskey and dance a highland whirl. They had no more problems justifying their taking of Spanish horses than their ancestors had in the taking of English cattle. The horses were running free wearing no mans' brand and "No papist bastard was going to say them no!" The group was to spend more than three months in Mexico before catching some 165 wild horses and getting them back to Arkansas but Thomas knew long before the trip was over that he would be coming back to the land known as Tejas. This land had everything a man could ask, the prairies were covered with sweet grass enough for one hundred times all the cattle in Arkansas, the bottoms had timber for homes and deep black soil for farms. The game was so plentiful and tame that even the poorest hunter could feed his family and there were even wild horses free for the taking. As soon as he could put together the things they would need and persuade Mary Jane Newman to marry him, he and his cousin David Jr. would move their families to this new land. Not often in the history of the world had people had such an opportunity to move into a virgin world and shape it to their own needs.

CHAPTER 12

On the ride back to the ranch house Mac and Bart discussed what needed to be done and agreed that the first order of business should be to reduce the load on the drought stricken grass by selling off part of the cowherd. They would bring the herd in tomorrow and sort it into the three groups that Mac had described, ship the culls, put the keepers back out to grass and get in touch with the Kansas rancher to see if he was interested in the remaining group. As they went over figures, it came clear that even if Macs' friends were willing to buy the cattle at the price they would bring in Kansas, less transportation costs, selling half the herd would bring in far less than half of what was owed on the ranch mortgage. They would have the remainder of the mortgage plus another IRS bill, operating and living expense all to pay with only half a herd to generate income. It was two very glum partners who rode into headquarters as the sun was setting. Supper was quiet as the enormity of their problems sunk in on Mac and Bart; Emiliano realized that something was badly amiss and with grace kept his own counsel.

After breakfast Mac and a very sore Bart rode to the backside of the Reese Canyon pasture and started drifting the herd back to headquarters. There were a lot of young baby calves so they moved slowly making sure that all the calves were mothered up. Bart was across the herd from Mac when one cow came out of the herd and started back up the canyon at a fast trot. Bart tried to turn her back to the herd but she dodged past him and broke into a run. Bart started after her but stopped when Mac hollered for him to "Let her go" and rode over to him. "She must have a new baby laid out, you go on following slow behind the herd and I'll go check. If the calf is able to travel, I'll bring them along and if not I'll leave them here for now. Just ride back and forth across the rear of the herd and be careful not to push them, remember that a horse walks four miles an hour but cattle only walk three miles an hour. Give them plenty of room and don't follow directly behind any animal; they can't see directly behind themselves and it makes them nervous to have any-thing but another cattle in their blind spot." Bart rode along behind the herd and was surprised to see that as long as he followed Macs' instructions, the cattle were perfectly content to amble along down the wide canyon bottom with no animal trying to run ahead or break off to one side. As a test, he fell in directly behind one cow and fol-lowed her closely and it was obvious even to his inexperienced eye that this made the cow uncomfortable in a very short time. At first the cow speeded up crowding into and upsetting the cattle ahead and then she tried to keep him in view by turning her head first one-way and then the other. When this didn't work, she turned sideways and would have disrupted the even flow of the herd had Bart not turned his horse away from her and backed off. Bart continued to work back and forth across the rear of the herd being careful not to linger in any animals' blind spot and to not crowd the animals. The herd moved quietly with none of the dashing about, bellowing and turmoil that years of watching western movies had led him to expect. In a little bit, Mac rode up to say, "She has a brand new calf and there's no point in making it travel right now. She's an older cow that knows how to take care of her babies and won't go far enough from it to let a coyote make supper out of it. Probably she will bring it along behind us; gentle cattle like these are more comfortable in the herd. If she doesn't bring it to the herd, then we'll come back and get them in a day or two." Bart told Mac about his experiment and how the cattle had reacted. Mac said, "Son you have just learned something that a lot of cowboys never learn. If you'll watch the cattle, they'll tell you how your actions are affecting them and what they are going to do. If you don't like what the cattle are about to do, then change your behavior until they are reacting like you want." "What about wild cattle, how do you handle them?" "Just like we handle the gentle ones except that we have to work from further away until they settle down and learn to trust us. Show me a bunch of wild cattle and I will show you a bunch of wild cowboys."

Before they left, Mac had opened the catch trap outside the pens and the gate leading into the largest of the corral pens so that when they arrived the cattle flowed directly into the pens without a hitch. Mac and Bart followed the herd into the pens and Mac explained what he wanted to do. "We have enough pens so that we can sort three ways. You open the gate into the south pen and I will bring you cattle that will be going to Kansas. Move away from the gate to let them in when I bring an animal down and then ride back to the gate to keep animals from coming out when I go back to the herd. After we get a bunch in the south pen, we will move them into one of the pens to the east and then we can pen culls that we are going to sell here or more Kansas cattle whichever is easy. We will keep that up until we have the three groups separated." Bart took a position out from the gate where he hoped he was out of the way and watched. The cattle had formed a loose group at the north end of the pen when Mac eased his horse into the herd and with no fuss and seemingly no effort separated an older cow and her calf from the bunch. As they started walking down the fence toward the gate Mac backed his horse up and let another cow follow; when an animal he did not want tried to follow, Mac swung Bald Hornets' head toward her and she turned back around the front of the bunch. Macs' horse never moved more than a step or two in any direction, sometimes only turning his head and not moving at all but he and Mac kept a steady stream of cattle flowing into the sort pen while turning back cattle that were to stay. After forty head or so, Mac followed a pair down the fence and told Bart, "I'll hold the gate while you ease through the cattle and open the gate into the lower pen on the east; swing the gate into the east pen so it doesn't block the opening." Bart started through the middle of the penned cattle but Mac called out, "Get over on the fence and give them time to move out of your way." By the time Bart got the gate open, the cattle were bunched on the fence line farthest away from him and Mac. Still on the ground Bart said, "Should I get behind them and push them out?" Mac said, "No, I'll show you a trick; step up on your horse and move to the center of the pen facing the cattle." Bart rode to the center of the pen and stopped with all the cattle watching him. "Now move toward the cattle just a little." Bart moved up a step and was surprised to see the cattle closest to the open gate began to move toward it. "If you want to slow them down, move toward the gate; if you want to speed them up, move toward the cattle." Bart moved back and forward once the cattle started moving and found that he could string them out and keep them moving slowly in single file by barely moving his horse. As the last cattle were starting out, he moved forward too fast and turned a lone cow back. He rode around behind her and she broke for the gate in a panicked run banging a hip on the gatepost as she went through. Embarrassed, Bart said, "That one's a little silly." Mac licked the smoke he was rolling and without looking up said, "Cattle just do what cattle do, if what they do is not what you want, it's your fault not theirs."

That night after a supper of Emilianos' chili con carne with fried eggs and homemade tortillas, the three of them sat outside the bunkhouse, Mac and Emiliano on old straight-backed chairs and Bart on a three-legged stool. Bart couldn't get used to how fast the dry air cooled off as soon as the sun went down; it must have been more then ninety degrees this afternoon and now an hour after dark, he was almost chilly. With the high humidity in New York, on a day like today they would be miserably hot all night; here he would need to pull a blanket up before early morning. They had turned out the bunkhouse lights so as not to attract bugs and the only sign of manmade light anywhere was the glow when Mac drew on his cigarette. Bart looked up at a sky that he had never before seen; the clear dry air and lack of light pollution made an unbelievable number of stars shine with brilliant intensity. He could pick out constellations that before now had existed for him only as pictures in a book and a meteor shower was in progress creating a steady stream of "shooting stars" large and small. As he watched the light show, an owl called "hoo-hoo uh-ooogah" from somewhere off to the south and as if commenting on the owls' musical abilities, first one and then a second coyote yip yip-yipped before harmonizing in a long drawn out howl. Bart was tired but tired in an entirely different way from what he felt after a long day selling televisions. They had sorted the cattle and then drove each bunch to a separate pasture, which meant that he had quadrupled his total previous time spent horseback in one day. He knew that he would be sore in the morning but right now he felt as relaxed as he could ever remember. Almost as if talking to himself,

Bart murmured, "People in the city would pay a lot of money for a day like I had today." Mac grunted and said, "Sure they would, they would be tickled pink to spend their money to get to breathe dirt behind a bunch of cows with an illiterate old coot, eat greasy food off tin plates and sleep on rope strung cots." Bart stood up and started walking back and forth in front of Mac and Emiliano; "Mac I'm serious there are people out there who would think they had died and gone to heaven to spend time on a Texas ranch with honest to God cowboys just doing the things you do every day. How many people could you bed down in the big house?" "Humph," "Well, there's five bedrooms that could sleep at least two each, more if they are real friendly, but do you really think that people would pay to come here? What would they do all day?" "You would teach them to ride and how a ranch really works instead of the way the movies show it. Emiliano, can you cook on an open fire for ten or twelve people if we took them out on trail rides? "Si Senor Bart that would not be a problem if I had Dutch ovens and a grill of some sort to put over the fire but I do not know how to cook the kind of food that people from the city are used to eating." "The kind of food you have cooked since I have been here would be exactly right. What they would want from a deal like this would be what working cowboys would get from the chuck wagon." Mac spoke up, "Emilianos' cooking would suit for sure but they wouldn't stay long for the grub that I've had thrown at me on some belly robbing outfits." "Mac, what about horses; what would it cost to get ten or twelve horses gentle enough for people that don't know the first thing about horses?" Mac was quiet a minute and said, "I bet I could get that many just for feeding them. This drought has got people trying to cut down on stock and I know several people with horses that are too old for hard work but that they are too soft hearted to sell for slaughter. But even if we got set up, where would we find these people that want to pay to play cowboy and would they pay enough to make it worthwhile?" "I expect that they would pay at least what a meals included bus tour would cost and that would be something like a hundred dollars a day." Mac choked on the smoke he was drawing in, coughed and said, "A hundred dollars? You have got to be dreaming! I can't make a hundred dollars clear money keeping a cow for the whole year." "It won't be all clear, we will have to feed them and the horses, laundry the sheets and towels and haul them to and from the airport but we should be able to clear at least half that." By this time Mac was up walking with Bart and said, "You know, I know a fellow down in Coke County that fixed up his Daddy's old chuck wagon. He used to take it around to parades and rodeos and such before he got too old. If he still has it and the teams, I bet he would let us use it. Can you handle a four mule hitch Emiliano?" "Si Senor Mac, I used to drive a freight wagon with a six mule hitch during the winter when I was not farming, surely I can still handle four." Mac stopped pacing, "We still don't know where we are going to find these people." Bart said, "I know a girl that works for a travel agency in New York City. I can call her and see what she thinks of the idea. What would it take to get a telephone in the big house? We would have to have one if we pursue this." "All we have to do is call them and tell them to hook it up. We had a phone until Susan died but had it disconnected. Didn't see no point in paying a bill for something Windy and I didn't use."

Next morning after a quick trip to the cattle to make sure that they had not mis-mothered any of the pairs and that everybody was where they were supposed to be, Bart took Susan's Buick into Sweetwater to see about getting the phone connected while Mac started around to his buddies to see who had horses to pension out. Mac still had trouble believing that anybody would pay the kind of money Bart was talking about just to be on a ranch. He couldn't believe it but Damn it felt good to be doing something besides just watching the grass disappear and the tanks go dry. It was even dryer in the country to the south and people there were getting desperate.

When he was in town last week, Mac ran into a friend that ranched out of Mertzon who told him about an old bachelor with a small place between Christoval and Eldorado. Old Tim had been a working cowboy all his life and was about as tough as they come; he was still breaking horses for the public when he was sixty-five. The old fellow had sold what little stock he had two years before and had nothing left but two old saddle horses that he was feeding every bite they got. He was in the habit of riding one and leading the other for a packhorse into Christoval every couple of weeks to get groceries and horse feed. He didn't show up so the storekeeper went out to check on him; he found him dead in the barn. He had put the last feed he had out for his two old horses, shot them while they were eating then went in the barn and shot himself. He left a note saying that he made it through the drought of the thirties and through the one in the fifties but he was just too old and too tired to fight it anymore. Mac didn't think he would ever get that beat down but he knew the helpless feeling of seeing everything you value disappearing and not being able to do a blessed thing to change it. He and Bart might lose Oak Creek but they would go out a kicking and a scratching. He had wrangled horses, he had wrangled cattle, though he didn't tell it, he and Windy even spent one winter feeding sheep on a big outfit in Nevada; he could learn to wrangle dudes if that's what it took.

Bart paid the fee and deposit to get the phone put back in service but found out that it would be at least three days before it was done. He decided that calling Lisa collect at the travel agency might not set the proper tone for future business relations so he bought a prepaid phone card. He got right through to her at her desk but then had trouble convincing her that: first, he was on a Texas ranch that he owned half of and second, that he was serious about the venture that he sketched out. He and Lisa had dated a few times and it looked as if she was having trouble getting past the fun loving, not too worried about anything attitude that he had shown her in the past. "I'm serious Doll; we can make a great vacation experience for your clients. We have over 5000 acres they can ride over loaded with all kinds of wildlife. We see deer, turkey, jackrabbits, roadrunners and rattlesnakes everyday and at night it sounds as if the coyotes and hoot owls are holding concerts. Every person will have their own horse and can ride everyday and even be able to help work cattle. My partner has cowboyed all over the west and can tell tales by the hour." So far Mac hadn't told him a single story but he was bound to have a bunch and that was no bigger fib than he told everyday at the electronics store. "We can pick them up and deliver them to the airport in Abilene and will have a chuck wagon so we can take them on overnight trail rides where they can sit around the campfire and sing along with Charlie and his guitar." Where the hell was he going to find Charlie and his guitar? "We have the greatest cook, I hope some resort doesn't hire him away from us, he is a dried up little guy but can cook like De Vinci paints. He is a genuine cowboy cook but can also turn out fantastic pies and cobblers and biscuits so light you have to hold them down while you butter them." Lisa laughed and said, "Slow down Cowboy, your salesman's golden tongue is going to have a heat stroke. Have you taken out liability insurance? You will have to have it or some Two Ton Tilley from the Bronx could do a prat fall off one of your horses and wind up owning your ranch. What about licenses? Do you need approval from any authority to open a dude ranch?" "OK, I'm a little ahead of myself but the ideal just struck me last night. What about the concept? Is it a pipe dream?" "Bart if you can get your ducks in a row and don't poison the first bunch I send you, I can keep a new bunch coming every week or so any time the weather isn't too hot or too cold until you are sick of the thought of a new bunch coming in. Bart? Bart, are you there?" "I'm here, what is a realistic charge for a week on Oak Creek Ranch?" "Some of the old established top end dude ranches get up to $1,500 a week per person and some of the low end charge as little as $75 a day per person but they may have twenty or thirty people at a time that eat like they were at a grade school cafeteria and are lucky if they get to ride an hour three or four times in a week. If you can bill yourself as a working ranch and give people that experience, $125 or $150 a day would be an easy sell." Bart said nothing for a minute and then, "Lisa, you have just earned yourself a gratis, lifetime, open ended invitation to Oak Creek Ranch. This could be the way that my partner and I get to hold on to the ranch. I love you, I love you, I love you and I will get back to you as soon as I instill a little Prussian discipline in this mob of quacking tribulations fluttering around my feet."

CHAPTER 13

Emiliano stopped and awkwardly shifted the egg basket from one hand to the other, trying not to fall or drop the eggs or his crutches in the process; crutches made carrying anything of any size a pain. Hopefully it would not be too long before he could do away with at least one of the cursed things. Lately his leg had been itching like crazy and his wife, Josepha, always claimed that was a sure sign of healing. "Be grateful old man, you have little enough to complain about. Think of a week ago, lying flat of your back and helpless in that arroyo. Had Senor Mac not come to check his cows, you would have long since been buzzard feed." Starting again his slow progress toward the house, he contemplated anew the debt he owed to Mac Connley. He knew that his two new friends were deeply worried about finding the money to save their ranch; they had included him in all of their discussions as if he were an educated man instead of a simple farmer. "I will do all in my power to help them; I could do no less and call myself a man but I have serious doubts about their scheme to bring paying guests to the ranch. The idea of people paying to ride horses instead of automobiles and to eat and sleep outside is a strange one but Senor Bart is from the big city and knows about such things. Still, I will use all of my skill to make certain that the food served to these people is the best possible. Just as when I was cooking for the labor crews, people that are well fed are less likely to complain and perhaps if the food is good enough, they will stay and pay their money. It would be nice to find the gold that Grandfather took from the bandidos and give it to my friends but in a country of such immensity even if the gold still exists, it would be as likely for me to find it as it would be for a politico to keep his promises." As unlikely as it was, he couldn't help but think again of Grandfather Juan's description of the place where he had hidden the gold and of the "oso piedra" or stone bear that guarded the site. He couldn't question Senor Mac without appearing to be a foolish old man but he would keep his eyes open when this blasted leg finally let him get around.

That night the atmosphere was upbeat. Bart reported on his conservation with Lisa and that a lady at the County Clerk's office had called around to several other county and state offices for him and found that there were no licenses needed or requirements except that the County Health Department would have to inspect the kitchen just like they would for any restaurant. He had also checked with an insurance agent and found that Texas law was designed to favor recreational use of agricultural land and that the needed insurance would not be cheap but it was affordable. He would write up a description of the facilities available and what Oak Creek Ranch had to offer guests and get this to Lisa.

Mac had made the deal with the Kansas rancher to take the cows they needed to sell. The trucks would be here at daylight two days from now so they would pen the cattle the night before and give them a feed of hay so as to be ready to load when the trucks arrived. The rancher had not quibbled about the price and had in fact offered to split the cost of trucking. Bart asked, "How can he know what the cattle are worth without seeing them"? "He knows what the cattle are worth because I told him exactly what the cattle are and he knows me. He sweetened the deal on the trucking because he knows that I would make sure that he gets the best of the deal." Bart didn't say anything to this but thought to his self, "Doing business like this is more different from the New York way than Reese Canyon is from Times Square." Mac had found six horses that were available and had a line on at least that many more that he would check on when he went to see about the chuck wagon. He had not found enough saddles but thought he could borrow enough one or two at a source given a little time so that they would not have to buy a bunch of tack. Emiliano chimed in to say that he had checked the big house and the storage room in the barn and they had all of the Dutch ovens, grates and other utensils they would need but that they would have to have more sheets, pillowcases and towels. They would also need bedrolls and ground sheets of some sort if they were to camp out overnight. Bart started a list of what needed to be done and who was to do it hoping that this would prevent them forgetting something vital. They sat up later than normal trying to think of things they might be missing and finally went to bed excited but more than a little apprehensive.

The trucks to take the cattle to Kansas arrived right on time and Bart was amazed how quickly and easily Mac loaded them. He had ordered three trucks to be sure that nothing was crowded and had separated the pairs from the cows yet to calve so that the pairs could be loaded in small groups in the smaller compartments of the trucks. After consulting with each of the drivers as to how many animals should be put in each compartment of each truck, Mac turned down their offers of help, separated out the proper number as needed and loaded them by his self. One young truck driver made the mistake of reaching through the fence with a "hot shot" to prod a cow he thought was moving too slowly. Mac didn't say anything he just snatched the hot shot away and sailed it out of the pens. He driver started to say something to Mac but the boss driver grabbed him by an arm and pulled him back away from the fence. Bart was close enough to hear him tell the young man, "These are his cattle, we are working for him and we will do it his way, besides, I've known Mac a long time and if you get in his face, he'll hand you your head. Go get your hot shot, put it in the truck and keep your mouth shut." As the trucks pulled away Mac stood watching them and said, "There's never a good time to sell a cow but Damn, I hate to do it while they are calving. At least these are going to a good home, they will be eleven hours on the road but Wally will have good hay and fresh water waiting for them and tomorrow they will be grazing some of the finest grass anywhere." Bart picked up a battery and a small spring from the side of the road and said, "Looks like that hot shot won't be used again for a while; how come he couldn't see that the loading was going as smooth as could be?" Mac thought a minute before saying, "Some people never learn to watch their animals much less understand that the way to keep animals healthy and to get what needs doing done right and in the least amount of time is to let animals move at their own pace without stress. Most people, even most cowmen, don't believe it but our most important job as stockmen is to make our cattle just as happy as it is possible for cattle to be. If we do that, the animals will do their part to make us money." Bart absorbed this and asked, "How long before we will get the money?" "Wally will pay the trucking and wire the balance direct to our ranch account; I gave him the routing directions when we made the deal. So tomorrow or the next day, depending on how busy Wally is, it will be in our account."

They split up for the rest of the day, Mac went south to check on the chuck wagon and more horses while Bart went into Sweetwater to buy the liability insurance and to start shopping for bedding and camping equipment and Emiliano started getting rooms ready and putting together menus and lists of groceries needed. Bart got the insurance easy enough but hit a snag on finding bedrolls and tents; no place in town carried them. A helpful clerk in the hardware store told him that while he could get what he needed at a big outdoors store in Abilene, he could get stuff that would do just as well a lot cheaper at the army surplus store in Big Spring. Bart asked how far it was to Big Spring and got a lesson in how distance is perceived in west Texas when the clerks, "Just a little ways to the west" turned out to be seventy miles. Bart got back to the ranch right at dark with the trunk and back seat of the Buick stuffed full of bedrolls, ground cloths and pup tents just in time to see Mac come in dragging a flat bed trailer with a chuck wagon on it and leading a one ton truck pulling a twenty-four foot stock trailer full of horses and mules. They unloaded the four little Mexican mules and five saddle horses first and got them settled on hay and water with only a little bit of squealing, biting and kicking. Then Mac backed the flat bed trailer into a ditch and the trucker helped them roll the chuck wagon off before he left. Mac pulled the truck into the hall of the barn so dew wouldn't wet the harness and saddles he had in the back and they shut it down for supper. They ate what Emiliano had fixed and then sat around the table with second cups of coffee. It had been a long day but nobody has particularly tired; Emiliano reported that he had found a bunch more bedding packed away in two cedar chests in the attic, probably enough of what they would need to bed down ten or twelve people. He would start airing it out on the clothesline tomorrow and get a better idea of what they needed to buy. Mac said that old man Malone was tickled that someone would be using his Dad's chuck wagon and only asked that he be allowed to come along on some of the trail rides; he even offered them the use of his Dad's old "hooligan wagon", complete with teams to carry bedding and tents. Mac said that he had found enough tack except that he would need to buy some bridles and some saddle pads and that he would haul in the hooligan wagon and its four-mule hitch and the other eight saddle horses he had lined up just as soon as he could get around to it. He also said that he had stopped by the house of the widow Gomez, who lived about four miles south, and she would be tickled pink to work part time cleaning, doing laundry and helping Emiliano in the kitchen. Emiliano protested that he could handle what needed to be done and that there was no need to spend the money. Mac said, "Maybe when you get back up to speed but you ain't there yet and besides this outfit needs the civilizing influence of a woman." Bart looked up from the pad he was scratching figures on and said, "What about if we asked Lisa to send us the first bunch Monday, two weeks from now?"

CHAPTER 14

Bart and Mac reined in at the creek to let their horses drink; the water was as clear as glass, flowing over white rock and waving strands of green moss as it wound back and forth from deep pool to shallows under the shade of tremendous old elm trees. Bart listened to the murmur of the creek as he enjoyed the delicious drop in temperature from hot sunshine to black shade and thought that he had never seen a more beautiful spot. "Mac this is just about as good as it gets." "I'd have to agree, the only thing that comes close to running water and shade is green grass with new baby calves on it." Bart had never had much of a mystic side but after just a few weeks he felt as if this ranch was as much a part of him as his right arm. He knew that he belonged here and could not imagine ever living anywhere else. Bart remembered his Dad laughing about some of his Irish friends, he called them professional Irishmen that after a drink of two turned maudlin and began to sing the praises of "the old sod" even if they had never seen Ireland; for the first time he understood and felt that same deep attachment of a man for his homeland. He wasn't born here but he knew in every fiber of his being that this is where he came from and this is where he was supposed to be.

The previous two weeks had gone by faster than any in Bart's lifetime; they had all been busy as hunting dogs trying to get ready for the first set of guests. He had gotten a crash course in the sad-dlers' art as he, Mac and Emiliano went over all of the saddles and other tack cleaning, oiling and repairing. They had cleaned the house from top to bottom and were proud of their efforts but when Senora Gomez arrived, she promptly did it over. They had made lists and shopped and thought of more stuff they would need as soon as they got home until they were all cranky. Bart took Emiliano with him on one shopping trip and got him outfitted with some new jeans and shirts; Emiliano thought that he should dress in white like the cooks he had seen in restaurants but Bart convinced him that white just wouldn't look right on the seat of a chuck wagon. Bart and Mac had ridden all of the borrowed horses several times each; they were all billed as "dog gentle and kid proof" but some of the people making these assessments would have called the great bucking horse Midnight, "Just a little bronky" and they didn't want to start their venture by scraping a guest off the caliche and hauling him to the emergency room. Mac had used the rides to show Bart every square inch of the ranch and they had agreed on the routes for two trail ride campouts, one short and easy and one longer and more challenging. The two campsites were ready with fire pits dug, firewood cut and his and her brush screened latrines built; they even peeled the bark off of the cedar poles they used to make latrine seats. They made a rough pole corral at each site and built feed pens so they could bring horse feed ahead of time and not worry about the cattle getting into it. Bart spent most of a day marking trails with signs and plastic tape so that people could walk out from headquarters to watch birds or just enjoy and get back without getting lost. Mac showed Bart the spring fed swimming hole on Oak Creek that had been used by generations of ranch kids. Bart got down and stuck his arm into the water and decided right quick that it would have to warm up some before he took a plunge. The first group was to land in Abilene at two o'clock tomorrow and Bart's mind was racing, making wild swings between euphoria at what could be and sheer terror of what might be.

Senora Gomez had arrived four days earlier and dust, grime and disorder fled before her; she and Emiliano seemed to get along well, though Emilianos' side of the conversations seemed to consist mostly of "Si, Senora." Lisa had booked eight people for six days at $150.00 a day each, two couples and a family of four. Lisa had questioned them as to their interests and passed this information on to Bart; she had also cautioned Bart not to try to structure every hour of every day but to give people the time to just enjoy. The Shapiros were both retired college professors very interested in the environment and in wildlife. The Overholts were also retired but from banking and their interest was history, particularly the settlement of the west and the Indian wars and they spent much of their time traveling from one historic location to another. The Kelly's were a young couple with two teen-age children; Jacob, fifteen and Tara, thirteen; Tara was the driving force of this group having been totally horse crazy since she was four years old. The plan was to pick the guests up in Abilene using the Buick and a minivan belonging to the granddaughter of Senora Gomez. After making one trip to town with Mac, Bart was secretly pleased that there was no way to fit everybody into the Buick and the pickup; the expense of hiring the van was small potatoes compared to having guests start their visit with a three hour road trip at forty-five miles an hour top speed bleeding down to thirty five on curves and forever waits at stop signs. Anyway they would have the guests at the ranch by five or five thirty get them settled in their rooms and feed them supper about six thirty. After supper, Bart would go over the options available and lay out a tentative schedule of activities. He would also caution them of the need to watch for rattlesnakes everywhere they went. "If you see a snake, just back away; they won't chase you and won't bite unless they feel threatened. Don't try to kill it, just call Mac, Emiliano or me if you see a snake around headquarters and we will deal it." He considered trying to explain that Mac gathered up every bull snake he came across and turned it loose around the house and barns because they killed or chased off rattlers but decided that probably that was a step too far for people who probably had never seen a snake of any kind in the wild. He didn't want to spook them off before they paid their money. Bart grinned to himself, "Four weeks ago I had never seen a rattlesnake and now I'm on the rescue squad."

Emiliano was walking without crutches now but he limped when he got tired and Bart and Mac were both on him constantly for trying to do too much too fast. He was incapable of just resting, even when they sat around talking after supper, his hands would be busy at something. Two weeks ago, he had asked Mac if he might have the deer hide that Mac had thrown across the fence when he dressed the deer Emiliano shot. He had soaked the dry hide first in plain water and then in a thick slurry of wood ash and water until the hair turned loose and he could scrape the hide clean. For several nights then, he cut around and around the hide making long strips about an eighth of an inch wide. When he got a strip twenty feet long, he folded it into a package about six inches long and tied it around the middle so that it stayed together but he could still pull the thong out from the center and unfold it. When he had sixteen of these packages, which he called "tamales", he began to braid. First he braided a sixteen strand round plait "bosal" or noseband complete with a large double "Turks head" knot where the reins would attach; he then used a eight strand flat plait to make the rest of the headstall complete with brow band

and a four strand flat throat latch secured with braided button and loops. Bart knew that Emiliano was working every night on a braided rawhide headstall but had not had a chance to examine it or even to see it in daylight until it was finished and Emiliano shyly presented it to Mac. Mac ran his hands over the gift, feeling the perfect fit and spacing of each strand and said, "Emiliano, I have seen rawhide work from all over and this is as good as any I have ever seen." "Oh no Senor Mac, my Mother's brothers from the state of Jalisco in Mexico tried to teach me but my work could never compare to theirs." "You may not think you are in a class with your Uncles but you could make a very good living making and selling work like this, thank you for this beautiful gift."

D-day arrived bright and clear, all hands were up long before day-light and after a hurried breakfast, though they had lots of time, they went over their lists once again. Groceries had been laid in, along with a half a beef from the Russ Ranch grass finished beef opera-tion and though it was not officially health department sanctioned, Emiliano had separated cream and churned butter to supplement the fresh whole milk Belle was supplying in such abundance. Mac and Emiliano had further descended into crime, even though the meat would be cleaner by a factor of ten then what came out of a USDA inspected Tyson plant by purchasing, slaughtering and adding two fat lambs and two cabritos, or young goats, to the larder. They had bought smoked bacon, sausage and ham from a little family run meat processor in Eden and eggs from Senora Gomez's flock of free rang-ing hens. They might crash and burn as a dude ranch but they would be well fed in the process. Senora Gomez's granddaughter, Selena, was to meet them at the intersection of highway 70 and Ranch Road 153 at twelve o'clock and they would go in convoy to the Abilene

Regional Airport so as to be there in plenty of time to meet the Southwest Airlines flight coming in from Dallas- Fort Worth at 2:00 PM. They were all anxious, Mac was talking more than Bart had ever heard; for him it was almost babbling. He admitted that he had not been this nervous since the first time when he, in his misguided and misspent youth, in search of fame and fortune, had climbed down onto the back of one of the bucking bulls in Goat Mayo's rodeo string. "I was shaking like a dog passing peach seeds and this old fellow helping me get ready; he must have been at least thirty, said, "Are you scared Son?" I said "No! — Maybe a little — Hell, I'm scared spit less!" and he says, "If you ever get over being scared, don't never get on another one." "I learned pretty quick why you don't see very many tall rough stock riders; the bull or the bronc has the leverage advantage. A tall fellow just has too much weight sticking out away from the animal and they can use it to pry you off. The really good rough stock riders are nearly always little wiry guys; least ways that's my story as to why I couldn't ride bulls and I'm sticking with it." Bart said, "That's the first tale you have told since I've been here. Can you spin some more yarns like that to entertain the guests?" "That's where your Uncle Windy would have shined. That old boy could tell tales all day and all night and never repeat himself. He could tell about something that happened when I was there that maybe rated a chuckle at the time but when he retold it, it was the funniest thing you ever heard. I'll see if I can't remember some of his stories that are fit for mixed company."

CHAPTER 15

Bart felt a little foolish standing in the unsecured area of the terminal holding a sign hand-lettered in Magic Marker saying "Oak Creek Ranch" as arriving passengers collected their luggage and streamed out past him. Most people glanced at him as they passed but one young girl wearing pigtails, blue jeans and a huge grin ran ahead of her family, slid to a stop in front of him and said without stopping to take a breath, "Hi I'm Tara, what's your name, how many horses do you have, can I help feed them, I hope I get to ride a mare, you do have some mares don't you, how long will it take to get to the ranch." Bart matched her grin with one of his own, took a deep breath, and said, "Hi Tara, I'm Bart, sixteen plus eight mules, sure, yes you can, yes and about an hour." Both of them cracked up with laughter and were still giggling when her family walked up. Bart stuck out his hand to the man and said, "You must be Mr. Kelly, I'm Bart Ryan." "Hello Bart, I'm Tom, this is my wife Liz and our son Jacob and it looks like you have met Tara." Mac came up pushing a baggage cart just as two older couples joined the group. Bart introduced himself to Sarah and Sam Shapiro and to Jan and Luke Overholt and then did a round robin introduction of the guests, Mac and Selena.

Mac rode with the Overholts and the Shapiros in Selena's van and Bart loaded the Kelly's into the Buick with him. The Shapiros started the conversation by asking Mac what he knew of the history of the area. "Well, Anglo history in the region really doesn't go back very far and neither the Spanish nor the Mexicans ever had much of a presence here. The early history of this part of the south plains is about the Comanche. This area was some of the last land fit for grazing or farming to be settled by whites because of the Comanche and their war like ways." Sarah spoke up, "Please go on, we have read about the area but would really like to know more." Mac bobbed his head and said, "Well, until about 1875 this whole part of the world was part of what the Spanish called "Comancheria" or the land of the Comanche and nobody else came here without their permission. Sam turned to Sarah and said, "We came to see the country and have found a historian to go with it." Mac ducked his head and said, "I shouldn't be running off at the mouth. I don't know that much but it is a subject that has interested me ever since my Grandfather told me stories about our family's' life on the frontier. He told about the struggles in their early days here and about his Father's adventures fighting Comanche with the Texas Rangers. Emiliano Cortez, who works with us at the ranch, had a grandfather who was captured by the Comanche as a young boy and lived with them for many years; almost all families who have been in this area for a long time have sad stories of death, rape and torture to tell about the Comanche and Kiowa." "Sarah and I have read scores of books about the settling of the west but no account of history can compare with the real life descriptions of people who lived it. We take maps of the areas we visit and try to fill in the location and times of historical events that have perhaps been over looked by the professional historians. I hope you can help us with this." "I'll be happy to tell you what I know but what we need to do is get you together with Bud Malone who will be coming to help with the trail rides. His people have lived here since 1872 and Bud has made the study of local history his life's work."

CHAPTER 16

Central Texas 1866

McAlester Connley was tired, down deep bone tired, as was every man and horse in the unit. The eight man squad of rangers had been out for almost a month; they had trailed two Comanche and one Lipan Apache war parties, fought skirmishes with and inflected casualties on the Lipans and one party of Comanche and caught and wiped out a six warrior party of Kiowa. They attempted to form a roving picket line on a north – south axis to intercept war parties coming into the settlements from the west; they rode back and forth looking for sign of hostiles and hoping to catch them before they reached the scattered farms and ranches. On the morning of the fourth day out, they struck the trail of six or eight Indians moving east on foot. Lt. Blount and old man Gabe Flowers, their most experienced Indian fighter, agreed that this was probably an Apache war party, no Comanche would be caught dead walking, and they took up the trail at a fast clip. They followed the Apache for two days and just before dark on the second day they smelled smoke and roasting meat. Lt. Blount sent Jim Malone ahead on foot and he was quickly back to report that seven Lipan were in a shallow depression three hundred yards ahead feasting on a mule they had butchered. There was still light enough to shoot so Lt. Blount formed them into a skirmish line and from two hundred yards they charged the camp. Two Apache were killed outright and several more were wounded. The survivors able to travel scattered like quail in all directions; Gabe Flowers followed one blood trail until it ended suddenly in the middle of an area churned up by the passing of a large buffalo herd. Gabe rode on to the edge of the buffalo disturbed ground and then with a wolfish grin on his face, he whirled his horse and rode back up the blood trail at a dead run. Twenty yards beyond where the blood trail ended an Apache jumped up from where he had back tracked and covered himself with dirt in the churned up ground. He made it about thirty feet before Gabe brained him with the three foot long rawhide and stone Comanche war club that he carried looped to his saddle horn. McAlester was with Gabe and asked him how he had figured out where the Apache was hiding, "The first Apache bastard that pulled that stunt on me put an arrow in my back; I ain't likely to forget that lesson." The rangers spent most of the next day attempting to trail down individual Apache with no luck. They also came up empty when six days later they followed a Comanche party west for several days before losing them when they split into small groups. Their luck returned when a Comanche party blundered into them as it was coming back from raiding to the east. The ranger riding point heard the sound of a lot of horses coming fast and signaled his comrades to take cover just before the war party burst through a narrow gap between two hills. The ten or so Indians were driving 25 – 30 stolen horses ahead of them; they had no captives with them and were moving fast. The rangers got off several shots per man and saw at least four of them take effect; two Comanche hit the ground but were quickly picked up by other warriors. The rangers gave chase but soon gave it up as it was obvious that their worn down horses were not up to the task of catching the Comanche with their supply of fresh horses.

The area they patrolled had once been fairly heavily settled but now was populated only with burned out homes and lonely graves. The Texas frontier was pushed more than a hundred miles to the east when the Comanche learned that most of the Texas men were away at war and unable to protect their homes. The women and children and old men who remained were no match for the blood thirsty savages that swarmed out of the wilderness seeking easy prey; the settlers' only hope for survival was to flee their homes and seek shelter to the east, many were to die horribly before they could reach safety. The rangers were far too few to halt the destruction and the raiders had recently learned new tactics that made the job of the would be protectors even harder; the war parties would no longer attack the first whites they found but rather would avoid contact while riding deep into the settled area. They would then ride hard to the west, killing and pillaging all in their path before fleeing back into their strong holds on the trackless plains. The rangers had been living off the land for the last week, their horses were exhausted, and they were down to a few rounds of ammunition per man; it was time to come home. They were not even legal Texas Rangers; the Reconstructionist government had disarmed and disbanded the Texas Rangers as one of its' first official actions. This in spite of the fact that Indian predation was the worst it had been in fifty years. With most able bodied Texas men away at war, the Comanche and Kiowa went on a rampage that made their earlier depredations seem mild by comparison. Even the Lipans who had been thoroughly whipped and driven far west back in the 50's were back preying on the unprotected and widely scattered farms and ranches. McAlester's group and a few others like them were the only full time forces trying to hold back the slaughter. These "ranging companies" as they were known were made up of volunteers, mostly young and single, who were supported as well as possible by the people of the area. Pay was almost unknown, there was no money, but usually the means were found to supply horses, food and ammunition. In 1866 the Texas frontier was a very bleak place; the U.S. Army was busy occupying the settled areas to the east, helping the Yankee carpetbaggers steal and making sure that honest Texans didn't have the means to protect themselves. If the savages were to be stopped it would be by the people themselves and done in spite of the U.S. Government.

The rangers reached the point where McAlester would turn off toward his home and he waved and rode off without saying anything. After twenty-eight days together, they were talked out; Lt. Blount told them to go home and get the wrinkles out of their bellies and meet him in Forestburg in six days. McAlester was almost eighteen years old and had been in a ranging company since he was fifteen; he had lost count of the number of patrols he had made and even the number of fights he'd been in. This trip had been the worst; they caught the Kiowa while they still had live captives; they probably would not have seen them at all if they hadn't heard Mrs. Gilpin scream in the night. They heard her scream from a half mile away and caught the Kiowa in camp tormenting the poor woman with fire after days of abuse. The bastards were rutted out after days of raping Mrs. Gilpin and her young daughter; they had cut the girls' throat just moments before and were burning Mrs. Gilpin with brands from the fire when the rangers arrived. All of the Kiowa went down in the first volley without firing a shot; they were so engrossed in dealing misery to the poor woman that none of them had weapons at hand. Lt. Blount was the first to reach Mrs. Gilpin; she was blind in one eye and burned over her entire body and she screamed and stumbled away when he touched her. "It is all right now Mrs. Gilpin, it is over and we will take care of you and take you home." She looked at him wildly with her one good eye and said, "I don't have a home, the black hearted devils burned it, they killed my Rufus and they burned Grandmother Gilpin and my two babies. They made me watch just now as they killed my daughter Betsy. If you want to do something for me, please kill me!" She collapsed in a heap and as Lt. Blount stepped to his horse to get his canteen, Mrs. Gilpin snatched a knife from one of the dead Kiowa and plunged it into her breast. They buried Mrs. Gilpin and her daughter in the same grave, drug the dead Kiowa away from the grave and started for home leading the Kiowa horses.

McAlister rode into the clearing around the house, stopped and shouted, "Hello the house." For a moment there was no answer but then Grandpa Thomas stepped out of the barn carrying his rifle and shouted, "Come on in." It was bad manners to ride up to the house unannounced and in these times it was also dangerous — unannounced visitors were often hostile. As he rode up to the barn, his Mother and Father came hurrying from the house followed closely by his little brother Ben. At the supper table Ben kept up a steady stream of questions wanting to know everything that he had seen and done while he was gone. McAlester tried to put him off with, "Mostly we just rode the hide off our rear ends and drank a lot of bad water." Ben wouldn't let it go and demanded details until Grandpa said, "That's enough, let the boy enjoy his Mommas' cooking; there will be time for stories later." After supper, McAlester, his Dad and Grandpa walked down to the barn. Grandpa lit his pipe and said, "It was bad wasn't it?" McAlester stood leaning on the fence looking out at the sunset and in a voice that he didn't recognize as his own, told them about finding the Gilpin woman and her little girl. He held it together pretty well until he told of carrying the girl to the grave and his voice broke. "She was just a little girl, didn't weigh hardly anything and those bastards treated her bad, it was bad enough for Mrs. Gilpin but no child should have to suffer like that. I was wishing that we hadn't killed those bastards so fast, I wanted to make them scream like that poor woman. Pa, I know you need me here on the place but I can't quit the rangers just yet. As long as those monsters keep coming, I have got to fight them." David Connley thought back to the day when his own Mother and brothers had died and his Father Thomas had almost died from three Comanche arrows in his body and said, "I know Son, I know."

CHAPTER 17

In the Buick, Bart was attempting to reply to the two adult Kelly's questions about how he, a New Yorker born and bred, came to own a Texas ranch and at the same time to answer a steady stream of questions, all horse related, from Tara. The only one not entering into the conversation was Jacob but by watching in the rear view mirror, Bart could see that he was following closely his answers to Tara's horse questions and to anything to do with the land or with animals. Jacob was a polite, well groomed young man but seemed to be as reserved as his little sister was out going; Bart made a mental note to draw him out when the opportunity arose. The ride back to the ranch went quickly with much exclaiming about how big and how empty the land was, how different it was from New York and how dry and barren it looked. Though he had never seen it any other way, Bart felt compelled to point out that it would be much greener and more appealing were it not for the drought. This created the need to explain that a drought in west Texas was measured in years rather than in weeks as it was in New York and that the current drought was already four years old. By the time they arrived at the ranch entrance, one of Brad's greatest fears had been laid to rest; it did not appear that guests, or at least these guests, would be hard to entertain; they were fascinated by all they were seeing and hearing. As Bart pulled up to the bump gate, Tom offered to open the gate and then cheered with delight with the rest when Bart nudged the gate open with the bumper and smoothly drove through. Selena though, who was following closely, lacked faith in her ability to get through without beating up her van and insisted that Mac get out and hold the gate while she got through. Bart kept up his dialogue explaining how the drought had forced them to sell part of their stock so as to have enough grass for what was left. He was saved from the possibility of having to admit that the guest ranching came about because of the income crunch when an armadillo chose the moment to appear at the side of the road rooting for bugs and doing his Mr. McGoo impersonation only feet from where Bart stopped the car. Selena stopped farther back and both of the Overholts came forward with cameras at the ready and Mr. Armadillo put on quite a show rearing up on his hind feet sniffing and peering around myopically in an attempt to figure out what all the commotion was about. He stood his ground until Tara let the car door slam as she clamored out over her Mother. Armadillo couldn't stand that; he whirled and went dashing off into the brush grunting like a pig with every jump. Tara was embarrassed by what she had done and apologized to the Overholts for ruining their photo opportunity; Mrs. Overholt put an arm around her shoulders and said, "No harm done, Honey, there will be lots of chances to get pictures of armadillos."

As they unloaded, Bart directed the Overholts and the Shapiros to the two first floor bedrooms and the Kelly's to two bedrooms on the second floor, explained the bathroom situation and told every-one that supper would be at six. Emiliano and Senora Gomez were on hand to meet the guests and help with the luggage and everyone got settled in quickly. For the last week, Emiliano had been agoniz-ing over the menu for the first meal; after much discussion, it was decided that it would be the all time west Texas favorite of chicken fried steak and cream gravy with mashed potatoes, red beans, sour dough biscuits, green salad and for desert a dried apricot and peach cobbler with fresh cream. Bart, in the dining room going over plans for the coming week, could hear Emiliano and Senora Gomez in the kitchen but could understand only a little of their Spanish. The conversation started off low key but seemed to become strained with Emiliano speaking more softly and less frequently and Senora Gomez's comments becoming sharper and more declarative until she exclaimed sharply, "Senor Cortez, la salsa nata le falta sal!" Emiliano said nothing for a count of five and then said flatly but calmly, "No Senora, no mas sal." "Pero Senor," "Senora, no!"——"Si Senor." Bart could not follow the back and forth but it was obvious to him that some sort of accord had been reached that had nothing to do with salt for the gravy. Never before had Bart heard Emiliano use the words Senora Gomez and no in the same sentence. All of the extension leaves had been added to the dining room table so that it could now seat ten comfortably; Emiliano and Senora Gomez would eat later after feeding their charges. When the food was on the table, Emiliano stepped to the back porch and loudly rang the dinner triangle that Mac had hung there. The Kelly family had walked down to the pens where Tara was trying, without much success, to get the horses to come to her and eat hay out of her hand. They got back to the house and the two older couples came into the dining room in time to hear Tara lose the argument with her Mother that she really didn't need to wash her hands again since, "All she had touched was hay." Bart told people to sit wherever they pleased and that all meals would be family style, "Just take what you want and pass the bowl to your neighbor." Mac passed the fried steak to Jan Overholt, who was seated next to him and was surprised when she passed it on without taking any. "Don't you like fried beef steak?" Jan smiled at him and said, "It's not that, it is just that we don't feel that it is right to feed grain to cattle when there are so many people in the world that are hungry, so we eat very little beef." Mac snorted and said, "Well you can eat this without feeling guilty because neither this beef nor his momma nor his grand momma or any other of his kin ever ate a bite of grain in their entire lives. They ate cows' milk and grass when they were little and nothing but grass and clean water after that." "But we have been told that cattle had to be fed grain to produce good meat." "I expect you got that from somebody that has money in a feedlot. I have eaten a lot of good beef and I doubt that I ever ate a piece of corn fed beef until I was grown. It wasn't until the farmers got cheap nitrogen fertilizer and grain got cheap because they were producing more than the market wanted that grain fed beef got common. For our use on the ranch, we used to kill fat calves or fat young barren cows but now people like the Russ's are making a business of finishing young cattle on grass and improving their country at the same time. They claim the meat is better for you and I know that it tastes better. Try a little piece of this and I'll bet you a soda pop that you come back for seconds." Emiliano's worries about whether city people would like his food were laid to rest; he and Senora Gomez made several trips back to the kitchen for refills amid constant compliments that redoubled when people got to the hot cobbler and cold cream.

As people finished their cobbler and began to push back from the table, Bart stood up and said. "Let's move out to the porch so that Emiliano and Senora Gomez can clean up." Bart led the way out to the veranda in the front of the house and when everyone had found a place to sit said, "We want to make your visit to Oak Creek Ranch as pleasant as we possibly can." Tom Kelly spoke up to say, "Food like that is a pretty good way to start." and a round of applause and murmurs of agreement seconded this view. "Thanks for the quality of the food go to Emiliano and Senora Gomez; we plan to feed you a west Texas diet while you are here with as much fresh and local food as we can manage. There will be a full ranch style breakfast at 7:00 a.m. but if you don't want to get up that early, there will be coffee made and milk and juice in the refrigerator and you can help your selves to pastries, fruit and cold cereal. About 8:00, Mac and I will be down at the pens ready to help anybody that wants to ride. For the time being, either Mac or I will be with anybody that is horseback and we will take at least two rides a day, mostly just for fun but sometimes to do ranch work. We will explain the rules as we go along; there aren't many, just enough to protect you and the horses. If you want to hike and explore on your own, feel free but first get with us so we know who is going where when and we can explain the layout of the ranch. We don't want you to get lost or wander on to the neighbors land. I have noticed that none of you smoke and I ask you not to build any fires; we are very dry and the danger of wildfire is very real. We will have campfires several nights in places where it is safe and we will take at least one over night trail ride. Let us know what you would like to do and we will try to make it happen." Sam Shapiro spoke up with, "Sarah and I would like to see Fort Chadbourne and Fort Concho if possible and talk to Mr. Malone about the local history and do you suppose Emiliano would tell us about his Grandfather?" Mac said, "Bud will be here Wednesday morning and I'll bet he would be tickled pink to take you on a tour of the forts; Emiliano is a little self conscious about his English skills but I bet we can get him talking one night after supper." Luke Overholt asked, "Would it be possible to go see the ranch where they are producing this grass finished beef? If they are doing all you say; improving their land, producing good beef and making money, that is something that the whole world needs to know about." Mac replied, "To tell the truth, I have been wanting to go see the Russ operation myself; one of their ranches is about a hundred miles southeast so we could go there and back in one day. I bet they would be happy to show us around; I'll call them tonight and see if we can set up a date. That is something else that Bud is up on. He has made quite a study of good grazing management and would be happy to explain what needs to be done." Tara piped up to say, "I thought we were going to be riding horses." "I tell you what "Short Stuff" you be at the pens in the morning at 8:00 and I will introduce you to the sweetest little mare you ever saw and you can ride to your hearts content." "Alright! What's her name?" "Her name is La Mosca, which means The Fly and she is a pretty little bay with four white socks and a little white star in her forehead. The only problem is that she has just weaned her last colt, who Emiliano named Picaro, which means rascal, because he is such a bad little boy that gets into everything and is always underfoot, and he will want to go everywhere with you and La Mosca." People began to yawn and Bart said, "We get up early and go to bed early but you all are welcome to do as you wish. If you want to ride in the morning, be at the pens by 8:00 and if you want to ride in the evening, be at the pens by 2:00. We will eat at 7:00, 12:00 and 6:00 every day but if you get hungry feel free to raid the icebox, just don't make a mess and get the cook mad or we will all be in trouble. We don't have much in the way of television but it is almost dark enough for the nightly starlight and meteor show complete with coyote and hoot owl chorus to began; if you have never seen the night sky without man made light, noise and air pollution, walk away from the house down toward the pens for a real treat. Last month, during the full moon, I was able to read a newspaper by its light. Not something that you can do in many places today."

CHAPTER 18

Emiliano was mixing biscuit dough while bacon and sausage fried and Bart and Mac had just sat down with their first cups of coffee after getting chores done when Tara came bouncing into the kitchen fresh scrubbed and ready to go. "Good morning Tara" said Bart, standing up "what would you like to drink?" "Good morning, some milk please but I can get it." "OK, glasses are on the counter and the milk is in the icebox in the glass gallon jug." Tara got the milk jug out and started to pour the milk when Bart said, "Let me help you, we need to stir the cream back into the milk." Bart tightened the jug cap and shook the milk vigorously before pouring Tara a glass. "I've never seen milk that had to be stirred; you just pour ours out of the carton." "This is fresh milk right from the cow and since it has not been homogenized the cream rises to the top after it sits a while." "You mean you make your own milk?" "Sure, at least our milk cow does, her name is Belle and you can meet her and her calf Susie Q later and even milk her if you like." "If we are drinking her milk, what does Susie Q drink?" "You don't need to worry; Belle gives more than enough milk for Susie and us too." Jacob joined them just then and Tara made a big production of showing him how to stir the cream back into the milk and explaining why it was necessary. Jacob didn't say anything but was obviously a little embarrassed by little sister's instructions until he looked over her shoulder to see both Bart and Mac smiling and Mac winking at him. "Thanks Sis, I will remember that. Mr. Connley, I have been reading about how some people think that grazing cattle is bad for the land and should be banned from all Federal land. A man from the Sierra Club come to our school and gave a talk at assembly about how greedy ranchers are ruining the west. Is this true? " "Jacob, it is true that a lot of damage has been done to the range by cattle and sheep grazing. I can show you place after place that was prime grassland when I was a boy that today is weedy brush-land and this has happened mostly because of poor grazing practice. I don't think that it has been done maliciously or out of greed, at least not since the early days of free range; most ranchers today try as best they know how to take care of the land; after all, this is where they make their living and they don't want to ruin it. Part of the problem is that even the college experts don't agree what should be done. It seems logical that most of the damage has been done by grazing too many animals too long without giving the grass time to recover between grazings. On our ranch we stock a little lighter than most folks and move the cattle between eight different pastures so that our grass gets a chance to rest. This makes sense to me and I think that it helps; in fact, I think that we need more pastures to give longer rest periods. There is a lot of discussion for and against with some of the college boys saying that rest doesn't help so it is hard for an uneducated old cowboy to know what to do. I do know that the grasslands all developed with grazing animals so I don't think that grazing itself is damaging but the way it is done can be. I do know that what happens when all grazing is stopped is not what people expect. I can show you some federal land west of here in New Mexico that the government took all of the cattle off of sixty years ago to save it from "over grazing" and it is in worse shape now than the private land right across the fence that has had too much stock on it for the same period of time. There is a piece of ground on the Sonora Experiment Station a ways south of us that has not had a hoof of stock, not a cattle or a sheep or even a deer on it for eighty years, it was healthy grassland when it was fenced and now it is nothing but a solid cedar break, no grass, no wildlife just cedar trees and bare ground. If you want, we will get Mr. Malone to talk to us one night and maybe he can explain things better than I can." " I would like that very much, Mr. Connley, I write a column for our school newspaper and I would like to do one on food production and its effects on the environment; I don't think that the American people are getting the whole story and I think that it is important that we do."

Just then, Emiliano stepped out the back door and clattered mightily on the triangle to signal that breakfast was ready and before the echoes had a chance to die people could be heard coming down the stairs and up the hall. This was not a bunch of slug-a-beds; these folks were up and ready to go. Emiliano had put out the promised "full ranch breakfast" with a huge mound of scrambled eggs, bacon and sausage, fried potatoes, cream gravy and hot biscuits. Along with the pitchers of sweet milk, orange juice and coffee the center of the table held jars of jelly and jam, a jug of cream and one of honey and for the adventurous, a bowl of fresh salsa picante made of chopped jalapenos, tomatoes, garlic and onions. The buzz of conversation that accompanied people serving their plates died quickly as people began to eat. Liz Kelly spoke up to ask, "Emiliano, what did you put in these eggs? They are fantastic!" "Senora, I put only a little butter in the pan to keep them from sticking, a little cream and some salt and black pepper." Bart said, "Emiliano can make most anything taste good but a big part of what you are tasting is fresh eggs from chickens that run free eating what chickens are supposed to eat, green stuff, grasshoppers and bugs as well as chicken feed. We get these from Senora Gomez and their shells are so thick that you have to whap them hard on the edge of the skillet to crack them and the yolks are dark orange with vitamin A instead of pale yellow; I'm afraid I'm ruined to ever go back to store bought eggs." Tara looked at her eggs as if expecting to see part of a grasshopper sticking out then shrugged, took a big bite and said, "I don't care what they ate, these are goood!" As people began to finish eating, Bart said, "Everybody that is going to ride needs to bring a hat, it will warm up pretty good later and the sun is a lot stronger here than in New York. Mac and I will both be at the pens to help so come on down when you are ready."

CHAPTER 19

Tara was, of course, waiting when they got to the corral gate; almost wiggling with excitement but doing her best to be adult. "I can ride pretty well; I have been lots of times to a camp in Pennsylvania where we got to ride every day. I know how to saddle and unsaddle and to curry my horses' back so they won't get saddle sores. Next year we are going to move to my Grandparents farm in Connecticut and Mom says then I can have a horse of my own. " "Sounds like we may have to make you assistant wrangler." said Mac. Let's catch La Mosca and find you a saddle that fits." Mac walked into the lot where the horses were finishing the last of a feed of oats and shook out a loop in his lariat. Bart had been surprised that Mac roped the horses to catch them even though they were gentle and Mac explained that this was the common practice when you had a large group of horses as it kept horses from trying to hide in the bunch and create turmoil. Not until he tried it himself, did Bart realize how much skill it took to settle a loop gently on the neck of one horse in a herd of sixteen without hurting or startling any of them.

It took almost an hour to get everyone fit to a saddle and mounted for the first time; Jacob had ridden some and his Mother had ridden competition show jumpers as a girl but no one else had ever been horseback. Liz took her two kids into the back lot and started working with them on their horsemanship while Picaro dashed in and out of the group at breakneck speed almost but never quite running into someone. This continued even after his Mother squealed and bared her teeth at him but stopped when she snatched the reins out of Tara's hand to stretch out her neck and nip his rump hard enough to turn the hair backwards. The two older couples listened to Mac's instructions with complete concentration but while he was listening, Bart could see that Tom Kelly was not looking forward to climbing up on the big, long legged dun that Mac had caught for him. Bart had ridden the dun, named Sonny, several times and knew he was fool proof but at sixteen hands he was big and to make Tom even more nervous, ever few minutes he would plant all four feet and shake like a dog shaking off water. Every time he did this, the stirrups flopped wildly, leather creaked and Sonny ended his performance by loudly breaking wind and blowing rollers in his nose before shaking his head and stomping out a quick rat-tat-tat on the ground with his big front feet. Tom was holding Sonny's bridle reins and started out right next to his shoulder but after three of Sonny's fits he was standing as far away as he could get and still keep the very end of the reins in a very white knuckled hand. Bart came up beside him and said, "Tom would you mind if we traded horses? I have ridden Sonny less than any horse in the string and I need to get to know him better." For a moment, Bart was afraid Tom was going to hug him but he just handed Bart Sonny's reins and said, "Sure, that's alright with me, glad to help." As Tom took the reins of Grayman, who Bart had caught for himself, Bart said, "You just listen to Mac and I will swap our saddles." Tom said, "OK", and looked fondly at Grayman who true to form was standing eyes closed and hipshot using the pause in activities to catch a nap. At last everyone was mounted with all feet in the stirrups and body masses more or less centered over their horses. Mac waved Bart to lead off while he followed along to spot trouble and as they passed, he muttered, "Thanks for thinking about bringing the stool, without it we either still wouldn't be mounted or else both of us would have hernias."

Bart led off at a slow walk; he and Mac had already decided that the first ride would be slow and short, only down to the creek and back and only level ground. Bart looked back to see Liz, Jacob and Tara right behind him chatting, reins in left hands and right hands waving and gesturing. Both of the Shapiros and both of the Overholts had two handed death grips on saddle horns with reins more or less forgotten while Tom Kelly had reins clutched in his left hand and his right hand not quite grasping the horn and an expression that looked more like a death head rictus than a smile on his face. Bart left the road and followed a cow trail that branched off the road and down into the creek bottom. As Bart approached a clump of grass wedged under a catclaw bush, a mother quail fluttered out into the trail in a limping, wing dragging run. Tara, who was close behind him, cried, "Oh look, the little bird is hurt!" Bart, feeling very worldly – Mac had explained this behavior to him last week – said "No honey she has a nest close by and that is an act that she puts on to lead us or any other intruders away from her eggs." "No she is hurt, see, her wing is broken and she can barely walk; we have to help her!" "OK," Bart said, "I will lead your horse and you can get down and try to catch her but I'm telling you that she is fooling you." Tara jumped down, tossed him the reins and ran after the quail. The bird seemed to be weakening and Tara got within a couple of feet before mama quail rallied and opened her lead to six feet. This happened several times, Tara following along for a quite a ways before the quail weakened enough for her to almost catch it, only to see it scoot ahead in a miraculous recovery at the last second. Finally, two hundred yards from the nest, the little quail exploded into flight and took off at a 90 degree angle until she was out of sight. Tara came back looking very dejected but Mac spoke up to say, "Don't feel bad, what you were trying to do was good and quail have been fooling coyotes and coons with that act for thousands of years; old Don Coyote knows a heap more about quail than any young lady from New York and he still gets fooled. Tell you what; we will bring mama quail some grain this afternoon for being such a good mother and to show her that we don't have any hard feelings." Obviously embarrassed, Tara came dragging back and climbed up on her horse. Finally she grinned and said, "She did fool me pretty good didn't she?"

When they arrived at the creek, every one dismounted and stood lined up along the stream edge to let the horses drink. Bart had brought them to the creek at the point where the ranch road crossed it so that they could return to the house by a little different route. Tara squatted down and to splash water up on her face and arms and yelped, "Ooo, that's cold", she looked up from drying her face on her shirttail and pointing across the creek said, "Mom, look, that big rock is shaped just like the Hopi bear fetish that Daddy brought you back from New Mexico." Mac looked and said, "I must have ridden by here a thousand times and I never noticed that but sure enough, it's a perfect bear when you look at it." The horses were through drinking so they started the process of getting everyone back on. Liz and the younger Kelly's mounted and moved out of the way while Mac and Bart helped the two older couples mount; out of the corner of his eye, Bart could see Tom make three attempts and finally with a look of triumph, haul himself into the saddle. The trip back was uneventful and as they reached the pens, Mac asked, "Who wants to ride again this afternoon? If you are going to ride again we will leave your horse saddled and tie them in the shade." All of the Kelly's raised their hands but both older couples said they had enough for the first day. "Go on up to the house and get washed up, Emiliano will have lunch ready in a few minutes; Mac and I will tend the horses and be right behind you." Tara jumped down saying, "Can I help?" and Jacob spoke up, "Me too." Mac said, "OK, you two take the horses that are to stay saddled, one at a time, to the hall of the barn and tie one to each ring set in the wall with the halter rope that is coiled on the left side of each saddle. Then loosen the girth until the belly band is almost clear of the belly and throw the end of the latigo over the saddle seat to remind whoever starts to get on the horse that the girth is loose." As the kids led their horses into the barn, Mac started unsaddling the two older couple's horses and said, "First time I ever had somebody pay to do my work." "That's just it Mac, it's not work if you are having fun and those kids are having a ball."

After dinner and a short rest, Bart only a little apprehensive, took the Kelly family out by himself while Mac and Emiliano worked on getting the chuck wagon ready. Tara remembered Mac's promise and insisted on bringing Mrs. Bob White a hand full of grain that she stole from the horses. With Picaro right behind them, she and Jacob walked ahead, after Bart cautioned them to watch for snakes, to spread the grain on the ground near the nest. Bart and Liz held their horses and watched while Tom led Grayman in a circle in an attempt to ease his cramping legs and sore butt. Liz watched her husband and said to Bart in a low voice, "You are a very kind man Bart Ryan." "What? I don't know what you mean." "I was watching Tom get more and more worried about getting on Sonny; he has never been around horses and didn't really want to make this trip. I was trying to figure out some way to save his pride when you saw what was happening and stepped in to trade horses with him, thank you." "Not necessary, Sonny is really just a big old teddy bear but he puts on a good show and we should not have put a novice rider on him. We are still new at this but we really want our guests to have the best possible experience." Jacob and Tara came back and Tara asked, "Are you sure this is the right spot Mr. Ryan? We looked under every bush around and didn't see anything." "I am not an expert on quail Tara but Mac tells me they are almost impossible to see when they are on the nest. They have a multi colored set of feathers that blends in with the background like camouflage and they know to be absolutely still when somebody comes around. Mac says when the babies hatch, they are even harder to see, just tiny little balls of fluff and if you get around where a nest has hatched, to keep from stepping on them you have to scoot your feet on the ground." Tom made it back into the saddle on his first try and rode over looking very pleased with his self and the caravan resumed its trek. Bart took them through Reese Canyon, up onto the mesa and down the other side before heading back to the ranch just in time to unsaddle and tend the horses before supper. Each of the Kelly's took care of his or her own horse leaving Bart with little to do but watch and think that, with the right group, dude wrangling was a snap.

CHAPTER 20

onversion at supper was animated and jumped from topic to topic with everyone joining in. The Overholts had gone out on a nature walk and had slipped up close enough to get good pictures of a bunch of thirty or so young wild turkey males or "jakes" that were feeding on grasshoppers in a small meadow above the creek. "They were just like a bunch of teenage boys" said Jan, "All long legs and awkwardness dashing here and there after grasshoppers and missing more than they caught." "Sounds like Jacob", piped up Tara earning a glare from her brother. "That's not nice Tara," said Jan, "I have watched Jacob and he is not awkward, especially around the horses; I am jealous how gracefully and easily he mounts and dismounts. We got some great pictures of the jakes and heard some big gobblers strutting and gobbling back in the brush but we never did get to see them." Sam spoke up to say, "You aren't the only one to get some great pictures, I watched Mac and Emiliano clean up the chuck wagon and start packing it. That thing is an engineering marvel; it is amazing how much stuff you can get in such a small area and still be able to get to all of it at anytime. I just may have to write an article for one of the history journals; I've read a lot about the chuck wagon but I have never seen anything that did justice to their efficiency."

Everyone seemed to be finished eating, so Bart said, "Let's move out to the porch and maybe we can talk Mac into telling us a tale." When everybody had found a place to sit, Tara said, "Mr. Connley, what was the most exciting thing that ever happened to you?" "Humph, well it might have been the time Windy and I got caught in a prairie fire up in Kansas, or maybe the time we had to out run the Mexican bandits in Arizona but probably the most exciting thing that ever happened to me was when I roped a grizzly bear down in the Sierra Madres of Mexico." "You didn't, why would you rope a poor little bear?" "I have you know, there wasn't anything poor or little about that bear! We were riding for Don Hernando Reyes-Ouzos on his ranch way down in Sonora and this grizzly was giving us fits. We were in the middle of calving season and every few nights that rascal would kill and eat another calf. Don Hernando had hired two fellows that were supposed to be first class bear hunters but in two weeks, they hadn't even gotten a glimpse of this bear. Windy and I decided the only way to keep that thing out of the cattle was for one of us to be with them all the time; he would ride around the herd for eight hours or so and then I would take over for a while. This worked pretty good; we never saw the bear but he didn't kill a calf for a couple of weeks and this was all we were after. One morning, I relieved Windy just after daylight and he wasn't much more than out of sight going back to camp when here comes Mr. Bear bold as brass across the creek and straight for where the cattle were bedded down. I squalled as loud as I could but Windy couldn't hear me, and the bear just ignored me; he hadn't had a calf to eat for more than a week and he planned to change that right now. I spurred up to cut him off from the cattle but he just dodged around me and kept on toward the cattle. My horse had got a snoot full of bear stink by now and was doing his best to stampede and put distance between himself and that bear. I got him back under control but saw that the bear wasn't going to stop unless I made him so I shook out a loop and charged him. He must have weighed eight hundred pounds or more and I knew that my only hope to control him was to catch him right behind his head where his neck wasn't so big so I could choke him down; that was my plan but it didn't work out." Mac stopped talking and started rolling a cigarette and Tara blurted out, "What happened? Don't stop now." Mac finished rolling his smoke, struck a match with his thumbnail; let the sulfur burn off before lighting the cigarette, taking a deep drag and continuing. "I made a pretty good throw but my horse "scotched" on his front feet just as the loop got there and I missed catching my slack to pull the loop tight; by the time I got the loop pulled tight, I not only didn't have the bear caught in the small part of his neck but Mr. Bear had his right front leg through the loop and I knew that there was no way that I would ever be able to choke him down. So there I was with a bear that I couldn't choke on one end of my rope and the other end of that rope tied hard and fast to my saddle horn with no way to get it loose." "What did you do?" Tara was the one to ask but everyone, Bart included, was sitting on the edge of their seats and listening with total concentration. "Well, I didn't think it would work but couldn't think of anything else to try so I whirled my horse to try to drag the bear. I was riding a hell of a good horse who was stout to the saddle horn but old Dan just couldn't stay hooked; just about the time he had a good pull started, he would get worried about that bear being behind him and would spin around to look at him. To make things worse, the bear figured out that if he came towards the horse, the rope got loose, so pretty quick we were going across that pasture just as fast as Dan could run backwards. All of a sudden, that bear reared up on his hind legs, planted his hind feet and started taking in rope hand over hand; he was reeling us in just like we were catfish on a throw line!" Mac paused to shift positions in his chair and to pinch out his smoke; a couple of the adults looked a little dubious but nobody said anything until Jacob said, "What did you do?" "Well, I stayed hooked as long as I could but finally I had to bail off and leave old Dan to his fate." "Oh no!" from Tara, Did the bear kill Dan?" "Well it was like this, I took off running about as fast as a broke up old cowboy could and thought I was going to be all right when out of nowhere a loop settled around my middle and jerked me to a stop. I looked back to see that bear setting in my saddle and would you believe that old Dan set up just like a rope horse is supposed to and held me while that bear came down the rope and ate me plumb up?" Groans came from all directions to be replaced with laughter and applause. Tara again, "OK, you got us but tomorrow night you have to tell us a true story."

Next morning Bud Malone drove his big Suburban in as Mac and Bart were walking down to the pens and announced that he was hunting a job. "I'm not worth a damn for anything anymore but I can still hitch a team and drive it and I'll work cheap; feed me and give me a cot in the bunkhouse and I'll still get the best of the deal. I haven't had a minute's peace or a cigar since my granddaughter and her three kids moved in with me so she could "take care of me." She just as sweet as she can be and means well but it's a tossup what will happen first: she smother me to death with her hovering or her brat kids drive me to suicide. I need some time off from being "Grampa." "Bud you know you are welcome but did you tell your granddaughter where you were going? She'll be worried sick and probably wind up calling the sheriff if she can't find you." "I didn't tell her where I was going, cause she would have beat me here, but I left a note saying I'd check in by phone and I called the sheriff so that fat gutted old fraud wouldn't get his bowels in an uproar." "Well if your granddaughter is as strong a woman as you say, she will worm your location out of Doyt pretty fast." "No she won't cause I told Doyt that if she did I would take out a half page ad in the Sweetwater Reporter telling all about the time I found him drunk out of his mind in a whore house in Villa Acuna and he knows I'd do it too." Most of the guests were lingering over second cups of coffee but Tara and Jacob had already caught their horses and were currying them. Bart was facing the pens as they talked and said, "Excuse me for interrupting but look there!" Tara was standing with La Mosca on one side and Picaro on the other currying first one and then the other. "Well I'll be," said Mac "I've never even touched that colt and she has him standing to be brushed. Bud, let's introduce you to Emiliano and the guests and then put your plunder in the bunkhouse." "With the build up that Mac has given you to the guests, you may not get much peace around here either; I feel like the "village idiot" most of the time because I can't answer their questions about ranching or the environment or the history of the area. I don't know if it is just a fluke and the next bunch will be total losers but these people are intelligent and they are interested in everything." They started back up to the house and Bart looked back to see Jacob and Tara leading in their parents horses.

CHAPTER 21

Bud's arrival and introduction to the guests caused a major shift in the orders of the day. Everyone had planned to go on a morning ride but instead all of the adults were seated around the table working on the fresh pot of coffee Emiliano brought in and listening to Bud field questions and hold forth on a half dozen subjects. Even Emiliano got a cup of coffee and stood listening in the doorway. Bud had the storytellers' gift of making each person feel that he was speaking directly to them. At the moment, he was responding to Sarah Shapiros' question about the Comanche and Emilianos' interest was obvious. "The Comanche came into the area from the north starting in the late 1600's. They acquired the horse by catching wild horses and by stealing horses from tribes already here and in only a few years, the horse completely changed their culture and way of life. With horses and millions of buffalo, hunting to feed their people was child's' play that took very little effort so they devoted their new found free time and mobility to stealing more horses and making war on their neighbors. They killed off or drove out all of the tribes' then living in the area and began to ride farther and farther afield looking for new raiding grounds. The one thing you can say about them is that they were equal opportunity bandits; they stole horses, cattle and captives from the early Texians to sell in New Mexico and then stole from New Mexico to sell to Louisiana. They sold Apache and Ute slaves to Mexico and Mexican slaves to American slavers. By the early 1800",s, they were raiding into what is now deep east Texas and the Gulf coast and into Mexico as far south as Guatemala; they would take the whole camp on the long raids into Mexico, women, kids, grandma, everybody and might be gone months. Routinely they would mount a raid into central Texas; kill, rape, steal horses and captives and in three days be a hundred and fifty miles away leaving behind a trail of dead or dying captives and exhausted horses. This was the situation when the first whites began to cross the area on their way to the west coast. The U.S. Army built some forts in the 1840's, 50's and into the 1860's; the closest to us were Fort Chadbourne just south of the ranch and Fort Concho down at San Angelo, but these didn't really change anything; mostly they were staffed with infantry that was useless in this country against mounted hostiles and the Comanche were some of the best light cavalry in the world. Both forts were abandoned during the War Between the States and not re-opened until well into the 1870's. The first civilian white settlement in Nolan County was the Lewis Ranch on Bitter Creek that was established in 1870 but the Comanche ran them out and they didn't come back for good until 1873; even then they had constant Indian trouble until the buffalo were killed off and the Comanche and other hostile tribes were starved into submission about 1875. The Comanche held the area from the Rio Grande to the Platte and from the mountains of New Mexico in the west to the west cross timbers in the east against all comers for two hundred years. They raided the Utes and Apaches to the west, the Cheyenne and Osage to the north, killed thousands of Texans to the east and Mexicans to the south and considered all of Mexico down to Nicaragua to be their private horse and slave breeding preserve. Their whole culture was based on stealing horses and making war against their neighbors. In their society, to be called a horse thief was a major compliment; no young man could hope to win a bride until he had stolen enough horses to show her father that he was a "solid citizen" and could take care of a family. The last big Indian raid in this area was in the late 1870's when a bunch of young bucks from the Comanche reservation in Oklahoma came down and stole every horse and mule from a cavalry detachment that was camped at Fort Chadbourne. They started north with them and were doing good until a roundup crew from all the local ranches saw them coming and ambushed them coming through a narrow cut on what is now the O bar O Ranch just north of here. The cowboy's pretty well wiped out the war party and recovered the horses. Sam spoke up to say, "But didn't the whites contribute to the problem by stealing Indian land?" "That was true for a lot of tribes, even some in Texas, but the Comanche and Kiowa were different; they lived far from the settled areas and nobody, Texan or Mexican tried to settle on their land until after they were defeated and pushed onto reservations. The only exception was the Penatekas or "Honey Eaters" who were the band of Comanche who lived in the southern edge of Comancheria; they ranged the hill country and south plains until they came in contact with the early Spanish settlers around San Antonio. They were moving south as the Spanish were moving north and conflict erupted when they met. Even this was more a clash of cultures than war over land; the Penatekas moved back north but continued to raid the Spanish, and later Mexican and Texan settlements. For over a hundred years, they routinely rode hundreds of miles to raid and then returned to safety in their sanctuaries far from any settlements. Even the trails to take cattle to the Colorado gold fields and to Montana went south and west to strike the Pecos River and follow it north rather than cross the heart of the Comanche lands.

Charley Goodnight and Oliver Loving laid out this route though it meant a drive of ninety miles without water from the headwaters of the Concho River to Horsehead Crossing on the Pecos River and even then Loving was killed by Comanche on the way home from their first trip." Just then Tara and Jacob came in and Liz said, "This is fascinating but I promised the kids I would ride with them." Bart asked, "Does anyone else want to ride this morning?" Tom got up but both couples indicated that they would rather listen to Bud so only Bart and Tom followed Liz and the kids back to the pens.

When the Kelly's and Bart got back from their ride, Bud was still holding forth with no loss of audience though they had moved to the front porch so Emiliano and Senora Gomez could set the table for dinner. Bud had offered to host a tour of old Fort Chadbourne and then on down to San Angelo to see Fort Concho, both the Shapiros and the Overholts had eagerly agreed. Tom and Liz Kelly said that sounded like fun but Tara was a little down in the mouth until Mac said, "The Tom Green County annual rodeo is going on, why don't we take that in while we're there?" Tara brightened up at that and positively beamed when Mac answered, "Sure" to her "Will there be any cowgirls in the rodeo?" After lunch they loaded up in the Buick and Bud's Suburban and drove the fifteen miles or so to the remains of Fort Chadbourne. There was a small museum and office building that was not open but not much remained of the original facility except the cemetery and ruins of some of the buildings. There were plaques and signs giving the history of the fort and marking the locations of various buildings but the group pretty well ignored these, except to take pictures, once Bud started talking. "The fort was established in 1852 to provide protection for the Butterfield Overland Mail Line and other people passing through on the way to

New Mexico and the west coast. It was named for Army 2nd Lt. T. L. Chadbourne, who was killed in the Mexican – American War at the battle of Resaca de la Palma. The fort wasn't very effective at doing anything besides guarding the stage station because the only troops stationed here were infantry. Companies A and K, US Army Infantry made up the first garrison detachment and to get anywhere they had to either walk or ride in mule drawn wagons. This was not what you would call a favored post by either officers or men; to give you an idea how isolated it was, the materials to build the fort, except for stone, had to be freighted in from the Gulf coast in wagons drawn by oxen. The Comanche were not too impressed – more than once war parties would swoop down – ride through the fort grounds whooping and a hollering, shoot at anything in sight and be gone driving any horses or mules that were handy. Water was a problem; the fort was located on Oak Creek where there was a good spring but in drought times neither the spring nor the creek supplied the amount of water needed. The Army hung on until the War Between the States broke out and then the fort was surrendered without a shot to Col. Henry E. McCulloch, CSA. After the War, Union troops were stationed here occasionally but the water problems and the lack of wood caused the main post to be moved south to the forks of the Concho and North Concho Rivers at what is today San Angelo. After the fort was officially abandoned in 1873, it at times served as a camp and supply point for Mackenzie's roving troops of cavalry that were so effective in finally bringing the Comanche and Kiowa to heel. These troops, usually with Tonkawa, Delaware, Lipan or Kickapoo scouts would crisscross the whole area until they struck the sign of hostiles. Then depending on how fresh the sign was they would either pursue the war party or back track them to the main encampment.

This was something new for the Comanche; they were accustomed to out running pursuit coming back from a raid but they had never before had to worry about being attacked on their home territory. They felt so safe that they did not even set sentries or watchmen on their camps or horse herds. It had been many years since any enemy had dared to come into their territory much less to attack them."

The expedition loaded back up and after a stop for cold drinks in Bronte proceeded on to San Angelo and Fort Concho. Fort Concho is much better preserved than Fort Chadbourne being newer but also much better built in the beginning. Bud once again had everyone's attention, even picking up two couples of tourists from Japan, as he related the history of the fort and its importance in the history of the area. "Fort Concho was one of the best located and best planned of all the Texas forts. German emigrant stonemasons from the Fredericksburg area were brought in to build the first buildings, which are still standing today. The fort was headquarters for the 4th US Cavalry from 1868 – 1873 and was headquarters for the 10th US Cavalry, the famed "Buffalo Solders" from 1875 – 1882. At various times it was also home to units of the 3rd, 8th and 9th Cavalry and units of the 10th, 11th, 19th, 24th and 25th Infantry and to units of the US Signal Corps. The fort was headquarters for the whole District of the Pecos the entire time that this huge area was under military jurisdiction. The cavalry patrolled the area chasing hostile Indians, Mexican bandits and Comancheros – the renegade whites and Mexicans that bought cattle, horses and captives from the Comanche with guns, ammunition and whiskey. The Infantry built roads and telegraph lines, mapped large areas of west Texas and guarded stage stations and survey parties. The fort became one of the most important in the west and San Angelo sprang up across the river to supply the legitimate and not so legitimate needs of the fort and the troops. Old timers tell me there was more soldier blood spilled in the dives along the river then there was in Indian fights. Several good men commanded at Fort Concho but the one who put it on the map and in the history books was Ranald S. Mackenzie, who was the first US Army commander to take the fight to the Comanche. He kept patrols out constantly and followed up every sighting of hostiles in force. He requested and got supplies of grain for his horses so that they could maintain condition during the winter and he continued his campaigns right through the cold months when the Comanche traditionally stayed in winter camp because their horses were thin and unable to travel long distances. Mackenzie had successful campaigns in 1872 and 1873 but his crowning glory came in 1874 when he found several hundred lodges of the largest Comanche band camped in Palo Duro Canyon along with some Kiowa and Southern Cheyenne. Mackenzie captured hundreds of Indians, burned all of their lodges and foodstuffs and killed some 1500 horses. This action, along with the extermination of the buffalo herds, effectively ended the reign of the Comanche as Lords of the South Plains. The survivors were herded into captivity at Fort Sill in Indian Territory with the last holdouts, Quanah Parker and the Quahadi band coming in to Fort Sill but refusing to surrender on June 2, 1875; Mackenzie was wise enough to accept Quanah Parkers pledge of peace without surrender and the Comanche wars were over. Fort Concho and its troopers were later to play an important role in the 1877 – 1880 campaign against Victorio and his band of Chiricahua and Mescalero Apaches with Lt. Col Benjamin H. Grierson and his black 10th Cavalry "Buffalo Soldiers" riding literally thousands of miles after the marauding Victorio before he and his band were killed by Mexican soldiers under Col Joaquin Terrazas in the Tres Castillas Mountains of northern Chihuahua Mexico."

CHAPTER 22

Mac looked up at the setting sun and said, "If we are going to the rodeo, we had best get out there before the grand entry is over and all the hot dogs have been gobbled up." Tara spoke up, "I'm ready for a hot dog but what's the grand entry?" "It's where all the cowboys and cowgirls that are competing in the rodeo plus all the sheriff posses and riding clubs, plus anybody else that wants to, come riding single file into the arena and back and forth around flag bearers until the whole arena is full of prancing horses and riders all decked out in their best "going to town riggings", it makes quite a show." They arrived a little late at the fair grounds and had to park quite a ways from the gate; Bart said, "I will go on ahead and get us tickets." Luke Overholt said, "No, this was not part of the deal, I will pay for the tickets." Sam Shapiro chimed in, "And I will pay for the hot dogs and drinks." Tom Kelly spoke up, "That's not fair, there are more of us Kelly's than anybody else, I ought to be paying for something." Luke pulled out his wallet to pay for tickets and said, "Don't worry; we will let you get the steak dinners." They had not much more got settled into their seats when the announcer said over the public address system, "Please rise for the parading of the colors and remain standing for our National Anthem." Every one stood and the men all took their hats off and placed them over their hearts as two young women, one blonde and one with hair black as a crows wing came thundering out of the gate under the announcers' stand on matching white horses and one to the left and one to the right circled the arena at a dead run with the United States flag streaming behind one and the Texas flag flowing behind the other. They made two complete laps and pulled up at the same time in the center of the arena facing the announcers' stand. The horses stood stock still as the announcer said "Miss Sonya Byrd" and another young woman took the microphone and sang a beautiful a cappella version of the National Anthem. The announcer took the microphone back and said, "Please bow your heads as the Reverend George Hill asks a blessing on this event." Tara and Liz each let out little gasps when both of the white horses simultaneously, kneeled down on one knee and lowered their heads to the ground. "Lord, thank you for this opportunity to come together in fellowship; we thank you for the blessings of freedom that we enjoy in this great country which, You have helped us to build. Make us mindful of the needs of those less fortunate than ourselves and please protect the contestants here tonight from harm. In Your Blessed Name we pray. Amen. "And now Ladies and Gentlemen, Miss Tommie Rae Wolf with the American flag and Miss Jill Carter with the Texas flag will lead the grand entry." The two flag bearers' rode back to the gate as eight sheriff posse members with red pendant flags flying from upright shafts came running in two groups to circle the arena in opposite directions and take up positions equally spaced four to each side of the arena. The two flag bearers led a long line of riders to the back of the arena where they dropped off facing the announcers stand while the line of riders wove back and forth across the arena using the red pendants as turning points until the arena was filled with horses and riders of every age, color and shape. When the lead rider cleared the last pendant, he turned up the right side and led the line around the arena and out. As the last rider left the arena, the pendant bearers once again went flying around the arena in opposite directions to come together two by two down the center and out the gate. The young women carrying the flags fell in at the back of the line and left the arena with their horses doing an exaggerated high stepping prance with arched necks and tails carried high. Tara had watched the whole process wide eyed and now plucked at Macs' sleeve, "Mac how did they make the horses bow at just the right time?" "What do you mean? They didn't have to make them! Those ponies are well bred young Texas horses and know that you are supposed to bow your head when someone prays; I did notice though that Tommie Rae's horse didn't close his eyes like you are supposed to." Tara swatted Mac on the arm and said, "You're teasing me; I'll find out for myself." The rodeo was a first for everyone except Mac; they had all seen rodeo on television but that was only a pale reflection of what they were seeing, hearing and smelling here, sometimes from only twenty feet away. The women were at first terrified that the horses and cattle were being brutalized and would be killed but as the night progressed through the roping events and barrel racing to bareback and saddle bronc riding to bull riding, their concern shifted to the well being of the human contestants. Sarah said, "I don't know how those boys they can absorb the abuse to their bodies and continue to function" Mac replied, "That is why most rough stock riders have a real short career. Every once in a while a Jim Shoulders or Freckles Brown comes along who is so tough that he is still contesting in his forties, but most are broke up, used up and worn out before they reach thirty. These boys take more punishment in just a few of years than most working cowboys get in a lifetime. Course this is when they are still young and bullet proof and are sure they are going to live forever. Steer wrestlers and calf ropers can keep going til they blow out their knees and team ropers can contest as long as they can get their tired old bones up on a horse but professional rodeo is a poor choice as a long term career." Just before the last couple of bulls were ready to be bucked out, Mac stood up and told Bart, "I'll meet you just outside the gate we came in." and walked down out of the grandstand and toward the area behind the bucking chutes. When the last bull threw his would be rider and added insult to injury by nose butting him in the seat of the pants as he tried desperately to get up on the fence, the crowd broke out in applause and started filing out of the stands as the announcer said, "God Bless and you all be careful going home. You hear?"

The Oak Creek bunch waited until the crowd thinned a little and then started back to the vehicles. As they came out the gate into the parking lot, Mac was waiting and with him was the black haired young woman holding her white gelding. "Miss Tara Kelly, I would like you to meet Miss Tommie Rae Wolf and Major" To her credit, Tara said, "I am pleased to meet you Miss Wolf." and shook hands before turning to rub her cheek on Majors' nose. Mac introduced Tommie Rae to everyone in turn ending with "My partner, Bart Ryan. Tommie Rae lives on her folk's' ranch northeast of here and trains horses. She has trained the horses used in a bunch of movies, commercials and TV series but so far hasn't left us country folks for the bright lights." Tommie Rae grabbed Mac's left arm in both her hands, hugged it to her and reached up to kiss him on the cheek. "Mac, you know that I could never move off and leave my best fellow." Bart was stunned to feel a jolt of jealous rage shoot through his whole being but he got control back, he hoped, before anyone saw the expression that crossed his face. Watching her profile as she spoke to Mac and then to Tara, he realized that he was looking at the most beautiful woman he had ever seen. She was not tall; perhaps 5' 6" but her erect carriage and slim grace gave her a presence far beyond her size. Tara turned to Mac and asked, "Could we go to see Miss Wolf work with her horses?" Liz broke in to say, "Tara, we are guests and can't be asking Mac and Bart to cater to our every whim." Tommie Rae spoke up, "I am going to be in San Angelo at daybreak on Thursday to shoot a commercial with Major and Sergeant; what if I stopped by the ranch about noon on the way home? I could make Mac and Bart feed me and then we could let Major and Sergeant show off a little. They are both terrible hams and are always looking for a new audience to impress."

CHAPTER 23

Bart and Mac rode home from the rodeo in different vehicles so it was the next morning as they were doing their chores before Bart had a chance to question him. "Tell me about Miss Wolf, is she Hispanic?" "Tommie Rae? No, mostly she is "Hill Country Dutch" but her Fathers' daddy was pure blood Tonkawa and there is some Comanche back somewhere in her Mothers' side of the family. I guess the Indian blood accounts for the black hair but did you notice that she has green eyes?" Bart had very definitely noticed but thought to himself, "They are not green; they're emerald with highlights of gold sparkling in the depths." "I have known her since she was just a sprout and she is just as pretty inside as she is outside. She is smart as a whip and when she went off to college, I figured she would be off to bigger and better things. She surprised us all when she got her degree and came back to the ranch. Her Folks' place is not much bigger than this one and they are bound to be having money troubles just like we are. She has done well with the horse training though and I expect that has helped the financial strain a lot." They finished chores and went into the kitchen for a cup of coffee before breakfast. "I thought that all Indians were moved out of Texas and into Indian Territory in the 1800's." "Nearly all were, except for some Alabama and Coushatta that have a reservation over in east Texas but there were several groups that just kind of blended in and stayed. Tommie Rae s' granddaddy was part of a group of several

153

families of Tonkawa that went to work on ranches owned by some old settlers down south of here and stayed when their kin was moved to Oklahoma. The Tonkawa had been good friends to these ranch families over the years so they returned the favor by giving them work and hiding them from the army until things quieted down. Tommie Rae s' Granddaddy's Grandfather started out as a cowboy working for wages, then leased some country and wound up owning a nice ranch." Neither Mac nor Bart noticed that Emiliano's ears perked up when he heard the word "Tonkawa" and that he listened carefully to the rest of the conversation. Mac had set up today for a visit to see the grass finished beef program at the Russ Ranch; the Overholts and the Shapiros wanted to go while the Kellies said they would rather ride. It was decided that Mac and Bud would go to the Russ Ranch and Bart would stay to ride with the Kelly's. Bart led his group off to the west to a part of the ranch that the guests had not yet seen just as Mac and his group rolled off in Buds' Suburban. Bart watched them go and thought, "We are going to have to put Bud on the payroll or make him a partner or something; he's working as hard as anybody."

Before they went their separate ways, Mac and Bart backed the chuck wagon and the "hooligan wagon" up close to the kitchen door and now Emiliano and Senora Gomez were busy stowing away all of the food, cooking utensils, tents and bedding that they would need for the overnight trail ride planned for tomorrow. As they worked, Senora Gomez raised the same questions that had puzzled Emiliano, "Why would anyone want to sleep on the ground on a hard pallet and eat off their knees from tin plates when they could be sitting in comfortable chairs eating from a table and sleeping in soft beds?" "Truly, Senora it is a mystery but they are very nice people who are paying to do these things so we must do our best to make it an enjoyable experience for them." "They are nice people, I have been surprised how nice they have been but just the same, I am glad that it is you and not I who is to cook and clean up in the dust and smoke and flies." "It will not be a problem, Senora. It will only be two meals, supper tomorrow night and breakfast the next morning and we will be back in time to eat the delicious lunch that you will have ready for us." Senora Gomez swatted at him with the dishtowel she had in her hand and flounced away, "Flattery will do you no good, old man, but at least my gravy will not need salt." Bart took the Kelly's on their longest and most difficult ride yet and when they came in for lunch, the elder Kelly's announced that they would not be going back out that afternoon. Tara started to object but Liz Kelly said, "Nope, we have ridden these horses hard this morning and we will ride them again tomorrow. They deserve a rest; if Bart agrees you and Jacob can spend the afternoon currying horses." "Can we Bart? Please" Bart had to swallow back the "Hell yes." That first came to mind and said instead, "That will be fine if you promise to remember what Mac and I have told you about safety around horses. None of these horses would hurt you intentionally but they might kick or run over you if you startle them so it is your job to see that doesn't happen." Liz said, "OK, let's get unsaddled and cleaned up and you can come back after lunch."

Bart ate a quick meal and then took the unexpected free time to run into Sweetwater on the pretext of picking up supplies; his real mission was to get a haircut. Emiliano and Mac had cut each other's hair but after seeing the results, Bart declined their offer to cut his. He hadn't had a haircut since he left New York and he wanted to neat up a little before Tommie Rae came in the morning. He was shaggy and needed a haircut but wished he knew more about which barber in Sweetwater to patronize. The lyrics to the silly Ray Stephens song, *Never Get a Haircut Out of Town* kept running through his mind but he gutted it out and went into the busiest barber shop he saw and turned out pleased by both the results and the price. It seems that west Texas barbershops are a lot like barbershops in his old neighborhood. The accents were different but there was the same bunch of loafers hanging out and by the time the barber was finished cutting his hair, everyone in the shop knew who Bart was, who he was kin to, where he was from and what he was doing in town. Bart was surprised to find that he didn't feel as if his privacy had been violated but rather that people were truly interested. One old man, Will Bryant, spoke up to tell Bart, "I worked on the rigs with your Grandfather when we were both young bucks. You look a lot like him, hope you got more sense than he did; if he hadn't married your Grandmother, he would have wound up either shot or in jail." Bart left Sarges' Barbershop pretty sure he would be back, picked up the stuff on his list and drove home to the ranch.

Mac called to say that his party would be late getting back so Emiliano went ahead and served supper for those who were there and insisted that Senora Gomez leave so that she would be home before dark. She objected saying, "It is only a little ways; I can stay and help you clean up before I leave." Emiliano took her by the elbow and gently led her to the door; "Thank you, Senora but there is not that much to do and I don't want to worry about you." "Very well, I don't want to worry you, buenos noches, Emiliano." "Buenos noches Maria y Adios." Bart heard only the last part of the conversation and wondered when Senor Cortez and Senora Gomez had become Emiliano and Maria.

CHAPTER 24

Both Luke Overholt and Sam Shapiro were excited about the business possibilities of grass finished beef and spent the trip home and on through a late supper quizzing Mac and Bud about the process and about what would be required to make it work. "Could you make it work on Oak Creek Ranch?" Sam wanted to know. "Not the whole process", replied Bud. "Native short grass range like Oak Creek has too short a green season to make finishing cattle feasible. You need to be able to keep cattle gaining rapidly for their entire lives in order to produce well marbled meat and to do this requires green feed for most of the year. The climate of this area pretty much dictates that our season of finishing quality forage will be limited to three or four months in the spring and early summer. This is fine for mother cows and their calves and can even be made to work for carrying the calves until they are 14-16 months old and weigh 700-800 pounds but we don't have the fall and winter green feed needed to put on the last 300-400 pounds. Russ Ranch moves their yearling cattle to another place they own 200 miles east where they can grow cool season forages to finish the cattle." "We have seen several patches of cultivated ground in the area." said Sam. "Couldn't you plant wheat or other cool season forages on areas like those?" "People try" said Bud, and have ruined a lot of good grassland in the process. The problem is that when you plow ground – especially in dry country – you destroy its' soil organic matter content. Soil organic matter absorbs a big percentage of the water that a soil can hold and is the fuel source for the soil life that provides much of a soils' fertility. In higher rainfall areas this is not as big a problem since rains are more frequent but here it means that you cannot rely on having good growth on cultivated land except in wet years. Most of the cultivated ground here should never have been plowed out. To produce grass finished beef Oak Creek would need to partner with somebody in a higher rainfall area." "Well it is an intriguing concept" said Luke, "The health benefits of grass fed meat and milk that Mr. Russ told us about give real value to the consumer and are a fantastic marketing tool. If you ever decide you want to get into the business in a big way, let me know. I am a member of a group of investors who are always looking for good business opportunities. We could help you with financing but also we keep a staff of bright young people that can help with everything from marketing to locating technical help of all kinds." Sarah spoke up to ask, "Could you produce the meat under an organic regime?" "What about that Mac?" said Bud, "What sort of chemicals or poisons do you use?" "Well, the last thing like that we used was six or seven years ago when coyotes caught our barn cat and I put some rat poison out to get the rats that got into our horse oats but we haven't needed anymore since we got another cat." "Oh!" said Tara, "I have been petting a kitty every morning at the barn. Is the coyote going to get her?" "No don't think so, she is a pretty smart lady cat and besides Susan had Windy and me fix cat size doors on all sides of the barn so she can always get away."

As people were starting to drift off, Bart asked, "Who wants to ride in the morning." For the first time since the guests arrived, Mac and Bart had no takers for a morning ride; everyone was looking forward to Tommie Rae's arrival and decided to wait for the afternoon trail ride. Tara was in the pens as usual when Mac and Bart got there; Bart nudged Mac and pointed to her working with her mount. She had a halter on La Mosca, which was nothing new but she had the end of the halter rope around Picaro's neck and he was leading right along just like his Mother. Tara stopped them at the feed bunk, picked up the brush she had left there and proceeded to brush La Mosca and then Picaro, talking the whole time without a doubt that they could understand every word. When he decided his mother was getting too much of the attention, Picaro would root his nose between La Mosca and Tara until she resumed brushing him. Mac watched a moment and said, "I have known men who worked with horses their whole lives and never had an animal trust them like that."

Chapter 25

West Texas 1876

Blue Wolf crawled the last few feet to the top of the ridge and carefully looked over. The small herd of buffalo was grazing into the wind along the floor of the valley below. They were the first buffalo he had seen in the twenty days he had spent making a big loop out from Ft. Griffin. He had been as far north as the upper reaches of the Twin Mountain Fork of the Brazos River as far west as the big spring on the old Comanche war trail to Mexico and now was south almost to Ft. Chadbourne. This was the heart of the range of the southern buffalo herd and as recently as six years ago had been home to more buffalo than he could count. It was also the home of his ancestors the people the Waco had named Tonkawa but who called themselves "People of the wolf." They were among the first of the southern tribes to get horses and move out on to the plains to follow the buffalo. They were not a warlike people and got along with everyone from the fierce Krankawa on the gulf coast to the farming tribes of the river valleys to the buffalo hunting Lipan of the western plains. Tonkawa craftsmen were skilled flint knappers and their arrow points and blades were in wide demand as trade with the other tribes. Though a peaceful people, Tonkawa history was full of strife; in the late 1600's the Apache moved into their lands from the west killing many and forcing the others into the hills to the southeast. Then the

Comanche came down from the north and at first the Tonkawa allied with them against the Apache but the alliance was short lived. As soon as the Apache were driven back west, the Comanche turned on the Tonkawa and nearly wiped them out. The remainder moved east to central Texas where they allied themselves with the early white settlers. The settlers would even bring their women and children to the Tonkawa camps for safety when Comanche war parties were in the area.

They were later moved farther west to a reservation in Texas where they remained friends of the settlers. This alliance came to an abrupt end when the Tonkawa were attacked and more of their number killed by a group of white settlers who considered all Indians enemies. The survivors were moved to the Indian Territory but the tribes already there despised them for their long and close association with the Texas settlers; they had scouted for and fought with the Texians against other tribes for many years. They were also feared and loathed because of their custom of ritually eating the hands of slain enemies. Although supposedly under the protection of the U.S. Army, they were set upon by a coalition of Delaware, Shawnee, Caddo and Wichita who killed all but a handful. The few remaining fled back to Texas to the Ft. Griffin area where the men worked as scouts for the U.S. Army and the tribe had some protection from the Comanche. The Tonkawa had been good friends to the white settlers, joining the Texians and later the U.S. Army in their fights against the Comanche and Kiowa but now that the Comanche were finally beaten and confined, the Army was going to move the last of the Tonkawa back to Indian Territory.

Blue Wolf had no intention of seeing his young family moved back to Indian Territory. The people there had already killed his parents and most of his kin; he would not see his children killed or at best vilified as "man eaters." Blue Wolf made this scouting trip by himself because he wanted no witnesses to what he planned. Two days ago his wife, Summer Rain, had left Ft. Griffin with their two children, supposedly to visit kin who were with the scouts at Ft. Concho but in reality, she was coming to meet him. The Tonkawa, as a people, were dead and Blue Wolf had decided that he would no longer be Tonkawa; his children would grow up in a different world. When the Tonkawa had first been moved on to a reservation by the Texas government, the father of one of Blue Wolf's friends refused to go and had instead moved his family to the ranch of a Texan who had befriended him. Blue Wolf did not see his friend again until two years ago when his scouting party met a herd of cattle being driven north. At first, Blue Wolf did not recognize his friend who in dress, manner and language was little different from the other drovers. Blue Wolf went home and insisted that his family start to dress in the manner of the white people and that they speak only English even when they were alone. The boy and the girl already spoke fair English; it was the common language at the fort where the native tongues of their playmates included Spanish, English, Lipan, Kickapoo and Tonkawa. Summer Rain had a harder time but now even she had a fair command of the language. She and the kids were to meet him tomorrow evening on the north bank of the Colorado River just above where Oak Creek meets the river. They were going southeast to the ranch where his friend worked. The ranch was in the hills north of the German settlements along the Guadalupe River and Blue Wolf didn't want his family traveling through the more thickly settled area without him. Blue Wolf had one more thing to do before going to meet his family. Two years before, Blue Wolf was with the buffalo soldiers chasing four Comanche and was the first on the scene where the hostiles had killed three men on Oak Creek. He saw sign where the Comanche had carried something heavy and hidden it under a ledge of rock and he found two packs with leather bags of gold. He knew that if the soldiers saw the gold it would be lost to him and while the soldiers couldn't follow the trail of a mule dragging a plow, Tall Horse, the other Tonkawa scout with the soldiers could read sign just as well as he. Blue Wolf took two of the pistols that were laying near the dead men and hid them in front of the gold and then hid the sign as well as he could in the few minutes before Tall Horse led the troopers into the camp.

As he thought, the first thing the soldiers did was to gather up everything left by the Comanche and pack it on mules. While the soldiers were burying the three dead men, Blue Wolf pulled Tall Horse aside and told him in Tonkawa "I have hidden two pistols left by the Comanche under the rock ledge directly behind my back. They are under the pile of sticks in front of the pack rat nest wrapped in a piece of oilcloth. I will share with you when we get a chance to recover them." They took up the trail of the fleeing Comanche and stayed on it until they found where troopers from Ft. Chadbourne had killed two of them. The black soldiers had heard tales about the Tonkawa and were disappointed when Tall Horse and Blue Wolf didn't pull out their knives and make a meal from the dead Comanche. So as to not spoil their fun, Blue Wolf told them "meat spoiled give belly ache" and he and Tall Horse went off to find the trail of the missing Comanche. They found nothing and to this day Blue Wolf was rankled that a Comanche bastard had out smarted him. They continued their scouting loop back to Ft. Concho and as it worked out Tall Horse was the first back in the area. He came back by the kill sight two weeks later while on another scouting trip. He found the pistols and offered Blue Wolf his choice when they again met. "It had rained while we were gone and they are a little rusty but it is a good thing that you didn't try to put them deeper under the ledge. There is a rattlesnake den there and I nearly got bitten twice."

Blue Wolf had not since been back to the site but he was going back now; if he was to live as a white man, some gold would be useful. Blue Wolf had decided that he would not try to take all of the gold. Until he and his family were settled, he would leave the gold where it was. Later, he would come back with something to carry it in and take the gold to a safe place; for now he was curious and wanted to see just how much was in the packs. When he first saw the gold he had been in a rush to get it back under cover before the soldiers and Tall Horse found his secret; he had only opened one pack enough to see that there were several of the small sacks.

On the way to the gold cache, Blue Wolf used all of his skills just as if he were on scout; making certain that he was neither followed nor did he stumble into people of any kind. There were scattered hostiles still out as well as buffalo hunters and soldiers; Blue Wolf didn't want to encounter anyone. He was careful to stay off of the skyline while traveling but would take every opportunity to reach high ground without exposing himself in order to check for people in the area. He had been watching from such a vantage point when he saw movement well off to the north. As he watched, the movement came closer until he could pick out four horses traveling in single file and finally could see that it was his family on their way to the rendezvous. Blue Wolf went back down to his horse and moved off on a course that would intercept Summer Rain and his son and daughter. Finding them now meant that he could show them where the gold was hidden without having to ride to the mouth of Oak Creek and back again. That night Blue Wolf broke one of the rules he followed when on scout and slept next to the fire where they cooked supper. Normally he would have put out the fire after cooking and moved well off before bedding down for the night but on this night the family sat late around the fire talking and enjoying being together. Before daylight, Blue Wolf made a big circle on foot around their camp to be sure they were still alone before saddling up and moving on. As they rode, he pointed out landmarks to his wife and children so that if need be they could return to the place without him. They crossed Oak Creek at a spot where buffalo had caved off both banks while crossing and to be sure they could recognize the place, Blue Wolf dismounted and put a head sized white rock from the creek in the forks of a big elm tree growing on the bank. From there it was only a short distance southwest to the campsite where the men were killed and to the ledge rock sheltering the gold. It was now full summer and the rattlesnakes using the den should all be scattered out on their summer hunting grounds but Blue Wolf was still very cautious as he raked the packrat nest aside and saw that the two packs were still there. Rats had gnawed on the packs seeking the salt from the horse sweat soaked into them but otherwise the packs were as Blue Wolf had first seen them. As he pulled the leather bags out from under the ledge, Blue Wolf realized that there was much more gold than he had imagined. Someone would be searching very hard for a treasure of this size; he didn't know what the coins were but they were old, some worn almost smooth, and not like the gold coins he had seen at the forts. This did not seem like a good time to spend or even have any of the coins with him. Blue Wolf decided that he would leave the gold where it was until he was settled and enough time had passed for any searchers to become discouraged and quit. The only person who could possibly know where the gold was hidden was the one Comanche that they had not found and after thinking hard about the chase, Blue Wolf had decided that there was very little chance that he was alive. Tall Horse had found the body of a young Comanche weighed down in the Colorado River after finding a spot on the banks where someone had carried something heavy into the river. Blue Wolf was almost certain that the body of the fourth Comanche was also in the river or some similar place; he did not believe that he and Tall Horse would have missed finding the sign if one horseman had split off from the group. He told the kids to gather wood and start a fire in the pit where the fire of the dead men had been. They would camp here tonight; the campsite would explain why they had stopped in this spot to anyone seeing the sign that they could not help but leave. Blue Wolf put the packs back under the ledge, arranged the packrat nest back as well as he could and then penned all five of their horses in a rope corral using the ledge as one side. They had watered when crossing the creek and the kids could cut them a feed of grass from the lush growth of the creek bank; by morning there would be no sign of his examination of the ledge cave.

After a scout before daylight, Blue Wolf led his family northeast for several miles before turning almost due east, he did not want to pass too close to Ft Chadbourne or Ft Concho both of which lay to the south. They would go east until they were well past the Comanche war trail that passed through Buffalo Gap before turning south. About noon, they dropped down into a broad valley covered with lush grass and came upon where buffalo hunters had killed fifty or sixty buffalo in a spot no bigger than a long arrow shot across. It was what the hunters called a "stand" where they shot each animal that tried to leave until the herd just milled in a circle until all were killed. Blue Wolf had seen many such spots in the last few years and knew in both his heart and in his head that the day of the free ranging hunter tribes was over. At the far side of the slaughter ground, Blue Wolf dismounted, took his knife and after murmuring a brief prayer, sliced off both of his braids next to his head. The children gaped at their Father as if he had lost his mind and Summer Rain broke into a wailing song of lament before he signed her to be silent. His hair had never before been cut and his head suddenly felt uncomfortably light. He coiled the two braids on the forehead of a tremendous bull skull and turned back to his family. "Blue Wolf the Tonkawa is dead, I am now Tom Wolf and we leave the old ways here with my hair and the bones of the buffalo."

CHAPTER 26

Tommie Rae rolled in at 10:00 am pulling a two horse trailer. Bart was the first one there as she opened the pickup door and stepped out but Tara was close behind, "How did you get here so quick? We thought you had a commercial to film." "I did and we got it done in record time. The script called for running horses silhouetted on the dawn sky and not even that prissy little director with his fake French accent could make the sun stand still for more than two shoots. Hi Tara, are you ready to see these two camera hogs perform? Let me get them unloaded and then, Bart do you suppose there is any coffee left? I left the house at 3:30 and I can't get my caffeine level up." "I'd bet on it, I have never yet caught Emilianos' coffee pot dry." Tommie Rae opened the trailer door and said, "Come Major, come Sergeant." and first Major and then Sergeant backed out and turned to face Tommie. Tommie took the halter ropes that were thrown over the horses' withers and tied first one and then the other to rings spaced down the side of the trailer. Tara spoke up to ask, "May I brush them while you are having coffee?" Tommie glanced sideways at Bart and seeing a slight nod, said "Sure but we won't be long." Bart and Tommie Rae went into the kitchen through the back door and found Emiliano and Maria just starting dinner. "Maria Gomez, Emiliano Cortez, this is Miss Tommie Rae Wolf. She has come to entertain us with her marvelously trained horses and she wants a cup of coffee as payment." Tommie stepped forward to kiss Maria's cheek then

169

turned extending her hand to Emiliano and said, "Maria and I are old friends, I am very pleased to meet you Sr. Cortez." Emiliano took her hand and with a slight bow said, "Con mucho gusto Senorita." "Why don't you all fix things so dinner can wait a little bit while Tommie and I drink a cup of coffee and then we will all go watch Tommie work her horses?" Tommie started down the hall toward the bathroom saying, "Excuse me a minute, if you will pour me a cup of coffee, I'll be right back." Maria poured two cups of coffee and set them on the kitchen table along with a plate of baked that morning cinnamon rolls. She giggled when Bart, reaching for the plate, said, "Maria, if you don't quit baking these things I am going to weigh 300 pounds." The first roll disappeared and Bart was taking the first bite out of the second when Tommie Rae came back in and said, "Maria, thank goodness you and Emiliano are here cooking, I saw Mac about a month ago and he looked like an escapee from a concentration camp. I don't think the man cooked at all after Windy died. You all have been a blessing and I thank you for putting some meat on my old friends' bones." She sat down and reached across the table to put her hand on top of Bart's saying, "Thank you for giving Mac reason to hope, the drought has been hell on earth and combined with losing his two best friends in less than a year, it is more than anyone should have to endure." Bart fought down the urge to take her hand in both of his and said, "Emiliano and I are the ones in debt to Mac; he saved Emilianos' life literally and I was just drifting through life with no purpose until I met Mac." Watching over Tommie's shoulder, Bart saw Maria turn and stare with raised eyebrows at Emiliano. It was obvious that Maria had not heard about the rescue and that Bart had inadvertently put his friend on Maria's bad list. Tommie Rae caught the byplay as well and thought, "I believe my friend Maria is interested in more here than just a paycheck." They finished their coffee and Bart said, "We ought to get back out there before Tara completely steals the affection of your horses. You have never seen anyone that loves horses like that girl." "Does she ride well enough to sit Major as he does one of his dance routines?" Mac walked in to hear this last and said, "That's not a problem, that little gal rides like a Comanche." "Oh, I'm so sorry to hear that, maybe she should come home with me so I can teach her to ride correctly like us Tonkawa's." Mac threw both hands up as if warding off attack, "Whoa now, don't lay your ears back; I didn't mean to start a tribal war." Tommie stood up and hugged Mac, "I'm just teasing you, old bear, but it would be nice to hear, just once, that someone rides like a Tonkawa. We were riding horses of our own breeding and living fat on buffalo for two generations before the Comanche dragged their raggedy asses out of the snow of the Rockies with everything they owned packed on the back of a dog. I ought to be ashamed of myself for talking like this; my only excuse is I grew up listening to my Granddaddy tell about what the Comanche did to our people. The only way you could make the old man mad was to say something nice about a Comanche. He used to scare us grandkids silly with what he claimed was a Comanche scalp his Grandfather took; looking back, I think it was probably part of a horses' tail. Let's go see if those two old crow baits remember anything that I taught them."

Everyone was gathered admiring the horses and watching Tara and Jacob groom their already silky coats. Bart asked, "Where do you want to work and where do you want us?" Tommie Rae looked around and said, "Right here between the trailer and the house would be fine; people can sit on the front porch and be comfortable. Jacob and Tara, thank you for grooming my old boys, if you will go up on the porch now, you can help me in a minute." As people started over to the porch, Tommie opened a door on the front of the trailer and took out two bridles; she slipped the halter off and replaced it with a bridle on first Major and then Sergeant. The bridles were fitted with round reins that ran from one bit shank to the other shank while the rein loop rested on the horses' withers where it would not interfere with the horses' movement. Tommie led the two horses out away from the trailer, positioned them about ten feet apart and put a bright red saddle pad and a surcingle with hand hold but no stirrups on the ground next to each horse. She then ducked into the truck cab, coming out carrying a long handled whip and wearing a white silk top hat with sequins and a dangling red ribbon. "Ladies and gentlemen, it is with great pleasure that I bring to you, all the way from suburban Ballinger Texas, those extraordinary examples of educated equine excellence, Major and Sergeant!" Tommie spread her arms in a sweeping bow and gestured dramatically to the two horses. Major ducked his head and with one leg extended, made a deep bow before coming back up to proud attention. Sergeant turned his head away from Tommie and looked up at the sky like he was watching birds. Once again Tommie made her sweeping bow and sang out, "Major and Sergeant." Major repeated his flawless bow and Sergeant again looked completely bored. Tommie Rae appeared ready to cry when she once again cried, "Major and Sergeant." Major made another grand bow while Sergeant turned to Tommie, rolled his lips up in an ugly grimace and blew rollers through his nose like a Bronx cheer. The audience broke out in applauding laughter as Major and Sergeant exploded into bucking, kicking runs around the trailer and back to their positions. At the call "Major and Sergeant", both horses dropped into perfect bows. Tommie Rae put down her whip and said,

"I will need some help for our next act but first I need to saddle up."
She picked up the saddle pad next to Major and after shaking it free
of dirt and smoothing down the hair, placed it on Majors' back. As
she turned to get the surcingle, Sergeant reached over to pull the
saddle pad off, drop it on the ground and look away. Tommie looked
puzzled, put the surcingle down and walked around Major to pick
up the pad. She brought the pad back to Major's left side and after
brushing and smoothing, put the pad back on. As Tommie turned to
pick up the surcingle; Sergeant started reaching for the pad again but
whirled back front and center when Tommie jerked her head around
and almost caught him. As soon as she turned her head back, Sergeant
jerked the pad off again and looked off in the other direction. This
time when Tommie came after the pad, she led Sergeant around
and put him behind her as she finished saddling Major. Tommie led
Sergeant back to his pad and surcingle and just as she finished saddling him; Major reached up to take the dangling red ribbon in his
mouth and run toward the porch with the fine silk hat. Tommie put
her hands on her hips, stomped her foot and said, "You bring that
back right this minute." Major looked chagrined and brought the hat
to Tommie but just as she reached for it, he danced sideways just out
of reach. This was repeated several times as they went around in a
circle, Tommie threatening and Major teasing until they got back to
Sergeant where Tommie called out, "Major and Sergeant." Major put
the hat in Tommie's' hand and he and Sergeant bowed deep. Tommie
Rae said, "Now if Tara and Jacob would like to help, we will go to an
old fashioned square dance. Tara came tearing out with a big grin and
Jacob followed looking a little more subdued. Tommie turned her
back to the audience and in a low voice told Tara and Jacob, "If you
two will just sit on the horses, you can grab the handle if you feel

the need but the horses won't be making any sudden moves; don't try to rein them or control them in any way. I will be giving them their clues. Ok?" Both Jacob and Tara nodded and Tommie first gave Tara a leg up onto Major and then helped Jacob mount Sergeant. Tommie reached into the truck to bring out a CD player which she placed on the hood of the truck. The horses were standing nose to nose and when the music started and the caller sang out "Bow to your partners" they both bowed and then wheeled toward the house and stepped off in time to the music at the call "Ladies to the left and gents to the right and promenade." They kept pace with each other and turned back right and left at the call, "Circle back home and Doe See Doe right." The two horses stopped beside each other head to rump and circled to the right with Major backing up and Sergeant going forward. At the call, "Doe See Doe left" they reversed the move with Sergeant backing and Major going forward. They repeated both moves at the call, "Do it all again and Promenade." As the horses reached the audience, the call came, "Bow to your partner and big circle left." The horses turned toward each other, bowed and then set off side by side in a slow lope around the pickup and back toward the audience. As they completed the circle the call came, "Big circle right." When this circle was completed, the caller said, "Circle back home and say goodnight." The horses peeled off left and right and stopped facing each other. They bowed to each other and then turned to bow to the audience. The whole group exploded in applause as both horses, Tara and Jacob all looked very pleased with themselves. Bart stepped down to Tommie Rae and said, "That was fantastic but we don't want to wear you and your horses out and if we are going on a trail ride, we had best let Emiliano and Maria finish up dinner while Mac and I pen the saddle horses and teams. Tara showed no sign of getting off of Major and said, "Tommie Rae, could you come with us on the trail ride, it's going to be lots of fun." Tommie looked first at Tara and then at Bart saying, "My folks expect me home tonight and I didn't bring anything with me." Bart said, "You can call your folks and I bet we can find you a toothbrush, nobody else will be showering tonight so you won't even have to stay down wind." Tommie swatted Bart on the arm and said, "Thank you Tara, I would like to come on the trail ride even if some people do act like smart Alecks."

CHAPTER 27

After they ate Bart went to the pens with Mac and Bud to begin his education on harnessing and handling teams. Emiliano and Maria had already loaded the chuck wagon with food and supplies and the hooligan wagon with horse feed, tents and bedding. All that was needed was to harness the teams and hitch up. They stopped by the saddle shed for bridles and as they started around to the back corral where the mules were penned, Bud said, "We need to caution your guests to be careful around the mules. I have been mule bit more times in the four years I have owned these little devils than in all the fifty years of handling mules that came before. They seem to delight in seeing which one can be the most ornery." They rounded the corner of the barn to see all eight mules in a circle around Tara who was feeding a carrot to each in turn and swatting the nose of any mule that tried to take a carrot out of turn. All three men stopped in amazement and listened as Tara told them in a serious voice that they must, "Mind their manners" if they expected her to bring them treats. "That little lady is either the luckiest or the best hand with mules that I have ever seen. Manners, is not in a mule's vocabulary; if I tried that, I would at best lose fingers and might wind up dead. Get her out of there, please before she gets hurt bad!" Mac eased into the pen and told Tara, "Come to me Tara but don't make any quick moves." Tara looked up with a puzzled expression but squeezed between two mules and came to Mac. "Honey, you shouldn't get in the pen with these mules. They are not gentle like the horses and could hurt you bad." "Oh they wouldn't hurt me Mac; Gertrude there and Henry were naughty and nipped at me the first time I brought them treats but I fussed at them and told them to behave and they have been fine." Bart spoke up, "Tara, I know you don't think they would hurt you on purpose and maybe you are right but we just can't take the chance. If you promise to only feed them through the fence, you can continue to bring them treats. Can you promise not to get in the pen?"

It took a while but eventually the teams for both wagons were hitched, everyone was mounted and with Emiliano driving the chuck wagon and Bud handling the hooligan wagon, the expedition got under way. Bart and Mac had decided that the group was skilled enough to handle the longer of the two trail rides they had planned so they stepped out on what would be about a four hour circuitous ride. Bart was leading while Mac stayed behind to watch for trouble and in general keep an eye on things. The three married couples were riding two abreast as were Tara and Jacob so it seemed natural that Tommie Rae fell in beside Bart. The line of march collapsed when they reached the creek crossing and all of the saddle horses decided that they desperately needed to drink. With the crossing full of drinking horses, Emiliano had no choice but to stop his team just short of the creek even though they were on a slight down grade and he had to set the brake to keep from rolling. Bart and Tommie Rae stopped their horses just across the creek and sat waiting for the watering break to be over. Tara called from the middle of the creek and pointed, "Tommie Rae, look at the rock leaning against the creek bank. Doesn't it look just like a Hopi bear fetish?" "It does for sure." said Tommie "If you will remind me tonight I will tell you about how a bear got turned to stone; it is a story that my Grandfather told me when I was a little girl."

Emiliano looked hard at the subject of this conservation and felt a chill run up his back, the shape of the big stone matched exactly the figure Grandfather Juan had scratched in the dirt many years ago as he squatted on his heels in the shade and told his grandson the story of the oso piedra that guarded the hiding place of the gold of the bandidos. Memories came flooding back and as he drove across the creek, Emiliano looked both up and down stream but the creek was brush lined and crooked in this spot and he could see only a short distance in each way. He could see no sign of the two smaller creeks that Grandfather said entered the big creek on either side of the stone bear but straight ahead to the east was a long flat topped mesa. As they drove up out of the creek bed, Emiliano could see a line of taller trees such as often marked a water course in this country winding off to the east toward the base of the mesa. He was as excited as he had been in a very long time but not wanting to appear a foolish old man to his friends, decided to say nothing until he heard the story Senorita Tommie Rae had promised.

CHAPTER 28

West Texas 1875

Coke Barton reined in his horse just before he topped out on the ridgeline and sat looking back south at the country they had ridden through. He could see a long way from this point; he could even pick out the little bunch of buffalo that they had passed an hour ago but he could see nothing else moving in that direction. Looking down, he could see his two companions and their pack mule moving north up the creek bottom. It had been seven days since they had seen any sign of pursuit and Coke was beginning to think that the Mexican cavalry must have either killed or captured Luis Robles and his entire bunch of cut throats. It was a sure thing that Robles would be hot on their trail if he were able to travel. Cokes' Mama always said that he was born under a lucky star but the events of the last two weeks had him fearful that maybe he was stretching his luck a little too far. It began two months ago when he agreed to drive twenty Hereford cross long yearling bulls from the Lewis Ranch on Bitter Creek to the ranch of Don Ramon Lopez in northern Coahuila. He got Hank Greenway and Jose Benavidez to go with him; they took an extra horse apiece and a couple of pack horses and, after he kissed his wife and two sons goodbye, they started the bulls for Mexico. Judge Lewis had threatened to "skin their heads" if the bulls got there poor or sore footed so they poked along giving the bulls lots of time to graze and in general just enjoying the trip. These Hereford cross bulls were something else; they were just eighteen months old and already bigger than most full grown longhorn bulls. Several ranchers in the Sweetwater area had brought Herefords out of Missouri; the Trammell's, the Newman's and the Lewis's all brought Hereford bulls from the east and though they didn't realize it, with the bulls from England came the horn fly which would become a major pest of American cattle. Coke had seen some of the purebred Herefords and he agreed with the observation that, "There was more actual meat on one Hereford than there was on two longhorns of the same weight." The longhorn cow would have a calf every year, walk ten miles to water if she had to and fight wolves off her baby but she was a little light in the meat department.

Coke and his buddies went heavy armed because there were reports of both bandits and Apaches being active in the area they would be traveling through but they delivered the bulls without seeing anything more threatening than a rattlesnake. They started back to Texas in fine shape and decided to stop over in the little town of La Rosana for a drink or two and a good meal. They had their meal and their drinks and then it seem reasonable to buy a five gallon keg of mescal to take with them. They were nipping a little on the mescal all day on the trail but got serious about it that night in camp.

Coke woke up just as it was getting light to find that he couldn't move; not that he couldn't move well, but that he couldn't move at all! His first thought was, "That damned rot gut mescal has give me the Jake leg and I'm paralyzed!" but just then he saw Jose and Hank beside him, both hog tied with pigging strings. As he was trying to sort all this out amidst the mescal fumes still floating around his brain, a short heavy set Mexican in a silver studded "Charro" suit stepped into his sight and holding up a tin cup said, "Buenas dias Senor, mucho gracias para este mescal bueno." Coke looked up at him through the one eye that wasn't stuck shut and said, "Who the hell are you? Cut me loose right now!" He had intended it to be a threatening growl but instead it came out more of a croak and not at all threatening. "Oh, pardon me Senor, I am Don Luis Robles - Ramos, Bandit Extraordinaire but I am afraid that I cannot cut you loose just yet. It would appear that you and I are the only ones here not passed out drunk. As soon as my men wake up, you and I will have a nice talk and you will tell me where you hid the money that you got from old Moneybags Lopez for the bulls but right now, I think a little siesta is in order." With that, he drained the cup and collapsed into a loose jointed heap. By twisting his neck Coke could see at least five or six men laid out around the remains of their fire. Jose was closest to him, lying on his side with hands and feet tied together behind him. Jose still had his boots on and Coke knew that he carried a knife in a sheath sewed to the inside of his right bootleg. Coke managed to roll over so that his hands and feet were touching Jose and felt a ray of hope when Jose grabbed his hand and said softly, "Pull the knife from my boot and cut me loose." It seemed to take forever but finally both he and Jose were free and he was quietly trying to wake Hank while Jose, with Robles pistol, was watching the drunken bandits. Coke managed to get Hank awake enough to function and sent him to catch and saddle their horses which were still grazing hobbled outside the camp. They found their guns and saddlebags still stacked on their saddles where they had unsaddled the evening before; evidently the bandits rode in to find them drunk and took only enough time to truss them up before hitting the mescal themselves. Coke and Jose gathered up all the guns that were easy to get at but were afraid to try to take the ones being worn by bandits. Four of the bandits' horses were grazing close bye, still saddled along with one big and two small pack mules. Coke got everybody mounted after having to threaten to brain Hank to keep him from bringing along the last of the mescal. They rode off slowly and quietly drifting the bandits' horses and mules ahead of them. After they got a mile or so away, they tied the extra guns to the pack of one of the mules and got serious about putting some distance between themselves and the bandits. They watered the horses and themselves at a flowing creek just before sundown but did not stop until they reached a small lake just after daybreak the next morning. The long hard ride on top of a mescal hangover from hell had them all whipped and they decided to stop long enough to make coffee and eat something. Hank made a small fire for coffee while Jose and Coke caught and unsaddled the extra horses. Nothing they had taken from the bandits was worth much; the horses were not the finest examples of horseflesh to begin with and were thin and ill used to boot. The saddles and guns were no better, old, worn and dirty. They threw the guns as far out into the lake as possible and turned the horses loose. One of the little mules had some corn meal and dried meat in its pack that they transferred to their saddlebags but nothing else on the little mules was worth keeping. Jose remarked that it looked as if the bandit business didn't pay too well in this part of the world. They unsaddled and turned the little mules loose and turned to the big mule. They had left their pack horses behind getting away from the bandits. They and their spare saddle horses had been tied to a picket line behind the drunk Mexicans and Coke decided to replace them with the big mule rather than take a chance of waking the bandits and starting a fire fight. The mule was carrying two rather small leather packs and when Coke unbuckled one to see what was inside and came close to having a heart attack! The packs were full of small leather sacks and in the sacks were full of gold coins. They had convinced themselves that the bandits would do the sensible thing and take the swap of three good saddle horses and two pack horses for their horses and mules rather than follow after three armed and now very alert men but the gold changed everything. They gulped down coffee cooled with lake water out of the can Hank boiled it in and leading the mule started for the border. About mid day, Coke rode to the top of the long ridge that paralleled their route and saw dust coming from the north towards them; looking south he could see dust rising faintly on their back trail. He rode back to his part-ners as fast as he could without crippling his horse and had them follow him west into a thicket of salt cedar. They dismounted and held their horses' heads to keep them from whickering and watched as a detachment of about fifteen Mexican Federales rode by going south. As soon as the mounted police were out of sight, Coke and his party rode on north. After a short time, they heard first one and then a flurry of gunshots coming from the south. The gunfight went on for ten minutes or so and seemed to be getting closer until there was a cluster of five or six shots and then silence. That had been seven days ago now and there had been no more sign of Senor Robles and his merry men. It seemed the famous Barton luck was holding they were back in their home territory; they would camp tonight on the good water of Oak Creek and be back at the Lewis Ranch with their gold the next day. Coke had already decided that the first thing he would do would be to buy a surrey and a good team of mares and take his Polly to Ft Worth to buy whatever she wanted; maybe then her Father, old Jake Malone, would finally believe that Coke could take good care of his daughter.

CHAPTER 29

Emiliano clucked to his mules to pick up the pace and shortly they arrived at the place where he and Senor Bud would leave the group and take a short cut to the camping spot. When Mac rode up and asked if they wanted him to come along and help get camp set up, Bud spoke up, "If two old farts can't unhitch two four- mule hitches and build a fire, having a third one around won't help much." Mac laughed and rode on, "Ok, we will be along in a couple or three hours." It wasn't far to the camp site where Emiliano and Bud unhitched the mules and put them in the pole corral but decided not to feed until the horses arrived. Bud said, "It wouldn't matter if they were full as ticks, these little heathens would still try to steal the horses' feed. Only way to have any sort of peace is to feed them all at once and we will still have cuss fights." They had pulled the chuck wagon up so that the chuck box and fold down work table were about ten feet from the fire pit where Bud started a fire while Emiliano got ready to start supper. He had thought to barbeque a whole cabrito done with his special sauce but Bart had vetoed that idea. "If Tara and the ladies see that little carcass turning on a spit, none of them will eat a bite of it." Instead of the whole carcass, he had the shoulders and hams cut out and even these he disguised by trimming off the shank bones and making an iron rack to hold them as they turned over the fire. He had cheated a little by bring along a big bowl of Senora Gomez' potato salad and a pot of red beans cooked with ham hock, onions and green chili. They would have hot Dutch oven biscuits with some of Susan's' wild plum jelly and for desert, peach cobbler. Having the extra room of the hooligan wagon meant a place for two big ice chests so they even had milk for the youngsters and cream for the cobbler. Mac and Bart had dug a second fire pit out away from the cooking fire and ringed it with rough pole benches where people could sit while they ate and to visit and enjoy the fire. Mac had been surprised when Bart took a pile of cedar poles and some bailing wire and turned out sturdy and comfortable benches. When Mac asked where he learned the skill, Bart said "My Dad was a builder, He and I built stuff together from the time I was five years old; he had me running a backhoe and a chain saw by the time I was twelve."

Emiliano set up the supports for the turning spit while the mesquite wood fire was burning down to coals and made a pot of coffee. Bud came back from laying a fire in the fire pit and dug out two folding canvas chairs from the hooligan wagon. He set up the chairs in the shade of the wagon and out of the smoke of the cook fire and poured each of them a cup of coffee; it was still a while before the trail riders were due back and they were caught up until time to start the cabrito roasting. Bud took out a cigar and lit it after offering one to Emiliano, "Mac tells me that your Grandfather lived with the Comanche." "Si Senor Bud, He was captured when he was ten years old and adopted into the tribe." "The guests would be fascinated to hear his story. Would you mind telling it to them?" "I would not mind, they are very nice people, but my English is not good." "Your English is fine but if you get stuck, I speak pretty good cow pen Spanish and could help you out." "Bueno Senor, after we eat, I will tell the story of my Grandfather."

After the wagons split off, Bart led the group in a big loop to the north and west before turning south and finally heading east toward the campsite. It had been a fun trip with everyone seeming to enjoy themselves. Even the wildlife cooperated, they saw turkey, a bobcat and deer several times, once a doe with two brand new fawns. They stopped once and dismounted when Tommie Rae pointed out an out crop of flint on a hillside and the chips where someone had obviously once made tools. "There is no way to tell who worked flint here but it might have been my Tonkawa ancestors. They lived in this area for many years before the Comanche drove them out and were known for making beautiful flint blades that they traded with other tribes." Tara was on all fours digging through the chips and Mac had just cautioned her to be careful because the chips are sharp when she squealed and held up an arrowhead. The point was perfect except a little at the very tip was broken off. They remounted and started on toward camp; it had been a while since dinner and everyone was beginning to have hunger pains.

CHAPTER 30

Headwaters of the Colorado River 1667

Long Stride looked up from his work and carefully scanned the area that stretched far and away to the north. He was sitting cross legged on the very point of a high ridge that jutted out north from the limestone hills behind him; these hills formed the divide between the watersheds of the Colorado and the Brazos Rivers and he could see for miles to the north and east across the rolling plains. Though Long Stride had never seen the ocean, the vast area of frost killed grass waving in the wind very much resembled waves on some large body of water. Long Stride was a member of the Mayeye band of the Tonkawa people; he was seventeen years old and an artisan skilled in the art of flint knapping. He had received his medicine vision in the fall and while he was not yet a proven warrior, he was a good hunter, a skilled craftsman and was accepted as a man full grown in the councils of the tribe. Today he was doing two jobs at once; final touch up and sharpening on a number of flint blades and keeping watch for buffalo. He had climbed to his lookout perch just below the top of the ridgeline in time to be in place to greet Father Sun; his uncle and clan chief, Points His Spear, had suggested that he come here to work where he could also keep watch for moving buffalo. His group had killed nothing larger than a white tailed deer for many days and they needed to find the buffalo. The winter had been hard and unusually long and all of the dried meat was gone; they were living on roots and what little small game they could catch. A group of the men even made a trip to the Colorado River and came back with a batch of catfish and some mussels, things most plains tribes would not eat. It was very early spring and the buffalo herds were on the move, chasing the first scant shoots of new green grass. Later as the grass grew taller, the herds would settle down, grazing mainly in big circles as they moved constantly to fresh grass; when this happened, they would be much easier to find and to hunt. Now with rain water ponds everywhere and short green grass in every direction, there was no way to predict where the herds might go and thus little chance to get in position to ambush a herd. Killing a grown buffalo with a bow and arrow was not an easy feat; killing an animal that was facing you was almost impossibility due to the heavy mane and dewlap guarding the location of the vital organs and shooting at the side was only marginally more successful because of the heavy ribs. The best chance to make a killing shot came by firing from a position just behind and on the right side of the buffalo. From this position a skilled marksman could send an arrow just inside the last rib to angle forward into the ribcage to strike at heart, liver or lungs. The problem was how to get into position; some tribes used a wolf skin disguise to creep in close but The People were brothers to the wolf and would never harm their brothers. With millions of buffalo within a two day walk, the people were often hungry because as his Uncle said, "No man can outrun a buffalo." They were often reduced to stealing the kills of their brothers the wolves.

Long Stride finished his examination of the horizon and returned to his flint work; he was building up a cache of blades and points to be used for a very special purpose; a family from the Catona band had been visiting with relatives in the Mayeye band and Long Stride was totally smitten with the charms of the oldest daughter, Pink Shell Beauty. As soon as things got back to normal, Long Stride intended to approach her father with a magnificent collection of his best points and blades as a brides' price for his daughter. At the moment, he was working on a piece that would not be a part of that collection; several months ago Long Stride had quarried several very large nodules of flint from a deposit in the canyon below and baked them in a fire that he tended for twenty four hours before allowing it to burn out. These nodules turned out to be the finest flint that he had ever worked with long blades of fine grain and uniform thicknesses striking cleanly off of the cores that he prepared. His normal procedure was to trim down the nodules that he mined into rough blades so as to reduce the amount of weight that he had to carry when they moved camp; the people did not have a lot of processions for this very reason. When they moved, everything they owned was either carried on their backs or packed on a travois dragged by a dog. After tiring of making several trips back and forth to gather his inventory at every move, Long Stride now had caches of flint and finished blades hidden in several places on their hunting grounds. One of the nodules from this batch split cleanly at his first blow leaving a face as long as his arm from knuckles to elbow and as wide as his hand; when he struck the first blade from this face, he was amazed when a perfectly flat blade the same width and length as the face popped off. Long Stride had never seen a blade of this size and perfection and decided at the moment that this blade must be turned into something special. After examining it from every angle and mulling over the question for several days, Long Stride decided that this would be a weapon of war rather than a tool for hunting. He held the almost finished weapon in his hand now; it was double edged, razor sharp, almost four fingers wide, a little over a half finger thick and it tapered smoothly to a slightly elongated point. When it was lashed to the elk horn handle that he had ready, the finished weapon would be over two times as long as one of his feet; Long Stride knew that the blade was apt to shatter when it first contacted bone in battle but he also knew that any warrior who looked on this weapon could not help but to covet it with all his heart. Long Stride intended to trade this magnificent weapon for one of the horses that the men of the Cava and Sona bands had began to capture and ride; having a horse would make hunting much easier and would allow Long Stride and his bride to have and move a tipi of their own.

Long Stride wanted a horse because he could see how it would make his life easier but he could not foresee the dramatic changes that having horses would have on all of the people of the plains. In a very short time the Tonkawa would become a prosperous and traveled people; with horses, hunting no longer took so much time and the people could visit and trade with others from the farming tribes of the east to the pueblo dwellers far to the west.

CHAPTER 31

As they got close to camp, Mac spoke up, "OK folks, here are some of those rules that I told you about. Nobody rides up to the cook fire or gets between the cook and the fire or his work table or raises any dust around the chuck wagon; the one thing that you absolutely do not want is to get the cook mad at you. In camp, the cook is king and woe be under your short bushy tail if you get cross wise with the cook." By that time they could smell delicious odors of mesquite wood smoke, roasting meat and baking bread so everyone was very careful to stay well away from the chuck wagon as they rode up and dismounted. With the Kelly's and Tommie Rae helping the horses were soon unsaddled and eating the hay that Mac and Bart had brought in ahead of time. Bart pointed out the latrines and the wash basin with its' can of water and roll of paper towels and went to light the campfire as people began to drift toward the facilities. Bud was hosting the coffee pot and as the adults took cups and doctored them to their taste, Bart turned to Jacob and Tara and said, "Kids I apologize, I did not even think about having soda pops for you." Liz spoke up and said, "Don't worry about that, I will fix them coffee milks like my dad did for me; they taste great and are a lot better for you than soda." Emiliano was carving the meat and had the beans, potato salad and biscuits lined up on his table so Mac called for everyone to get a plate and silverware and serve themselves. As Emiliano served Liz a slice of meat topped with sauce, she said "Emiliano that smells delicious, what is it?" "Senora this is a favorite dish of my Country that we serve on special occasions. It is called cabrito asado." When people had their plates, they moved to the benches around the fire pit and conversations changed from the events of the day to the food, with the cabrito getting rave reviews. Liz said, "Mac, Emiliano told me that this is called cabrito asado but what kind of meat is it?" Mac looked to be sure everyone had tasted their meat and said, "Asado means roasted and cabrito means little goat." "You are kidding. This is goat meat? It is absolutely delicious; I thought goat would be tough and taste bad." "I know, here in the southwest, we have told bad tales about it for years; we tried to keep the fact that it is so good a secret so we wouldn't have to share but the truth has gotten out and now most of our goats are sold to the northeast." People began to finish their meal and, after asking if anyone else wanted seconds, Emiliano brought around bowls of hot cobbler and cream. Mac spoke up to say, "We operate on cow camp rules, when you finish eating everybody tends their own eating utensils. Scrape any food scraps into the garbage bag and then put your dishes and silverware in the wreck pan but hold on to your cup if you want more coffee. If we help Emiliano get cleaned up, he has promised to tell us about his Grandfathers' life with the Comanche." As darkness fell, the heat of the day – it had been over ninety degrees – quickly dissipated into the dry air and clear sky and suddenly the warmth from the campfire felt very good. Emiliano had a big kettle of water boiling on the fire and the dishes were quickly washed, scalded and dried ready for tomorrow. Bart helped put food away while Bud made another pot of coffee. He took it around serving seconds and then poured Emiliano a cup and said, "Emiliano, come join us at the fire, everyone would be very interested if you would please tell us about your grandfather."

Emiliano sat down between Bud and Mac and said," I do not speak English very good but if you wish, I will try to tell the story of my Grandfather. My people have lived for many years in northwest Coahuila Mexico. Where they live is very dry and has poor land; it is not easy to make a living in this place but it is the home of my people. For two hundred years life was made even harder by raids from the west by Apaches and raids from the north by the Comanche. At ten years of age my Grandfather was stolen from his Fathers' corn field and taken north by a Comanche war party. He was treated very badly during the trip and for days he expected to be killed at every moment. When they got deep into Comancheria, the Indians began to treat him a little better; they still slapped him or struck him with the quirt they all carried if he didn't move fast enough to suit them but they untied his hands and gave him enough food and drink. He was still very frightened but tried hard not to show this to his captors. There was a boy not much older than Grandfather with the group who was especially harsh to him. The boy put a rope around Grandfathers neck and led him around like a dog or a horse, screaming at him and at times beating him with a stick. One day after they had been traveling for about a week, the boy had Grandfather gathering wood for the fire and as he brought in a big load, the boy hit Grandfather from behind causing him to fall forward into the fire. Grandfather rolled out of the fire and came up with a big stick which he used to beat the boy about the head until he quit trying to fight and ran away. Grandfather expected the warriors to kill him but instead they laughed and clapped their mouths in —Senor Bud, Como se dice aprobacion en Ingles? —Ah approval, si gracis. The way he acted met with their approval and one even put some grease on the burns from the fire. That was the last time that any Comanche

197

ever mistreated him; from then on, he was treated in all ways as if he were Comanche born. When they reached the band to which most of this party belonged, Grandfather was taken in by an older couple who had lost their children to sickness. He soon looked upon them as his parents; the woman, Bright Cloud, made clothes for him and good things to eat and the man, Osage Killer, gave him a pony, a knife and a bow and arrows. He learned the language quickly and was accepted into the group of boys that ran wild through the camp. The band moved every few days so there were always new things to do and new places to explore. He became skilled with the bow and was soon bringing in small game to his parents lodge. He told me that the proudest day of his life was when he brought an antelope that he had killed in to his adopted Mother. She called her friends to see what her son had done and cooked the liver for his supper. Osage Killer spent a lot of time with him as did Slow Bear, Bright Clouds' brother. They taught him the ways of the Comanche and made him proud to be one of the Nurmurnuh. The warrior leading the war party that captured him called him "Head Knocker" after his fight with the older boy and the name stuck; it would be his name until he became an adult. He was horseback much of the time and soon became expert; a favorite game of he and his compadres was to leap from the back of their pony to the back of an untamed horse and ride it with only a handhold on its' mane. It was the ideal life for a young boy, the play that took up the days of he and his friends was prepa-ration for the work they would do as adults. Grandfather told me many stories about his life, tales of buffalo hunts and horse stealing raids against the Utes, the Pawnees and the Texicans. I know that they raided into Mexico as well but he did not tell of this and I did not ask. The last years he was with the Comanche were very hard; the buffalo were gone and the U.S. Cavalry chased them all the time. Finally all of his band was either killed or captured and Grandfather returned to Mexico to start a new life. It is late and I have talked too much." The group broke into applause with everyone speaking at once to thank Emiliano for sharing his Grandfathers' story with them. The Overholts were especially grateful and asked if he would tell them more if they had time before they had to leave.

CHAPTER 32

Mac took this time to tell people that there was a bedroll and ground cloth for each of them and also flashlights in the hooligan wagon and that there were pup tents that he and Bart could put up if anyone felt the need for more privacy than distance and a dark night could provide. Bud spoke up loudly to say "Be sure and shake your boots out before you put them on; it wouldn't do to squash some poor little scorpion that was just looking for a warm bed." This caused some groans and a couple of nervous laughs but no one seemed interested in a pup tent as they picked up their bedrolls and began to unroll them in family groups out away from the fire. First Mac and Bud and then Emiliano and Bart refilled their coffee cups and converged on the fire. Bart had never been a big coffee drinker but that was rapidly changing; evidently coffee was the life force of the cowboy, he had yet to catch the coffee pot empty on Emilianos' stove. As they sat congratulating each other on a successful, so far, first trail ride, Tommie Rae joined them causing all four men to come to their feet, she poured herself a cup of coffee after telling them to please sit down and not make her feel like a stranger. "Emiliano, did your Grandfather ever mention the Tonkawa to you?" "Si Senorita, he often told of the Tonkawa scouts that helped the U.S. soldiers to find the Comanche. The Comanche did not worry very much about the blue coats unless they had Indian scouts with them and the Tonkawa were the best of the scouts. Grandfather said that the Tonkawa could track a red ant across a slick rock; there were Tonkawa with the Buffalo Soldiers that killed or captured my Grandfathers band. They were some of the last Comanche still free and were captured after being chased for many miles, my Grandfather barely escaped with his life and returned to Mexico." "Emiliano, it is very likely that my Grandfathers' Grandfather was one of those scouts. He told stories that have been passed down in my family of those last days and one of his stories was about a band of Comanche that the Buffalo Soldiers followed from up close to the Red River to south of where we are now before all were captured or killed. He was afraid that one warrior had gotten away but he could not figure out how he did it and it bothered him to the end of his days that he had been outsmarted." "Senorita, it is late now but you and I should talk more about our ancestors. I know how Grandfather got away; it was one of his favorite stories. If we compare the stories we have been told, perhaps we will know if my Grandfather was the warrior who escaped your ancestor."

The camp woke to the smell of coffee and bacon frying to find Mac and Bart finishing up feeding the stock. There were more than a few groans as bodies not used to sleeping on the ground were forced upright. Sam Shapiro limped up to the coffee pot and said, "Mac, you all have done a great job taking care of us but you might want to get some air mattresses for your next bunch of tenderfoots. I feel like I have been in a rock fight with an octopus." Mac grinned, handed him the coffee he had just poured and said, "Have some of Emilianos' coffee, it's good for sore backs, bunions and most anything else that ails you. If it makes you feel any better, the ground has gotten a lot harder since the last time I slept on it and about four o'clock this morning I decided that we would have mattresses of some kind before the next sleep out." Tara and Jacob were already brushing their mounts as the horses finished their morning feed. Tara was completely in love with La Mosca and had brushed her at every opportunity until the mares' coat was as sleek and shiny as a new penny. Jacob was less demonstrative but it was obvious that he felt much the same about the black gelding, Mirlo. Mirlo was the last horse Windy broke before his death and he had told Mac several times that this horse could be one of the really good ones. Windy named him Mirlo or Blackbird because he looked like a low flying bird when he raced across the ground with his long mane and tail streaming in the wind. Mac had been a little dubious about putting Jacob up on Mirlo, the horse was not going to hurt the boy but Mac worried about what the boy might do to the horse. It turned out, he need not have worried; the boy was a natural rider with a good "hand" and he and Mirlo soon were melded into a single unit. Emiliano dumped the skillet full of scrambled eggs he was cooking onto a platter and beat on the skillet with his iron spoon. The announcement was not really needed since everyone except the kids was already in place with coffee and plates in hand. Bart was acting as biscuit server while Mac poured coffee and as the last person was served and moved off to sit on the fire pit benches, Emiliano said in a low voice, "Senor's, I think that it would be a good thing if the three of us and Senorita Tommie had a talk soon."

Mac helped Bud hitch the teams while Bart and Tommie Rae saddled the horses for the two older couples; the Kelly's saddled their own mounts after Tara and Jacob finished currying both their own and their parents' horses. With so many hands helping they were soon mounted and ready to go. Mac stayed behind to help break camp and load the wagons while Bart led off on a different route back to the ranch. Tommie Rae and Bart were riding together and he told her about Emilianos' request that they all meet. "Do you have any idea what that could be about?" "I think I might, one of my Grandfathers stories was about his Grandfather finding where some Comanche that he was chasing killed three men and stole their horses. He said his Grandfather found where the Comanche had hidden some gold and took his wife and his son and daughter to the hiding place when they were on their way to Gillespie County where they first settled. Old Tom told them that when the time was right, they would come back and get the gold but they were not to speak of it to anyone. Evidently my ancestor was smart enough to realize that it would not be smart for a blanket assed Indian to start his life in civilization by showing up with a bunch of gold. I was never able to get a straight story about why they never went back for the gold."

Chapter 33

Tom Wolf did well for someone who had grown up in an entirely different culture. He brought his family safely to the Lemke Ranch on Grape Creek northeast of Fredericksburg and, thanks to the recommendation of a boyhood friend whose family worked on the ranch, got a job as a cowhand. He sent his kids to the school in Willow City, saved his money and eventually leased a small ranch and began ranching on his own. The cows made a little money but the family prospered mainly because Tom and his boys soon earned reputations as the best horse trainers in the country and always had a string of horses being worked at the ranch and more waiting in line. Tom considered it a personal failing if a colt ever showed anger or fear of him and it was a disaster if one tried to pitch or run off. He would not work with a horse less than three years old and much preferred that they never have been touched when they came to him. Horsemen swore that with a Wolf trained horse all you had to do was to think of what you wanted him to do. The gold occasionally crossed Toms' mind but he was busy and making money; it just never seemed to be the right time to go back.

When the last buffalo was gone and the hostiles confined, the open range country north of the Colorado River and clear to the Canadian line was heavily over stocked by cattlemen pouring in from both the east and from New Mexico. Fast buck promoters formed land and cattle companies left and right and when the early investors made big returns, the areas still in open range were covered up with cattle. This was the situation when the worst drought anyone could remember hit the entire high plains region; record dry weather started in 1884 and continued through 1888. Cattle all through the area were thin when a three day blizzard with heavy snow and record low temperatures blew in early in 1887 to be followed by a series of storms one after another; cattle died by the hundreds of thousands from Montana south almost to the Rio Grande. The wild expansion of cattle ranching fueled by eastern and British money ended in three months' time. When the drought finally ended, most of the syndicate ranchers were broke and the ranchers who had managed to protect their grass and to hold on to breeding stock suddenly found that they were in very good shape. So many cattle died in the great die off that numbers were very low and demand and prices were high. Money was not a part of his culture but trading very definitely was and Tom had a surprising head for business. When cow prices got high, Tom sold his cattle and used the money to buy a better ranch than he had been leasing and to buy a really good stallion and some good mares with colts at side. Many small ranchers had quit during the drought and a lot of land was available at give away prices. At this time land was valued at about what it could be expected to return in a year of normal production so the sale of his high priced cattle paid for the land at distress prices with money left over. The horse training still brought in good money but with Tom plus his two sons and now two grandsons on the place they were running short of horses to train; Tom decided that they would raise, train and sell good horses of their own breeding. Buying the ranch and horses started Tom thinking about what he could do if he had even a small part of the Comanche gold. Land was cheap and with money, it would be possible to put together a ranch that would guarantee the security of his family for generations. For the first time in a long time, Tom was seriously thinking about trying to locate the gold and put it to work. In the spring of 1890, as sort of a scouting trip, Tom rode along with several Lemke hands to deliver a set of heifers to the Newman Ranch north of Sweetwater. Their route took them to within about ten miles of the hiding place of the gold and Tom was amazed at how the country had filled up; small ranches and farms were everywhere and the roadsides were so heavily grazed that they had trouble finding grass for their herd. Tom had no doubt that he could find the right spot but with so many people around it would require some thought and care to get to the gold and out again without being discovered. He would have to polish up his scouting skills; the task would not be as dangerous as a scout against the Comanche but it might be just as difficult. Wealth had never been that important to Tom; the Comanche gold was a challenge but he was very comfortable training horses and watching his Grandkids grow up. On the way home from the trip to Sweetwater, Tom decided that the time to retrieve the gold cache had still not come. Though he would not admit it, even to himself, Tom had a strange feeling about the gold and it's' legacy of violence and death. Life was good for him and his family and he was fearful about doing anything that might jeopardize that.

Ten years were to pass before nature intervened and caused Tom to realize that if he was going to get the gold, he would have to do it soon. All though he had hidden it well, Old Tom was losing his eyesight and he didn't want the gold to be lost if he were unable to return to it. Tom took his oldest son, now known as Young Tom, aside and told him that the time had come to retrieve the gold. Together, Father and Son came up with a plan to accomplish this goal.

Young Tom and his Father rode out from the ranch on a fine spring morning with Young Toms' son Jason following behind in a light wagon carrying camping equipment and several heavy canvas sacks full of horse hobbles. They were going to go north and west buying brood mares and young horses. The plan was to go from ranch to ranch buying horses as they went but with the goal of camping at least one night on the banks of Oak Creek above where it runs into the Colorado River. They would retrieve the gold, load it into the wagon and circle back south and east toward home buying horses as they went. The new grass was growing, their horses were fresh and they were not rushing but taking their time and enjoying the trip. Jason got his Grandfather talking about his early life and heard several stories that he had not heard before. He had learned that he could always get a response from his Grandfather by making some comment about the Comanche; the old man saw through the ploy but pretended that he didn't and came up with new tales on cue. He had ridden this land as man and boy and the landmarks and the history were as much a part of him as his right hand.

The plan was to get out of the hill country and into the rolling plains country where the ranches were larger before starting to buy horses. They spent their third night out camped at ten mile crossing on the San Saba River. As they started north again on the fourth day, they had still not bought a horse but they were having a fine time. Just after noon, a dark and angry looking cloud boiled up in the northwest and Old Tom began to look for a place to camp. He and Young Tom rode ahead and as they topped a rise, the storm broke with a fury, strong wind and a flurry of hail followed by heavy rain and vivid lightning. Jason pulled a slicker on and in the moment of inattention almost lost control of the mules who wanted to turn tails to the storm. Jason got them started back up the road just in time to see a bolt of lightning strike the road ahead with a blinding flash and an explosion of sound so loud that he was deafened. The mules did their best to run away again and by the time Jason got them under control and headed back in the right direction, the storm had slackened into just a steady rain. It had been raining so hard that he could not see much past his mules' heads. As the rain lessened he could see to the top of the rise where he had last seen his Father and Grandfather and a sick feeling flooded his whole body. Jason could see two horses lying in the road and as he got closer two men as well.

Jason brought his Father and Grandfather home to be buried and his Grandmother responded to the tragedy in the old way; she hacked her hair off short, wailed as she gashed her arms and withdrew from everyone. After four days Grandmother Summer appeared at the supper table. She had bathed and wore a long sleeved blouse and head scarf. "This family has lost much in lusting after the gold of the cursed Comanche. So long as I am alive, no one is to speak of this gold." No one ever did.

CHAPTER 34

The trail riders got back to the ranch just in time to wash up and eat the dinner, still lunch to the guests, Senora Gomez had ready. Both older couples voted for naps after dinner and the Kelly's asked if they might go out for a ride by themselves. After telling everyone goodbye and helping to unhitch and unload the wagons, Bud announced that he had best check in with his granddaughter and be Grampa for a while and drove off home. Tommie Rae helped Maria with the dishes and talked a moment before going to load her horses. Mac, Bart and Emiliano were finishing up stowing the camping equipment as Tommie Rae got to the barn and Bart asked her if she had time to visit a little with Emiliano. They gathered in the shade in the hall of the barn; Emiliano dug out the canvas chairs and they sat in a circle looking at each other. Tommie Rae laughed and waving her hand at the group said, "This looks like a council of war, does anyone have a pipe we could pass?" Bart said, "I am gobbled up with curiosity to know if your two ancestors really did play out a drama a hundred and something years ago. Emiliano, you said that you know how your Grandfather escaped, why don't you lead off with that story?" "Si, I can do that but first, Senorita, did your Grandfather say anything about a treasure of gold?" "He did, Emiliano. He said that he found where the Comanche they were chasing had killed three men and stolen their horses and that they had hidden a leather pack with some gold under a ledge rock." "Esta seguro! It is certain then; my

211

Grandfather killed those men and hid their gold because he knew that he could not escape the Buffalo Soldiers burdened with such weight." Bart spoke up, "Burdened with what weight? How much gold was there?" "My Grandfather told me that there were two leather packs full of gold coins and that each pack was the weight of a grown man." It was very quiet for maybe a count of five before Mac let out a low whistle and said, "Three hundred pounds of gold, maybe more; what would that be worth today?" Tommie Rae looked up from the scrap of paper she was figuring on and said, "Three hundred pounds of gold at $400 a troy ounce would be worth something like 1.75 million dollars but my ancestor also said that the gold was in coins, old coins unlike any he had ever seen. If it is all in coins, they could be worth many times the value of the same weight of gold bullion." "Senorita, Senor's, I must speak. I came to your house, Senor Mac, how do I say "con engano fradulentemente" en Ingles?" "Under false pretenses, but you made no false claims my friend." "Si, but I came looking for the gold and not looking for work as I allowed you to think. Had you not found me and taken me in, I would have long since been dead. If we find the gold, I want you and Senor Bart to have any share that might be due me." Mac spoke up to say, "If we find any gold, I think that the four of us should share and share alike, equal partners." Bart was nodding in agreement and Tommie Rae said, "I agree that it should be equal partners but I also think that it is very unlikely that we will ever find anything. The only location that came down in our family legend was that the location was on a creek the Tonkawa knew as "The creek of sweet acorns" and that it was marked by a big white rock in the forks of a tree. Even if that creek is Oak Creek, the gold could be anywhere from the headwaters ten miles north of here south to where the creek empties into the Colorado. Nearly every tree on Oak Creek died during the drought in the 1950's so it is likely that even the rock in the tree is gone." "Senorita, I know where the gold is hidden." "You know?" "Si, I have been trying to think of some way to tell what I know without sounding like a crazy old fool. My Grandfather made me memorize the landmarks that lead to the gold. The final landmark is the oso piedra, the stone bear that we all saw at the same time." Mac said, "At the creek crossing, Tara pointed out the rock shaped like a bear!" " Si, Senor, my Grandfather saw the stone bear as they were leaving and took it for a sign of good luck since the bear was his special guide. The gold is under a ledge of rock that sticks out of the base of a long ridge just west and south of the creek crossing." Bart said, "We have to take our guests to the airport after noon tomorrow so it would be at least day after tomorrow before we can go look. We don't have any more guests scheduled yet. Tommie, could you come back on Sunday and help us look?" "You couldn't keep me away with a shotgun; I will be here shortly after daylight on Sunday prepared to stay awhile but I do think that we would be smart to say nothing to anyone about our little venture until we have something solid."

CHAPTER 35

When Bart and Mac got to the pens at first light, they found Tara brushing La Mosca and Picaro with tears streaming down her cheeks. She turned her face away and wiped her eyes on a shirt sleeve. "I know I am being a baby but I can't help it. I am going to miss them so much and I will never, ever see them again!" Mac choked a little but said, "Sure you will Honey; you can see them in your mind anytime you want. I can picture horses that I rode forty years ago just as clear as if they were standing in the corral. Good memories never go away, just the bad ones." After breakfast, both older couples declined a final ride. The Shapiros had another photo safari planned and Emiliano had agreed to tell the Overholts more about his Comanche Grandfather. The Kelly's again asked to be allowed to ride alone so as they rode off, both Mac and Bart found themselves at loose ends.

"Mac, tell me about the Wolf family." "Well the oldest of her folks that I knew were Tommie Raes' Granddaddy Jason and his wife Ingrid. It was before my time but they created quite a stir when they decided to get married back about 1915 or so. They had known each other since childhood and the Wolf family was well respected but it didn't sit well with some to see a white woman marry an Indian. There was even some talk about running them out of the country but that stopped pretty quick when two of Ingrid's' brothers, Dolf and Henry, took turns thumping the heads of some of the loud mouths. Those were two big rough Dutchmen and nobody was going to say anything bad about their baby sister. Anyway Jason and Ingrid had two kids, a girl, Helen, who married and moved away and Tommy who is about my age. Tommy is the one I know best; he married Joann Schutze who grew up with Windy and Susan and me and we got to know him when he and Joann were courting. Susan and Joann were big friends and when Windy and I came back, we got to know them better and to be honorary uncles to Tommie Rae. When you meet her folks you will see why Tommie Rae is so special; they are good people. Tommy and Joann wound up with the ranch after everybody else either died off or left to do something else and they have had to struggle to keep it. They were determined to keep the ranch but also determined to see that Tommie Rae got an education. Tommy kept up the family tradition of training horses and built a lighted arena so he could work young horses at night after working all day on the ranch. Tommie Rae grew up helping both with the ranch work and with the horses and by the time she was twelve or so was almost as good a hand as her Daddy. I think that Tommie Rae went to college mainly to please her folks but she graduated at the top of her class in business even though she took her horses with her and was on the rodeo team. A lot of that German work ethic shows up in the whole family."

CHAPTER 36

South Central Texas 1850

It had been a good summer; the crops were the best they had raised in their six years on this land. It had been hard with a lot of setbacks but at last the Nimitz clan was firmly established in Texas and even gaining a little prosperity. They had lost two family members killed by Comanche and several wounded in the raids that also cost them in the loss of livestock and burned crops. They had suffered through three years of drought when they first arrived but ever since, the weather had been good and their hard work was now paying dividends. Every family unit now had their own good stone home and the storage bins, root cellars and pantries were full. Every man and boy older than ten was a good shot and always had weapons at hand; some of the younger women could shoot as well and all of the women could load weapons when needed. The Comanche still came raiding but had learned to bypass the Nimitz settlement which was built in the fashion of the villages in Germany. Rather than each family living out in an isolated home, the houses were clustered together with their barns and corrals and the fields radiating out from the easily defended central grouping. In addition, when the danger of raids was highest in the fall, during daylight hours a boy or young man was always keeping watch from the tower in the village center. With a spyglass, they could see all but the most distant fields and had on several occasions brought the farming crews hurrying home when Indians were sighted. The farmers kept saddled horses with them and were always alert for the sound of a gunshot followed by the ringing of an iron rod beating on the iron rail hanging in the watchtower. When an alert was sounded, the women quickly gathered the young children inside, dropped the heavy shutters on the outside windows and laid arms and ammunition out ready for the defenders. Once a party of mounted Comanche came racing and screaming through the settlement before the men got in from the fields. They were greeted with blasts of buckshot delivered from behind two foot thick stone walls. Three of the ten or so warriors were hit along with several horses; the war party left carrying its' wounded and with several horses carrying double.

There was a good market on the coast for all that they could produce; this was especially true of their beer and of the wine that they were producing since their grape vines began production. Since they now had excess grain, they brought in hogs to add cured hams and bacon and sausage to their larders and to the products they could sell. Several families newly arrived from Germany had been welcomed and children were being born; the first to be born in the village was Hilda Nimitz, daughter of Freida and Ernst Nimitz, who was born late in the summer of their first year. She was a dark eyed little imp that quickly became everyone's favorite with her bright smile and loving ways. In many ways, the good things of life in Germany had been brought to Texas while the bad had been left behind.

Grandfathers Hans Nimitz and Carl Schutze were the first to come over from Germany and theirs had been a hard lot. They came in a group of other family men brought over by a promoter who supposedly had a charter from the Mexican government to found a colony of German settlers on the middle reaches of the Colorado River. Each head of household was to receive 320 acres of land suitable for farming, a team of horses, tools, seed and provisions for a family for a year. The men were to come first and help each other build shelter for their families who would come later. The group landed in Matagorda Bay to find that the promoter was not there and no one knew anything about him or his colony. A few of the men had enough money to buy return passage but Hans Nimitz and six others did not. They were farmers with no land to farm and no tools and no supplies. Most of the men found work as farm hands making barely enough to survive but Hans and his friend and cousin, Carl Schutze, found work as deck hands on a coastal freighter that plied the coastal waters from New Orleans to Matamoros Mexico. For two years they saved every penny they could and traded their labor to the ship's owner for the right to transport goods they bought in New Orleans back to the settlements springing up along the coastal bend of Texas. At the end of two years, they had enough money and merchandise to open Nimitz and Schutze Mercantile at the mouth of the Colorado River on Matagorda Bay. They agreed that Nimitz would run the store while Schutze continued on the freighter where he was now first mate. The arrangement worked and they were able to save enough to send for their wives and children. Almost four years after the men sailed for Texas, the families were reunited.

The store made good money but both Nimitz and Schutze were men of the soil and wanted land of their own. They also wanted more of their kin to join them so once again they started saving. Hans had three younger brothers in Germany and Carl had two brothers and a brother-in-law that wanted to come. Several of the charter companies had gone bankrupt, the Comanche were raiding deeper into the Colorado Valley and land away from the coast was cheap. The partners bought a twelve thousand acre tract on the upper Colorado River and sent word for their kin to come. The

German Immigration Company or Adelsverein was actively promoting German immigration into Texas and the extended Nimitz and Schutze families were soon on their way. When the families arrived, Hans and Carl sold the Mercantile and prepared, at long last, to move to their own land. The new immigrants were successful farmers in the old country and had brought a lot of farming tools and seed with them; they could not bring their work teams or their cattle but Hans assured them that there were plenty of horses and cattle in Texas. It was late fall and everyone was anxious to get to their farms and be ready to put in a crop as soon as spring arrived. They hired a group of Mexican freighters who moved freight from the coast to San Antonio with oxen drawn wagons to transport them and their households to their new homes. The mood was festive; the whole clan was together and they were on the road to great adventure. Over the years, there had been several marriages between the Nimitz's and the Schutze's and another had occurred just before they left Germany; Ernst Nimitz, the son of the second oldest Nimitz brother married Freida Wolle, the daughter of Hans' sister Gerda and her husband Ben Wolle. The lack of privacy and the fact that both were seasick the entire voyage had not contributed to a romantic honeymoon but things were much better now with the solid ground under them and their own little tent at night. The oxen traveled at their own bovine pace and required time to graze as well so ten to twelve miles was a good day's travel. They were ten days from the coast but still six or seven days from their goal. Ernst and several others of the young men had taken to riding out ahead of the caravan to hunt. The coastal plains were alive with deer; it was common to see herds of more than one hundred animals and even these rather inept hunters could keep the group well supplied with venison. On this day, the hunting party had ridden farther out than normal and was coming in with three deer and a small bear. They had ridden out at an angle to the line of travel and were now circling forward to intercept their party. They were crossing some broken country several miles north of the River when they heard a woman's scream that chilled their blood; the first was followed by more screams and women's voices of which they could understand only, "Nein, Nein!" All three hunters dumped the game they were carrying and spurred their horses into a run toward the source of the screams. Ernst arrived first to see his beloved Freida stripped naked and pinned to the ground by a naked Indian. The Indian made one last shuddering thrust and rose to his feet; Adolf Schutze's young wife was likewise being raped while two more Indians watched. Ernst threw up his rifle and shot at the buck that had been on his wife but in his fury, he jerked the trigger and missed his target. Instead the ball from his .65 caliber jaegers rifle took most of the head off of one of the Indians waiting his turn at rape. Ernst heard both of his friends shoot but was charging his horse directly at the Indian who had violated his wife. The warrior tried to run but was no match for the running horse, Ernst swung his empty rifle like a club and smashed it into the head of the running Indian who collapsed like his bones had turned to water. Ernst jumped off his horse to smash the rifle twice more into the bloody mess that had been a man before dropping the rifle and running to his wife who was sobbing incoherently and trying to cover herself with the torn remnants of her dress. His friends had killed the other two Indians but not before one launched an arrow that struck Adolf

Schutze in the leg. Luckily the arrow had gone all the way through Adolf's' calf so they were able to snap off the head and pull the arrow out. They handed Adolf's wife up to him and with Frieda ridding in front of Ernst and wearing his coat, they started for the wagon train. Freida kept sobbing that, "I am dirty, I am ruined, I can never hold by head up again and you will have to divorce me." Ernst tightened his arms around her and said, "Hush little one, you have done nothing wrong. You are my wife and the love of my life and nothing could ever change that." Frieda snuggled in his arms and cried softly against his chest and seemed to become somewhat calmer. When her breathing had returned to normal, Ernst asked, "How did they catch you?" Frieda said that she and Anna had been walking beside the wagons and, "We went into some roadside brush to relieve ourselves when two Indians grabbed us from behind and threw us up in front of two other riders. They held hands over our mouths so we could not scream and rode hard away from the wagons." Suddenly she jerked rigid and whispered, "Oh Ernst what if he made me pregnant? What if I have a half Indian baby? Ernst stiffened with the thought and then said, "You are my wife and any baby you have will be my baby as well and we will love it with all our hearts."

CHAPTER 37

Selena showed up right on time at 1:00 pm and by 1:30 everyone was loaded and ready to go to the airport to catch their 4:00 flight. All three couples left their addresses and phone numbers and told Bart to feel free to use them as references with potential guests. Tara wore a necklace and bracelet of plaited hair from La Mosca's tail that Emiliano had made for her and Jacob wore a bracelet Emiliano had plaited of hair from the tail of Mirlo. Tara was ecstatic when she saw the necklace, it had as a pendant the arrowhead that she had found and thought she had lost. When Emiliano told Liz what he had in mind, Liz snitched the arrowhead from Tara's' box of treasures and brought it to him. At the airport, there was a final round of "thank you, thank you" all around with handshakes from the men and hugs from all the women, Liz took the opportunity to whisper in Bart's ear, "Don't you let Tommie Rae get away from you." Bart surprised himself by responding, "I don't intend to." With the guests on their way, Mac thanked Selena and paid her for her help. As Bart and Mac started back to the Buick, Mac said, "Partner, if you will stop at the liquor store at the edge of town, I will buy a bottle of good whiskey and we will celebrate; I think we have earned it."

Bart and Mac pulled up to the ranch house to see the clothes lines behind the house loaded with bed linens and bath towels and Maria and Emiliano, each with an empty laundry basket, walking toward the kitchen door."Senor's, thank goodness you are home. This

woman has been driving me all day like a rented mule, all of the bedrooms and baths have been cleaned, the last load of laundry is now
on the line and the master bedroom is ready for Senorita Tommie
Rae. It is truly sad that my weary old bones are too feeble to work
more today and so we will all go hungry tonight." Maria swatted at
Emiliano with her laundry basket and said, as he danced away from
another swing of the basket, "Hush you old fraud, you know very
well that there is a roast cooking in the oven and that we did no
more than an honest day's work." Mac and Bart watched the byplay
and then looked at each other with a couple of knowing grins as the
two continued their banter and proceeded on to the kitchen with
obviously no interest in anything but each other. After having had so
many people for meals, the table seemed empty with just Maria and
the three men. They finished supper and Mac paid Maria and thanked
her, "I don't know how we would have made it without your help and
I sure hope you will come back if we have more guests." Emiliano
walked Maria out to her car and came back looking very pleased with
his self. Mac turned to Bart and said, "Did I ever tell you about the
old dog I knew that chased mountain lions? We were working out in
the Big Bend Country and the rancher had this old coon hound. He
had been a damn good coon hound but he was getting old. There was
lots of lions in that country and that fool dog got to chasing them. We
would hear him at night, O-O-O-AO, O-O-O-AO til all hours but
he never could catch up to a lion. The old fool should have quit while
he was ahead." "What do you mean", said Bart. "What happened?" "A
real old lion came by one night and that old dog chased after it and
caught it. All we found was his collar." Emiliano had standing been
listening intently to the story but when the punch line was delivered, he turned and went into the kitchen muttering in Spanish. In

a minute he stuck his head back in, shook his finger at Mac and said with a grin, "At least the old dog enjoyed one last chase."

Mac and Bart had just finished their chores when Tommie Rae drove up and got out looking ready for work in a sweat stained Stetson, faded jeans with leather gloves sticking out of a rear pocket and an often washed mans blue jean shirt. "Let's go, daylight is wasting. Are you two just now doing chores?" "We have done a half days work while you were driving down the road." Said Bart, "And if you are going to be sarcastic, you won't get any of Emilianos' hot cakes." She grabbed his upper arm in both of her hands and matching his stride said, "If I were strong, I'd lie and say I ate hours ago but I'm starving. I guess since the gold has been in the ground for over a hundred years it can wait until we eat breakfast." Emiliano had the food on the table and very shortly they loaded into the two pickups and started for the stone bear. Bart rode with Tommie Rae while Mac and Emiliano led off with the back of the ranch truck loaded with axes, shovels and rakes. At breakfast, Mac had said, "I know where the ledge of rock must be; there is a long ridge that parallels the creek about 150 yards west of the high bank of the creek and it has exposed rock at its base for part of its length. There is one place about a hundred yards from the road where someone has quarried building stone at some point in the past. Let's hope that they didn't pick our spot to dig their rock." The road to the creek crossing dropped off the ridge and into the creek bottom so Mac turned south down the creek bottom and drove up as close to the ridge as he could manage. Brush was heavy in places in the bottom with chittamwood, honey locust and green briar forming dense thickets; most of the bottom was more open with elm, oak and Spanish walnut trees scattered on grassland. They unloaded and Mac pointed due west, "The rock quarry is straight through there and if I remember right, there are some shallow holes under the ledge rock that runs from there south. Everybody be careful, there are rattlesnake dens in several places along the ridge. The snakes should be scattered out from the dens now but I still see lots of snakes up and down the creek." Emiliano took a machete from the truck while Bart took an ax and Mac and Tommie Rae picked up garden rakes. It was not possible to travel in a straight line but rather you had to wind around and between thickets while trying to maintain progress in a general direction. They reached the base of the ridge about fifty feet north of the old stone quarry and Mac cautioned, "Look real close where you put your feet, this is a real snakey spot. They mostly should have left the den site by now but be careful; I have ridden by here in the early spring and seen bunches of rattlers sunning on these flat rocks." The ledge of rock that the miners had been working was about three feet thick and was made up of layers ranging from eight inches down to four inches thick. The material under the ledge rock was soil with limestone gravel and rocks scattered through it; where the material had a lot of gravel, it was loose and easy to move. Looking at the old workings, you could see where people had, after digging the soil off of the ledge, driven wedges in between the layers of rock to peel them off like the layers of an onion. The miners had chosen a spot to dig where there was less over burden on the rock ledge; the ridge in that spot was not as high or as steep as it was for the rest of its length. The ledge was obvious all along the ridge but in most places only a little rock showed through the dirt and for long stretches, there were no openings under the ledge. Since there were no openings under the rock from the quarry back to the creek crossing they walked south along the ridge, trying to find the most likely spot to start looking. Both of the old stories had stated that the packs were hidden in pack rat nests so they looked for nests as they peered into every opening under the ledge. In several places Bart and Emiliano cut brush that was hiding openings and they found seven shallow caves, four with rat nests, along the ridge in the quarter mile from the quarry south to where the ridge melted away into Oak Creek. Since they were already there, they started at the opening farthest to the south. Using the garden rakes, they pulled everything out from under the ledge rock. The pack rat nests were mostly leaves and twigs but there were also walnuts, acorns and trash of all kinds mixed in, everything from beer cans and snuff can lids to plastic sacks; in two places, they raked out very indignant rattlesnakes. As they raked out each opening in turn, they found pieces of glass and pottery and even some buttons but no leather sacks full of gold. The sun was getting hot when they got back to the trucks so with one opening left, they called a break to have a drink and cool off. Bart handed Tommie Rae a bottle of water from the cooler and offered bottles to Mac and Emiliano, both refused the cold water and instead poured cups of hot coffee from a thermos bottle. Bart took a long pull from his water and said to Tommie Rae, "If you have your heart set on having a sure enough rough tough cowboy, we may have a problem, I might be able to learn to ride bulls and bend horseshoes with my hands but I don't think I will ever be tough enough to drink hot coffee in one hundred degree weather." Tommie Rae laughed and surprised him by going up on tip toes to kiss him on the cheek and say,"Oh well, a girl can't have everything, I will just have to live with the disappointment." Bart grinned, as Mac told him later, "Like a possum eating chicken guts." and took up a rake and went to work, mainly so he wouldn't grab up Tommie Rae and run off with her like a coyote with a stolen hen.

The last opening was a deep one with a lot of trash but was barren of anything of value just like all the rest. The floor of this last opening was of softer dirt than the rest and Bart began to rake this out from under the rock more in frustration than anything else. He had pulled out most of what was loose when Tommie Rae squealed and fell to her knees and started pawing through the dirt. "I saw something shiny." Bart kneeled down to help her look and immediately came up with a corroded brass buckle with a piece of dried out leather still riveted to it. "Here it is" he said. Tommie Rae glanced at the buckle and said, "No that isn't what I saw. What I saw was shiny." She sifted through the last of the dirt and held up a gold coin. Mac let out a low whistle and asked, "Is it old? It looks shiny new." Tommie Rae was looking closely at the coin and said, "It is a Spanish eight escudo cob coin minted in 1611 and is probably worth something like 4,000 dollars." Bart stared at her and said, "How in the world do you know all that?" Tommie Rae grinned up at him and said, "I know it was minted in 1611 because 1611 is stamped right here and I know the rest because I spent a bunch of time yesterday on the internet. I figured if we were going gold hunting that I needed to know a little about the subject." They attacked the cave once more and raked out every bit of loose material without finding anything; the floor was solid rock like the roof and the back wall was undisturbed soil and gravel except for some tunnel holes dug by rats. Nobody said anything but, at the same time, all four of them looked at the rock quarry a few feet away. Finally, Mac said, "I am afraid that the rock miners left with more than just building stone." Bart spoke up, "Emiliano, are you sure your Grandfather said the gold was south and west of the creek crossing?" "Si, Senor. He made me repeat the directions many times. The camp of the bandidos where he hid the gold was south and a little west of the creek crossing." "Well it was fun thinking about being rich." said Bart and started walking toward the rock quarry, hoping to see an opening that they had missed. They searched every nook and cranny from the rock quarry to the creek crossing without finding as much as an armadillo hole. Suddenly, Emiliano looked across the creek and said in a thin voice like a little boy reciting his lessons, "They left the campsite riding south and then Grandfather saw the stone bear. Senor Mac! Is there another place where you could cross the creek to the north of here?" "Not that a car or truck could cross but, yeah, just below where Bear Creek comes in you can cross horseback." "That is it, Compadres; we have been looking south of the wrong crossing. The crossing we use now was not here when Grandfather found the gold!" The first opening was sixty yards north of the road and they tore into it with a vengeance but the results were the same, leaves, twigs and junk but no gold. The next opening was also empty and when they reached the next cave, they were within sight of Bear Creek. This opening was the deepest that they had seen and had obviously been used heavily by both rattlers and pack rats. There were shed snake skins mixed into the huge mound of rat nest that took up most of the cave. Bart kneeled down after looking carefully for snakes and began dragging rat nest out with a rake. Tommie Rae was kneeling beside him and as he dragged out the first rake full, she pounced like a cat and held up a leather pouch. It was a dried out scrap of leather but clearly it was a pouch; the neck was still closed with a knotted leather thong but there was a hole in the bottom of the pouch and it was empty. Mac joined them with another rake and he and Bart pulled the nest out where Emiliano and Tommie Rae could go through it. They quickly found another pouch and then several more but all had been torn open and were empty. It took an hour but finally the cave was empty. They found the remains of two leather packs and dozens of small leather sacks but no gold. The floor cave was identical to the one where they found the coin, rock floor and ceiling and back wall solid except for tunnel openings used by rats and snakes. They walked out the rest of the rock ledge, all the way to where it disappeared into the junction of Bear Creek with Oak Creek. They found one other small opening but it too was empty except for a few leaves. The stories were true, the gold had been here but someone had found it before them.

CHAPTER 38

It was a melancholy group that gathered up their tools and the rat chewed leather scraps and started back to the house. Emiliano got the coffee pot started and a pot of stew warming and they all sat down at the kitchen table. Bart framed the question on everyone's mind with, "Why would anyone tear open the sacks, take the gold and leave the sacks? The coins would be a lot easier to carry in the sacks." Mac was turning one of the packs over in his hands when he suddenly stopped and looked closely at the straps that had been used to close the packs. "Look here; there are four straps per pack but no buckles. The straps are old and stiff but they are still strong; why would all of the buckles be gone?" Tommie Rae said, "We found one buckle in the cave with the coin but none anywhere else." Mac looked at his friends with a big grin, "It's not a question of who got the gold but what? Everyone looked puzzled, "It was the rats! Those pack rats could no more leave pretty shiny things like those coins alone then a duck could walk off from a June bug! That's where the buckles went too; they chewed the straps in two and took the buckles and the coins to a hidey hole. Seventy eleven generations of pack rats have lived and died in those nests since Emilianos Grandpa hid the gold in their house and there is a reason they are called pack rats. The gold isn't gone; we just have to find where the rats hid it." Bart said, "The snake dens, the holes back under the rock, would the rats go into the snake dens? "You bet they will." Said Mac, "They go into the den in the summer after the snakes leave to be cool and they go back for warmth in the winter when the snakes are hibernating. Sometimes they even play a little catch up and make supper out of a chilled down rattler. I have never seen it but people tell me about uncovering a snake den in the winter time and seeing snakes and rats all bedded down together like puppies in a basket." Emiliano was the first to react, he jumped up and got four glasses out of the cabinet and then brought a gallon jug in from the pantry. "Compadres, this calls for a celebration, I started this working a while back. It is not the best wine in the world but it is all we have so it is the best we have." He poured wine into each glass, serving Tommie Rae first and then picked up his own glass and said, "Salud! Let us drink to the gold that we are sure to recover from the rats and the rattlesnakes." They all drank and Tommie Rae said, "Emiliano, this is very good! Aside from being a truly good man you continue to amaze me with your many talents; I see why my friend Maria is so interested." Bart didn't think that saddle leather could blush but Emilianos' face took on a reddish tint that grew even brighter when Tommie Rae kissed him on the cheek. "Forgive me for teasing you but do know that I only tease the people that I like." "Senorita, no man could be angry about attention from an angel." Tommie Rae broke out a long delighted peal of laughter and said, "Oh be careful Maria my friend, be careful, there is more to this book than the cover suggests."

"Mac," said Bart. "How far back do you suppose those tunnels go before they reach the den?" "Son, I don't have no idea; all I would know to do is to just start digging and see what we find." "Do you know where we could find a backhoe?" asked Bart. Mac answered, "Terry Blackmon has one that he uses to put in septic lines and such. He lives close and I expect we can make a deal with him if he is not using it." "Let's go see him." Said Bart, "but let's pretend that we are digging a storm cellar; I would just as soon not have the world know that we are digging for gold at least not until we find some. Let's eat some dinner and go see Mr. Blackmon." Mac and Bart drove the five miles to the Blackmon place and caught Terry just coming in from a fencing job. After hearing what they wanted, he said the backhoe was ready to go but he was too busy to run it for them. If they wanted to run it, he would charge them fifteen dollars a running hour plus fuel. They could take his diesel tank on wheels to the job site and settle up when they were through. Though Mac protested, Terry and Bart both doubted the ability of his old truck to safely pull the backhoe trailer so they decided that Bart would drive the tractor back to the ranch. Terry gave Bart a quick rundown on the quirks of his machine and they were off for home; Bart driving the tractor and Mac pulling the fuel browser behind the pickup. As he drove the loose jointed old tractor down the gravel road, Bart hoped that he had not let his mouth cause him to make a fool of himself; he had run a backhoe but he was never really good at it and it had been a long time ago. Oh well, as Emiliano said about the wine, he may not be very good but he was the best they had. They got home to find Tommie Rae and Emiliano finishing up chores; having all the extra horses and the mules meant that they had to keep them up in the pens and feed them their total diet and this added to chore time. They ate a light supper and moved out to the cool of the front porch to talk. Mac asked Bart how he planned to attack the snake den. "The over burden is thinnest over the rock ledge at the north end of the cave. I thought I would dig in at an angle there and see if we find anything before I try to move all of the dirt off of the ledge. If we find something, I will have to move the dirt off so I can peel the rock back so I can finally get to the dirt and gravel where the den tunnels are located." While they watched, an almost full moon began to rise and flooded the scene with white light. Bart watched it grow lighter and said, "It's light enough for me to see to drive. Tommie, if I drove the tractor down to the site, would you follow me and bring me back? It would save us a few minutes in the morning." The old tractor started on the first try and Bart led off with Tommie Rae following in her pickup. Bart didn't try to wind through the brush to the snake den but instead just pulled the tractor off the road so Tommie Rae had room to turn around. She got out of the truck and walked over to where Bart stood watching the moon and said, "Beautiful isn't it?" Bart looked down and touched her upturned face and said, "It is the most beautiful thing I have ever seen" and folded her in his arms. Tommie wrapped her arms around his neck and pulled his head down for what started as a tender kiss but quickly changed to something with a lot stronger feelings. After a long moment, Tommie lay her head on his chest and said, "I don't know whether to be flattered that you find me so attractive that sweat and dirt don't matter or to be worried that you like your women to smell like packrat nests and horse lots." "I like this woman regardless of how she smells and I hope she doesn't mind because I plan to make my number one job being close to her." "She doesn't mind at all but she must tell you that the aroma of diesel fuel clashes just a bit with that of eau du packrat nests. Come on we can continue this when both of us have had a shower but if we don't get back, my "Uncle" Mac will come looking for you with his shotgun. I saw his face and you didn't fool him for a minute with your tractor moving ploy." Bart looked down, kissed her again and said, "Maybe I didn't fool Mac but it worked just fine."

They rushed through chores and breakfast and were at the snake den shortly after sunup. Bart positioned the backhoe so that he could pile what he moved where it would be out of the way and began to move dirt from the top of the rock ledge at the north end of the cave. When he had an area of rock about ten feet by ten feet clear, he folded up the hoe and used the front end loader to peel off the layers of rock. The last layer of rock over the den tunnels was about six inches thick and when Bart lifted the front edge, a piece of rock six feet square came loose; Bart flipped this slab over like you would open the top of a chest and he could see cavities and tunnels in the dirt underneath. Bart backed the tractor out and all three of his companions swarmed into the opening. Bart was still getting down from the tractor and could see nothing when the whoops and shrieks of his partners told him the good news. The area under the flat rock was a honeycomb of little rooms connected by now open topped tunnels and in every room they could see the glitter of gold coins. All four of them lined up at the front of the uncovered den scooping up coins and when everyone's' hands were full, it dawned on them that they hadn't brought anything in which to carry the gold. Mac carried the coins he had found out and put them on a flat rock and announced that he would go back and find containers of some kind. The other three kept gathering coins and found that the layer of coins in some of the cavities was four and five inches thick. Evidently as new coins were brought into the den they were laid on top of those already there until in places, the rooms were full almost to their rock roof. Mac returned with a bunch of empty quart jars that Susan had used canning fruits and vegetables. "I started loading up five gallon buckets until it dawned on me how heavy five gallons of gold would be." They had picked up all of the visible coins so they transferred these to jars and Bart moved the tractor back into position to move more rock. He had to drag the slabs off with the backhoe and then push them out of the way with the front end loader but when he peeled back the last layer, the same scene of gold filled rooms was repeated. They worked steadily through the day, stopping only at noon to eat the sandwiches and drink the coffee that Emiliano had packed. By dark they were all exhausted but they had uncovered what seemed to be the entire snake den and had gathered all of the visible coins. Even the quart jars were heavy if they filled them too full and putting them in the six jar carrying racks that Mac had used to carry the jars made for too heavy a load even for the men.

They got back to the house and unloaded and while Emiliano started supper, Mac and Bart when to do chores and Tommie Rae started counting coins and weighing gold on Susan's kitchen scales. When Bart and Mac got back, Tommie announced that they had a total of 363.5 pounds of gold coins. She had all three men's undivided attention as she explained that she had not had time to count them all but they seemed to average about six tenths of an ounce each which would mean that they had something like 9700 coins. The bullion weight of the gold would be worth something like two million dollars but the value as coins would be much more; it might be as much as 10 to 15 times as much. It was obvious that they would have to have some help from someone who understands the coin market if they were to get the true value out of their find.

After a quick trip to Abilene to find a jewelers scale, Tommie Rae and Bart photographed each coin front and back with its weight to the hundredth of a gram visible in its photo. Tommie Rae scanned the photos into her computer and created several copies of the inventory. They arrived at a total of 9778 coins with a total weight of 366.683 pounds and both Tommie Rae and Bart were exhausted by the time they finished. The coins were packed in cotton wool in small lock boxes and locked away in safety deposit boxes in the vault of the First State Bank of Bronte. Oak Creek Ranch was a long time customer of the bank and the President, Ted Smith, arranged for them to deliver the boxes when only he and his Vice President were present. Everyone drew a sigh of relief when the coins were safely locked away; Mac put away his old Colt thumb buster and Emiliano put the old double barrel ten gauge Parker he had been wagging around back in the closet it came from. Knowing that they needed to get their legal affairs in order, they had met with, Henry Wolle, a cousin of Tommie Rae's and a partner in a large law firm in San Angelo; on his recommendation, they had him form the Oak Creek Partners limited liability partnership. Each of the four of them had equal shares in the partnership and equal claims on the assets of the partnerships managed through individual capital accounts. Wolle explained several benefits, tax and otherwise, to having the LLP own the gold and distribute income. Tommie Rae nodded in understanding as he explained but the three men were quickly lost in the "there fore" and "provided that" of legal jargon. As Mac said later, "It's a damn good thing we have Tommie Rae or the lawyers could wind up with the whole shebang." The law firm also started the process of getting Emiliano a visa so that he could be in the country legally and eventually become a legal resident. By the time all this was done, Bart and his three friends had spent the most hectic week of their lives.

CHAPTER 39

Luke Overholt sat at the head of the dining room table in the Oak Creek Ranch house and spoke to the other six people present. "Miss Wolf, Emiliano, Mac, Bart, you have met Tom Weidman and Dr. Philip McKitrick but let me tell you a little about them. Tom is the head of the antiquities investments department of Jackson Sole and Associates — a very successful investment bank that specializes in investments in art, antiques and rarities; there are larger investment banks but none with more expertise in these types of investments. Both I and my investment group, Synergy LLP, have used Tom and his bank for many years and have always been pleased with the results. One of the strengths of Toms' bank is their knowledge of the tax laws and their ability to structure investments to maximize after tax returns. Dr. McKitrick is another old friend and associate and is one of the most respected numismatists in the world; few people know more about the value of old coins than Philip. It was he, Miss Wolf, that I showed the photographs that you sent me and I have never seen him as excited as he became when he realized the extent of your find. I have talked to my group, without revealing your identities, and to Tom and Philip and I would like to put forth a proposition to you. A problem with marketing a find such as yours is the depressing effect on the market if the size of the find should become known. The depression in price would be temporary; the demand for antique gold is so huge that even a hoard such as yours could not over load the market long term but there would be a short term reduction in price. What Tom and Philip recommend, and I concur with, is that the coins be marketed over a prolonged period of time in several different venues. In order to have funds immediately available to the four of you, we suggest the following arrangement; it is a little complicated but if you will, hear me out and then we can go over the arrangement in detail. Toms' bank would take possession of the coins as deposits from you as Oak Creek Partners LLP and would be paid the standard storage fee based upon the appraised value of the deposits and the length of time that they are held. The bank would also act as agent for the Oak Creek Partners LLP to oversee all transactions and make certain that your interests are well served and they would be compensated for these services. Synergy LLP would advance funds or letters of credit to Oak Creek Partners LLP as needed and would be compensated with interest bearing loan notes secured by the deposited coins. Philip would then began marketing the coins and be compensated with a percentage of the net sale proceeds. As funds come in, they would be used to retire the loan notes. To obtain the most value, the sale of the coins might need to be spread over a number years and we feel that this arrangement allows that to happen while benefiting all parties. If you agree in principle, we will need to agree on the various fees and interest rates and then turn the lawyers loose to draw the various agreements." Bart spoke up as the agreed upon spokesman for the group, "Give us today and tonight to talk things over amongst ourselves but regardless of what arrangements we make, we do know that we would like Mr. Weidman to arrange secure transportation for the coins from the Bronte State Bank in Bronte, Texas to his bank to hold in trust for Oak Creek Partners LLP."

CHAPTER 40

Bart and Tommie Rae were in her pickup on the way to introduce Bart to her parents and Bart was about as nervous as any time he could remember, terrified that he might fail to pass muster with her folks. He was showered, shaved and wearing clean jeans and a nearly new shirt but he still worried about his appearance and about the impression he would make on the Wolfs. Bart had never given much thought as to how he looked to other people but today he had found himself looking at his reflection in every mirror he passed. He noticed for the first time that he now sported the classic cowboy two tone face; his face from mid forehead down was tanned as dark as saddle leather while the portion that was normally covered by his hat was pasty white. As he dried himself after his shower, he realized that he no longer had around his middle the roll of fat that he had brought with him from New York and that his face had lost the start of a double chin that had become a too familiar feature. He looked different from the overage adolescent that arrived in Texas and Lord knows he felt different. With the exceptions of the deaths of his parents, in the past seven weeks he had experienced more strong emotion than he had felt in all the preceding years combined. The euphoria he felt when he saw Oak Creek Ranch and knew that it was his was no stronger than the anguish he felt when he realized that they might well lose it. The discovery of the gold and the wealth that it would bring them was fabulous but even that paled in comparison to Tommie Rae looking up into his face and saying, "I am afraid that I am very much in love with you. I hope that doesn't frighten you off." In these few short weeks, he had made more real friends, gained more confidence in his own abilities and developed more insight into what was really important than in the whole of the rest of his life. The four of them had sat up late last night and had agreed that Oak Creek Partners LLP should be more than just a mechanism to parcel out the money from the gold; they would be partners in the ranching business, they would all work in the business and the gold would give them the means to expand. Emiliano again tried to give his part of the gold to his friends and when they again refused; he said," But Amigos, I am just a simple farmer and cocinero; I know nothing about how to run a ranch. How can I do enough to earn my part?" Mac spoke up to say, "Amigo, I know a little about ranching but nothing about business. Tommie Rae knows about business, Bart knows about people and you know about farming and you understand animals. We will all do what we know how to do and help each other. That is what partners do."

They turned off the highway, clattered across a cattle guard and followed a ranch road about half a mile before Tommie Rae pulled up in front of a big worn looking but neat ranch house with a deep porch that stretched completely across the front. They got out of the truck and Tommie Rae took Bart's hand, leading him toward where a couple was sitting in the shade of the porch. The couple stood and came down the porch steps as Tommie Rae said, "Mom, Dad, this is Bart Ryan. Bart these are my parents Tommy and Joann Wolf." Bart stepped forward reaching his hand out to Tommy Wolf and said, "Mr. Wolf, I am very pleased to meet you, Tommie Rae has told me a lot about you." Tommy stretched out his hand and with a grin said, "Welcome to our home Bart, the name is Tommy and I doubt that Tommie Rae has told you as much about me as she has told her Mother about you." Joann Wolf swatted her husband on the arm and said, "Tommy Wolf, you behave yourself." Before reaching out her hand and saying," Bart we are so glad to finally meet you, come in and let's get something to drink." They all sat at the kitchen table for the obligatory coffee and Bard found the tension bleeding off from him as the conservation was immediately comfortable and easy. Tommy Wolf was a small wry man, just the body type Mac claimed made the best riders but unlike some small men, he was neither pugnacious nor hyper. He had a calm level gaze and seemed to radiate confidence and good humor with no sense of needing to prove himself to anyone. Joann looked at Bart and said, "We had just about decided to come to Oak Creek and find out what was going on when Tommie Rae broke down and told us about the gold. That is a story so fantastic that no one would believe it if you wrote it in a novel." Tom spoke up, "Yeah, young lady, I'm still mad at you for not letting us in on what was happening from the get go." "Hush, Tommy, she explained how they had to get arrangements made to safe guard the gold and to set up the legal requirements of dividing it before word leaked out and things got crazy." "Well she ought to know that we wouldn't tell anybody." "Tommy Wolf, you mean well but your daughter knows as well as I do that you have never been able to keep a secret in your entire life. You are the best man I know but your face is an open book; the inscrutable red man you are not." Bart said, "Mr. Wolf, the four of us were scared to death when we had that gold stacked up on the kitchen table. Looking back, we made some bad decisions but all I can say is none of us had ever been in a situation even vaguely like that. All we could think of was what some people would do to get their hands on that gold and the only safeguard we could think of was to not let anyone know it existed until we could get it locked away." "You all did things just right and Tommie Rae knows that I am not mad at her. I never could stay mad at her even when she was a rotten little teenager. Now that you have things lined out, what are you going to do with the money?" Bart looked at Tommie Rae and said, "We have decided to keep the limited liability partnership that we formed to handle the gold active and go into the ranching business in a larger way. Tommie Rae thinks and I agree that ranchland is priced about as cheap as it is going to get. I don't think that you could buy it and pay for it with its production but I do think that it will increase in value. We are talking about buying more land in this area and also maybe some farther east. We are intrigued with the idea of finishing animals on grass but we need to know more about it than we do now before we jump into a big project. We are getting financial advice from some people that we trust but thank God for Tommie Raes' business knowledge; the three males in this partnership know nothing about business." "Bart that is not so, Mac and Emiliano may not have much education but they as well as you have a wealth of common sense and that is what business is about. We will have to hire accountants and lawyers to make sure we know what the rules are and to guard our backs but any one of the three of you has a better sense of right and wrong and of what will work and what will not work than most of my college professors. I think we make a pretty good team but right now, we had best get on the road; we promised Emiliano that we would be on time for a special meal that he is preparing to celebrate our good fortune." Tommie Rae and Bart got up to leave and Joann came over to hug Bart before kissing her daughter. Tommy held out his hand to Bart and said, "Son, you look after my little girl." Bart took his hand and surprised himself by saying, "Sir, I hope to make that my life's' work."

CHAPTER 41

The four partners sat late at the supper table, as full as ticks after eating a great meal but still eating some of Emilianos' homemade ice cream. They had agreed upon the arrangements with Synergy LLP and with Dr. McKitrick and funds were now available; Mac and Bart wanted to settle the tax debts against Oak Creek Ranch and Tommie Rae wanted to pay off a mortgage against her folk's ranch. Both of these debts that had seemed so huge could now be paid out of petty cash. When Tommie Rae asked Emiliano what he would like to do with some of his money, he said, "Senor Mac, what would something like the headstall that I braided sell for here in the United States?" Mac thought a minute and said, "If you got it in the right stores, it would probably bring something like one hundred to one hundred-fifty dollars." Tommie Rae spoke up to say, "If someone took that kind of work around to events like the PRCA National Finals Rodeo and the Calgary Stampede, you could probably double that." Emiliano was quite a moment before saying, "If it can be worked out, I would like to take some money into the state of Jalisco in Mexico and start a factory were my cousins and nephews could earn a decent living." Tommie Rae said, "I don't know what all it would require to get that done but I'll bet our friend Luke Overholt and his whiz kids can tell us what we need to do. In the morning, I will call the woman that runs his office and get them started digging out information."

The partners had decided that they wanted to be in the ranching business together so the question now was where to go from here? Mac had heard rumors that the lawyers who bought the 9R were becoming a little disillusioned; it seems that a lot of the romance had gone out of ranching for them when they found themselves hooked to a property that brought in little in revenue and had a seemingly endless requirement for expenditures. They hired a man to manage the place as a hunting ranch and he brought in more money in fees from hunters but also he spent more for advertising, deer blinds, quail feeders and hunting guides and the ratio of income to expense got even worse. They ran off the hunter and put out feelers for buyers. They were more than a little put out that no one was interested in paying them a profit for the ranch, in fact — as the drought worsened — no one wanted the ranch at any price. From a return on investment standpoint, it was not attractive to business people and it was too big a chunk of money to be in wide demand as a play thing.

The partners were trying to decide whether or not to try to buy the 9R and if so, how to go about setting up the deal. Bart asked, "Mac what is a fair price for the ranch?" "That's hard to answer, the ranch will carry about 1400 cows in normal times but I don't know how to translate that into a price." Tommie Rae spoke up to say, "What would the ranch lease for in normal conditions?" "Well if you figure that providing feed for a cow shouldn't cost more than two thirds of what her calf will bring. If a calf is worth three hundred dollars and it takes twenty acres to run a cow, it would be something like 9 to 10 dollars an acre plus the hunting rights will bring maybe 5 dollars so call it 15 dollars an acre lease." Tommie Rae said, "The rule of thumb for figuring property values has long been that a property should sell for something like ten to twelve times its annual rent but with people buying ranches just for recreation, the relationship between what land will produce and what it will sell for is being lost." Bart said, "We know that the lawyers bought just for recreation but if they are trying to sell out so soon maybe they have had a change in their economic status and the cost of being ranchers has gotten too high. Fifteen dollars an acre times ten would be $150 an acre; why don't we see if they will take $125? We can always come up if we need to but let's decide what the top dollar we will pay is before we start negotiations." As people nodded agreement, Tommie Rae spoke up to say, "There hasn't been an oil play the area for a long time but oil prices are rising again and the oil companies are looking for new areas to drill, let's make sure that we get the mineral rights on anything that we buy." Mac knew the foreman for the 9R and a phone call told them that both of the lawyers were expected to be on the ranch this weekend. Mac got the office number of one of the lawyers and set up a meeting for the coming Saturday.

CHAPTER 42

Mac drove the ranch pickup slowly up the graded gravel road toward the ranch headquarters that backed up to the line of low flat topped hills forming the edge of the Callahan Divide. Mac pointed out the rise in elevation of the divide and told Bart that water falling on the south side of the divide would flow into the Colorado River while water falling on the north side would wind up in the Brazos River. The house was built up close to the hills so that a steep bluff sheltered it from the north wind; barns, out buildings and corrals were arranged in a fan shape down slope in front of the house. The house was a long two story white stone building with a stone chimney on each end and a functional wide porch across the front. On the east end a door on the second floor opened onto a roofed and screened in balcony built on top of an attached garage. An unusually tall windmill on the west side of the house pumped into a large galvanized storage tank mounted on top of a tall circular stone base; the over flow from the storage tank went into a big round stone pila or reservoir. They had passed a series of small fenced pastures that Bart now knew were called traps and were designed to hold animals for short periods of time handy to the corrals. According to the truck odometer, they had come six miles since they turned off the highway and they were still a little ways from the headquarters. Bart had seen more grass in that distance then he had seen in all the rest of his time in Texas; Mac told him that much of it was too old to be of much use to cattle but it would cover the ground and help the water soak in when it finally did rain. As they got closer, Bart could see several buildings aside from the big house. One long low building that he assumed was a bunkhouse and another smaller building, both with porches and chimneys, were close together near a large barn and the corrals while a small house complete with clothes lines and flower beds was visible behind the main house. Several enclosed sheds were located along the road and a new looking galvanized grain bin on stilts flanked the barn. Looking at the workmanship on the buildings, the fences and the corrals, it was obvious that care and thought had gone into their design and construction.

The partners had decided that Mac and Bart would approach the lawyers about the possibility of buying the ranch and they wanted to do it before the word of their bonanza leaked out. They planned to tell the lawyers only that they represented a group interested in investing in ranch land and to use a letter of credit from Synergy LLP to prove capability. They felt it was better tactics that the lawyers assume that they represented a group of hardnosed New York money men rather than just themselves. Mac had called the day before and they had appointments to see J. Harrison Claus and Jeffery N. Thompson at 2:00 this afternoon. They parked the truck close to the gate of an iron yard fence where each fence post was a carved limestone hitching post with a hand forged iron ring attached. Bart glanced at his watch and was pleased to see that they were right on time as they started up the brick walk. When they approached the door, they heard dogs barking from somewhere behind the house, which was the first sign of domestic animals they has seen or heard since entering the property. Bart rang the doorbell and after a moment it was opened by a middle aged Mexican woman wearing a maid uniform. Mac and Bart both removed their hats and Mac said, "Hello Rosita, we are here to see Mr. Claus and Mr. Thompson." Rosita smiled and said, "Come in Senor Mac and I will tell them that you are here." She left them in the entrance foyer and knocked before opening the second door down the hall and announcing, "Senor Mac and his friend are here to see you." Rosita stepped back and gestured into the room with a smile and a "Por favor." Mac thanked her and he and Bart entered what appeared to have been a library at one time but was now fitted with easy chairs, a bar, and a large television tuned to a baseball game. One of the two men seated in front of the television rose and said, "Connley, come in." He turned to Bart and said, "I am Harrison Claus and you are?" Bart retracted the hand that he had extended and Claus had ignored and said, "My name is Bart Ryan." Claus turned to Mac, the other man was still watching the ball game, and said, "Connley, I thought we were going to meet your principles, I really don't care to waste my time dealing with hired hands." Mac took a deep breath and said softly, "Bart is my partner and he is the man that has final say as to whether we buy your little pea patch or we go on to the next ranch on our list." Claus looked as if he had bitten down on something sour and said, "Of course, come in please and sit down, Jeffery, turn the television off and come meet our guests." Jeffery got up finally, turned the television off and came over carrying a highball glass dark with liquor and said with a bit of a slur, "Where are you from Ryan? You don't look like any New York investor I ever saw." Bart spoke up, Oh, I am from New York all right but I have been spending some time learning the ranching business." Claus was all sweetness and light now and said, "What can I get you to drink?" Mac held up his hands in a nothing for me gesture and Bart said in his best New York staccato while ticking off points on his fingers, "Business first, drink later. Can you provide clear title to the property, is the abstract up to date, are all mineral rights intact, how much do you owe, how far are you in arrears on your payments and what are you asking for your interest? It would save time if you answer my questions truthfully as I assure you that our lawyers and accountants have and will go over everything concerning you and this ranch with a fine tooth comb any discrepancies between what you tell me now and the truth will be a deal breaker. We want to invest a considerable sum of money in the next few weeks but I assure you we always get fair value on anything we buy. We are business men not dilettantes looking for play things which we later find we cannot afford. If the property meets our needs, I will write you a check but I will not haggle like a fishwife. I will make you a fair offer and you can say yes or no. Do we understand each other?" Jeffery had been getting redder in the face as Bart spoke and finally got right in Bart's face shouting, "You can't talk to us like that, I'll kick your New York ass and" Claus pulled him back, shoved him down in a chair and said, "Shut up Thompson and stay out of this."

Mac drove them slowly back toward the highway and home and said, "Son, you plumb amaze me, in all the time you have been here, I have never been around a milder mannered man. Where did that hard as nails guy that took the hide right off those two four flushers come from? How did you know that the bank was about to repossess the ranch and how did you get them to admit it? "Mac I have dealt with bums like that all my working life, I used to sell appliances on credit and I can spot a liar and scam artist as soon as he opens his mouth. The kicker though was Pete telling you that none of the help had been paid in three months; if you can't make payroll, you sure can't make mortgage payments on a three million dollar note. If you are three months in arrears on a note that size, the bank is going to be seriously concerned and moving to protect their interest. Maybe I ran a little bit of bluff and maybe I was a little hard on those bastards but they pissed me off with the way they treated us and I felt like playing a little catch up. We lucked out, they were closer to the wall than we suspected and our offer of $130 an acre was just enough and just in time to get them out without being foreclosed. I am ashamed though that I was so small as to refuse to shake hands with Claus after the deal was done." "Don't be, when you went to the truck to get your clipboard, that toad said, "Connley, if you can get him to give us two hundred thousand under the table and knock that amount off the purchase price, there will be fifty thousand in it for you." "Well," said Bart, "we had best check in with our partners and then get in touch with our high powered staff of lawyers and accountants, all two of them, and get them started on a sales contract and title search."

CHAPTER 43

Mac drove the old ranch pickup through the 9R entrance with Bart in the passenger seat beside him. They were enjoying being on the ranch after having spent most of three days with lawyers, bankers and accountants. After the one meeting with Claus and Thompson, the partners had no further contact with the two; the Fort Worth bank that held the mortgage took over the sale negotiations and it was soon evident that the bank was extremely pleased to be dealing with Oak Creek Partners instead of with the two lawyers. Clyde Norris, the officer representing the bank, could not have been more accommodating. The one sticking point came when he rather hesitantly said that since the some two hundred deer and quail feeders on the ranch were not "permanent parts" of the ranch, he would have to charge the partners the amount still owed on the feeders. Bart and Tommie Rae looked at each other but before either could speak, Mac said "No!" in a very forceful voice. Norris looked a little chagrined and said, "Well perhaps we can come down a little on the price." Mac held up a hand and said, "I didn't mean that the price was too high. I meant that we don't want them. We probably will lease to hunters but I'll be damned if I am going to bait deer and quail up to a feedlot to be shot." Norris again looked pleased and said, "I understand and I will see that we get the feeders off quickly."

Mac and Bart were on their way to speak with the five people that had been employed on the 9R. Mac had known Jake Malone, the foreman for years and hoped that he would stay with them. He also knew Rosita and Evidencio Morales; Rosita worked as cook and housekeeper while Evidencio was a general ranch hand and a pretty fair hand with horses. There were two other hands that Mac had never met and they wanted to talk to Jake before meeting with the others. Jake lived with his wife Anna in a neat little house nestled under two huge old oak trees just four hundred yards from the main gate off the highway. Jake came out to meet them as they drove up and offered what Bart had found to be the almost universal salutation to visitors in this part of the world of, "Get out and come in." Amongst the older folk, it often came out, "Get down and come in." Mac introduced Bart to Jake as "my partner and somebody that you will like once you get used to the funny way he talks." Bart grinned and offered his hand with, "I am pleased to meet you." They met Anna, a pleasant faced women smelling of fresh baked bread and accepted her offer of coffee and a seat on the front porch. Anna brought the coffee and a plate of fresh from the oven cookies and excused herself back into the house as Mac and Jake both rolled smokes. Mac led off with, "Jake my three partners and I are looking to combine the 9R with Oak Creek and see if we have sense enough to run a good cow outfit. We are talking about eventually running around a thousand cows and carrying most of the calves over to sell as feeders the next summer. Do you think you might be interested in being part of something like this?" Jake looked at the tip of his cigarette and said, "Mac the bank started hauling those damn deer and quail feeders out today and every time a truck load came bye, it was all I could do to keep from running along behind cheering like a kid at a fourth of July parade. For nearly three years I have put up with rude arrogant and incompetent would be hunters, trailed down their gut shot deer and poured more corn into feeders than I did when I was working at the feedlot. Damn right I would like to be part of a real cow outfit." Mac said, "OK, I know Rosita and Evidencio but tell me about the other two hands." "Joe Tubbs is just a kid really but he grew up on a ranch and he is willing. I haven't had a chance to teach him much on this job but he will do if he has a chance. The other guy, James Heller, was hired by Mr. Claus and I don't have any use for him; he makes me think of some of the big city thugs that I ran into in the army. He gets along with the hunters, especially the ones that like their whiskey but he is not much good for anything else. He shrugs off all the work he can on Joe or Evidencio and I have caught him smoking dope twice on company time. I tried to get Claus to let me fire him but he not only said no but told me to leave Heller alone. I needed a job too bad to do what I should have done and quit. I had one other fellow, a good hand, Henry Dobbs, but he quit when Thompson told him to get his suitcase out of the car and carry it into the house. Henry apologized for leaving me shorthanded but said he had taken all the crap he was going to take from those two Nancy boys." Mac asked, "Did you all ever get your back pay?" "Not hardly! We got a notice that the corporation Claus and Thompson formed to buy and run the ranch was in bankruptcy and that we would have to enter claims with the court." "Do you know what everybody is owed?" "Yeah I do, Anna kept the payroll but the checks had to come out of Claus' office in Dallas; they are the ones that told us to file our claims with the court." Mac looked at Bart and said, "What do you think Partner?" Bart said, "I think we need to start with a happy crew. Jake, if Anna will tell me what everybody has coming, I will write checks and we can take them with us when we talk to the rest of the crew." Anna must have been discretely eavesdropping because she very quickly had out the book listing names, social security numbers and amounts due for all the help. Bart watched her copy from the bound ledger that showed all of the payroll information recorded in a neat and legible hand; Bart could see that she was tracking all of the other ranch expenses as well and complimented her on her work. "The way you have things organized reminds me of my Mother; she was a bookkeeper and a stickler for everything being in place and done so anyone could read it." Anna handed him the list of names and amounts and said, "Thank you, I had to learn to do this when Mr. Claus told Jake it was part of the job. Neither of us had ever kept a set of books so I bought a course and tried to learn to do it right." Bart read the list and said, "Well it looks good to me but you didn't put your salary on the list." "Oh I don't get paid; this is just something I do to help out." Bart sat down at the kitchen table and quickly wrote out checks including one equal to what Rosita was paid for Anna and put them all with the ranch checkbook in the dust and water proof plastic folder that he had started carrying. Mac had called ahead and the rest of the crew was supposed to meet them at the headquarters office at 9:00 am. They thanked Anna for the coffee and cookies and started up to headquarters with Jake following in his own truck since the bank had picked up all of the ranch vehicles including the ancient road grader and the even more ancient John Deere tractor that were there when the lawyers bought the ranch. Jake mentioned the grader and tractor to Bart and he made a mental note to jump Clyde Norris about getting them back. They weren't much but they did the job of keeping the ranch roads passable. The trucks were bought after the lawyers bought the ranch but the grader and tractor were part of what the Partners had bought. He also decided that he would withhold the money he had just paid out in back wages when it came time to settle up; he didn't doubt that the bank could get their money back from the lawyers' bankruptcy or no bankruptcy. The lawyers would find the bank a little harder to fleece than a set of uneducated ranch hands.

The ranch office was the separate building located between the big house and the bunkhouse and all of the rest of the crew was present on its' front porch when Mac and Bart drove up. Jake arrived and said to the group, "Folks, I want you to meet Mac Connley and Bart Ryan. They are part of the group that has bought the 9R. Mac and Bart meet, starting from my left, Joe Tubbs, James Heller and Rosita and Evidencio Morales." "Rosita and Evidencio I know and I am glad to meet you Joe and you James. My partner has checks for each of you to cover what the lawyers owed you in back pay, this isn't something that we had to do but we felt bad about the way you were treated. We will be changing up how things run around here; this will be a cow outfit rather than a hunting operation. Evidencio, Rosita and Joe we would like to stay on if you want to but James, you don't fit what we need." Bart was handing out checks as Mac talked and he received thanks from Joe Tubbs and the Morales but Heller looked at his check, got right in Macs' face and shouted, "What the hell is this? You keep two Mexicans and a punk kid but cut me loose and don't even give me severance pay? I will stomp your ass old man and kick the shit out of your pretty boy friend as well." Heller drew back a fist to hit Mac just as Jake stepped between them and Jake took the blow on the side of his head; it knocked him off the porch and down hard on the ground. Mac turned to check on Jake and Heller hit him in the back of the head and sent him stumbling off the porch to fall on top of Jake. Bart stepped up behind Heller and said, "Hey." Heller whirled around with his right fist cocked and took three quick straight left jabs to the face and a powerful right hook to the belly that doubled him over gasping for air. Heller was taller than Bart by half a head and out weighted him by fifty pounds so Bart decided to not take any chances. He stepped up and slammed his cupped hands over both of Heller's ears at the same time — which has about the same effect as a hand grenade going off in your head — Bart then stepped back and kicked him hard in the solar plexus as he fell. Mac got back to his feet and turned around just in time to see Heller collapse on his back like a rag doll with lips mashed in on missing teeth, his nose pointing off towards his left shoulder and his eyes rolled back in his head till nothing showed but white. Mac looked at Bart who was unmarked and not even breathing hard and asked, "Damn Boy, what did you hit him with?" Mac was OK, just embarrassed, and Jake was back on his feet saying, "I'm alright, I'm alright" with Rosita holding a clean handkerchief to the cut on his cheek. As Heller groaned and coughed and began stirring, Mac reached down to grab a handful of greasy lank hair and jerk him upright into a sitting position. Heller's eyes finally came back into focus and he glared at Mac and then at Bart who was standing beside Mac. "You bastard, you sucker punched me and I am going to cut your fu" The rest was garbled as Macs' left hand jerked Heller's head forward to meet the punch from his right fist that came from behind his body. Heller screamed and the blood flew and suddenly Heller's nose was more or less back in the center of his face. "I am only going to say this once pachuco. You have ten minutes to get your plunder and get the hell gone. I am going to call the Sheriff and we will all give statements as to what went down here today. I have a pretty strong suspicion that you don't want my old buddy Doyt to run your fingerprints and mug shots through the system. If I was you, I would put some distance between me and Nolan County and

I wouldn't even think about coming back unless you want to stay here for good. Now git!" Joe Tubbs and Evidencio had been grinning at each other like a pair of pet possums and as Heller got to his feet and staggered toward the bunkhouse, the grins got even wider. Mac turned to Joe and said, "Does he have a gun?" "Yes Sir, he has a little chrome .25 caliber automatic that he can hide in the palm of his hand and he brags about how many times he has used it to put men down." Jake and Mac both walked out to their trucks. Jake took a bolt action deer rifle out of the rack on the back window and Mac took his old thumb buster out of the glove box and then reached behind the seat for a 30-30 saddle gun that he handed to Bart. The three of them stood waiting behind Macs' truck with no guns in sight until Heller came out of the bunkhouse; he threw an old suitcase and a duffel bag into the trunk of his car and started toward the office with his right hand held low behind his leg. The three stepped out where Heller could see their guns; Mac eared the hammer back on his .45 and said, "That's close enough. I surely hope that you don't have a pistol in your hand because I would surely have to shoot you if you did." Heller looked at the guns pointing at him and stood real still turning pale. He opened his hand to drop the little pistol behind his back and turned back toward his car without saying anything. Heller cranked his old car and left in a shower of tire thrown gravel; they watched as he reached the highway and turned south toward Coke County.

Jake put his rifle up and said, "Damn if I don't like the way you fellows operate. That thug made life miserable for all of us for too long." Mac turned to Bart and said, "Just about the time I think I know you, you come up with something new; where in the world did you learn to fight like that?" Bart grinned and said, "It's no big deal, I fought in the Golden Glove matches in high school and when

I joined the Army my company commander was a boxing nut that wanted more than anything to win the regimental boxing championship. Those of us that could box a little were given the choice of motor pool mechanic duty or training for the boxing matches. Not too hard to choose between training and eating at the training table or fixing truck flats and eating chow hall food. I spent nearly my whole hitch boxing; our coach was an ex-special forces unarmed combat instructor who was a good boxing coach but also taught us a couple of dozen ways to kill or cripple a man with your bare hands. We won the regimental championship twice for our Capitan and I thought he was going to cry when I told him I wouldn't re-up when my hitch was over."

CHAPTER 44

The Morales and Joe Tubbs went about their business and Mac and Bart sat down with Jake in the office. Jake looked at Mac and Bart and said, "I want to thank you for the chance to be part of the new 9R. My Daddy worked for the 9R until the 1940's and I was born in the Company house over on Eagle Creek; my Mothers grandfather helped drive the first cattle to graze the 9R from Navarro County. He came with Tom Trammell, the man who founded the 9R, and was killed by Comanche somewhere north of here on Oak Creek. I feel like the 9R is a part of me and I will do my damnedest to help you make it work." "Jake," said Mac, "we are glad to have you; we are going to do some things that are a little different from the way most folks operate and to make it work we will need good people. While the lawyers ran up their bills getting the sale finalized, we four partners have spent some time visiting with Bud Malone and with several ranches that have gone to what they call high stock density grazing. You have seen what we started several years ago on Oak Creek; putting all our cows in one herd and moving them through eight different pastures. It has made a big difference in our grass; we finally had to ship some cattle this summer but we had grass for two years after most of our neighbors had to completely de-stock. From what we have seen, we are pretty sure that both the grass and the cattle will do even better if we had even more pastures per herd so that we could stay in each pasture for shorter periods and still give plenty of time for the grass to recover. Some people are moving to fresh pasture every day and only grazing each pasture one time during the growing season." Jake was trying hard but could not help but let a look of sort of sick disbelief creep onto his face. "Mac, we would run all the meat off of them just gathering and moving." Bart spoke up for the first time, "Mac, tell him about the San Pablo." "Jake, do you know the country south of Carrizo Springs?" "Yeah, I do, it's some of the worst brush country that I have ever seen." "We were down on the San Pablo Ranch last week and saw a four man crew gather and ship four thousand Mexican steers off forty thousand acres in eight hours. Really heavy brush and their final tally was four head off the book count." Jake started to say something but Mac held up a hand and said, "They had been moving the cattle every second day through thirty six pastures by tolling them with a siren on a truck. They started training them by blowing the siren and feeding cubes to however many cattle showed up; pretty soon they were all coming to the siren and then they used the siren to move to fresh pasture with riders just drifting up stragglers. Before long, they didn't need the riders or even to feed cubes; the cattle learned that the siren would take them to fresh pasture and were ready to go anytime it sounded. The day we were there, the siren truck came wailing through a 2000 acre pasture and you could hear those big steers popping brush on a high lope coming from every direction to the siren. The truck pulled right into a trap and on into the pens with the steers right behind just like kids chasing the ice cream truck. They had riders there but they just followed along behind and shut the gates. It don't seem possible to old codgers like you and me who have spent days cleaning a 1000 acre pasture but most of the people doing this don't even saddle a horse when they move cattle. Cows that are raised with this management get dog gentle; it takes all the cowboying out of gathering or moving cattle." Jake still looked dubious but said, "I guess it makes sense, moving to fresh pasture would be a good thing to cattle and once they came to the siren a time or two without something bad happening they would get comfortable with the deal." Bart spoke up, "Jake how many pastures are there on the 9R?" "Right now there are fourteen big pastures and about twelve traps. There was almost a lot less; the first thing the lawyers wanted to do was tear out all the interior fences. We tore out fences for two weeks before they realized what it was going to cost in labor and they decided that they could live with fences after all. I was hoping that they would come around so we started the tearing out on fences that were in bad shape and needed to be replaced anyway. How many pastures do we need to make this work?" "Jake we don't know for sure, we have Tommie Rae doing some research but we think that we need at least 65-70 pastures counting both ranches." said Bart. Jake looked real dubious now, "That is going to be a bunch of fence, probably some more water points and a bunch of money; is it going to be worth it?" Mac looked at Bart and said, "You tell him." "What Mac thinks will spook you is Tommie Rae and I hope to put the subdivisions in with electric fence." "Well Bart, Mac is just not as modern as some of us; I worked for an outfit up in the panhandle for a while and we fenced in wheat pasture cattle with electric fence right on a busy highway. If the fence is hot and the cattle are trained to it, there is no problem holding them. That will work, we can split the big pastures three or four times and it will be fast and not cost anything like what a net and barbed wire fence would cost." Bart said, "We have some maps being made up; as soon as we get them, we will get with you and start deciding how to do the subdivision. How much net wire fence is on the ranch? Emiliano brought up getting some hair sheep, both to have lambs to sell and to make better use of weeds that the cattle don't like. I think that is something we may want to explore." "All of the big pastures are sheep and goat tight. They used to run both Angora goats and fine wool sheep here back when we had markets for hair and wool. The biggest problem I see with sheep would be coyotes and cats. Since sheep and goats left this country, people have stopped fighting predators and their numbers have exploded. If we bring in sheep, we will have to have good guard dogs."

Mac said, "Jake if you will, have the boys check the fences and the water on the Red Rock Crossing pasture that borders the southwest corner of Oak Creek; I want to move the Oak Creek cattle just as soon as we can. We will leave my pickup here for them to use if you don't mind running us home in your truck. When they get back from checking pasture, they can come hook on to our stock trailer and start bringing horses and mules to your horse trap. They can move all of them except the saddle horses that we have in the north trap. Tell Evidencio to watch those damn little mules; the little heathens will ambush you. Tommie Rae has us going to Angelo this afternoon for something but we can move the cows in the morning if things are ready. Also, tell me about the trucks that the bank picked up; they moved them to a lot in Abilene and I bet we can buy them worth the money if you can tell us which ones are solid." "There were two nearly new one tons that we used for feed trucks and three three-quarter ton pickups. Two of the pickups are solid but the green one that Heller was driving is sick; he cracked the oil pan on a rock and ran it out of oil. It will still run but I wouldn't trust that motor." Bart looked at his watch and said, "We had best go or we will be in trouble with Tommie Rae."

Mac turned to Jake with a grin, "Can you believe that, he hasn't even asked the girl yet and he is already hen pecked." "You talk big Mac, but you're just as scared of her as I am; let's go."

Tommie Rae and Emiliano were sitting on the front porch dressed for town when Jake dropped them off and shortly they were on the road with Mac and Emiliano in the back seat, Tommie Rae driving and Bart beside her. Tommie Rae said, "Good news, my lawyer cousin called and he has the visa for Emiliano. It even has an entry stamp that I don't know how he got but Emiliano is legal as soon as we pick it up. We are going to do that first then we are going to go eat and then we are going to go to the men's clothing stores and get all three of you outfitted so you look like the gentlemen of substance that you are. Boots, suits, shirts, hats, we buy the whole bit for all three of you." Mac started, "Now wait a minute, I don't need no" "Hush Mac, we are going to Mexico to help Emiliano start his factory and maybe east to buy more land and you all need to look the part of successful men." "But" "Hush Mac." Bart was trying his best to keep a straight face but when he saw Macs' expression, he lost it and broke out laughing. Mac glared at him and said, "Watch it boy, you I can still handle." Later with a good meal under their belts and Emilianos' visa in his pocket, Tommie Rae herded them into the best men's clothing store in town and announced that she needed three clerks. The manager appeared and she told him that she wanted all three of her partners outfitted from top to bottom starting with good quality light weight business suits but also shirts, ties, slacks, sport coats, underwear and socks. As the clerks brought out items, she then went from partner to partner approving or vetoing each selection and cajoling and threatening to get the needed fittings done. Emiliano pretty quickly surrendered to a "Si Senorita" attitude and seemed to enjoy modeling the new clothes. Mac scowled ferociously and muttered constantly under his breath but Bart caught him several times checking his appearance in the mirrors. Bart quickly got into the novelty of being able, for the first time in his life, to buy what he wanted without having to worry about cost. When Mac exploded with, "I ain't gonna pay three hundred dollars for no suit!" Tommie Rae came right back with, "No you are not paying, the Partnership is paying because these are your new working clothes and a business expense that is deductible." When the last pair of slacks had been marked for alteration, Tommie Rae led them across the street to one of the several good boot makers in town for dress boots and both straw and felt hats. This time there was no argument from Mac about being fitted for a couple of pairs of custom handmade boots. Bart was flabbergasted at the dozens of kinds of exotic leather and the options of heel height, toe shape, top height, inlays, appliqués and fancy stitching that were available but finally settled on two pair of low heel conservative boots in calf skin, one pair black and one pair brown. Emiliano was likewise conservative but Tommie Rae and Mac both expressed a little more individuality in their choices. Mac voted for soft kangaroo for the feet of his boots with shark skin heels and at his suggestion they all had the 9R brand inlaid in their boot tops. Tommie Rae had one pair made up of black patent leather and one pair of cream colored calf covered with a cut out filigree of scarlet leather. It would be several weeks before all the boots were ready but Bart nearly choked when he saw the size of the required fifty percent deposit check that Tommie Rae wrote out. By the time hats had been selected and steam creased to the owners' preference and belts and buckles selected from an amazing selection, it was closing time for the shop and time for them to go home.

CHAPTER 45

Next morning Tommie Rae saddled up before daylight with Mac and Bart and they rode out in the cool of the early morning to gather and move the cowherd on to the 9R. This was the first time since before the guests arrived that Bart had been horseback in what Mac called, "the best time of the day." All three of their horses were blessed with the ability to travel in an easy riding running walk. This gait covers ground almost as fast as a trot but with none of the trots' bone rattling jarring. Mac said, "You could be damn sure that any horse that Windy kept for his own personal use would have a running walk. Windy would put up with any number of faults in a horse but if one didn't have a running walk, he wouldn't keep him around." Jake had called this morning as they were finishing breakfast to report that the Red Rock Crossing pasture was ready; both windmills in the pasture, one to the south and one to the north were pumping, the drink tanks had been cleaned and the pilas had enough water to hold this number of cattle for several days even if the wind died. The sun had not yet touched the horizon but in the gray light of dawn the daylight world was just waking up and the night time world was going to bed; they saw deer starting to bed down in thickets where in the top most branches birds were singing their hearts out to announce to the world that they were back on duty. A coyote crossed ahead of them carrying a half-grown jack rabbit back to its' pups and a great horned owl sailed silently bye on its' way to a daytime perch.

In another hour it would be hot but right now it was pleasant and there was even a hint of moisture in the air. The weather forecast the day before out of Angelo said that a tropical depression was forming west of Cuba and just maybe west Texas could get something out of it. Bart had learned that people in west Texas follow the hurricanes in the Gulf of Mexico just as closely as do the people that live on the coast. This time of year, a hurricane coming ashore and tracking inland was one of the few chances this country had for general rains over a large area. You could have scattered thunderstorms at any time but even if you were lucky enough to be under one, the moisture didn't do a lot of good and got sucked right back into the atmosphere when the ground and the air was dry all around the wet spot. It's considered bad luck to talk about the possibility of rain in a drought but all three partners noticed that the wind had shifted from the normal southwest to an almost southeast direction and that long strings of high clouds were appearing in the north flowing from east to southwest in flat arcs.

The cattle were in the pasture next to the 9R and were up grazing when the partners arrived. The cows were calved out with the last calf born being three weeks old and ready to travel. The three spread out and began drifting the herd towards the gate into the 9R pasture. Bart guessed that this qualified as work but if so, he was for sure working in the right job. He liked everything about it from the company to the motion of the horse under him to the sounds and smells of the animals; right now, he was that rarest of people, a happy man doing exactly what he wanted to do. He and Tommie Rae planned to go to Abilene this afternoon to see about the 9R trucks and he also wanted to buy a truck for his own use and one for Mac if he could talk him into it. He hated dealing with car salesmen but looked forward to having Tommie Rae all to himself. The cattle seemed to know that something special was afoot and they stepped out a good clip; the older calves had formed what Mac called "hoodlum gangs" and every once in a while a bunch of them would gang up and run ahead bucking and playing as if they were going to quit the country. The first time this happened, Bart was about ready to circle around to bring the runaways back to the herd when suddenly the "hoodlums" realized that "Mama" was not with them they didn't know where "Mama" was and the whole bunch came thundering back bawling for their mothers. As they got to the gate, Mac eased ahead to open the gate and then rode through it calling to the cattle. The cattle didn't know this gate but they knew Mac and they knew the call that he used and they picked up the pace anxious to see the treat that it promised. One of the older cows pushed through several cows that had stopped at the gate and broke into a little bucking run before dropping her head to graze the deep forage. The herd filed through the gate as Mac circled back to where he could control the flow and get a count. After the last cow cleared the gate, the three rode the six hundred yards or so south to the north most 9R windmill. On the way, the wind picked up and shifted from southeast to east with a smell and feel of moisture on it. They could feel the temperature dropping and high clouds began to blow in from the east. As they sat their horses watching the cattle graze, Mac turned his face to the breeze and said, "It looks like the storm is trying to come ashore south of us, if it holds together and it doesn't turn north too quick, we will be on the wet side of it and just might get lucky; keep your fingers crossed."

By the time they got back to Oak Creek headquarters, the sky was filled with masses of high swirling clouds moving from east to west and spits of rain were falling spasmodically. They unsaddled quickly and went in to see if they could catch the noon weather report from the TV station out of Abilene; when they tuned in the forecaster was pointing to a map showing the predicted path of what was now a category II hurricane named Carmen. The storm was expected to come ashore probably tonight, somewhere between Corpus Christi and Brownsville; it was a young storm and not violent as hurricanes go but it had blossomed over the warm waters of the Gulf of Mexico into a huge storm that covered most of the central Gulf. The computer forecast was for the storm to come in just south of Corpus and track to the northwest; if this happened, most of west Texas should get good rains but the weather forecasters were still playing it cautious. As they listened, the weather man explained that if the storm came in south of Brownsville, its' most likely tract would be due west into Mexico and they could be left high and dry. Mac got up, turned off the TV and said, "It will do what it's going to do and we can't change it; if it is as fickle as the last Carmen I knew, it may just turn around and go back out to sea just to spite us. Let's go see if Emiliano will give us some dinner." As the four of them ate, Bart asked Mac to go with them to Abilene to see about the trucks. "No you two handle that; I need to get with Jake and figure out how to divide the Eagle Creek pasture." "You had better come along Mac; Tommie Rae is liable to buy you a pink pickup if you are not there to tell her what you want." Mac got red in the face and said, "I have told you two, I don't need no new pickup, I don't want no new pickup and don't you two go buying me no pickup; the one I got is just barely broke in good." Emiliano had a smirk twitching at his lips and Tommie Rae had to hide her grin behind her napkin to say. "Bart, quit deviling, Mac; He will be ready to trade in that old rattletrap when he sees our new trucks."

Bart had called the banker, Clyde Norris, about getting their tractor and road grader back; he apologized profusely for their having been taken and assured Bart that he would see that they were returned immediately. Norris also apologized that the trucks had been removed; he had intended to offer them to the partners at what was left on their notes. He read off the amounts due for each truck and told Bart that if they wanted them at those prices, he would see that they were moved back to the ranch. The trucks had been taken to the Ford dealer in Abilene; Bart called the service department and arranged for a mechanic to check out the truck Heller had run out of oil. Bart and Tommie Rae started into Abilene as soon as they had eaten with the Ford dealership their first destination. They found the service manager and Bart introduced himself and asked about the condition of the suspect truck, "My lead mechanic just told me that he went out to drive it in to a service bay but the engine rattled so bad when he started it that he shut it down without moving the truck. The motor is shot." Bart thanked him and borrowed his phone to call the banker and tell him that they would pass on the crippled truck but would take the others at the prices he quoted; Norris thanked him and said that he would see that everything was delivered back to the 9R tomorrow. They had discussed on the way in what Bart wanted in a truck and Tommie Rae had drawn it up in a list.

They were pounced on by a salesman as they walked in the showroom door and while they tried to convince him that they knew exactly what they wanted, that they would pay cash and that they were not interested in the special deals with special financing that would be good on selected vehicles for only a few more days, the salesman was too wound up in his pitch to listen until Tommie Rae held up her hand in the universal "stop" sign said, "Whoa", handed him the list and said, "We are going to buy a truck rigged out just as it shows on this list and in the next year or so we will probably buy two or three more; if your price is right, we will buy from you and if it is not we will go somewhere else. I bought a truck here last year and I swore that never again would I be jerked around like I was on that deal. Here is what we want, figure your best deal and we will either say yes and pay you or say no and go somewhere else but we will not haggle. We have some errands to run and will be back in about an hour. Is that time enough for you to price out want we want?" The salesman gaped at her with his mouth open, looked at Bart who just shrugged and grinned and finally salesman shut his mouth said. "Yes that should be plenty of time." Tommie Rae smiled brightly at him and led the way out of the showroom. Bart held it together until they turned the corner and were out of sight of the salesman and then he broke up in a fit of laughter so violent that tears rolled down his cheeks and he couldn't talk. When he finally got his breath, he said, "When you cut him off in mid spiel, I thought he was going to faint; is he the one who gave you a bad time last year?" "No, he is not but he is one of the same breed and I just got tired of him not listening to us."

They ran their errands and Tommie Rae had the opportunity to introduce Bart to another of her friends; they ran into Cecilia Collins in the grocery store. Cecilia – a pretty black women Tommie Raes age – was in TCU at the same time as Tommie Rae. Her folks ranched on the South Concho south of San Angelo and had been in this part of the world as long as had the Wolf clan. As they pulled back into the dealership parking lot, they saw their salesman polishing the windshield of a white three quarter ton four door crew cab; they decided on a crew cab for Bart since they knew that the four of them would likely be taking several trips together in the near future. Tommie

Rae pulled her truck up beside the new truck and she and Bart got out; "Here it is rigged just like you wanted and I was able to make you a whale of a deal." "That's good," said Tommie Rae, "because I have been pricing this very truck on the internet and you would not believe how much difference I found in asking prices for the very same truck." Bart walked around the new truck and then leaned on a fender and watched the salesman sweat; you could read his thoughts just like they had appeared over his head in one of those little balloons over the heads of cartoon characters. Did she really know what the truck should sell for and would she really walk if he priced it so as to really make some money? He told his sales manager what was going on and the manager checked with a contact at the bank to see if they really might buy more trucks; the contact said yes they were real and could buy a dozen trucks if they wanted but when the salesman tried to get the manager to set the price all he got was, "You are the salesman, sell." Salesman turned to Tommie Rae and while he looked like a man about to play Russian roulette with an automatic, he finally said, "I got the sales manager to agree to $25,090 and let me tell you that is a very good price for this truck. We got a special deal on three trucks and this is the last..." Tommie Rae held up her stop sign again and said, "That's fine, we'll take it." The salesman said, "Huh oh, OK! Let's go get the paper work done." They rode back to the ranch in their separate vehicles but when they were in the kitchen drinking Emiliano's coffee, Bart said, "I have got to know, did you really know what the truck should sell for or were you bluffing?" "I will have you know, Sir, that I am more than just a beautiful face on a fantastic body, when it comes to money, I am the tightest broad you ever met. I used the internet to check sale prices all over the state and we did make a good deal."

CHAPTER 46

Pecan Creek 1880

Seth Collins stopped his horse just below the ridge line and looked down at the creek bottom below and knew that he was coming home. He first saw this valley in 1874 when he was chasing Comanche as Corporal Collins 10th Cavalry US Army. Company D rode into the Pecan Creek Valley on their way back to Fort Concho after a hard twenty day scout. The clear cold water of Pecan Creek was a treat after days of August sun, dust and gyp water but the real delight was the black shade of the big pecan trees; trees – in this part of west Texas – were as rare as hens' teeth. There was sometimes brush in the rough draws and along ridge crests but real trees were mostly limited to rare spots up and down the river and creek bottoms. The most common of these spots were where the water flow had changed course and created an island on which trees could take root and grow with some protection from the wildfires set by the lightening of summer thunder storms. Corporal Collins was just plain Seth Collins now but he was about to be rancher Seth Collins.

He spent ten years in the 10th Cavalry and those ten years turned an ignorant slave boy into a competent and confident man. Seth learned many useful things in those ten years starting with reading, writing and a little arithmetic – thanks to a missionary lady at Fort Concho – but perhaps the strangest thing for a black soldier to learn and prosper from was how easy it is to make money if you have money. Before he received his first month's pay, Seth had turned his two dollar signing bonus pay into six dollars and thirty-five cents by loaning money to other troopers. It wasn't long before every trooper at the Fort — black or white — knew they could always get a dollar or two to see them over till payday from Trooper Collins in D Company; the longer it was until payday, the higher the interest rate but it was always at least get one dollar and pay back two. A few times at first, Seth had a little trouble collecting; one time three troopers borrowed money and when it came time to pay up, all three stood together and told Seth to "Go to hell, we ain't paying you nothing." Seth didn't say anything and watched as they walked off laughing and slapping each other on the back; that night he caught the biggest of the three coming back from the latrine and beat on him till he was blue where he used to be black. Next morning, all three paid up and that was the end of Seth's collection troubles. Taking care of the rapidly increasing pile of money was getting to be a problem until Seth found that he could deposit it with Mr. Greenhaw, who had a store across the river in San Angelo; Mr. Greenhaw loaned it out to officers and business people at five percent a month and he and Seth split the profit 30- 70.

When his second hitch was up, Seth mustered out, bought civilian clothes and a good horse and started for the site on Pecan Creek where two of his ex-troopers were building him a stone house. Seth had been buying up un-located land script for several years; land script or un-assigned deeds granted to various people over time served almost as currency on the frontier and could be redeemed as land. Seth had redeemed six sections (3840 acres) along the course of Pecan Creek where it parallels the east bank of the South Concho;

by controlling access to the only water available, he controlled an area five times what he bought. Soon after they got the roof on the house, three ex-buffalo hunters rode in with rifles across their saddle swells and announced that "Niggers weren't allowed in this valley and that they were taking over." Seth and his hands buried the three deep in the horse lot and went on with their building. Nobody came looking for the three but since they had spent quite a bit of time in various dives bragging about how they were going to "Run the darkies out" rumors circulated and the general consensus became that it was better not to mess with Seth and his troopers. The next step was to go east into the older settled part of Texas and buy cows. After the ranch was stocked and operating he hoped to bring Miss Nellie Sanderson – a niece of Sgt. Benny Miller – home as his bride.

CHAPTER 47

The next ten days were to become the grandest time period Bart could remember; it started with the rain, a gentle rain that spread over Texas from the Gulf of Mexico to El Paso and beyond like a mothers' love. Carmen did prove to be a fickle lady; she came ashore at Corpus, stalled out and went back out to sea and sat there for a while pumping moisture ashore before coming inland again and tracking slowly off to the northwest. The wind died down to no more than a breeze and for four days running it rained on Oak Creek Ranch; every once in a while there would be a hard squall like rain storm but most of the time it was just a gentle fall of steady rain. Mac was back and forth to the rain gauge on the yard fence so often he wore a path in the yard; he checked the gauge and came back in to announce the new amount and record it on the calendar where he kept a running account of the year's weather events. When the rain finally stopped, they had received eight and a half inches; a lot of it ran off simply because the ground could not hold more water but the soil profile was full for the first time in over four years and all the dirt tanks were full and running around. They would not grow a lot of grass this year; it was too late in the season but the grass plants would green up and have time to replenish their energy reserves and would be ready to grow when the warm temperatures and lengthening days of spring arrived. The cool season plants would explode; the filaree and the winter fat and the rescue grass would come to life and

Emilianos' new flock of sheep would have green feed all winter. The only downside was that since it rained over all of Texas and a lot of Oklahoma, everyone wanted cattle and prices had gone straight up; it would cost a lot more to get the cattle they needed to stock the 9R but that was a small price to pay for seeing the drought broken. The rain was magnificent, especially when after five warm sunny days, a cool front brought more clouds and rain and they got another two inches. The creek was running strong, babbling like a bunch of kids on holiday and all of the walls in Reece Canyon were seeping water; Bart and Tommie Rae rode into the Canyon late in the day and the light of the sunset reflecting off of the seep water clothed the canyon walls in sheets of silver and gold. Bart took Tommie Raes' hand as they sat their horses side by side enjoying the view and she made the whole thing perfect when she said, "Oh Yes" when he asked her to marry him.

CHAPTER 48

Salas, Martin and Salas Attorneys at Law
261 General Flores Ave.
Chihuahua City, Chihuahua Mexico

Father Ramon Lopez
Church of the Holy Mother
San Miguel, Coahuila Mexico

Dear Father Lopez:

I have been instructed by my clients, Sr. and Senora Emiliano Cortez, to inform you that they wish to donate to the Church of the Holy Mother, in the name of Sr. Cortez's' deceased first wife, Josepha Anita Santos de Cortez the property that he owns in San Miguel. I will be in San Miguel on the tenth of this month and I will call on you at that time to complete the details of the transfer.

Sincérele,

Antonio Roberto Salas-García Esq.

Antonio Roberto Salas – García Esq.

Longtree Farm, Hillsboro, Connecticut

Liz Kelly walked to the stair case and called upstairs, "Tara, Jacob come down, there is something here you will want to see." It was four o'clock on Monday afternoon and the kids had just come in from school. They had changed out of school clothes when they first got home and were both ready for their normal 1500 calorie snack which would hold them until suppertime. Tara arrived first clattering down the steps in a shambling, loose jointed descent that differed from her falling down the stairs only in that she remained upright. Tara jumped the last three steps into the living room with a "What's happening, Mom?" Jacob came down the stairs more decorously and was surprised to see his Father standing at the front windows with his Mother. "Hi Dad, what brings you home so early?" Tom waved his kids over to the window and said, "Come look." They reached their parents side just in time to see a white pickup with a long white fifth wheel horse trailer pull off the County road and start up the drive towards the barn. Tara looked at the truck and back at her parents, "Who is that?" "What are they hauling?" "Are they looking for us?" Tom spoke up, "Maybe we should go down to the barn and see." Tara was well in advance of everybody else and reached the truck just as it rolled to a stop and a young man in blue jeans, a white dress shirt and a black Stetson got out from the driver's seat. A similarly dressed young woman in the passenger seat looked up from a clipboard and got out as Tara approached. The young man came around the front of the truck and said, "Hello, we are looking for Longtree Farm." The rest of the family arrived and Tom said, "This is Longtree Farm are you looking for anyone in particular?" The young woman said, "We are Stella and Tom Taylor and we have deliveries for Tara and Jacob Kelly." Tara was straining to see into the small windows of the horse trailer but turned toward her to say, "I am Tara Kelly and this is my brother Jacob. Mom, Daddy, do you know about this?" Stella handed Tara an envelope and said, "Maybe this will explain." Tara opened the envelope and took out a note and started to read to herself until Liz said, "Read it out loud Honey."

Oak Creek Ranch
1901 Ranch Road 91
Maryneal, Texas

"Dear Kelly Family,

All of us at Oak Creek Ranch have been blessed with unexpected good fortune and we want to share with some of our favorite people."

Your friends,

Mac, Bart and Tommie Rae, Emiliano and Maria

Tara handed her Mother the note and raced to the back of the trailer where Tom was opening the rear door; she was so excited that she couldn't form a complete sentence but was bouncing up and down and making squealing noises until a horse inside the trailer whickered and Tara shouted, "La Mosca, Oh it is, it is you." Tom lowered the walk ramp and Liz had to grab and pull Tara back saying, "Wait just a second Honey, give him a chance to get them out." Tom came out of the trailer leading La Mosca and Picaro and close behind, Stella came out leading Mirlo. La Mosca lowered her head so that Tara could wrap her arms around it and Tara stood hugging and petting her with tears running down her face until Picaro shouldered forward and stuck his nose between Tara and his Mother demanding his share of the attention. Jacob led Mirlo off to the side and stood quietly rubbing his hands over the silky face and neck of his horse. He was not blubbering like his silly little sister but he did turn his head away from the group when the wind made his eyes water. Tom recovered his manners first and asked if the Taylors would stay and eat with them. Stella said, "Thank you very much but we have another horse to deliver about fifty miles from here so we had best be going." Tom began to reach for his bill-fold but Tom put up his hand and said, "Mac said you would try to pay us but it is not necessary, we have been well paid." Liz and Stella stood off to one side talking like the two conspirators they were; it had taken several phone calls to time the delivery to when the kids were home and it was still daylight. Tom and Stella turned back to their truck as first Tara and then Jacob led their horses over to thank them both.

Sweetwater Reporter
Sunday Edition
Local Events

Tommy and Joann Wolf of The Wolf Ranch in Runnels County are pleased to announce the marriage of their daughter, Tommie Rae Wolf to Mr. Bart Ryan. The couple was married last Friday night by the Reverend Mr. Harold Peterson in a private ceremony at the Wolf Ranch. The bride was given in marriage by her Father,

Tommy Wolf and attended by maid of honor Miss Jill Carter. The groom was attended by his best man, Mr. Mac Connley. The bride is a graduate of Texas Christian University and is very active in the family tradition of horse training; her equine pupils appear regularly in movies and commercials as well as in competition arenas all over the West. She is also a partner in Oak Creek Partners LLC, which has extensive ranching interests in the area. The groom is also a partner in Oak Creek Partners LLC; he is a native of New York City with roots in west Texas.

The couple plans a combined wedding and business trip to Mexico after which they will make their home on Oak Creek Ranch.

CHAPTER 49

Bart stretched his neck, rolled his shoulders and scooted his rump forward and back trying to find a softer spot on the fallen block of rim rock where he was sitting and getting progressively stiffer in the predawn chill. He was careful not to make any quick movements even though he was screened by some low brush and it was still several minutes away from being light enough to see into the valley below him; he had been in place for ten minutes or so and the daytime world was just now beginning to awaken. The nocturnal animals were calling it a night and seeking out their daytime resting spots; he glimpsed its' silhouette flying against the lighter eastern sky and felt rather than heard it as an owl passed by his head on silent wings headed for the big cottonwoods farther down the valley. Mac called this the best part of the day and Bart was in total agreement. When he lived in the city he had always dreaded getting up in the morning but here on the ranch, morning found him up and ready to go; impatient for the sun to come up even when he and Tommie Rae had been out late the night before. This morning, Bart was playing a role that was still new to him, this morning he was a hunter. Born and raised in New York City he had never been exposed to hunting; his first experience with firearms came when he joined the army. Smart and anxious to learn, Bart paid close attention to the instructors and found that marksmanship came easy to him; he qualified with everything he trained with and shot expert with the M16 and the

Berretta 92 pistol. After he and Tommie Rae married, her father, Tommy Wolf, had taken it on himself to teach Bart to hunt. Tommy stressed the fun of hunting but Bart was pretty sure that his main purpose was to make sure that Bart could handle guns well enough to take care of his little girl if push ever came to shove. Tommy started him on shotguns and after a few sessions with hand thrown clay pigeons had taken him quail hunting. Bart had been feeling pretty good about his performance on the clay pigeons but quickly learned that getting a bead on one quail out of an exploding covey of fifteen was a different deal entirely. They had hunted quail three times now and dove twice; when he came in from his first dove hunt with two doves out of fourteen shots, he told Tommie Rae that she had best hope that he never had to hunt for their supper. He started carrying a 22 caliber rifle in his truck and practicing on the jackrabbits that were in one of their population explosion stages; it was no fair shooting sitting rabbits and he burned a lot of ammunition before getting the hang of leading the running rabbits.

This morning was not recreation or education; this morning he was out to stop a killer. After they formed Oak Creek Partners LLP with the proceeds of their beyond miraculous gold find, Emiliano expressed two wishes: to open a leather working factory in Mexico where his cousins could use their talents to earn a decent living and to have a flock of hair sheep like the pelo de buey or hair of the ox sheep he had herded as a boy. Emiliano was now in Mexico tending some business for the factory; he had felt that he must go even though something had started killing their sheep. They bought two different groups of ewes but they didn't get guard dogs with either bunch and so far had not found grown dogs for sale that were bonded to sheep. Bart promised that he would do his best to catch the culprit; his first reaction was to call the government trapper and get him to come but Emiliano refused. "Bart, there is only one coyote that is killing and I can tell by its tracks that it is crippled. If we can kill it, the killing will stop. If the trapper comes and kills many coyotes with snares and traps, he may or may not catch the killer but he will destroy the territorial balance that the local coyote clans have established and we will have a constant stream of young cast out coyotes coming and going; they will all be hungry and apt to become sheep killers. If the coyotes you have are not killing, they are a sheep man's best friends since they will not allow strange coyotes to enter their territory." Bart was somewhat dubious about Emilianos' explanation but promised to spend as much time with the sheep as he could and to not kill any coyote that was not crippled unless he caught it in the act. When they bought the sheep, most of them were bred to lamb in the wintertime and Emiliano said at the time that this would be a problem since none of the wild animals had their young in the winter and the new baby lambs would be irresistible to predators of all kinds. In the future, Emiliano planned to breed the ewes so that they would lamb in the mid to late spring when there was green grass but also when there were lots of baby rabbits, rats and deer to take the predator pressure off of the lambs. Bart was constantly amazed at how much a city boy had to learn about the ranching business; he had excellent tutors in his wife and his partners but Bart was impatient at being ignorant. He was reading <u>Holistic Management</u> by Savory and Butterfield and had finished <u>How to Not go Broke Ranching</u> by Walt Davis. He promised himself that he was going to do a lot more reading; the Texas extension service had some great material for ranchers. He also wanted to go to some of the grazing management schools and stockmanship schools that were beginning to be held in various parts of the country.

The sheep were still bedded down where he had left them last night, on a small knoll in the valley below him; he could hear them just beginning to stir with lambs calling to mama and vice versa. The coughs, sneezes and snorts of the awakening sheep sounded a lot like a barracks full of soldiers waking up. Bart could tell the difference in the voice of a grown sheep and the bleat of a new lamb but could not begin to recognize individuals. Emiliano assured him that every lamb knew its' mothers' voice and every ewe knew her lambs' voice as well as any human mother knew the voice of her child. Bart had been coming to the sheep first thing in the morning and last thing at night for several days now but had not seen a coyote of any description much less the crippled killer. As he waited for daylight, Bart found himself caressing the glossy stock and finely cut checkering of the rifle he held in his lap; it was without a doubt the most beautiful thing he had ever owned. He had never been poor but neither had he ever had access to anything like the kind of money that Tommie Rae and he now had as the result of their place in Oak Creek Partners. Most of the gold coins they had found were still to be sold by the numismatists they hired in New York City but even so, they had money at their disposal beyond any of their wildest dreams. So far, with the exception of new clothes for all of the men that Tommie Rae had insisted on, they had spent money only on things that should make money: land and livestock mainly. Bart felt a little guilty that he owned something as expensive as the rifle that he was holding; he had gone into Ike Gossetts' gun shop in Sweetwater to buy 22 shells and saw this rifle lying on Ikes' workbench. Ike built the rifle for himself; it was a 22-250 built on a pre-World War II 98 Mauser action with a custom medium weight barrel made by Liji. Ike reconfigured the bolt handle to a more graceful shape, hand honed the action until it worked as smoothly as silk, polished all of the exterior metal parts to perfection and skillfully blued them to a deep blue almost black sheen and then stocked the rifle with beautifully figured walnut. He glass bedded the action into the stock to insure a perfect fit and hand cut checkered designs into the pistol grip and forearm. Bart admired the rifle and Ike picked it up and handed it to him; it was fitted with a Redfield 2X to 9 X variable powers scope and balanced superbly when Bart raised it to firing position. As he was looking at the rifle, Ike opened a drawer and took out a stack of paper targets that he had shot with the rifle. There were six targets each one representing a string of five shots fired from a bench rest at 100 yards; as Ike demonstrated with a coin from his pocket; a penny would cover the entire pattern on all but one target, which had a small portion of one hole peeking out from behind the penny. Bart knew that a minute of angle was one inch at 100 yards and a minute of angle accuracy was considered to be very good; this rifle had five of six targets measuring .375 inches from center of hole to center of hole at the widest point. Bart handed the rifle back to Ike and said, "You had best take this back before I slobber on it. That is a beautiful piece of work, Ike." Ike nodded his thanks and said, "I have never made a better one; it is the only thing in this shop that is not for sale."

That night, Bart told Tommie Rae about the rifle and said that he was thinking about getting Ike to build him one like it.

Things were busy on the ranch, they were still working hard to get their newly purchased 9R ranch fenced and watered for high stock density grazing. The 9R was well equipped when they bought it but they were changing their method of grazing to one similar to the way the bison herds had grazed this land for eons. When nature was in charge, the grazing animals stayed close to each other for protection from wolves; with a lot of animals on a small area, the herds had to keep moving so that all could receive adequate feed. The high stock density program they were developing mimicked this behavior; a large number of animals on a small area for a short period of time followed by a period of rest from grazing. The partners traveled over several states talking to ranchers that had made the changes before starting their project and the more they saw, the more convinced they became that high stock density grazing with good time control was the way they should manage. Ranchers were getting good results with both animals and range conditions while increasing profitability. They were convinced but the required fencing and water development was taking time plus all four partners had spent time in Mexico getting the rawhide and leather factory started in Tenamaxtlan in the state of Jalisco. The other partners had intended the factory to be Emilianos' alone but he had insisted that it be kept in the partnership. Emiliano had proven to be a good businessman in spite of his lack of formal education but he still doubted his own abilities in some areas and his faith in Mac, Tommie Rae and Bart was absolute. Bart had more or less forgotten about the rifle until he came in from work one evening to find it lying on his desk. Tommie Rae would not tell him how she talked Ike into selling it or what she paid for it; she just smiled and said, "Never mind, you wanted it and I wanted you to have it." She had thought to buy ammunition as well and Bart had started carrying the rifle with him anytime he was on the ranch. He had shot the rifle at various ranges from fifty yards out to five hundred yards and was still amazed at what it could do; Ike had sighted it to hit dead on at 200 yards which meant that from 100 yards to 300 yards, he could hold on the center of a coffee saucer size target and be pretty sure of a hit even if he miss-judged the distance by a little.

It was beginning to get light enough to see movement so Bart stopped his wool gathering and started scanning the slope above the sheep that was slowly coming into view as the sun rose behind his back. He saw movement of some kind four or five hundred yards away and carefully raised his rifle to check it through the scope. What he had seen was the flick of a deer's tail and he watched as a doe and two yearlings came up from the valley floor and bedded down in a patch of shinnery oak about half way up the slope. Three hundred yards closer to him, Bart saw a covey of Bobwhite quail still in their overnight sleeping circle under an agarita bush and watched as they began to stir. The birds stretched exactly like he did when he got out of bed in the morning, extending first one arm or rather wing and then the other before stretching their necks out as far as possible and shaking to loosen out the kinks; some began a desultory pecking about the area while others found a spot of bare ground and began dust bathing. Tommy Wolf told him that the quail always flew when they were coming to or leaving their night time roost so that skunks, foxes and other predators couldn't track them by their scent trail and fall on them at night. These didn't seem to be in any hurry to leave; maybe they were waiting for the sun, what Emiliano called "la estufa de los pobres" (the stove of the poor) to get a little higher and warm things up.

The valley was getting light now so Bart shifted his attention to the sheep and to the area closer around them. The sheep had not yet started drifting off the bed ground but most of the ewes with lambs were up and their lambs were chowing down with a great deal of tail wringing and nose butting of their poor mothers' udders. Between

Bart and the sheep there was a patch of knee high weeds of some sort (Bart still couldn't name all of the local plants in spite of the efforts of Mac and Tommie Rae) and Bart caught a glimpse of movement at the edge of the weeds. He eased his rifle up to look through the scope and sure enough, there was coyote. The animal was creeping toward the sheep and even at this distance and with the coyotes' slow progress, it was apparent that the coyote was crippled in its' left front leg. Bart felt a surge of adrenaline and was surprised to see a decided tremor in his arms and that the barrel of his rifle was making random movements seemingly with no input from him. He lowered the rifle and wrapped his left arm in the sling just as his army instructors had taught him; it wouldn't do for him to miss the coyote because of buck fever. Bart raised the rifle again, pleased to see that the tremor was gone, and searched for the coyote. He located it just as it stepped clear of the weed patch; Bart took a deep breath and let half of it out as he had been taught and with the crosshairs fixed on the coyotes shoulder started to squeeze the trigger. Before his shot when off, something came flying out of nowhere to hit the coyote in the side of the head; blood flew and the coyote went down on its' side to kick several times and lie still. Bart looked to his left and saw a man – or maybe a boy – step into the clearing; he was watching the coyote intently and carried a leather sling shot with an egg sized rock pouched and ready. Here sat Bart with two thousand dollars worth of rifle in his hands and a skinny little kid with a rock in a sling shot beat him to the sheep killer; he was not looking forward to the comments that were sure to come from Mac. As Bart watched, a young woman stepped out from the brush and drawing close to the young man, clapped her hands and said loud enough for Bart to hear, "Bravo, Miguel, Bravo". The sheep were all watching the action and a few ewes were stamping their front feet in warning that nothing had better threaten their babies but the flock showed no signs of wanting to run away. The young couple walked closer to the dead coyote and Bart took the opportunity to come down from his perch and approach them. He had his rifle slung from his right shoulder in what he hoped was a non threatening manner but when the boy heard him approach, he stepped forward to put himself between Bart and the girl, held his sling ready and looked extremely tense. Bart held both his hands up palm out and said in his terrible Spanish, "Gracis Miguel, gracis para usted mata el coyote" hoping that Miguel could understand that he was thanking him for killing the coyote. The tension bled away from Miguel and he said, "You are welcome Senor, I once had sheep of my own and I could not stand by and watch the coyote kill when I could prevent it". Bart, thankful that Miguel spoke English better than he spoke Spanish, held out his hand and said, "I am Bart Ryan and I am glad that you came along when you did and for your skill with the sling." Miguel took his hand and said, "Con mucho gusto Senor Ryan, I am Miguel Olivera and this is my sister Glorietta." Bart took off his hat and said, "I am pleased to meet you Senorita Olivera." Glorietta ducked her head and said, "I am pleased to meet you Senor Ryan." Both of the young people were tired and as Mac would say, "Looked gaunt as a gutted snowbird." Bart shifted his attention back to Miguel and said, "Do you like working with sheep?" "Very much Senor, it is what I did from the time I was very small up until last year." "Maybe you would like to take care of this flock? I promised my partner I would look after them while he is in Mexico and if the truth be known, I don't know the first thing about sheep." "I would like that very much Senor; I need work and sheep are what I know best." "Good, let's go to my house and get my wife to feed us and we can talk about it over breakfast. Let me get something from my truck to drag the coyote with so his fleas don't get all over us. If I don't have the carcass, my partner Emiliano will not believe that we got the killer." "I can do it with this Senor" and fashioned a noose from his sling around the coyotes' neck. Glorietta ran back to the edge of the brush and came back with two small bundles and Bart led the way back to his truck.

Brother and sister were very quiet on the way back to headquarters and Bart noticed that they looked both ways intently when he came out on the highway and seemed to shrink into the truck seat when he met a truck coming from the other direction. Bart was pleased to see that Tommie Rae was still at home; he knew that she planned to go into town today. He led the Olivera's in through the kitchen door and found his wife frying bacon; they often left early to do chores after just a cup of coffee and came back in later to eat breakfast. Bart stepped into the kitchen and said, "Tommie Rae, I have brought guests for breakfast. This is Miguel Olivera and his sister Glorietta; Miguel killed the sheep killing coyote before I could and he is going to be helping with the sheep. Miguel, Glorietta, this is my wife Tommie Rae." Tommie Rae wiped her hands on her apron and smiling said, "I am pleased to meet you, please come in. You can get washed up in the bathroom, first door on the left and then we will eat. Bart would you put out fresh towels for our guests?" Bart washed up himself, put out clean towels and came back to find Tommie Rae and Glorietta having a spirited conservation in Spanish; he had spent nearly an hour with the couple and Tommie Rae less than five minutes but Bart was sure that Tommie Rae knew a lot more about the Olivera's at this point than he did. Glorietta excused herself to wash up and Bart poured himself a cup of coffee and joined Miguel and his coffee at the kitchen table. "Bart they are very tired, they have been walking more than twenty four hours; after we eat, why don't you take them down to the bunk house, they can rest and we will talk this evening." Glorietta came back with face scrubbed and hair combed and asked, "What can I do to help Senora?" Tommie Rae pointed to the cabinet and said, "You can set two more places at the table if you wish." Bart noticed that Glorietta had changed back to English now that he was in the room and mentally gave her a gold star for politeness. Tommie Rae took in the starved look of the young couple and started making pancakes to go with the bacon and eggs that she had under way. Tommie Rae was not quite as good a cook as Emiliano – though torture could not make Bart admit it – but she did make a mean breakfast and she piled the young couple's plates high. Bart noticed that both crossed themselves in silent grace before starting to eat. They were polite and had good table manners but their food disappeared at an amazing rate and both accepted second helpings after being urged to do so by Tommie Rae. When everyone finished eating, Tommie Rae refused Glorietta's offer to help clean up and Bart took Miguel and Glorietta down to the bunkhouse. No one was using the comfortable little house where Bart, Mac and Emiliano had lived when Bart first came to Oak Creek Ranch. Emiliano had moved into the home of his new wife Maria while a house was being built for them on the 9R, Mac had moved into the big house on the 9R where Rosita Morales, the wife of Evidencio who worked as a ranch hand, cooked for him and generally spoiled him. Bart, of course lived with Tommie Rae in the Oak Creek Ranch house so the bunk house was empty. Bart opened the door and motioned for Miguel and Glorietta to go in, "No one else will be here so you all make yourselves at home. There is bedding in the closet right there in the hall, just take the bunks you want and I will be back a little before sundown. If you get hungry, there is food in the refrigerator and the pantry and wood for the stove."

Chapter 50

Emiliano managed to keep a pleasant expression on his face but it was getting harder with every passing minute as the officious little clerk shuffled papers, made a big show of reading various clauses while periodically sighing dramatically as if he were being worked to exhaustion. Emiliano understood the problem with getting the contracts filed; the clerk felt that because of his position and expertise he was entitled to "un mordito", a little bite, and Emiliano was dammed if he was going to bribe the little bastard to do the job he was being paid to do. Emiliano had been in Guadalajara for six days meeting with construction people, lawyers, bankers and politicians, he was tired and right now, he wanted nothing more than to be home with his new wife, Maria. Finally, Emiliano said, "Senor, I would not presume to rush you but I am scheduled to have lunch with the Governor of Jalisco and the Major of Guadalajara in fifteen minutes and I would not like to have to explain to these gentlemen why I was late for my appointment." The clerk, who from his rough hands, manner and speech had categorized Emiliano as a peon in borrowed finery just in from the hills, took a second look and from his level gaze and serious demeanor decided that Emiliano really was going to lunch with the Governor and that he had made a potentially serious mistake in attempting to use his position to extract a little extra from an important man. "Certainly Senor, all is in order here and I will personally see that all is properly filed and the receipts are mailed to the address you have given me." Emiliano said, "Gracis." and walked away; he really was going to lunch with the Governor and Mayor, it was not every day that someone wanted to start a factory and employ fifteen or twenty people in one of the most economically depressed areas of their state and the politicians were grateful. They were particularly impressed that the company had a profit sharing plan for their employees and that all of the employees, even management, would be Mexican; at the present time, the Oak Creek Partners were popular people in this part of Mexico. The partners had been very pleased how smoothly things had gone; their friend, Luke Overholt, and his people at Synergy Investments LLP had done an excellent job of educating them on what needed to be done to set up a business in Mexico and how to go about it in the most efficient manner. The factory was up and running with a young business college graduate as business manager and one of Emilianos' cousins as shop foreman and lead craftsman. They hired eight skilled braiders and leather craftsmen and were in the process of training ten more; the first rawhide items, reatas, quirts and headstalls had been shown around the U. S. rodeo circuits by Jill Carter, one of Tommie Raes' friends and rodeo buddies and they had been very well received. Emiliano and his cousin Jorge were already planning to expand into tanned leather items like headstalls and breast bands. One of Emilianos' female cousins, a weaver, approached them to produce wool and mohair items like saddle blankets and girths and Jill Carter came to them with designs for ladies purses and for tooled leather belts, hat bands and spur leathers. The partners had formed a company and hired Jill, who had a degree in marketing, to run it to market the items to venders, retail stores and on the internet; Emilianos idea of a modest little shop where his cousins could make a living was taking on a life of its own. In the morning, Emiliano would get on an airplane and fly home; he was still a Mexican but home is where your heart is and Emilianos heart was back on Oak Creek with his wife and his friends.

CHAPTER 51

Bart got home sooner than he expected and found Glorietta helping Tommie Rae in the house and Miguel busy mucking out horse stalls. "Ho Miguel, I thought you two would still be asleep." "We rested Senor, but it is time that we began to earn our keep." Bart pointed to the horses standing in the lot and said, "Do you ride Miguel?" "Si Senor, since I was this tall" holding his hand about two feet off the ground. "We will find you a saddle that fits and a horse but right now let's go see how the ladies are getting along." They went in the back door into the kitchen where Glorietta was cooking something that smelled great and Bart poured them each a cup of coffee and said, "Sit a minute while I check with Tommie Rae." Bart found his wife on the computer in the room they had set up as an office and bent over to kiss the top of her head. "Hi Babe, have you had time to decide what you think of our two strays? Tommie Rae turned her face up to get a proper kiss and said, "I like them, I never did get to town but I talked to Glorietta for quite a while; they have had a really hard time, you need to hear their story, but she didn't whine about their troubles, just said that they would have to work hard to get back on their feet." "Would you like to have Glorietta to help in the house?" "I really would, I am going to be busy as a hunting dog with all the deals we have going and she has worked as a cook in good restaurants in Mexico. Some of the dishes she described made my mouth water." "What do you think? We pay Miguel the same that the boys on the 9R are getting and Glorietta the same as Rosita?" "I think that that would be fine but you need to come hear their story before we make a decision."They went back into the kitchen to find that Mac had come in and was talking to Miguel and Glorietta. Tommie Rae went over to kiss Mac on the cheek and said, "Mac I'm glad you got here in time to hear this. Glorietta, come sit down and tell Bart and Mac what you told me about los coyotes?" Glorietta sat down on the edge of a chair and said, "Senors y Senora, It may be that you would rather that Miguel and I leave as it is possible that we put you in danger by being here. Miguel and I lost our home and little rancho in Mexico when we could not repay a mortgage that our Father had taken out before he died. There was no work and we had no way to support ourselves. We took what money we had and paid it to a smuggler, a coyote, to get us into the United States; we were supposed to be taken to Arkansas where we would have jobs in a chicken processing plant. Fifteen of us, four young men and eleven young women crossed the Rio Grande at night north of Cuidad Acuna on rubber rafts and were met by men in two vans; they drove us to an abandoned house somewhere south of here. We got there about an hour before dawn and they told us that we would continue the journey as soon as it was dark again. We lay down to sleep on the floor but I got up to relieve myself and as I was coming back to Miguel, over heard the coyotes gloating about how much money they would get from, pardon my language, the whore master in Dallas for the eleven young women. I went back to Miguel, put my hand over his mouth and when he awoke, pulled him outside; when we were well away from the house, I told him what I had heard and we set off walking. Twice during the next day, we saw the coyotes looking for us but we stayed off the roads and they did not see us.

When I was listening to them at the window of the abandoned house, I heard them laugh about how it was too bad that there was not somewhere that they could sell the men instead of just killing them after extracting all their families could pay for their freedom. These are very bad people and they are looking for us; if you want us to leave, we will understand." It was very quiet for a moment and then Mac said, "Senorita, they may be bad people but I guaran damn tee you that they are not bullet proof and if they come hunting trouble around here, we will prove it. We need help and if you and Miguel want to sign on, you are welcome."

After supper, Maria called Tommie Rae to report that Emiliano would arrive on the 2:00pm Southwest flight into Abilene from Guadalajara and to ask if Tommie Rae would go with her to pick him up; for someone who had spent most of his life on a small farm in rural Mexico, Emiliano was turning into quite the accomplished traveler. Tommie Rae suggested that Maria come to Oak Creek about noon and they would go to pick up Emiliano and all come back to Oak Creek for supper and to hear about Emilianos' trip.

CHAPTER 52

Joey Heller drew hard on his cigarette and used the glow of the burning tobacco to look at his watch for the fourth time in thirty minutes. He didn't like dealing with Mexicans in general and he damn sure didn't like dealing with Domingo Sanchez and his crazy body guard Jorge. Heller was disgusted with himself for popping off to Ralph Tucker and saying that he didn't need any help and would make this run by himself since his brother Jimmy was too sick to go. He should have brought at least one other man to watch his back while he was doing business with Sanchez; these bastards killed people for any reason or for no reason. They killed people even when they knew it would bring all kinds of heat down on them. Heller knew that Sanchez was heavy into using his own products; the word was that he had been run out of the Zetas for being so doped up that he couldn't tend to business. Heller had $200,000 of Ralph Tuckers' money to pay for a load of meth that Sanchez was bringing from the lab he ran south of Acuna. Heller had traded money for dope with Sanchez twice before but it would not surprise him at all if the crazy bastard decided to just blow him away and keep the money and the dope. Heller promised himself that if he ever met with Sanchez again it would be on his own turf and with plenty of backup. Heller also was uncomfortable being this close to the 9R ranch; he didn't want to run into anyone who knew Jimmy when he was working, or rather hiding out, on the 9R. Joey and Jimmy were identical twins and not even their own mother had been able to tell them apart even on the rare occasions that she wasn't drunk or stoned out of her mind. Their mother had an ever changing but steady stream of boyfriends – most of whom were as dysfunctional as her; the attitude of these men toward the brothers ranged from indifferent to sadistically hostile and by the time they were five or six, they knew that the only people they could count on for help of any kind were each other. Joey was worried about his brother; Jimmy came back from his vacation on the 9R beat all to hell and had not been himself ever since. He would not tell Joey what had happened, just that, "He had some killing to do." He spent three weeks with his broken jaws wired shut and then had to have a bunch of dental work done; with the new false teeth and broken nose, for the first time, people could tell them apart. Joey was worried that his brother would do something stupid. They had both been in trouble with the law since they were twelve years old but after a short jolt in reform school, neither had ever been convicted of anything. They stayed out of jail by being smart and thinking through their actions; Joey was afraid that Jimmy would let his hatred for whoever clobbered him over ride his good sense.

Sanchez had insisted on meeting some place on a country road with little traffic and no more than forty miles north of San Angelo. This intersection of two ranch roads north of the 9R fit that description and was familiar to both of them. He was also bothered that Sanchez had insisted that he bring a pickup with a camper body; they had one they used to haul grass but he wasn't supposed to be getting anything but meth on this trip. It was almost four o'clock, Sanchez was over an hour late and Heller was tempted to haul ass back to Ft. Worth and tell Tucker that the doper didn't show. He threw his cigarette out of the window and was about to start the truck and leave when he saw lights coming from the west.

The vehicle stopped a couple of hundred yards away just short of the intersection of the road he was on with one that ran north and south. The vehicle sat there with its' lights on for a minute then turned them off for a count of three back on for a count of three then off for a count of two and back on. Heller repeated the signal with his own lights and the vehicle started up and came toward him. Heller could see that it was a white cargo van with Texas tags. Heller sat in the truck cab with his hand on the butt of the pistol in his lap as the van pulled up and stopped alongside. Sanchez looked over from the drivers' seat of the van and said, "Hello Heller, do you have the money?" "I have the money. Do you have the dope?" "Oh Heller would I come all this way without bringing you Tuckers merchandise? I have the meth plus a little more as appreciation for a little favor you are going to do for me." Heller could see Jorge grinning at him from the passenger seat of the van. "What sort of favor?" "Nothing danger-ous, I just need you to give Jorge and the six ladies here in my van a ride into Dallas. We had a little trouble shortly after we got across the border; this van is hot, I need to ditch it and I can't be prowling around looking for another ride with six putas on my back. You take Jorge and the girls to Dallas; I will swap vehicles and come to pick up Jorge. No sweat, no strain and you get an extra five percent on your order of meth." Sanchez pulled the van forward until the rear ends of the two trucks were almost even and Jorge had the camper hull open before Heller could get out of his seat. "Wait a minute," Heller squalled as he came around the truck to find Jorge leveling a forty five at his belly. Heller slid to a stop and put up his hands just as Sanchez opened the rear door of the cargo van and said, "Come out" in Spanish to someone inside the van. A young woman carrying a backpack stepped out gingerly and was quickly followed out by five more. Sanchez told them to get into the camper but the first girl was too short to be able to jump up on the tailgate of the truck. Sanchez motioned for Jorge to help them; the moment he stuck his pistol in his belt and reached for the first girl, two of the other girls darted around the van and ran into the darkness. "Alto putas" screamed Sanchez as he reached through the window of the white van to turn on its' headlights. The two girls were running down the center of the gravel road and were no more than twenty-five or thirty yards away when Jorge's' forty five barked five or six times. The girl in the lead fell flat on her face like a rag doll and didn't move but the second girl struggled to continue on while dragging her left leg. Sanchez said, "Finish it" and waved Jorge toward the staggering girl. Jorge ran up behind and caught the girl by her long hair, pulled her head back and slashed her throat with the long knife that had appeared in his hand. Heller was already moving toward the cab of his truck and when the blood gushed blackly in the harsh light of the headlights; he jumped in the truck, started the engine and sprayed gravel as he accelerated as rapidly as possible. Sanchez screamed at him and pulled an AK-47 rifle from the van to loose a stream of automatic fire at the retreating truck. Sparks flew like fireworks as bullets struck the truck and glass fell in showers from its' shattered windows but the engine continued to roar strongly as the truck gained speed and pulled rapidly away. Suddenly the noise of the engine dropped to just a mutter and the truck coasted to a stop about two hundred yards from the van. As the truck stopped in the center of the road, gasoline flashed into flames beneath it and by this light they could see Heller slumped over the steering wheel.

CHAPTER 53

art and Tommie Rae were drinking coffee in the kitchen with all the windows open and enjoying the predawn coolness when the phone rang; Bart got up to answer it. Tommie Rae heard him say, "Hello" and nothing else for several minutes when he said, "I will be there in about fifteen or twenty minutes." "What is it Bart?" "That was Tom Gillette; there has been a shooting about ten miles east and he wants me to see if I can identify a body they think is James Heller. I shouldn't be too long." Bart picked up his hat, bent to kiss his wife and went out the back door to the driveway where his truck was parked. Since the drought had broken this summer, the weather had been unusually cool; Bart shivered slightly in the morning breeze and briefly considered going back for a jacket.

Bart and Mac had met Tom Gillette last year when the Texas Ranger spoke about preventing livestock theft at a Texas and Southwestern Cattle Raisers Association meeting in San Angelo. Both Mac and Bart were impressed with Gillette and when Bart learned Gillette was an avid quail hunter, he invited him to hunt with him on the 9R. Over the fall and winter the two had become close friends. When Tom asked Bart to come to the shooting scene, he suggested that Bart not bring Tommie Rae as "It is pretty bad." Bart could see revolving emergency lights on several vehicles when he topped the hill two miles from the intersection and he was flagged to a stop by a deputy sheriff as he approached the scene. The deputy bent to speak to him through the open window, "Sir, you will have to wait here until they have cleared the road." I am Bart Ryan, Deputy; Tom Gillette called me to try to identify a body." "Sure thing Mr. Ryan, just stay to the right edge of the road and stop when you get to the crime scene tape. Ranger Gillette is at the scene." Bart slowly drove the hundred yards or so to where he could see Tom Gillette talking to another sheriff's deputy and a man dressed in a business suit. Gillette looked up and waved Bart forward as he stepped out of his truck. "Bart, thank you for coming; this is Deputy Joe Black of the Nolan Country Sheriff's Department and Robert Hunt of the Border Patrol. Bart Ryan is a local rancher and I called him because I knew that he had met James Heller and might help us identify our male body." Bart shook hands with both men and followed Gillette as he walked toward an ambulance parked on the side of the road. "It is not a pretty sight, he was burned after being shot but his face escaped major damage. He was carrying papers identifying him as Henry Turner but Deputy Black stopped Heller about a year ago for running a stop sign and thinks that this may be him." Gillette opened the back door of the ambulance and shined his flashlight on the exposed face of a body encased in a body bag. The stench of burned flesh and hair was over powering but Bart stepped closer and after a long look said, "That's James Heller but he has had some dental work done since I last saw him." A second zipped up body bag lay next to Heller's' body and after moving back from the ambulance Bart said, "What happened here?" "We are still trying to put it all together but we have two dead; Heller and a Mexican national named Anita Lopez who was shot in the leg and then had her throat cut." Another Mexican, Angelina Cortez was shot and left for dead but the bullet only grazed her skull and after she came around she was able to tell us her name and the name of the other girl. She said that two men who she knew as Jorge and Sanchez brought six women here and met a man in a pickup. She and the Lopez woman tried to run away and that is the last thing she remembers until she awakened about an hour ago. She is in the Hospital at Sweetwater and I will follow up with her later. It is a good bet that Sanchez is Domingo Sanchez, a known smuggler of people and drugs that we have been trying to catch up with for quite a while. Ms. Cortez was able to tell us that Sanchez was driving a white enclosed van and we have alerts out to all law enforcement agencies for a hundred miles in all directions. They machine gunned Heller's truck and shot the women with a 45 ACP; I hope some lone cop somewhere doesn't try to play hero and take them down by himself. We are waiting for someone from the District Attorneys' office to show so we can close down the crime scene but there is not a lot we can do right now. We have roadblocks up on all of the roads leading away from here; we got a real break in that Don Phillips, the local game warden, was watching for people spot lighting deer from the hill south of us and saw, from a distance, the whole thing go down. He called it in and we had roadblocks up within twenty minutes of the first shots being fired." "Tom, which way did the van go when it left?" "Don said they circled the burning truck, stopped at it just a moment and left going back west the way they came; we have a roadblock where this road crosses the Maryneal road." "Tom, the north gate into Oak Creek is on that road and Tommie Rae is at home alone; I am going back right now." As Bart sprinted toward his truck, he heard Tom shout, "I'll be right behind you."

Bart pulled out backwards from the side of the road in a gravel throwing," bootleggers' turn" and was accelerating rapidly toward home before Tom Gillette reached his SUV. Bart grabbed up the handset of his newly installed shortwave radio and called, "9R Ranch base one this is mobile one, come in." "Come in base one." Bart was mouthing a silent prayer when the radio crackled alive with Tommie Raes' voice, "This is 9R base one, go ahead Bart." Bart made a real effort to hold his voice calm and level, "Tommie, it is probably nothing but we have some thugs running loose. I want you to get Glorietta and Miguel in the house with you and lock all the doors. Get your twenty gauge out and load it with heavy shot; I am on the way and will be there as quick as I can." Tommie Rae knew from the tone of his voice that Bart was seriously concerned so she didn't ask questions she just said, "I will go right now. Be careful!" She hung up the handset and went to the gun closet in the office for her Browning twenty gauge and a box of number four shot. She smiled when she took out the trim little semi automatic and saw the identical except larger twelve gauge next to it; she had given the twelve gauge to Bart for Christmas and was more than a little surprised when his gift to her was the twenty gauge. She loaded the shotgun and started out to the bunkhouse; it was starting to get light and Miguel came to the door immediately when she called out from the porch. He was obviously surprised to see her carrying the shotgun and said, "Senora, what is the matter?" "Miguel, get Glorietta and your rifle and come quickly to the house; Bart called and there some bad men in the area." Miguel ducked back inside and reappeared almost immediately with Glorietta and the Henry twenty-two magnum rifle that Bart had bought him to use guarding the sheep. Tommie Rae ran to her pickup and pulled the keys out of it and locked the doors; normally they didn't lock anything on the ranch. She didn't know if they even had a key to the house; as Mac said, "Locks only keep honest folks out and they might need to get in." Once inside, Tommie Rae picked up the radio hand set, "9R Ranch base one to mobile one — come in Bart." "This is one, Tommie are you alright?" "We are fine, we are in the house with the doors locked and Miguel has his rifle so slow down before you have a wreck!" "Will do Babe; Tom is right behind me and we will be there pretty quick, keep your eyes peeled. 9R Ranch base two, this is mobile one come in base two." After a moment Bart heard Jake's voice, "This is base two Bart, we have been listening. What do you want us to do? Over"

"Jake, get Anna and everybody else together at the big house. They probably are long gone but these thugs have already killed two people. Is Mac with you? Over" "Yes, Mac got here a few minutes ago; what's going on Bart?" "James Heller was shot and killed about twelve miles east of the Oak Creek headquarters in what looks like a drug deal gone sour. Two Mexican thugs have four women in a white panel style van and they will probably try to steal another vehicle. Pull the trucks up where you can see them and be careful; I will holler if I find out anything. Over"

Bart was approaching the seldom used north gate into Oak Creek and he slowed down and stopped as he came up on the gate. It was now light enough to see and Bart's heart jumped up into his throat as he saw the gate leaning crookedly open; it was off the hinges and being held up only by the padlocked chain on the other end. There was a fresh set of tire tracks going through the gate and out of sight on the ranch road. Tom Gillette drove up behind him and Bart ran back to Tom's vehicle, "Tom, they are headed toward the headquarters, can you get us some help?" Bart heard Tom start talking into his radio but was already back in his truck and accelerating down the ranch road before Tom had time to connect to anyone. This track ran up and through a line of low hills before dropping back into a broad mesquite flat; about a mile ahead it forked with the left fork lead-ing to the headquarters and the right fork going down into the Oak Creek bottoms before turning south east to eventually come out on the highway on the east side of the ranch. It got very rough close to the creek and Bart doubted that the van would be able to manage the crossing. Every once in a while Bart caught glimpses of the tire tracks still on the road; as he came up on the fork in the road Bart found himself holding his breath. If they took the left fork, the thugs were less than three miles from Tommie Rae. Bart rolled up to the fork and said a heartfelt "Thank you Lord" when he saw the tracks on the right fork of the road. Tom rolled up behind him at that moment and Bart went back to tell him where the track the thugs were on came out and to tell him that he was going to Tommie Rae; Tom waved him to go without lowering the radio handset from his mouth.

The road was rough here and Bart had to slow down from the reckless pace he had been setting; as he rounded a curve to his right, he caught a flicker of movement to the right and as he watched a white van appeared weaving through the mesquite trees toward him. It was the thugs but Bart was between them and Tommie Rae and he damn sure intended to keep it that way; two hundred yards ahead the road crossed the deep gully of Hanson Draw at the only place a vehicle could cross for a half mile in either direction. Bart reached the crossing and pulled his truck crossways in the road com-pletely blocking the crossing. He grabbed his rifle and a box of shells from the back seat and after checking that the magazine was full and chambering a round, leaned across the hood of the truck looking back down the road. The van, with two men visible, appeared mov-ing slowly; when they saw Bart they stopped completely. They were about two hundred-fifty yards away and Bart stepped into the open so that they could see that he was armed; as he cleared the truck, a man got out of the passenger side door with a gun and turned loose a long ripping burst of automatic fire. Bart dove back behind the truck as bullets kicked up dirt on both sides of and in the road in a pattern twenty-five or thirty feet wide; two or three struck the truck. The gunman stopped to change the magazine on his weapon and Bart shot him center mass just as Sergeant Brownlee taught him; he fell but got up on his knees and aimed the gun at Bart again so Bart shot him in the head. The driver of the van jumped out and screaming curses in Spanish ran around to snatch up the machine gun. This time Bart didn't wait, as soon as he touched the gun Bart shot him in the head as well.

Bart waited a minute or so and when no one else appeared, began walking towards the van with his rifle reloaded and at the ready. Almost immediately, he saw dust coming and stepped out of the road so that Tom, who was coming up behind the van, could see him. To this point, Bart had not felt the slightest twinge of fear but with Tommie Rae now safe from the two coyotes, he decided to wait for Tom before investigating the van. He was suddenly terrified that he might be killed and taken away from Tommie by a scared little woman with a gun.

Tom stopped his truck fifty yards from the van and stepped out with a rifle in his hands, "Are you alright?" "I'm fine but two of them are dead; I don't know about in the van." Tom stayed behind the open door or his truck and shouted to Bart to get down before shouting to the van, first in English and then in Spanish for the occupants of the van to "Come out with your hands above your head." He repeated this again and then eased up on the back side of the van and jerked the rear door open, at the same time jumping out of the line of any possible gun fire. Tom looked into the van and then came around to check the two dead gunmen before motioning for Bart to come to him. As Bart walked up, Tom turned to him and red faced said, "You crazy fool, you could have been killed! Dealing with scum like this is what they pay me for; it is not your job to risk your life to stop bastards like these." Bart looked at Tom with more than a little color in his own face and said, "These bastards were going toward my wife and I was the only thing that could stop them; if you think that I was going to back out of that situation, you don't know me very well Buster!" A sheriff's car pulled up behind Toms' vehicle and Tom put a hand on Bart's shoulder and said, "Hell Bart, I'm sorry; you are absolutely right and I'm wrong. Put it down to after action nerves, please. Go to your wife and I will be along as soon as I can." Bart turned toward his truck but turned back when Tom shouted, "That wasn't bad shooting for a damn Yankee!" Bart gave him a single finger salute over his shoulder and suddenly weak kneed, climbed into his truck and headed home.

As Bart drove up to the ranch house, Tommie came out still carrying her shotgun; Miguel and Glorietta followed her out, Miguel with his Henry and Glorietta lugging the huge old ten gauge double barrel that Emiliano kept behind the kitchen door. Miguel was the first to see bullet holes; the windows of both rear doors each had two holes in them, the box of the pickup had two holes through and through and there was a bullet crease across the top of the hood. Bart reached out to Tommie Rae and took the shotgun from her (she was trying to hug him with the gun still in one hand) and crushed her to him. Tommie stepped back wiping her eyes and started looking at and running her hands over Bart, "Are hurt? Who was shooting at you? Are they still out there?" "It's OK Babe, I'm not hurt and the thugs won't be bothering us. Let's go in the house and disarm this posse and I will tell you what happened. I need to call Mac and the others and let them know the danger is over."

It was thirty minutes before Bart finished telling his story (he had almost finished when Mac drove in and he had to start over). Glorietta had made coffee and the whole group was gathered in the kitchen, Emiliano and Maria were on their way, when Tom Gillette drove up. Bart met him on the porch and from the look on his face, knew that what he feared was true. He kept his voice low and said, "The women are dead aren't they?" Tom nodded and said, "In the worst way, it is a good thing those bastards are dead, I have never abused a prisoner but I would be hard pressed to keep from killing those two in cold blood." Maria and Emiliano arrived and everyone moved into the living room where there was more room.

When everyone had found a seat, Bart said, "Tom you are the only one here who knows the whole story; would you tell the group what took place?" Tom stood and said, "At 4:30 this morning Nolan County game warden Don Phillips was watching from a high point east of here for people spot lighting deer. He saw two vehicles stop on the road close together and shortly after screams and gunshots and then automatic weapon fire and a vehicle burning; he could not see what was happening from his vantage point but after twenty minutes or so, the other vehicle turned around and left in the direction it had come from at a high rate of speed. Warden Phillips called in to the Nolan County Sheriff dispatcher as soon as he heard automatic weapon fire. The dispatcher notified Deputy Joe Black and Deputy Black called for backup from the Sheriff Department and, because of the automatic weapon fire, called me and asked for assistance. I arrived on the scene at 5:05 am and found two people dead, a male who Bart identified as James Heller dead of gun shots and a young woman identified by her friend as a Mexican national named Anita Lopez. The woman friend, a Mexican national named Angelina Cortez, was wounded and is in Sweetwater Memorial Hospital."Tom paused because Emiliano had made a gasping noise and half risen from his seat. "Ranger Gillette, do you know the age of the Cortez woman?"Tom looked at his notes and said, "She gave her age as nineteen Emiliano." Emiliano stood and said, "My brother Jorge has a granddaughter nineteen years old named Angelina; I think Maria and I had best go to Sweetwater to see this woman. Is she to be charged with a crime Senor?" "I wouldn't think so Emiliano but she would need to be available to testify at an inquest. If it is your grandniece, I am sure we can get her released to you and Marias custody when the doctors release her." Bart rose and asked, "Emiliano, would you like Tommie and me to go with you?" "Thank you Bart, we don't even know for sure that this is my grandniece. I will call if we have any difficulty." Tom waited as Maria and Emiliano left the room before continuing his narrative. "Bart is the only one involved in this mess that deserves any praise; if he hadn't realized that the suspects could get off the County roads and take to the ranch tracks, they might have gotten to the headquarters here or to some other ranch house while we in law enforcement were waiting for them to show up at one of our roadblocks. He probably won't tell the story correctly so I will. When he found the north gate standing open and fresh tracks headed this way, he took off down that track like a mad man. The suspects took a wrong turn down into Oak Creek bottom before doubling back toward here; Bart got ahead of them while they were down in the bottoms and wedged his truck crossways in the crossing of Hanson Draw so that the thugs would have to take him out before they could get to the headquarters. They opened up on him with a machine gun so Bart shot the gunman twice and when the second man picked up the machine gun, Bart shot him. Bye the way Bart, the reason the first guy got up after you shot him in the chest – he was wearing body armor. Bart managed to get his truck out of the cut he had wedged it in and came on here. By that time help from the Sheriff's office and the Texas Highway Patrol had arrived so we back tracked the suspects and found four women murdered." All during Tom's narration Tommie Rae had held Bart's hand as if afraid he would leave but she grabbed hold of him with both hands and buried her face in his chest when Tom said, "I started to give Bart hell for putting himself in danger but he shut me up with, "There was no way in hell I was going to let them get one step closer to Tommie Rae."

The group broke up with Glorietta going into the kitchen to start something for lunch while Miguel and Mac went out to do the morning's neglected chores. Tom said, "Bart you will need to give a statement as to what happened; do you want to go find the rep from the D.A. office and get it over with?" Bart leaned over to kiss Tommie Rae on the forehead and gently disengaged his arm from her clutch, "Yeah, let's get that over with so things can get back to normal around here. I won't be long Babe."

Bart and Tom rode back toward the scene of the fight in Tom's SUV. Bart was quiet for a few minutes before asking, "Have you ever killed a man Tom?" "Yeah, Bart, on two different occasions; is it bothering you?" "That's why I asked, I don't feel anything except relief that it was them instead of me. Does that make me some sort of monster?" "If it does then I guess I am one too; I have had a few nightmares about what happened but it was because of how close I came to getting killed. Both of the men I killed were trying to kill

me and I have never had a minutes regret about killing them first."
They arrived back at the scene of the fight to find Nolan County
Sheriff Doyt Hayward talking to a young man in a business suit and
Dr. James Coffey, the Nolan County Medical Examiner. Both the
Sheriff and Dr. Coffey had met Bart and both stepped forward to
shake his hand and Sheriff Hayward said, "Bart thank goodness you
and yours came through this alright. This is Ben Hollister of the
District Attorney's office." Bart said, "Mr. Hollister and held out his
hand." Hollister ignored Bart's hand and said, "I need to ask you some
questions Mr. Ryan, do want to have an attorney present during my
interrogation and where is the weapon used in the two killings?" "I
don't think I need an attorney; I was attacked on my own property
and shot back in self defense." "Whether it was self defense has not
been determined and I must say that it looks somewhat like an execution; both of those men had been shot in the center of the forehead
and I seriously doubt you could do that from the distance you claim
to have fired from." Bart opened his mouth to reply but Tom pulled
him back and said, "Bart didn't tell you where he fired from, I did
and it was not a claim it was a fact. I have seen Bart shoot and from
that distance he can make those shots all day long. I don't know what
your problem is but I am the one who called Bart into this mess and if
he hadn't realized that the suspects could leave the County roads on
the ranch tracks, we probably would have more innocent causalities
and the suspects would still be running loose. You are way out of line
treating Bart as a suspect; so far he and the game warden are the only
ones to do good work on this case." "I don't need you to tell me how
to do my job Ranger Gillette; I have two homicides and if Mr. Ryan is
such an excellent shot, why did he not shoot to disable instead of killing those men?" At that Sheriff Hayward let out what could only be

termed a snort and said, "Hollister have you ever been shot at with a spit ball – much less a machine gun? When you are in a fire fight only an idiot would shoot to disable. I vote with Tom, you are way out of line. You should be thanking Bart instead of harassing him." "I am not harassing him, I am investigating him and I want the weapon used in these killings put in my custody immediately. It may have been used in other crimes and we won't know until the crime lab has checked it out." Tom stepped up close to the now sweating young man and said, "Hollister, do you have any evidence – any reason to believe that Bart's rifle has been used in the commission of a crime? You have just made a serious accusation and if you pursue this course without evidence, I will recommend that Bart sue you and the District Attorney and I will testify on his behalf." Sheriff Hayward spoke up to say, "Son, don't let your alligator mouth overload your jaybird ass. If I was you, I would apologize to Mr. Ryan and hope like hell he is a bigger man than you are." The conversation was interrupted by the arrival of another car driven by District Attorney Henry Myers. Myers got out of the car and strode up to the group calling each man by name; he stopped in front of Bart and extending a hand said, "You must be Bart Ryan, I understand that all of us owe you a debt of gratitude." Hollister spoke up, "Sir that is the man that shot the two victims killed here." Sheriff Hayward said, "Young Hollister seems to think that Bart here should be charged with something; he just hasn't quite figured out what." Myers motioned for Hollister to follow him and walked back to his car. The two men talked for a moment before Hollister walked to his vehicle and drove off without out speaking to anyone. Myers came back to the group and said, "Mr. Ryan, Hollister had some things to tend in town; if it suits you, I have a tape recorder in my car and we could get your statement out of the way." "That would be fine, Mr. Myers." Myers turned to Tom Gillette, "Tom come sit with us, after Bart's statement, I would like to hear the whole story from you." The three walked back to Myers car and Tom got in the back seat while Bart and Myers sat in front. Myers put a fresh tape in his recorder and after giving the date, time, location and names of those present said, "Mr. Ryan would you please tell us in your own words what transpired today?" "Tom Gillette called me this morning about 5:30 am and asked if I could come to a location about twelve miles from my home to see if I could identify a shooting victim. I identified the man as James Heller who was employed on the 9R Ranch when we bought it. Tom told me what they thought had happened and that the people involved had left going west on Ranch Road 91 toward Maryneal. I told Tom that there was a gate into Oak Creek Ranch on that road and I left to get back to my family. Tom followed me and we found the gate into Oak Creek broken open and tracks leading into the ranch. Tom called for help and I followed the tracks; about a mile from the gate the road forks and the van took the right fork which leads down to Oak Creek and a very rough crossing. After telling Tom where the road the van took would come out, I took the left fork towards home. Just before I got to Hanson Draw, I saw a white van weaving toward me through the brush. I got to the crossing on Hanson Draw and wedged my truck crossways in the cut going down to the crossing. I got my rifle and some extra rounds and waited behind my truck. In a short time, maybe three or four minutes, the van came into view where it is now. I stood up so they could see that I was armed and the man in the passenger seat jumped out and opened up on me with an automatic weapon. I jumped back behind the truck and when he pointed the reloaded weapon at me, I shot him in the chest. He went down but got back up on his knees and pointed the weapon at me again, so I shot him in the head. The driver ran around the van and grabbed the machine gun so I shot him in the head. By this time Tom was coming down the track behind the van so I came up on the road where he could see me and started toward the van. Tom stopped maybe fifty yards from the van and took shelter behind his vehicle with his rifle; he asked if I was alright and then told me to get down. Tom checked the interior of the van and the two dead men and I went home to make certain that my wife was OK. Tom, did I leave anything out?" "No I don't think so; that covers your part very well." Myers said, Mr. Ryan did you know or had you ever met either of the two men in the van?" "No, I had never seen either of them before today and at this point I still don't know their names." Myers gave the date and time again and said, "This concludes the statement of Mr. Bart Ryan." Myers turned the machine off and said to Bart, "I want to apologize for Ben Hollister; he is young and still suffering culture shock after moving down from the Ivy League. He will make a good prosecutor someday if he doesn't wise off at the wrong man and get his head pinched off. I will see that he apologizes for his treatment of you." "Don't worry about it; he was just doing his job as he saw it."

Tom took over then and recounted in a straight forward way everything that occurred from the time he was called to the scene until the present time. Bart said, "Tom if you will run me back to my truck, I need to go to the hospital and check on Emiliano. Mr. Myers is the Mexican girl that was hurt in custody?" "No, I checked on her just before I came out here and Doctor Price wants to keep her overnight for observation. I need to get a statement from her and she needs to be available if an inquest is held. Dr Price said that she has kin here that have asked to take charge of her." "That would be my partner Emiliano Cortez and his wife; they went to see if she was their grandniece when they heard her name. She will be in good hands with them."

Myers once again shook hands with Bart and said, "I can't say it publicly but you did a very good thing taking those two out. Aside from the atrocities they committed here today, they were both wanted on multiple felony counts for everything from drug trafficking to murder. At least these two won't be back on the streets in a few years like so many of the felons that we send to prison. Thank you!"

Bart and Tom were both quiet for most of the trip back to the headquarters before Bart asked, "Tom how did you wind up a Ranger?" "I guess it is kind of the family business, my Dad was a U.S. Marshall, my Grandfather was a Texas Ranger and my Great-grandfather was a Chickasaw Light Horseman. I always knew that I wanted to be a lawman and of course (with a shy smile) the Rangers are the best of the bunch. I got a degree in criminal justice, spent four years in the Highway Patrol and the happiest day of my life was when I was notified that I had been accepted to compete for a position as a Ranger."

CHAPTER 54

Chickasaw Nation 1876

Jean-Paul Gillette looked up from the pile of furs he was sorting on the store counter and smiled as he listened to his wife Marie and their son Tim laughing as they raced to see who would be first to finish hoeing out their row of corn hills. It was early summer in the Chickasaw Nation and the weather was perfect; spring had come early after a mild winter and their crops were as good as he remembered. Jean-Paul had been in the Chickasaw Nation for twelve years; he came from Mississippi as an itinerant peddler with everything he owned packed on two mules. He went first to the Nation's Capital, Tishomingo, and petitioned the Grand Council of the Chickasaw for permission to establish a trading post in their Nation. His request was granted mainly, he thought, because some of the older council members remembered his grandfather, as an honest man. Grandfather Gillette had been a trader to the Chickasaws before they were removed by force to the Indian Territory.

Jean-Paul leased a shack of a building on Pennington Creek north of Tishomingo and opened for business. Business was slow to develop but began to pick up as people found that Jean-Paul spoke fluent Chickasaw and indeed was one quarter Chickasaw. His Grandfather Gillette married Grandmother Anna just before her family and the other Chickasaws were sent to the new homeland carved out of the western side of the Choctaw Nation and though none of her children were enrolled as members of the tribe, Grandmother Anna made certain that they knew of their Chickasaw heritage and that they spoke the language. Things got much better for Jean-Paul when he met Marie Walkingstick; he courted her all summer before she finally agreed to marry him in the fall. As a tribal member by marriage, Jean-Paul was now allowed to own land in the Nation and he bought 160 acres on the Blue River east of Tishomingo. Jean-Paul contracted with Henry Anatubby and his sons to build them a combination house and store where a strong spring flowed out of a hill above the river bottom; they moved in just as the redbud and Chickasaw plums began to bloom.

The years that followed were full of hard work but also full of fun; their son Timothy was born just after their second wedding anniversary and Jean-Paul started work on a new and larger house that would be separate from the store. He needed more room as he had become a major buyer for produce of all kinds; the store room, a lean to shed out back and parts of their home were stacked high with bales and boxes of everything from furs, to pecans to dried meat and with kegs full of honey, lard, apple cider, hickory nut oil and homemade plum brandy. Jim Curly made regular trips with his freight wagons hauling produce to the steamboat landing at Fort Towson and hauling merchandise back but at times the produce came in faster than they could haul it out; they badly needed more storage space. The trading post had prospered because Jean-Paul was scrupulously honest with his customers and also because he went out of his way to look out for their best interests. His standing in the community went up tremendously when two Choctaw con men got old man Greencorn drunk and convinced him to trade his farm for a "gold mine" they had found. The three came in drunk to the trading post wanting liquor which Jean-Paul would not sell them. When he realized what was happening, Jean-Paul ripped up the paper Mr. Greencorn had signed – kicked the two Choctaws out – made Mr. Greencorn a pallet in the storeroom where he could sleep off his drunk while Jean- Paul sent Tim to tell the son of Mr. Greencorn what had happened.

Marie and Tim finished their hoeing and came to the front porch where the big clay olla of water was sweating moisture; this water evaporating kept the water inside delightfully cool. One of Tim's chores was to keep the olla full of fresh spring water and to make sure gourd dippers were hanging close by for anyone who wanted a drink. Tim and Marie were bantering good naturedly about who had won the race when a flurry of gun shots shattered the morning quiet and the sound of running horses came from the east. Marie grabbed Tim by the arm – shoved him into the store and quickly followed him inside. Jean-Paul picked up the rifle he kept behind the counter and got to the front door just as four loose horses ran into the front yard followed closely by two mounted men who were shooting back at someone chasing them. As Jean-Paul watched first one and then the second of the two men were hit by gunfire. The first fell backwards off his horse and lay still in the dirt while the second dropped his pistol and slumped forward clutching his horse around the neck to keep from falling. The loose horses ran into the open corral, slid to a stop in the far back corner and whirled to face out, snorting in fear. Tim managed to escape his Mother and stick his head out between his Father and the door jamb; he missed most of the action but was on hand to see three men ride into the yard with guns at the ready. Tim turned to his Mother and yelled, "That's Uncle Toby". Marie pushed her husband out of the way to see her younger brother Toby and two other Chickasaw Light Horsemen ride in just as the second wounded man fell from his horse in a boneless heap.

The Chickasaw Light Horsemen had been organized by the tribe to combat the rising tide of lawlessness that was sweeping all of the Indian Nations; the northern, the eastern and the southern borders of the Indian Territory were alive with thugs and outlaws of all sorts that used the border to escape the reach of local law enforcement. The United States Marshals were charged with enforcing the law within the territory but they were few and the territory they were commissioned to protect was large. Outlaws could steal and kill in the Nations and be back in Texas or Arkansas or Kansas before the marshals knew a crime had been committed. The Chickasaw took matters in their own hands and organized the Light Horsemen to serve as the national police force.

The whole family was out in the yard now and Tim was peppering his uncle with questions. Toby held up his hand and said, "Hold off for now Tim, I need to talk to your parents." The three adults went back into the store and Tim inched up closer to where the other two Light Horsemen had drug the two dead men. Tim knew one of the Horsemen slightly and asked him, "Who are they and what did they do?" Before the man could answer, Tim heard an anguished scream from his mother and raced back to the house and through the open door but froze when he saw his father holding his sobbing mother to his chest. Both his father and his Uncle Toby had faces that appeared carved from stone. Tim started forward to his parents but Toby put a restraining hand on his shoulder and said, "You must be brave Timothy, the horse thieves lying dead outside killed your grandparents."

The next few days were a blur for Tim, people came from miles around to pay final respects to John Walkingstick and his wife; they were two of the most respected people in the Nation. There were more people camped on his grandparents' farm than Tim had ever seen in one place; but he had never felt more alone in his life. The outlaws had taken from him two of the four people he loved most in the world and sitting alone on the hill above the farm, Tim swore a private oath that he would spend his life fighting the scum that preyed on innocent people like his grandparents.

CHAPTER 55

When the white van — the last remaining evidence of the thug invasion — was towed to Sweetwater, things gradually returned to normal. The partners spent quite a bit of time discussing where they wanted to go with the ranching business; Tommie Rae, in particular, was infatuated with the idea of controlling the entire process from pasture to final consumer. It became obvious that they needed to know more about grass finished beef and about what was required to produce and sell it. Traveling to ranches producing grass finished beef and talking to ranchers from all over the country who were involved in the business provided some answers but also raised questions that they had not considered. They commissioned Luke Overholts' whiz kids at Synergy LLP to do a thorough study of the benefits and potential as well as the problems of producing and marketing grass fed meat and milk. The more they learned, the more fascinated they became with the concept. Apparently, there are very real health benefits for humans in consuming meat and/or milk from ruminant animals that have not been fed grain. Synergy LLP put together an exhaustive study of the research literature on the subject that none of the partners read in its entirety — there were dozens of research papers reproduced in total — but the summary was clear enough. Grass fed meat and milk are rich in nutritionally beneficial compounds that are in short supply in the diets of most people. These compounds are present in green forage and they accumulate in the meat and milk of animals that graze fresh green forage. They would be producing a product that improved the health of their customers and that would be a advertizing agents dream to promote – Cattle grazing in green pastures rather than standing in crowded feedlots and mothers telling their kids, "Eat your hamburger, it's good for you." Tommy Rae announced that, "Even the idiot professor that taught my marketing course in college could sell that product." Aside from this, it soon became evident that given the right type of animals and good grazing management, the process could be very profitable even if the product did not sell at a premium. It was also apparent that to be successful finishing cattle on grass they would need a much longer green period than they had in west Texas. The problem was water; they needed to have green forage over most of the year in order to keep cattle gaining and to have this, they would have to go to either to where they could irrigate or to where it rained more. At this point, Mac spoke up, "I have been around irrigated pasture a little over the years and that is a whole lot like farming. I vote we look first at country with higher rainfall." Tommie Rae started looking on the internet for ranches for sale in different areas and soon had a long list of candidates. Bart suggested that they make a list of attributes that they wanted or didn't want in the new ranch and use this to cull the list to manageable size. Mac spoke up, saying that they didn't want to get into an area where rainfall was too high. He and Windy spent some time in east Texas and western Louisiana and he wanted no more of damp cold winters and steaming hot summers. "We damn near froze to death up into March and nearly killed our horses with heat stroke in the summer. We waded mud till our boots rotted off and fought swarms of mosquitoes day and night. It rains so much that the grass doesn't have nothing in it; a cow can stand belly deep in that grass and starve flat to death. As far as I am concerned, the catfish and alligators can have that country." Bart grinned at Tommie Rae and Emiliano and said, "I believe we can rule out anywhere that has alligators." Tommie Rae said, "Mac is right about the grass in high rainfall areas, too much water leaches minerals out of the soil and you can wind up having to spend a lot of money on fertilizer to get decent animal performance. From what I read, the best animal performance comes from areas with a lot of calcium in the soil; these are also the soils that can grow legumes like alfalfa and clover that are needed to provide nitrogen to the grasses and to lengthen the period of high quality grazing. I suggest that we look for a ranch with deep, high calcium soils that is in a rainfall belt of maybe 35 to 45 inches a year." Mac spoke up, "We could find that in parts of the hill country of Texas but that whole area has been run plumb out of sight in price by people from the cities buying ranches for recreation."

Tom Gillette had become a frequent visitor at Bart and Tommie Raes – Tommie Rae had a suspicion that the presence of Glorietta might have something to do with the frequency of his visits. Tommie Rae's lawyer cousin in San Angelo had gotten legal status for Miguel and Glorietta and Glorietta in particular had blossomed with her new legal and financial security. Tom was with them now and said, "You might want to look at the area where my Dad's family lived; the Chickasaw Nation, which is in south central Oklahoma has a lot of what you have described." Mac said, "I've worked in that area and Tom's right, there is a lot of limestone country with strong native grass as good as the Osage country in northern Oklahoma or the Flint Hills in Kansas. There are also river bottom areas of several rivers where they grow alfalfa and all kinds of crops. One of the prettiest ranches I have ever seen was on the Blue River; that ranch had it all – clear cold water in the river with huge pecan trees in the bottom and good bluestem pasture on the upland. Jake has a pretty good handle on what is going on with the fencing and water development on the 9R and since we got the guard dogs, Miguel has the sheep well in hand. What say we take a little trip into that part of the world and see what we can find? I kind of like the idea of having some country that stays green all summer" Emiliano begged off on the trip saying that he had been away from home too much lately, "It would not do for Maria to realize that she can do without me." This earned him a swat on the arm from his wife but she smiled when she did it and was obviously pleased saying, "Good the new house is getting close to being ready and you can see about getting accommodations made for my chickens. We can't move until my ladies have a safe new home."

The partners decided that they would like to have enough country to run at least a thousand cows or the equivalent number of yearling cattle in one location and Tommie Rae made contact with several realtors in north Texas and southern Oklahoma to see what was available. Ranches of this size are not common and none of the realtors they contacted had a listing that fit their needs. Told of the trouble they were having finding a ranch, Tom Gillette suggested that he contact an uncle and some cousins who lived in the area and see if they knew of land for sale; some people didn't like to deal with realtors but his kin had been in the area for a long time and would likely know who wanted to sell.

The realtors they had contacted kept the phone lines hot trying to interest them in various smaller places but didn't come up with anything approaching the size they wanted. Bart and Tommie Rae were beginning to think that they would have to look for land in another area when Tom Gillette called to say that his cousin Mark Gillette had a lead on a ranch that sounded like what they wanted. Mark lived in Tishomingo Oklahoma and was a friend of an older man, Henry Pierce, who owned ten thousand acres on Blue River. Mr. Pierce's health was not good and the ranch that had once been his passion in life was now too much for him to handle. None of his kids cared anything for the ranch and he told Mark that he would rather sell it to someone who would keep it operating rather than see his grandkids split it up into hobby farms and horse traps before he was cold in his grave. Bart called Mark and made a date for the partners to get together with him in Tishomingo in two days to meet Mr. Pierce and to see Pierce Ranch. When Bart told Mac about the ranch, he thought a minute and said, "Pierce Ranch – hell, Windy and I went to Pierce Ranch to receive a string of yearlings when we were working for Woodlaw and Scott Cattle Company thirty years ago. That's the ranch I told you about; they raised really good Hereford cattle on some of the prettiest country I have ever seen." Bart, Tommie Rae and Mac left the next morning and after spending the night in Ardmore, met Mark Gillette for breakfast in Tishomingo. Mark was a tall robust looking man a little older than his cousin Tom but the family resemblance was striking. After introductions were made all around and the waitress left with their orders, Bart said, "Mark we appreciate your help in this and if we can make a trade, we want you to have a finder's fee for your efforts." "Bart, thank you for the thought but that is not necessary; Henry Pierce was like a father to me at a time when I needed the support. He gave me a job but also taught me the business and taught me how a man is supposed to live. I worked for him for ten years before he helped me go out on my own. All I want is to make this as easy for him as possible."

After breakfast they loaded up in Bart's four door truck and drove the fifteen or so miles to Pierce Ranch; they turned off the highway at the Pierce Ranch entrance and followed a ranch road across a rolling tallgrass prairie. Mark explained that most of the ranch was upland native grass like this prairie but that there was also about three thousand acres of Blue River bottomland stretching for five miles on both sides of the river and about a thousand acres of flat ground – second bottom – that was farmed in wheat. When Tommie Rae asked what "second bottom" was Mark explained that this was land that was formed by the river in ancient times but was higher than the true bottomland and no longer over flowed. This information led Bart to ask how often the river flooded the bottoms. "There are some low bottoms on the ranch – maybe three hundred acres – that flood every few years but it is very rare that any amount of the bottoms flood; I have only seen the river out big one time in all the years I have lived here and then it was back in banks in twenty-four hours. Farther downstream Blue can get pretty wild but it seldom is a problem this far up. A big part of its stream flow is from springs; up here the water is so cold the Oklahoma Fish and Game Department stocks trout in it in the fall." At this point the road turned south to parallel the drop off into Blue bottom and they could see the river winding through scattered big pecan trees with green forage growing beneath them. Bart stopped the truck as they all took in the view; finally Mac said, "I expect that if our cows saw this, they would think they had died and gone to heaven."

They came to the headquarters where a comfortable looking old rock house presided over several barns and a large set of working pens. Mark pointed to a large rock reservoir on the slope above the house and said, "Our ancestor Jean-Paul Gillette built that reservoir to hold the water from a spring that comes out from under a rock ledge on the slope. The spring supplies water to the house and pens and has never stopped flowing; Jean-Paul built his trading post — it burned about 1900 — where the ranch house is now. They parked outside the small yard and as they reached the porch, the front door opened to reveal a pleasant faced middle age woman. "Mrs. Greencorn takes care of Mr. Pierce; Mrs. Greencorn, meet Bart and Tommie Rae Ryan and Mac Connley." Mrs. Greencorn shook hands with everyone and said, "Come in Henry is in the living room." Mark led them into a large room where a slight and rather short man was, with some difficulty, rising from a leather easy chair; Mr. Pierce came forward with the aid of a cane and shook hands with everyone as Mark introduced them. The room had a large plate glass window looking out over Blue bottom and Henry had his chair turned so that he could see out of it. They all found seats and Mac broke the ice by saying, "Mr. Pierce, you wouldn't remember me but I came here many years ago to receive a set of yearling heifers that you sold to Woodlaw and Scott Cattle Company." Mr. Pierce looked closely at Mac and breaking into a grin said, "You are right Son, I didn't remember your name but I haven't forgotten how you knocked that smart aleck truck driver off the chute for hitting my little girls with a hot shot." Bart spoke up, "He is getting mellow as he gets older; the last truck driver that did that to one of his cattle just got his hot shot broken over a fence post." The atmosphere had been a little strained but suddenly they were a group of friends talking over the coffee that Mrs. Greencorn served. "Mark tells me you might want to buy my ranch; what do you want to do with it? Bart looked at Mac who motioned him to go ahead. "We own some country in west Texas that is good cow calf country but a little short on length of green season to be a top stocker country. We would like to have a place to carry our calves over to heavy feeder weights and maybe grass-finish some." "So you wouldn't want my cows?" Mac spoke up, "Mr. Pierce if you still have the kind of cattle you sold Woodlaw and Scott, we very definitely would like to have them." "Oh, they are the same kind all right, I am the only Hereford breeder in this part of the world that isn't raising white faced camels and calling them Herefords; my cattle can get fat and raise a calf on nothing but grass. The feedlot boys hate them – they can't sell enough corn and lot time because my cattle are fat and ready to kill before the gutless monsters they are breeding now get warmed up. My cattle are not tall but they mash down the scale because they are thick and deep. We don't have any trouble selling bulls even though we don't register them; people know that my bulls will put muscle on their calves. I think the thing about selling this ranch that I dread most is seeing my cattle dispersed." He paused and leaned back in his chair with a grimace. "I am going to let Mark show you the ranch, he knows it as well as I do; you all go see and when you get back, we will see if we can make a trade."

They spent several hours riding over the entire ranch; it was easy to see since the only brush was where areas had been allowed to grow up to provide wind breaks. Mac exclaimed several times about the health of the native grass; Pierce Ranch had been practicing rotational grazing for many years and it showed in the vigor and variety of the native forage. They rode down through the bottom land where a mixture of alfalfa, fescue and clover was growing under big pecan trees and crossed Blue River on a low water crossing. Bart stopped the truck on the crossing and they sat for a moment watching the clear as glass water surge and ripple over the boulders that formed the bed of the river. Mac spoke up to say, "It looks more like a Colorado trout stream than a river in Oklahoma." Mark said, "It heads not too far north of here in some limestone country and springs keep the flow pretty uniform even in dry weather. We swam in it all the time as kids and those deep holes where the springs come in are so cold that you can't stay in them." They crossed the bottom land on the other side of the river and climbed up to another area of tallgrass prairie where they found the main cowherd. Bart drove slowly through the cattle that were finishing up a grazing period and beginning to lie down for some rest and rumination. The cows, like Henry Pierce said, were not tall but they were thick and deep bodied and even though nursing big calves they were as Mac said, "Fat as town dogs." Bart reached the far side of the pasture and Mac asked him to circle back through the cattle, "I didn't know that there were any cattle like this left. These are 1940 model Herefords! The whole industry has gone crazy breeding cattle bigger, taller and heavier; it used to be that just the exotics from Europe were outsized but now even Herefords and Angus have been selected for size until the cattle can't make it on grass alone. The feedlots and the packers have been calling the tune for a long time and they want big cattle that can eat a lot of corn without getting fat and will dress out a huge carcass. The bigger the carcass, the less it costs per pound to process. It has worked pretty good for the feedlots and packers but the cowman is out of luck; they can't maintain a cow that can produce the type animal that the trade wants without spending a lot of money on feed supplements. These ladies can do it on grass and if we want to be in the grass finished business, we need these cows." Bart looked at Mac and said, "Partner, that is the longest speech I've ever heard you make; I believe we had best try to buy Mr. Pierces' ranch and cattle." They drove out the rest of the ranch on the east side of the river and crossed back toward the headquarters on another low water bridge. As they approached the house, they could see Mr. Pierce sitting on the front porch; he stood as they approached and said, "Come on in, Mrs. Greencorn has some dinner ready for us."

When the partners left Pierce Ranch five hours later they had agreed to buy the ranch and equipment for 5.5 million dollars and the cattle – 1200 grown cows, 50 herd bulls, 140 yearling heifers and 75 yearling bulls – and six saddle horses for $1,443,500. The cattle would be paid for immediately and the land would be paid for in ten equal annual payments – plus interest at seven percent – after a down payment of one million dollars; the two hands on the ranch would be offered jobs at their present salaries. Mac was a little dubious about hiring the two without knowing anything about them but Mark assured him that the two were good men. The deal allowed Mr. Pierce to remain in his home as long as he wished; Mark thanked them for this on the way back to town saying, "The old fellow is dying and I would hate to see him uprooted in his last days." They still had to get the lawyers involved and a title search done but that should not pose a problem – the ranch had been in Pierce hands for over one hundred years. When the deal was done and they had shaken hands, Mr. Pierce said, rather pensively, "I suppose you will be changing the name of the ranch?" He was inordinately pleased when Mac said, "Why no, this is the Pierce Ranch and will be as long as we own it; we will begin using our 9R brand but the name of the ranch won't change. After dropping Mark in Tishomingo, the partners recapped the day on the way to the motel in Ardmore; they agreed to approach Mark to see if he would become manager of the unit. Bart said, "He is smart and I get the feeling that he has been manager in everything but name for some time." Half way to Ardmore, Tommie Rae began laughing so hard she couldn't talk before getting control back to say, "Do you two realize that we just spent almost seven million dollars in one afternoon and this time last year we would have been sweating bullets to come up with a hundredth of that." Mac chuckled and said, "It's been a change alright but I think that we did good today. It is a good ranch that fits right in with what we want to do but I am just as excited to have the cattle; they will give us a big leg up on building a grass finished beef business." "Mac will they do alright if we send some of the Pierce cows to the 9R?" asked Bart. "They ought to do fine; in general you can move cattle west or north or from a weak country to a strong country without trouble but it gets dicey if you go the other way. When we ship calves from the 9R to the Pierce, we will want to do it as soon as they are weaned and straight and try to have green feed for them when they arrive. I'm not thrilled to get into farming but a patch of wheat could be a great place to start fresh weaned calves." They rode on a few miles before Mac said, "I'd rather take a whipping with a wet rope than say this to you two smart alecks but you had better buy me a new pickup. It looks like I am going to be on the road pretty regular."

CPSIA information can be obtained
at www.ICGtesting.com
Printed in the USA
LVHW081248281120
672778LV00025B/1076